Proud Mary

Iris Gower was born in Swansea where she lived all her life. The mother of four adult children, she wrote over twenty bestselling novels, many of which are based around Swansea and the Gower peninsula, from which she took her pseudonym.

She received an Honorary Fellowship from the University of Wales Swansea in 1999 and was awarded an MA in Creative Writing from the University of Cardiff.

Also by Iris Gower

Sea Witch
House of Shadows
Emerald
Bomber's Moon
Spinner's Wharf
Proud Mary
Fiddler's Ferry
A Royal Ambition
Destiny's Child

Iris Gower

Proud Mary

CANELO

First published in the United Kingdom in 1984 by Century Publishing Co. Ltd

This edition published in the United Kingdom in 2021 by

Canelo
31 Helen Road
Oxford OX2 0DF
United Kingdom

A CIP catalogue record for this book is available from the British Library.

Print ISBN 978 1 80032 025 3
Ebook ISBN 978 1 78863 958 3

Printed and bound in Great Britain by Clays Ltd, Elcograf S.p.A.

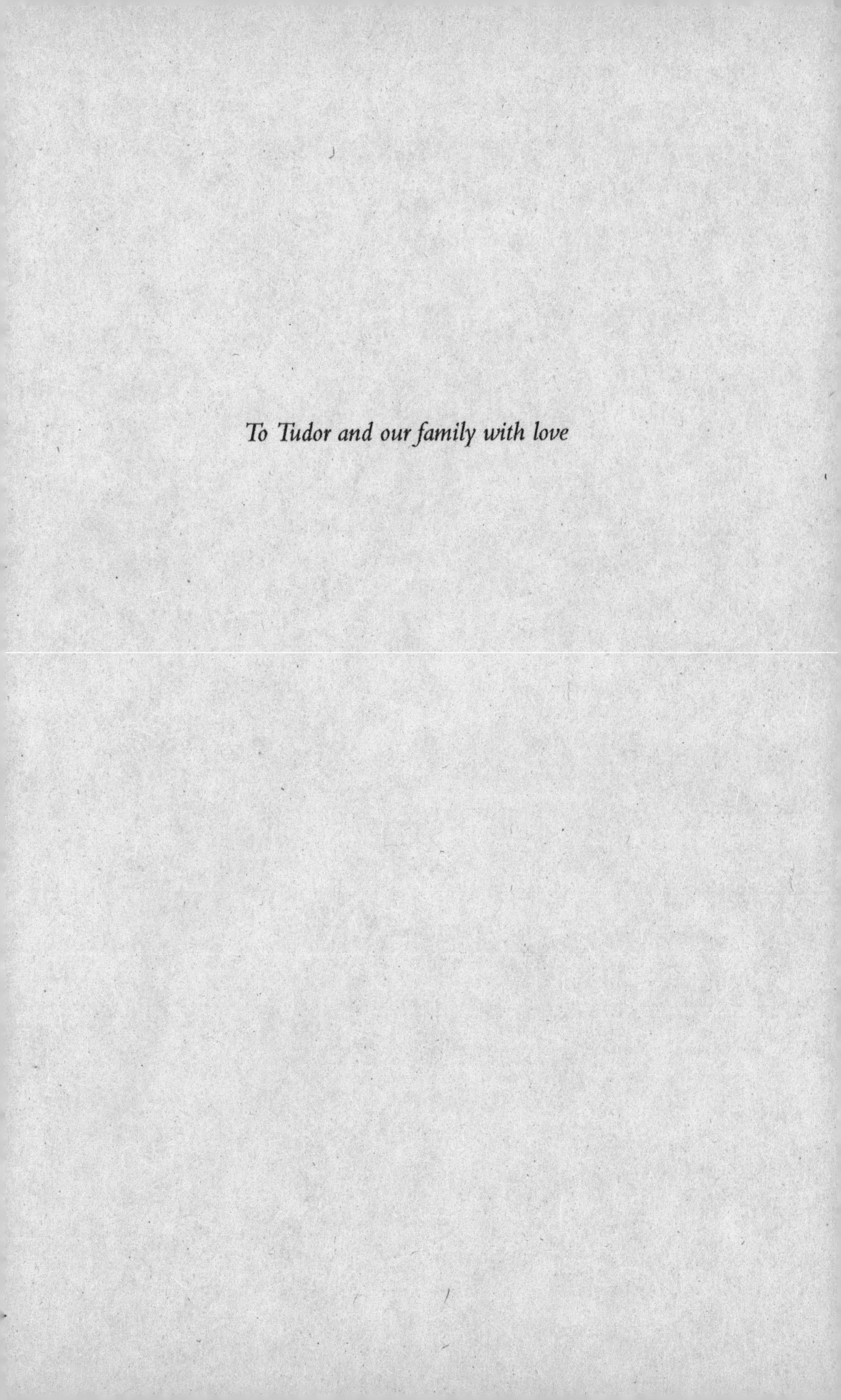

To Tudor and our family with love

Chapter One

Sweyn's Eye lay soft and grey in the harsh early morning rain. Clouds moved over the silent hills towards the east where the copper works belched forth green smoke from a forest of chimneys that invaded the skies. The prison, stark and ugly, hugged the line of the shore, facing the heavy rolling seas with mute defiance. And the old gallows creaked mournfully in the wind.

Mary Jenkins stood outside the heavy oak door, steadfastly gazing at the sodden wood and the huge iron hinges that guarded the prison entrance. Behind her clustered a group of bedraggled women waiting, as she was, to be admitted into the stern building.

She bit her lip and tears blurred her vision, but she swallowed her pain, unwilling to make a display of her emotions. Standing tall, with head aloft and back iron-straight, she was unaware that her raw-boned elegance and the darkness of her heavy-lidded eyes set her apart from the other women. She only knew that she was lost and alone in an unfamiliar world. She wished herself away from the prison and safe within the welcoming warmth of the Canal Street Laundry, breathing in the scent of hot clean linen, checking sheets or issuing orders that she knew would be obeyed with good humour.

There was a grumbling among the women behind her; they were weary of the rain that soaked through heavy woollen shawls, running in streams from black straw hats. She felt a momentary pity for them, but then she was one of them now – waiting as they were to visit menfolk imprisoned behind the forbidding walls.

'There's hoity-toity you are, Mary Jenkins.' A voice thickened by gin hissed towards her with the venom of a snake.

'Come down in the world now, 'aven't you? No better than the rest of us and you standing there like you was a queen.'

Mary ignored the sneers though her shoulders were tense, but the voice continued mercilessly.

'Murderer, that's what Billy Gray is! Shouldn't wonder if they hang 'im by the neck until he's dead.'

Mary turned and stared angrily at the woman who was taunting her; she was a sorry sight, her face lined and yellow, her eyes anguished and Mary's anger melted away.

The old gallows swung in a gust of wind and Mary shuddered. Public hangings were no longer the custom in Sweyn's Eye, but the gibbet that stood behind the prison walls was no less fearsome.

'Oh, Billy!' she whispered his name, her heart heavy with bitterness. He was no murderer and although she had not been allowed to speak to him since his arrest, she felt with a deep certainty that he would be able to explain everything if only he were given a chance.

A silence had fallen on the women and Mary turned to see a man striding towards the prison gates. He was taller than she by several inches, his shoulders broad beneath the good serge of his topcoat.

'Aren't you Mary Jenkins?' His voice was low and melodious, sounding foreign because of the American overtones.

'What's it to you?' she asked flatly and he took her arm, propelling her forward, rapping on the prison door imperiously. 'I feel a certain responsibility,' he said and then shrugged. 'Never mind, I don't suppose you'd understand.'

A small section of the great door opened, creaking as though in protest. 'Oh it's you, Mr Sutton, sir.' A grim-faced warder doffed his hat, stepping back a pace and Mary found herself within the yard. Wondering why she was allowing a stranger to manipulate her, she glanced up at him almost against her will and a tremor shuddered through her. He looked mysterious in the dim light, his eyes appeared turquoise and the breeze lifted dark curls from his brow. Then he smiled and it was as though the clouds had suddenly parted to reveal bright sunshine.

'Who are you?' she asked. Her voice was light, insubstantial and she hardly recognised it as her own.

'Brandon Sutton.' His reply was brief and to the point and Mary felt unnerved by his presence. She moved away from him, unaware of the silent warder waiting to lead them into the main prison building until the American took her arm firmly and drew her forward.

'What are you doing here?' She forced herself to speak as she was hurried along the windswept yard towards a flight of steps.

'The same as you, I guess. I wish to see Billy Gray.'

'Why?' The word came out hard and flat and Mary stared at Brandon Sutton, her chin lifted as though defying him to deny her an answer.

'I'd like to question him,' he replied lightly, but a narrowing of the turquoise eyes showed his displeasure at her abrupt question.

'Go on ahead, sir,' The warder spoke with gruff diffidence and Brandon nodded.

'Thank you, Griffiths.' He moved swiftly up the steps, leading Mary up the short flight and into a dingy hallway.

'You'd best wait here; at least you'll have some privacy.'

Mary felt strangely bereft as Brandon Sutton vanished from sight and she was prevented from following him by the outstretched arm of the warder, his rugged face impassive.

'Why am I being kept here?' she asked breathlessly. 'I have more right to see Billy Gray than that stranger, surely?'

The warder looked at her without interest. 'You will have to wait until you are called. This isn't the Mackworth Arms, you know. Grateful to Mr Sutton, you should be; he brought you in out of the rain, didn't he?'

Mary swallowed her anger and seated herself on a bench, staring round the dingy walls unrelieved by even a single window. She clasped her hands together in her lap and looked down at her neatly polished boots, trying to quell the frustration and anger that flowed through her. She felt demeaned, as though she had become tainted by the very sight and smell of the prison. This was no place for her love, for her dear, gentle Billy.

She closed her eyes, forcing her thoughts away from her surroundings. She wondered how the girls were faring at the laundry. Three long weeks she had been absent from work, for since Billy's arrest she had been too worried to think of anything but him.

She realised that the Canal Street Laundry could function perfectly well without her and that everything would run along on oiled wheels as usual. The checking would be done properly, the delivery rounds would be as regular as ever and Doris would still be hauling her scuttle full of coal to stoke the boilers – yet a tiny part of Mary hoped that she would be missed.

She had been relieved and grateful when Mali Richardson, owner of the laundry, had advised her to take some time off work and had grasped the opportunity with both hands, knowing that Billy would need all the support she could give him. Not that she had done very much in that direction so far, except try to cheer his Aunt Agnes with false optimism and to find young Rhian a job in the packing room. Billy's sister had taken the position with the utmost reluctance; irritated rather than pleased at Mary's intervention, she made it quite clear that there was no love lost between them.

Mary brushed the disquieting thoughts aside and gave herself up to reminiscing about the happy and satisfying years she had spent at the laundry. She could picture Mali Richardson as she had first seen her, Mali Llewelyn as she was then: small and white-faced, a girl who had arrived at work with an anxious frown creasing her high, intelligent forehead.

Mali had been given the task of stoking the boilers, a challenge she had accepted with more courage than skill. And over the years she had shown great strength of character. It had been no surprise to Mary to see Mali eventually rise to a high position in the company, for she had streamlined and reorganised the laundry with great insight and when Mr Waddington (the previous owner) had died it had been Mali who had taken over the business.

Mali had been with child when she had married Sterling Richardson, the copper boss, and the event had caused a sensation in the town. Many had predicted the early downfall of such an alliance, yet the glow that these days shone from Mali's green eyes proved beyond all doubt that she had taken the right course and was happy. That the role of wife and mother suited her was beyond question.

Mary got to her feet abruptly, her hands twisted nervously together. At twenty-seven years of age, she knew that she was well past the time when she should have a brood of her own babies hanging round her skirts. She loved Billy Gray, of course she did, hadn't she known him since they both were little more than infants themselves? Yet she had shrunk from him whenever he had become too passionate, feeling a strange reluctance to give herself completely. Perhaps she needed to keep the independence she had fought so hard to gain.

She shivered. Her first home had been a hovel, her earliest memories sleeping with her baby brother on stained matting alongside a sick father and a drunken mother. She brushed the thoughts aside – the prison was affecting her badly, for she had not dwelt on the privations of her childhood in years.

The door at the end of the hallway opened suddenly and Mary turned to see Brandon Sutton re-emerge from the heart of the prison. He glanced neither right nor left and seemed not to notice her.

Mary trembled as he walked past her; he was magnificent, his broad shoulders proudly held, his back straight, his movements lithe like those of a powerful animal.

'Mary Jenkins,' Griffiths loud voice broke harshly into her thoughts, 'you can go in now.'

Trying to gather her wits together, she blinked rapidly and stared at the hard-faced warder, forcing down the sudden wave of nausea that threatened to overwhelm her. She realised suddenly that she was afraid to see Billy again – how, she wondered, had the trial affected him?

She took a deep breath and moved forward and it was as though she had entered an underworld, a place of darkness where the sun could not penetrate. The coldness of the room struck her forcibly and then she dimly perceived the figure sitting at a table in the corner overshadowed by two uniformed men.

'Billy?' Mary's voice came out slowly, her tongue seemed suddenly to fill her mouth as she stumbled forward and sat opposite him, her heart drumming painfully within her. She was separated from him by the long stretch of wooden table and the invisible barrier of authority erected by Griffiths, who took up a stance at the door alongside another warder, arms folded uncompromisingly across his chest.

'Mary, you shouldn't have come, I didn't want you to see me like this.' Billy's head was sunk low on his chest and as her eyes became accustomed to the gloom she drew in a sharp hissing breath. His hair had been shaved almost to the bone, he had become thinner and there were dark circles beneath his eyes. A sudden anger filled Mary and, oblivious to the men standing guard, she reached out her hand and grasped Billy's cold fingers.

'Are you all right?' she asked urgently. 'Tell me if you are being treated bad, boyo, and I'll do something about it.'

His heavy sigh seemed like the last gasp of a dying man. 'Don't go making a fuss now, girl,' he said at last. 'They are treating me proper, just like they'd treat any other man accused of murder; don't ask soft questions.'

'But Billy, you're not to blame, I know you well enough to understand that much.'

A thin smile appeared on his face and for a moment Mary glimpsed the old Billy Gray.

'Come on love, tell me all about it,' she said softly. She jerked her head in the direction of the warders. 'Never mind them, what they think now doesn't make any difference, does it?'

Billy shook his head as though in bewilderment. 'Look, Mary girl, I don't know what happened and that's God's truth. Like I said at the trial, I just heard someone running about outside the house.' His shoulders slumped. 'That night when it happened, I heard this sound by the back door, soft it was like the rustling of footsteps. As groom to Dean Sutton, I thought it only right to find out if anything was going on.'

Mary's heart ached for Billy as she sat in silence waiting for him to continue. He shook his head. 'Oh, I suppose I should have minded my own business, but I didn't and that's where I went wrong.' He looked at her almost pleadingly. 'I went outside in all innocence like and I wish to God I'd stayed indoors; I wouldn't be in this mess then.'

For a moment his voice quivered and Mary felt a knot of protectiveness heavy within her. She longed to take Billy in her arms and cradle his head on her breast, but that was the act of a mother, not a woman in love with a man.

'Go on Billy,' she said softly, 'I'm listening.' She squeezed his fingers, ignoring the pointed look given her by one of the warders.

'I saw the face of the older man, Twm Price-Nightwatchman it was. I shouted to him, asked why he was snooping around in the dead of night; then his son Gerwin was on me, threw me to the ground – didn't recognise me in the dark, I don't suppose. I got up in a fine rage, bellowing like a wounded bull I remember and Gerwin ran for it. Twm made off like mad towards the old quarry. I shouted to him to take care, but it was no use; in a blind panic, he was. Went straight over the edge and to my dying day I'll never forget his scream.' Billy's shoulders sagged. 'I didn't push him, whatever the men in wigs said.'

'Of course you didn't.' Mary's voice wavered as Billy's beseeching eyes met hers.

'There was money in my pocket, see, that's what went against me.' Billy's voice shook. 'Said I stole it and the notes were from Brandon Sutton's safe. Planted on me, they were. Must have been, there's no other explanation.'

Billy looked down at his clenched fists. 'He's been to see me, asking me about some book and did I have pages out of it.' He shrugged. 'What would I want with such things?'

'Why, the mean hypocrite!' Mary bit her lip, her thoughts in a turmoil. So that's what Brandon Sutton meant by feeling responsible.

'Never mind him,' Billy was saying. 'Look after yourself, Mary, and try to do your best for Rhian too while I'm in here,' he said earnestly. 'She's a headstrong girl, I know, and needs a firm hand to keep her steady, but she's true and honest for all that.'

Mary tried to marshal her thoughts. 'Don't worry your head about your sister,' she attempted to smile reassuringly. 'I've already found her a position, a packer in the laundry. It's nice clean work and steady pay at the end of the week. She'll be set up for life there if she puts her back into the job.'

Billy's eyes glowed with gratitude and Mary felt tears sting her eyes. He was like a whipped dog, with all the life gone out of him. He had always been cheerful and good-natured, a big man with a fine head of hair and a smile that would set any girl's heart alight, but now the fire seemed to have gone from his belly.

Griffiths' harsh voice broke into Mary's thoughts. 'You, Mary Jenkins – shift your backside, time's up.' She rose to her feet at once, her hands clenched at her sides, her colour high.

'There's no need for such vulgarity, mind,' she said fiercely. 'I'm not some floosie in off the streets.'

The warder's pale eyes narrowed as he stared at Mary. He appeared bewildered by her outburst and for a moment it seemed he might apologise; then he flushed a dull red and ran his finger around the stiff collar of his shirt as though it had suddenly become too tight for him.

'Back to the cells, scum!' He caught Billy by the scruff of the neck and shook him like a dog with a bone. Billy offered no resistance, though his humiliation was clear to see in the sudden pallor of his face.

Mary gasped in outrage but before she could speak again, Griffiths had lashed out at Billy's ankles with a heavily booted foot.

'Your woman doesn't understand how we work things here, boyo, it might be good for your health if you told her to mind her lip. Go on, I'm waiting.'

Billy stared at Mary as though begging her forgiveness. 'Just shut your mouth, girl, and go on home.' She watched as he was dragged unceremoniously from the room, almost crying in impotent rage.

'Best go, girl.' The younger warder appeared to have more compassion than Griffiths. 'It's no good to kick against the pricks, don't the good book tell you that?' Mary moved out of the room and along the hallway into the yard where splashes of sunshine had broken through the clouds. She felt as though she was leaving behind her some sickening nightmare and returning to normality once more. Griffiths appeared behind her, a grin on his broad face. 'See, I'm the boss here, girl, got a lot of pull I have, so why not be civil to me?' He rested a moist hand on her shoulder and she pushed him away angrily.

'I want to see the governor.' Her voice trembled and the warder shook his head almost pityingly.

'Don't learn very fast, do you?'

'I mean to see the governor,' Mary repeated, though her knees were trembling and she had never been less sure of herself in all her life.

'Well, you can't see him, Mary Jenkins! Not now or ever and don't show your face back at this prison because you won't be allowed past the gate.' Griffiths smirked. 'Knew your mam and dad, I did. Bad blood they had, both of them, so don't go puttin' on airs and graces with me, my girl. Now get out.'

Mary hurried out into the street, throbbing with pain and anger. Billy was being ill-treated, his pride torn to shreds and Griffiths was not fit to be in charge of animals, let alone human beings. Yet what could she do? She stood, trembling in the roadway with the gaunt building hovering over her like a bird of prey. Then she moved across the cobbled street towards the beach and stared at the rolling sea shimmering in the patchy sunlight, breathing the air in deep gulps and striving for calmness. Perhaps she would have been better advised to grease the palm of the warder instead of trying to fight him with her puny strength.

She walked along the sand listening to the waves sucking at the shore as a greedy babe sucks at its mother's breast. She felt helpless and friendless, bitterly blaming herself for her outburst of temper.

Brushing the raindrops from a fallen tree trunk she seated herself, arranging her skirts around her ankles with trembling hands. She smiled ruefully – who would believe she was the same Mary Jenkins who rules the laundry with a rod of iron? She found herself relaxing a little, the salt breeze taking the heat from her cheeks and the calling of seagulls in the empty sky bringing her a sense of calmness.

'Big Mary', that's what she was called behind her back, but there was no spite intended by the name. She was a hard task-master but fair and she had always been so sure of herself until now. She sighed softly and thought of Billy's eyes staring at her in mute appeal; she would not, could not allow him to waste away behind prison bars.

As she looked towards the hazy horizon, she thought angrily about Brandon Sutton. She would go to see him, convince him of Billy's innocence and ask him to withdraw his accusations.

Before she knew it, she was on her feet as overhead a flurry of seagulls called plaintively. The clouds that had earlier obscured the sun had completely rolled away and a blue bowl arched above her head as she made her way back to the road.

She did not look at the prison or at the creaking gallows standing stark and vaguely threatening near the wall, but walked swiftly towards the tramway terminus before she could lose her courage.

She had only a very hazy idea of where Brandon Sutton lived, but she was sure it was somewhere on the western slope of the town where the grass was sweet and verdant and where, in summertime, gracious displays of flowers were bedded in carefully landscaped gardens. Certainly the elder of the Sutton brothers owned the Big House, named in Welsh *Ty Mawr*, which stood almost at the top of the hillside. Mary had heard gossip about the family, for the Suttons were Americans and outsiders, their ways not those of the inhabitants of the Welsh valleys. There was talk of a family quarrel and of old Mr Grenville Sutton's wish that the brothers should be reconciled, but how much truth was in the rumours Mary did not know.

The tram rattled into sight, the late sunlight glancing off the advertisement for Cherry Blossom Boot Polish. Mary climbed on board and as the tram jerked into motion, slid into the nearest seat. At her side was a dainty woman dressed in green serge, wearing a large hat which cast a shadow over one side of her face but Mary would know that wide generous mouth anywhere.

'Mali! I was only thinking of you a short while ago, there's strange to see you now.'

'Not strange at all when I live up on the hill, but what are you doing venturing so far outside town? Lost your way, have you?'

Mary shook her head slowly. 'I'm sorry to put a damper on our first meeting for ages, Mali, but the truth is I'm trying to get some help in freeing Billy from prison.'

Mali frowned and laid her gloved hand on Mary's arm. 'I'm sorry,' she said. 'I've heard about Billy, of course, but in my joy at seeing you I suppose I forgot all about it.'

The two women were silent for a moment, staring through the window of the tram, watching the landscape change before their eyes. The hill where the rich of the town had built their homes was free of the effects of copper smoke. Grass grew green and fresh and wild flowers were much in evidence.

'Do you know Brandon Sutton?' Mary asked at last. 'I'm trying to find out where he lives.' She became aware that Mali's eyebrows were raised in surprise.

'But I understood that Billy was jailed largely on Brandon's evidence,' Mali said gently. 'What good will it do to speak to him?'

Mary nodded. 'I know it must seem hopeless to you, but I must try to change Mr Sutton's mind. Billy isn't capable of all the things he's been convicted of and I'm going to tell Brandon Sutton so to his face.'

'Oh, Mary, you make me feel so ashamed,' Mali said remorsefully. 'I should at least have come to see you before this – how you must have been suffering.'

'Don't fret.' Mary shook her head. 'With a small child to look after, you've doubtless got your hands full.'

'Nevertheless, the laundry is still my responsibility,' Mali persisted. 'I've let you carry the burden for the running of the place for too long. I should be taking more interest in what's happening there, I suppose. Anyway, to come back to your question – yes, I do know where Brandon lives. I have to pass the gate as it happens.

As the two women alighted from the tram, stepping out on to the broad sweeping roadway, the air was like wine bringing with it the clean salt smell of the sea and Mary breathed deeply. Below, spread out into the distance was the town of Sweyn's Eye, the long curving road thrown down between the folding hills like a question mark, the sea incredibly blue as it washed onto the golden beach, the foam that edged the waves white and frothy in the sunlight. It was a different world, Mary thought. The stink of the copper works, the sound of the sparks shooting into the sky when the blast furnaces were tapped – it all seemed remote from her now. Even the grey of the prison seemed like a painful but distant memory.

'Here we are!' Mali spoke brightly. 'This is *Ty Melyn;* Brandon lives here with his father. Grenville hardly ever leaves home and he's a likeable old man, though a bit gruff on times.' Mali pressed Mary's arm. 'If not, promise you'll come up to *Plas Rhianfa* and have tea with Sterling and me.'

Mary nodded without replying. She had no intention of intruding upon Mali's privacy. She waved as Mali moved away and then turned to walk through the wide iron gates and along the pathway overhung by budding trees.

Her heart was hammering inside her as she stood before the great door. Should she go to the back of the house, she wondered, but then anger swept over her. She was not here as a servant, so why should she behave like one? She lifted the knocker and, as it slammed downwards, the noise reverberated through the house.

The maid who opened the huge door stared disdainfully at Mary's shawled figure. 'Yes?' she asked haughtily as Mary moved nearer.

'Tell Mr Sutton that Mary Jenkins wants to see him, and don't look down at me, my girl, or I just might fetch you a clip across the ear.'

The young maid stepped back quickly. 'Wait by here and I'll see if the master will speak to you.' She moved away huffily, the ribbons from her cap fluttering behind her.

Mary stood on the step, her hands icy cold in spite of the sunshine, and wondered what exactly she could say to Brandon Sutton. He was a man who seemed an enigma with his strange turquoise eyes and tall strong figure.

The maid returned with a smile of satisfaction on her young face. 'Mr Sutton can't see anyone at the moment, I'm sorry.' She was closing the door even as she spoke and Mary felt a swift sense of disappointment.

'Tell him I'll wait,' she said fiercely. 'I'll wait all night if need be, he must see me.'

'Please yourself.' The maid closed the door with a bang and Mary was left staring at the dark carved panelling, her heart beating rapidly and anger running like a tide through her veins. Who did this Brandon Sutton think he was? Well, he would not turn her away so easily. She moved to the garden seat at the entrance of the drive and sat down, her hands folded resolutely in her lap. He would see her even if she had to keep vigil outside his home all night. And yet, as her anger ebbed away, she felt suddenly as though she had been betrayed.

Chapter Two

Dirk Brandon Sutton was newly come to Sweyn's Eye, but already the old town with its hills and sudden valleys was in his blood. He stood now on the quay breathing in the scent of tar and salt, listening to the sound of fussy tugs leaving the harbour and feeling some of the tensions ease from his shoulders. His visit to the prison had not been an unqualified success – Billy Gray had shown a dumb hostility, refusing to answer any of his questions and Brandon had grown impatient.

'I expect my brother put you up to stealing the manuscript, didn't he?' His voice had been fierce and Gray had shaken his head in apparent bewilderment. He was either too stupid or too loyal to Dean to give anything away.

Griffiths, the weathered old warder who had spent half a lifetime on the prison's 'death cell', had not helped matters. He was by nature a bully and his harsh treatment of the new prisoner resulted only in an obdurate silence. If Billy had been merely a pawn in some devious game played by Dean, he was never going to admit it. Brandon frowned; his brother was not above trying to spike his guns and there had been an abiding hatred between them for many a year.

He sat on the low sea wall, his long legs stretched before him as he watched a Chinese walking surefootedly across a narrow plank that reached from the ship's side to the quay. The man's face was yellow, his eyes sloping, almost almond-shaped. Under his arm he carried a box from which came the distinctive sound of a cockerel crowing. Brandon smiled; the sailor would doubtless arrange a quick sale down at the Cape Horner, making enough money to keep him in ale for the rest of the day.

Brandon loved the sea and the colourful hustle of the dock, yet today the matter of Billy Gray worried the fringes of his mind. He remembered the night some weeks ago when he and his young works manager had disturbed an intruder at the office.

It was by mere chance that Brandon had decided to return to the works. He and Mark had spent the evening in the Mackworth Arms drinking ale and outside the weather had become cold with a hint of rain in the air. When Brandon entered the office with Mark close behind him they had found it in a shambles. Drawers of the desk and cabinet had been thrown to the floor and Brandon had known at once what the intruder had been after. But he had been out of luck.

Brandon smiled to himself, for the manuscript of his handbook for tinplate men was locked away in a safe at the bank. When it was published – and, by damn, Brandon intended it to be – it would revolutionise the scale of payment made to the workers. It would become the bible of the trade – a guide to tinplate sizes, so ensuring an equality in wages.

By going ahead with the project Brandon had made himself unpopular with the other owners in the area, not least his brother, Dean, who had a stake in most of the works in the vicinity of Sweyn's Eye. But Brandon had spent several years working on the book. Philadelphia had been rich in steel and he had made good use of the time spent there. He had no intention now of wasting his research, which he had expanded considerably since coming to Britain. Brandon's thoughts were bitter. His brother would never change, he would for ever harbour a grudge, blaming Brandon for his exile from America.

He moved from the quayside and strolled along at the water's edge, wrinkling his nose at the stink of the copper works higher up the valley. Then he paused and, irritated by his thoughts, thrust his hands in his pockets. He now fully recognised that he had made an error of judgement on the night of the burglary, but when he and Mark had picked up the trail of the intruder, following the tracks up to *Ty Mawr*, he had been coldly angry.

He had entered his brother's house without ceremony and accused Dean of treachery. Billy Gray had been standing in the hallway, his hair wild and his eyes haunted. When Mark had held him, searching his pockets, he had found a roll of banknotes. It had been enough for Brandon to send for the constable, but Dean of course had come out of it all as clean as a whistle.

Now Brandon left the seafront and made his way back onto the road. He ought to look in at the works before he returned home. Grenville Sutton would be eagerly waiting for him, drinking in anything Brandon had to say, for the old man did not have enough to occupy his time.

As Brandon strode through the gates of the Beaufort Steel and Tinplate Company, he reflected that as yet he was something of an unknown quantity to the men, a new broom who would presumably sweep clean and a foreigner to boot. Brandon sighed; it had been his father's idea to come over from the States in his declining years, for Grenville Sutton had evinced a sudden longing to return to the birthplace of his ancestors.

Yet even in those few months Brandon felt that he had proved himself to the hard-working men of the Welsh valleys. Indeed, it amused him to know that already he was referred to as the Iron Prince.

'Afternoon, Mark,' Brandon nodded to the young manager. 'Everything under control?'

'Aye, there's nothing for you to worry about sir; been keeping my eye on things as usual.' Mark half rose from the polished wooden chair but Brandon waved him back and sat on the edge of the table.

'I've been to the prison,' Brandon said abruptly. 'Tried to talk to Billy Gray.' He shook his head. 'I'm sure my brother is behind all this; Billy was working as his groom for some time, wasn't he?' He continued to speak without waiting for a reply: 'He wouldn't tell me a thing, he's a stubborn cuss.'

Mark nodded in agreement. 'Aye, he's the type to keep his trap shut all right. I don't suppose we'll ever know the truth of what happened that night, why old Twm Price was killed and that halfwit son of his frightened to death.'

Brandon ran his fingers through his thick unruly hair. 'I suppose you're right, but I feel it in my bones that Dean is mixed up in it all somehow.' He rose to his feet and his tone was brisk. 'Is everything under control here?'

'Oh, there was one nasty incident, sir.' Mark's eyes avoided Brandon's gaze. 'One of the openers cut her hand – not too bad, but I thought it best to send her home.'

Brandon looked up sharply. 'I'm willing to bet it wasn't one of the older women; they're all far too skilled to fumble the separating of the sheets.'

'No it was one of the new girls.' Mark's face had turned a dull red and Brandon hid a smile. It was quite clear that the lovely young girl had been distracted and it was not too difficult to find the culprit.

'Wish you'd learn to curb your urges, at least in working hours,' he said dryly and Mark's sheepish grin told Brandon he had come to the right conclusion.

'Been giving her a bit of incentive on the side,' Mark grinned widely. 'Sweet little thing, she is, good to take out on the mountaintop for a couple of hours, just to instruct her in her job, you understand.' He sighed. 'But it's Katie Murphy I've really got a fancy for; she's got beautiful red hair and skin like the cream off the milk.'

Brandon sat in the polished wooden chair before his desk and leaned back staring up at the younger man.

'Before you know it, your Katie'll have a ring on her finger and you'll have one through your nose,' he said slowly. 'I know what women can be like.'

Mark's expression changed. 'Anyone would think you didn't like the ladies. Had a bad experience with one of them, have you?' Then he grinned sheepishly. 'Sorry, it's none of my business, forget I spoke.'

'I've forgotten already.' Brandon spoke evenly, but a host of bitter memories were rising inside him. He was back once again in the heat and dust of his father's large estate in America: a young man eager for life, full of ideals and rarefied opinions. When he had become engaged to the local beauty, his life had seemed to stretch ahead in one long sunlit pattern.

Mary Anne Bloomfield had been soft and lovely, the belle of the small Southern state where she had been born. She was so sweetly innocent that Brandon had been enchanted with her. He had courted her slowly, curbing his hot blood, reluctant to lay so much as a finger on her and risk frightening her away. That had been his mistake, as he soon learned when she had run away with his brother, leaving a note to the effect that she wanted a man and not a young idealistic boy. The scandal had rocked the neighbourhood and Brandon had become obsessed with a longing for revenge.

But retribution had come swiftly upon Mary Anne, for Dean had very soon tired of her. He had deserted her, uncaring that she was full with his child, and when she had returned home in disgrace it was only to find herself packed off to an aunt in a distant country town. The ensuing scene in the Sutton household had been bitter. At least Dean had been forced to leave for Britain and it was clear that Grenville Sutton considered him a son no longer.

That was all a long time ago now. Brandon sighed, for memories of the past still had the power to burn in his gut. He could never forgive Dean and his brother knew it, but they had agreed to keep up appearances for their father's sake. In his declining years, Grenville Sutton wished for peace and harmony, not understanding that some wounds went too deep ever to be healed.

Brandon rose to his feet in one swift movement – power in the rippling muscles of his body, yet with a grace unexpected in such a tall man. 'I'm going to look over the new furnaces,' he said abruptly and then he was outdoors standing with the sunshine warm on his bare head.

He stared around in satisfaction, reflecting that he had made a good move in buying the Beaufort Steel and Tinplate Works. The twin stacks of the blast furnaces that reduced the rough ore to molten metal rose almost a hundred feet high, dwarfing the buildings of the steelworks which sprawled over two hundred acres of land separated by the curving line of the river Swan. The site was small by most standards, but was unusual in that it was equipped to process the metal from the first melting of the rough ore to the final stages of tinning. Adjacent to the works was the Great Western Railway line, which already had proved to be an asset in providing ready transportation as well as orders for the renewal of rails.

Brandon moved into the melting shop and stood for a moment accustoming himself to the noise and the searing heat. The air was acrid and it hurt to breathe too deeply of the smoke-laden atmosphere. But the men took it in their stride, working short shifts before the furnace mouth. Towels held over the lower part of the jaw and clamped between the teeth defeated some of the abrasive dust and a quick draught of ale or water kept the throat lubricated.

On taking up the ownership of the Beaufort Works Brandon had cut the time of each shift by an hour. To his satisfaction, production had increased in spite of the shorter hours, which proved his theory that tired men did not work at their best. And in the last few months the blast furnaces equipped with Cowper's patent stoves had turned out almost six thousand tons of pig iron a week, which for a small company was a not inconsiderable achievement.

Brandon stopped and nodded to Joe Phillips, who was a rugged fifty-year-old and perhaps one of the most experienced of the workers. He was certainly the most vigorous in his demands.

'Morning, boss.' Joe did not smile and Brandon paused, knowing there was going to be some complaint or other.

'What is it Joe?' he said affably. The man was a solid worker and an honest man, well worth listening to.

'All I want is a bit of *chwarae teg*, boss,' he said. 'Fair play is what the men in this foundry need and I'm the only one who will open my big trap and say so to your face.'

'All right. Go on.' Brandon concealed a smile.

'Well, for a start, those steam hammers, bloody dangerous, they are. Weigh nigh on eight tons a piece, and need maintenance they do.'

'What's wrong with them?' Brandon was suddenly alert, for accidents cost dearly in terms of manpower as well as money and he did not want to look for trouble.

'Going awkward somewhere in the innards,' Joe replied laconically. 'Clogged up, I shouldn't wonder, but it's not my place to say so, mind.'

Brandon ran his hand through his hair. He should have had all the equipment checked before he bought the place; there might be a great deal else going wrong and he had no capital for extensive repairs.

'I'll have the hammers seen to, Joe.' Even as he spoke, Brandon recognised that he had been so impressed by the two new open-hearth furnaces in the melting shop that he had assumed everything else would be in good working order; it seemed he was about to learn differently.

'Now is there anything else I should know?' He felt the acrid sting of heat and dust blast into his face as one of the furnaces was opened. Joe nodded, unaware of the particles of metal drifting downwards in a shaft of sunlight.

'It's the cutting of the taw, boss. There's one man doing small sheets of iron who is getting more wages than the fellow next to him who is working the bigger sizes. No sense in it!'

'I'm aware of the discrepancy in the wages, Joe,' Brandon said, 'and I am trying to do something about it, but all I can say at the moment is be patient.'

Joe tugged at the ends of his greying moustache, his eyes narrowed thoughtfully. 'Patience, it's not a lot to offer the boys, is it, sir? Patience is not what those boyos are used to. Live hard and work hard they do, and need a good pocketful of money to make life worthwhile.'

Brandon smiled and laid his hand on the older man's shoulder. 'Things are going to improve around here, Joe,' he said soberly.

'You can take my word for it.' He thrust his hands into his pockets and the thought of the manuscript locked away in the bank safe gave him a feeling of immense satisfaction.

He returned to the office and sank down into his chair, rubbing irritably at the dust on his face.

'Get a brew going, Mark,' he said. 'My throat is like the Sahara Desert. How those men stand the heat for so many hours a day, I'll never know.'

Mark pushed the blackened kettle onto the stove. 'They're used to it,' he said reasonably. 'Most of them have been doing nothing else but work in the steel and tinplate since they were boys. It's either that or go down the mines, nothing else round here.'

Brandon studied the young manager in silence for a moment. 'And what makes you different from the rest?' he asked at last. 'How did you escape the furnaces and the pits?'

Mark's youthful face was suddenly sober. 'My mam scrubbed floors,' he said simply. 'Took in other folks' washing; did anything so as to make money to get me an education. She died begging me not to go into the Morfa, the pit that killed my father and two older brothers.'

In silence, Mark made the tea and as Brandon watched him he warmed to the young man. Mark had character and determination written clearly into his strong features; he neither asked for nor expected pity; he was merely stating facts. Brandon took the cup Mark held towards him and sipped the steaming tea thoughtfully. He believed he had a closer affinity with Mark than to his own brother. Which reminded him that tonight he had promised to take his father to Dean's house. It would be a chore, not a pleasure, but Brandon would not willingly allow his father to see the hostility that existed – would always exist – between himself and Dean. He rose to his feet and placed the cup on the desk.

'Look after things here, will you?' He shrugged on his coat. 'I'm taking the rest of the day off.'

Mark nodded willingly. 'You can trust me, sir.'

Brandon's gaze was level. 'I guess I can at that,' he said quietly.

Then he left the office and strode out along the road. He had a great deal of thinking to do and he was at heart a solitary man. He loved the silence of the seashore in the early light of the morning with nothing but the cry of the seagulls overhead to distract him. But now it was late afternoon. The sun was dropping in a sky that was cloudless except where the issue of smoke from the conglomeration of works along the line of the river gushed upwards like an abuse.

Yet it was the industry, the copper, the steel and tinplate that was the heart of the place. Sweyn's Eye was growing fast, Brandon had seen that much in the six months that had passed since he had arrived in the town. Men needed the works and the works needed men; it was a union that could not be broken.

But it could be improved and this was what Brandon meant to do. For example, he could push through the publication of the handbook which would help put the wage structure on a fairer basis. He realised that making reforms was not the way to gain popularity, but when had he ever worried about that?

His thoughts took him back to the morning at the prison and determination grew in him to make Billy Gray talk. He was sure that the man was as guilty as hell; it was clear that through the young groom Dean had made yet another attempt to betray him. His bid to steal Brandon's manuscript left a bitter taste in the mouth, but then Dean showed loyalty to no man or woman for that matter.

His mood softened as he thought of Mary Jenkins, tall and statuesque. A proud woman, wearing her dignity like a cloak. There had been a fierce passion smouldering in her eyes, a dreamy sultriness not yet fully awakened that intrigued him. He would not be averse to taking her in his arms and teaching her the power of love, bringing the subdued sensuousness of the woman into full glory, for if he was not mistaken she was still virginal. And was there some element of revenge because she bore the same name as his first love, he wondered?

Since Mary Anne there had been many women in Brandon's life. He had enjoyed them, giving them his vigour and passion, but somehow nothing of his inner self had been touched. Perhaps it was a family trait, he mused, maybe the Suttons did not have it in them to give of themselves to any woman.

But now Mary Jenkins had stirred a chord and it made him uncomfortable to think of her eyes looking into his. He moved on across the golden sand. It was about time he went home to the house up on the western slope of the hill, not too far from *Ty Mawr* where his brother lived. Brandon sighed, knowing that his father would be waiting impatiently for his return, excited at the prospect of bringing his two sons together now that he had at last forced them into agreeing to a meeting.

Not that there was the remotest chance of that happening, not in reality, but Brandon would go along with his father and indulge him in his dreams. He would pay lip service to a friendship that could never be, knowing there was nothing but enmity between Dean and himself.

Brandon moved reluctantly away from the beach, thrusting his hands into his pockets and turning his back on the sea.

–

Mary had sat up on the hill with the cool breeze playing on her face for what seemed like hours. The sea far below rolled gently in onto the shore and the sun, moving lower now, slanted across the lush grass at her feet turning the buttercups to pure gold.

There was an air of peace and tranquillity here up on the western slopes that soothed the mind and brought relief, for Mary's thoughts had been in a turmoil when she had alighted from the tram several hours ago.

No one had left the house, or even sent the uppity young maid to Mary with a message. She wrestled with her disappointment and anger, knowing she must leave the fine imposing house before she made a complete fool of herself, for her urge was to hammer on the door closed so finally against her.

Yet there was a knot of pain inside her as she remembered the strange turquoise eyes of Brandon Sutton. She leaned back against the soft warm bark of the tree that spread sheltering arms above her head and tried to clear her mind, but it was an impossible task.

'It's soft in the head, you are, Mary Jenkins!' she said aloud. Yet she remembered so clearly the way Brandon Sutton had looked into her eyes back there at the prison, almost as though he would fight her battles for her. As he had led her inside the gate, away from the taunts of the other women, staring down at her as though she was a lovely, desirable woman, she had felt herself to be so. She pushed the thought away, for this was the man who had put Billy behind bars. He must be a rogue and a liar into the bargain and she was a simpleton to give Brandon so much as a moment of her time.

She rose to her feet reluctantly and stood for a moment looking down into the valley. She could see the line of the river and the huddle of buildings that squatted toad-like on the banks. Further away were the coffin-shaped docks with one tall-masted ship leaning drunkenly against the outward flow of the tide. She was achingly proud of her town; it was monumental in grandeur, with the shooting of sparks from the copper works and the blaze of lights from the foundries as the furnaces were tapped.

There was dirt and poverty in abundance and as a young woman, Mary had been seized by a wish to help the unfortunates who lived in narrow alleys untouched by sunshine in the slum areas of the town – the slums from which by hard work she had managed to drag herself and her brother.

She had often wondered why no one ever opened a shop that would bring the basic items of food such as flour and vegetables and also cheap tough clothing to the people at reasonable prices.

The Cooperative Movement was the nearest thing to salvation for the poor, yet even that offered no solution to the problem of those who wished to eat today and settle the account on payday.

She had often toyed with the idea of starting such a shop herself, but she had no resources. In any case, she had been busy working her way up to the position of overseer at the Canal Street Laundry. Mary prided herself that she could do every job herself from stoking boilers to ironing sheets, so when she had reason to reprimand a worker it was with a full knowledge of what difficulties were involved.

She shivered a little as she stared around at the large elegant villas that turned away from the stink of the town and looked out to sea where the lovely waters of the Channel separated the coast to Wales from Devonshire. Here lived the privileged of the town, wealthy steelworks owners and copper bosses. It was difficult not to feel some resentment, yet Mary recognised that it was these same people who had brought prosperity to Sweyn's Eye.

She looked towards the turreted roof of *Ty Mawr* and with a firm set to her lips began to walk towards the Big House. If she could not talk with Brandon Sutton, then she could at least see his brother. The elder Sutton son had been Billy's boss and a good one too as far as she knew. Surely he would do all he could to help the boy who had once served as his groom.

The maid who answered the back door to Mary was reluctant to let her in, yet there was something in the stance of the tall composed woman that spoke of authority.

'Wait by here. Mr Dean is expecting visitors, I don't think he'll be able to see you,' she said at last. As Mary stood listening to the soft whinnying of the horses across the yard, she tried to picture Billy stepping out of his home above the stable one night and finding himself sucked into a whirlpool of misery.

The girl returned after what seemed an endless wait and gestured for Mary to enter the house. She led the way along a narrow passageway past the kitchens that were bustling with activity and then Mary found herself in a spacious, well-lit hallway. She took a seat and linked her fingers in her lap while the maid stared down at her with large curious eyes.

'Mr Dean says I'm to bring you a cup of tea; he'll be some time yet.'

After what seemed an eternity, Dean Sutton came hurrying down the stairs smiling at her. 'Miss Jenkins, or shall I call you

Mary? Come on into the sitting room, honey.' He smiled down at her, a big rugged man with a large handsome head and a thick mane of hair. Mary knew him by sight, for he had been part of the fabric of Sweyn's Eye ever since she could remember.

'Sit down, Mary. I think I can guess why you've come; you're worried about Billy, aren't you?'

Mary nodded, overawed by the luxury of the room. Carpet gleamed, set against the floor in jewel colours; the furniture was large and highly polished and everywhere there was an air of light and spaciousness.

'*Duw*,' she said at last. 'There must be something an important man like you can do, Mr Sutton?' She floundered a little, wondering at her own audacity, but though she was trembling she forced herself to continue. 'Billy did nothing wrong, he was only looking after your interests, mind.'

Dean sat beside her on the sofa and covered her hand with his own large fingers.

'I know that, my dear, and I'll do all in my power to see that any injustice is put to rights.' He leaned closer. 'My brother is a hothead, flinging accusations without waiting to consider matters. He had a down on Billy right away, sent that manager of his for the constable. He vented his spleen on the first person he saw.' Dean paused a moment. 'For my part, I'm sure that whoever it was broke into my brother's office that night, it wasn't Billy Gray.'

Mary felt tears of gratitude rise to her eyes, but she held her head high and her face was impassive.

'That's a great relief to me, Mr Sutton.' She spoke with more confidence now. 'I'm so glad to know you're on Billy's side.'

The door opened suddenly and she blinked in surprise. Brandon Sutton had entered the room and behind him an older man, tall and broad of shoulder, his hair grey yet with the same stamp of strength on his features. That the three men regarding each other silently were related by blood was obvious at a glance.

'Father!' Dean was rising to his feet, holding out his hands warmly. 'And Dirk,' his voice faded. 'How good of you to come calling.'

'Do you have to call me Dirk?' The voice was clipped. 'You know I prefer Brandon.' Mary was unaware of the tension between the brothers; she was so angry with Brandon Sutton that she could not think straight.

He had condemned Billy without a hearing and had refused to face her when she had called at his house. Yet he stood before her now, proud and arrogant, as though he had done nothing wrong.

'You hypocrite!' she said in a low voice. 'How dare you go to the prison to see Billy when you were the one who put him there?'

She strode towards the door, her skirts swirling around her ankles. Then Brandon was standing over her, his hand on the doorknob as his eyes held hers. It was Mary who turned away first.

'You don't understand,' he said briskly. 'Billy Gray was put just where he belonged by the force of the law.'

'Oh, come on now, Brandon,' Dean drawled. 'Don't try to deny that it was you who accused my groom of trespassing on your property and stealing your money.'

Mary saw Brandon's eyes narrow. 'I don't deny anything. Billy Gray deserves all he's got and there are others who should be behind bars with him so just keep your mouth shut, Dean, no one is asking you to interfere in the matter.'

'Come on now, boys.' Old Mr Sutton moved forward: 'This is supposed to be a pleasant social evening for the three of us.' He looked icily in Mary's direction. 'Perhaps you would oblige me by leaving, young woman.'

Mary lifted her chin and defiantly returned the anger in the old man's eyes.

'Yes, I'll leave,' she said. 'But I'll say this much first. Your son is a liar and is not fit to be in decent company.' She moved into the hallway and as she glanced back over her shoulder, the three Sutton men were standing silent, like figures in a play. Mary let herself out into the cool of the early evening and as she made her way down the hill, there was a sadness deep and aching, growing within her.

Chapter Three

Mali Richardson stood near the window enjoying the warmth of the afternoon sun. The fragrant breeze drifted towards her, heavy with the scent of roses, and she felt a deep sense of peace. In her arms lay her young son, his bright head close to her breast. The boy was growing fast, she thought proudly and sighed softly, achingly aware of the happiness that had been hers since her marriage.

The small chapel where she had stood with Sterling almost two years earlier was the one she had attended all her life. And it had not worried her unduly that she was even then big with child or that the wedding between copper boss and working girl had caused a sensation in the town. All she had cared about was the happiness that filled her being as she stared up at the stained-glass window depicting the Lamb of God and felt the coolness of the plain gold band on her finger.

The door opened, startling her from her reverie and Sterling entered the room. His bright hair was shining in the sunlight and Mali's heart leaped with joy as it always did at the sight of her husband. She held out her hand towards him.

'Come here, *cariad*,' she said softly. 'There's something I want to tell you and it just won't wait a moment longer.'

As Sterling sat beside her, leaning over to kiss the boy in her arms, the child stirred, golden lashes fluttering against smooth rounded cheeks. Tears burned her eyes as Mali felt the weight of Sterling's head against her shoulder. She was safe and warm in the circle of his arms, the love between them almost tangible.

'Don't wake David,' she said gently. 'He's only just fallen asleep, so now pay attention while I talk to you.'

Her voice was light and teasing and Sterling looked up at her, his violet eyes bright. 'You're getting above yourself, Mali, giving orders like a martinet. Who would think you were once a little skinny waif who fought like a she-cat outside the gates of the Canal Street Laundry?'

Mali smiled reprovingly. 'I was never a skinny waif there's a fibber you are, Sterling Richardson.'

He leaned back consideringly. 'No, perhaps skinny is the wrong word. After all, you did provide a good show when you put Sally Benson on the floor like a champion fist-fighter.'

Mali felt herself blushing. 'I suppose I must have looked like a hoyden,' she said sheepishly, 'but that girl was asking for it, mind.'

'And she most certainly got it,' Sterling said wryly, 'and in the process your blouse was torn to shreds, which gave me ample opportunity to view the goods.'

He pinched at her breast playfully and Mali slapped his hand away.

'Be serious, now, and let me get a word in edgeways.' She smiled softly, unable to conceal her happiness as Sterling took her face between his hands questioningly.

'All right, I can see you're bursting to tell me; you look like the cat who ate the cream, so what is it?'

Mali's colour was high; she felt exhilarated and, strangely, just a little nervous. She wanted to savour the moment and yet have it over and done with.

'David is going to have a brother or sister,' she said softly. Once the words were spoken, she felt a fluttering of apprehension. It was strange how she had never entirely shaken off the strictures of her upbringing. In the Llewelyn household, intimacies had not been encouraged. Anything to do with the flesh was put aside, spoken of only in whispers and childbirth was something to be got over with as little fuss as possible. Slowly Mali lifted her head and looked into her husband's face.

'Say something, Sterling, you don't mind another babba round the place do you?'

As she fell unwittingly into the Welsh vernacular Sterling smiled. 'Of course I don't mind.' He moved away from her and thrust his hands into his pockets. 'But I can't help being concerned about you. After all, David is little more than a baby himself.'

Mali laughed spontaneously. 'Well, you should have thought of that before you came to my bed with such eagerness every night.' She blushed, knowing that she had always been as anxious to receive Sterling's love as he to give it.

'Come here.' Her hand lovingly caressed the crispness of the hair at the back of his neck. 'I'm a strong Welsh girl, remember? I'm just built for childbearing. Why, wasn't little David born without scarcely a pain? So don't be worried, now.' She kissed his mouth. 'Tell me you're pleased or I'll be grieving inside me.'

He smiled and to Mali it was like the sun breaking through the clouds. He was so handsome, his eyes alight, his gleaming hair falling over his brow, that she wanted to hold him close to her.

'Of course I'm pleased,' he said firmly. 'But I'm going to insist that you take things easy from now on. This supper party tonight for example – I've a good mind to call it off.'

'Oh, no, don't do that,' Mali said quickly. 'It's all arranged and I don't have anything to do but enjoy myself. You really have no idea how easy my life has been since I married you.'

Sterling smiled. 'Well, I should hope so, my wife has no need to lift a finger. Which brings me to the subject of the laundry.' He stared at her, frowning a little, and Mali felt a sudden sense of unease. She watched in silence as Sterling moved across the room to stand near the ornate fireplace.

'I've been wanting to say this for some time, Mali.' His deep blue eyes regarded her steadily. 'I want you to sell the business.' He paused. 'I might be old-fashioned, but I've never liked the thought of you working, especially now with the increased responsibilities you'll have at home.'

Mali fidgeted in her chair and the boy on her lap stirred, his eyes fluttering open for a second before closing sleepily once more.

'Let me think about it,' Mali said at last. 'The laundry means so much to me, Sterling, you know that. It gives me a sense of fulfilment to think of the way I've built it up into a thriving concern.'

'But you'll have all the fulfilment you want in looking after our children surely?' His tone became softer. 'I worry about you, Mali, you are not half as strong as you'd like to believe.'

She could read his anxiety plainly in the furrowing of his brows and she relented.

'If it troubles you so much, then of course I'll sell the laundry,' she said brightly, but her heart was heavy and she felt somehow bereft. The business was so much more than a source of income, it was a symbol of her rise from poverty and despair. But Sterling was right – her first duty now was to her family.

'You won't regret it.' He smiled at her from across the room and it was as though he had touched her with loving fingers. 'I take a great delight in being able to provide whatever you want,' he said. 'And now that the copper company is running so successfully, there's no need for you to burden yourself with responsibility for a business we don't require.' Mali was about to deny that the laundry was any sort of burden, but the words died on her lips at the loud imperious knocking on the door.

'Excuse me, Mrs Richardson, but it's time for Master David's tea.' The young nanny took the sleeping boy from Mali's reluctant arms, carefully holding him against the starched whiteness of her apron. David opened his eyes and smiled at once, his green eyes still misted with sleep.

'Thank you, Primmy.' Mali rose to her feet, clasping her hands together, knowing that she would never become used to handing over her son to another woman. She forced herself to smile at Primmy as she left the room. She was a good nanny and fond of David, but rather inclined to take charge in a high-handed manner almost as though he was her own child.

'What's wrong?' Sterling placed his arms around her waist and drew her close to him. 'You look as if you had bitten into a peach, only to find it was bitter.'

'You are too nosey for your own good, my boy.' Mali wound her arms around his neck and clung to him, breathing in the familiar scent of him, a mingling of soap and fresh air and masculinity. It would do no good to tell him that she wanted her son with her at all times, wanted to bring David up at her knee, the way she herself had been raised. Sterling's ways were those of the rich and it was a foregone conclusion that his children should have a nanny, a trained nurse who would take upon herself all the difficulties of child-rearing.

'Come along, I think you should rest before supper.' Sterling drew her towards the door. 'I shall come and sit with you for a while, smooth your forehead if you like until you fall asleep.'

'That would be nice.' Mali held on to the warmth of Sterling's hand as together they mounted the curving staircase. *Plas Rhianfa* was an elegant house, large and comfortable with ample room to bring up an enormous family. Mali smiled to herself, remembering the first time she had set eyes upon the mansion in which she was to spend her married life. It was such a far cry from the little house in Copperman's Row where she had been born that at first she had felt she was living in a palace. Strangely, it had not taken her very long to grow accustomed to spacious high-ceilinged rooms and servants who danced attendance on her every whim.

'Come on, you look half asleep already.' Sterling led her into the sunlit bedroom and drew the blinds across the windows. Gently he unfastened her gown and as she lay upon the softness of the bed, he settled himself beside her.

She reached up towards him, her arms warm as they clung to his neck, her eyes shining with an unspoken invitation. 'Suddenly I don't seem to be sleepy,' she whispered.

Sterling held her close, his hand cupping her breasts, his breathing ragged. 'Will I ever stop wanting you?' he asked hoarsely and Mali smiled happily.

'I hope not, *cariad*,' she whispered.

It was much later when Mali was dressing for supper that she realised how tired she was. She studied her reflection in the long mirror that swivelled to and fro on a gilt stand. 'Three months gone,' she said aloud, turning sideways for a better view of her figure, smiling with pleasure to see that only the fullness of her breasts revealed any sign of her condition. But she was too pale, she decided, and there were dark shadows beneath her eyes. She sighed, conceding that Sterling was right; she did need rest and the laundry was becoming too much for her. Not that she did a great deal of work there, it was mostly a matter of studying the books and checking the delivery dates against the records in the office.

The great bulk of responsibility was taken off her shoulders nowadays by Mary Jenkins. Mali smiled. Big Mary had been her friend ever since the days when she had stoked the boilers in the laundry wash house. Then she had thought of Mary as a martinet, for the overseer was strictness itself. But she was also fair; she had seen Mali's potential and had encouraged her to rise from her lowly job to the position of office worker she eventually held.

Mali felt a pang of remorse, for in her own joy and excitement over the discovery that she was again with child she had neglected Mary. She had given her time off from work, it was true, but she should have done more. Seeing Mary on the tram so unexpectedly, she had recognised lines of strain in the strong features and pity had flowed through her for Mary was so much a part of the past. Mali stared at her reflection unseeingly now, unaware of the sadness in her face. She was back in the dust and the stink of Copperman's Row and memories crowded uninvited into her mind.

When her father had died so tragically, seared and mutilated by the molten copper he was smelting, she had been in the depths of despair. However, the customers from the Mexico Fountain as well as the men from Maggie Dick's public bar had rallied round her. They had made a collection for Davie Llewelyn, bringing her money as well as their condolences. The sum had been large enough for Mali to approach the laundry boss and ask if she could buy shares in the firm. He had accepted gladly, for Mr Waddington had become old and sick and was fond of Mali as well as being impressed with her business acumen.

Mali sighed, recalling that the money had been stolen before she could hand it over, taken by the floosie who had hoped to marry Davie. It had seemed then as though all her hopes and dreams were to come to nothing, but Mr Waddington had taken her under his wing anyway and on his death, she found he had left the laundry to her.

Mali shook back her long dark hair impatiently. Living in the past was not going to help her now; she had agreed to sell the laundry and, although it would be like losing a part of herself, she would not go back on her word. But whoever took over the business would have to abide by one stricture, which was that Big Mary be kept on in her present capacity.

The supper party was not all that Mali had hoped it would be. She had invited few guests, mostly with a view to repaying past hospitality, but had buoyed up her spirits with the hope that the evening would be a pleasure as well as a duty.

Now she glanced discreetly round the table. No one appeared to notice her; it was strange, she reflected, how alone she felt amid the chatter. Opposite her sat Dean Sutton and beside him his delicate wife Bea. Bryn Thomas, the old doctor who had attended Mali at her confinement, sat with his back half turned towards his waspish wife, though whether by accident or design Mali could not say. Marian Thomas, unlike her husband, had no sense of humour and her lynx-like eyes appeared to miss nothing of what went on around her. Then there was Grenville Sutton, Dean's father; he was an unknown quantity as yet, though Mali had liked him on first sight. He should have been seated now with Sterling's mother, but at the last moment Victoria had pleaded some minor indisposition and begged to be excused. In all honesty, Mali thought dryly, she couldn't blame her mother-in-law one bit.

The immaculate white tablecloth was spread with fine silver that shimmered in the light from the chandeliers. The room was elegant, the furniture polished and gleaming, the carpet rich and deep. She was surrounded by luxury, but at this moment Mali felt she would rather be anywhere than playing hostess at *Plas Rhianfa*.

She sat back in her chair, content to remain silent while the men endlessly discussed business matters and the women enthused over the latest clothes displayed in Ben Evans' window. She knew that however gushing Marian Thomas might be, she could never accept Mali as one of her own kind. Bea Sutton was different; she offered genuine friendship and, catching Mali's eye, she smiled warmly.

That Bea's health was failing was painfully obvious, for her bones jutted from beneath the soft silk of her gown and though the evening was cool, beads of perspiration formed above the too well-coloured mouth.

Bea held Mali's glance, grimacing wryly as Marian Thomas chattered ceaselessly at her side. The men had fallen to discussing the possibility of a coming war and Mali shuddered. Placing her napkin carefully at the side of her plate, she rose.

'Let us go into the drawing room, where we'll be more comfortable.' She spoke quickly, conscious of the broadness of her Welsh accent. None of her guests spoke as she did, even though to Mali's knowledge most of them had been born and bred in Wales. The fine schools to which they were sent must have ironed out all traces of the language, she thought absently.

Bea slipped her hand through Mali's arm. 'You are looking particularly well tonight,' she said gently. 'If I'm not mistaken, there's a special reason for that extra bloom in your cheeks?'

'That's very observant of you, Bea.' Mali leaned closer: 'You're right, I'm going to have another baby.' Bea smiled, though there were lines of strain around her mouth and Mali felt her heart constrict with pity. It was common knowledge in Sweyn's Eye that Bea had once been in love with Sterling, had even carried his child. But that was before the awful discovery that Bea and

Sterling were related by blood. Mali wondered why she had never felt any jealousy for the other woman in her husband's life; perhaps it was because Bea was so genuinely warm and friendly.

'I know what you're thinking,' Bea whispered, 'and truly, it doesn't hurt any more. It was all a long time ago and now I'm truly in love with Dean.'

Mali remained silent. To all outward appearance, Dean Sutton was likeable enough, yet some inner core of distrust plagued her. She could not forget the talk about his being involved in the explosion at the Kilvey Deep some time ago. The mine, which was owned by Sterling, had been flooded bringing disaster to the town. There was no proof that Dean was implicated in any way, just gossip whispered by serving maids from one house to another. But Mali would never forget the dreadful scene at the pithead, the dead and dying lying around the blackened earth and her fear that Sterling was among the victims. For that reason Mali could never feel it in her to offer friendship to the big American but his wife Bea was different; she was a warm and generous woman and it grieved Mali to see her looking so ill.

'Come and sit down,' she gently. 'I'll pour you some iced tea. There's silly you were to come out tonight when the air is chilly, you should have stayed at home and got some rest.'

'I'll rest long enough when I'm dead.' Bea's words, though lightly spoken, carried conviction and Mali shivered.

'Don't talk like that Bea,' she said reprovingly. 'It's like tempting fate.'

'No need to tempt fate, Mali dear, it's here knocking at my door.' Bea smiled suddenly and lifted a strand of greying hair, tucking it into place absent-mindedly. 'Enough of me. What would you like this time, another boy to keep David company or would you prefer a daughter?'

Mali returned Bea's smile. 'I don't really mind. Perhaps a girl would be nice to dress in frills and fripperies but so long as the child is healthy, I shall not complain whatever it is.'

Mali glanced towards the dining room, wishing Sterling would join them. She found herself faintly uneasy without his presence to give her confidence.

'Where's poor dear Victoria?' Marian Thomas moved nearer to Mali, a speculative look on her face. Her eyes were long, almost oriental and thick black brows met over a prominent nose.

'I must say I thought she would grace us with her presence tonight. The poor dear has practically shut herself away since she had to move into that little house,' she continued stridently.

Mali managed to smile, though the implication behind Marian's words was that in moving to *Plas Rhianfa*, Mali had ousted Victoria Richardson from her rightful home. In fact, it had been Victoria's choice that she moved but Mali was not prepared to explain herself to the doctor's inquisitive wife.

'Since the death of Bea's father, Victoria has become a virtual recluse,' Marian continued mercilessly. 'It was all such a terrible shock to her, she and James were such good friends.'

Mali was angered by Marian's lack of sensitivity in reminding everyone present of the affair between Sterling's mother and Bea's father, an affair which had caused havoc particularly for Bea herself.

'Victoria keeps her own life very private,' Mali said evenly, 'and she doesn't pry into anyone else's business either.'

Marian didn't even blink at the implied reproof. 'What a charming way you have of speaking, dear, so sweet and funny.'

Bea tugged at Mali's arm, leading her away from where Marian Thomas was sitting. 'Don't let the old harridan upset you with her snobbish airs and graces. It's people like that who make my hackles rise – only an upstart grocer her father was, but she rides along on her husband's coat-tails, for everyone likes old Bryn.'

To Mali's relief the door opened and the men entered the room talking loudly. One of them laughed and the air of tension in the room was suddenly dispelled. Sterling came straight towards Mali, taking her hands in his.

'You look beautiful tonight,' he whispered. 'Motherhood suits you!' As Mali reached up to touch her husband's cheek in a brief gesture of affection, she felt Bea's eyes resting on her. Quickly she sat in a chair and folded her hands in her lap, feeling as though she was rubbing salt into old wounds. Not that Bea would think any such thing, she was far too sensible a woman for that.

'I'm quite pleased with myself.' Sterling sat on the arm of Mali's chair, looking down into her eyes. 'I think I've found a buyer for the laundry.'

Mali felt her heart contract. 'So soon?' she asked shakily. Sterling rested his hand on her shoulder.

'Not going to change your mind, are you?' He spoke with a hint of reproof in his voice and Mali shook her head.

'No, but I did ask for time to think it over. The laundry has been an important part of my life, you know that.'

'I know, darling, but I just happened to mention that we were considering selling up and Dean made me a very good offer for the place.'

Mali glanced over to where the American stood beside his father. The two men were very much alike, both big with large shoulders and leonine heads. The older Mr Sutton was still handsome, the lines of his face clear and firm. Dean caught her eye and smiled and Mali inclined her head, her thoughts racing.

'I'll bring him over to talk to you,' Sterling said and before Mali could protest he was striding across the room, catching Dean's arm and engaging in animated conversation with him.

'So you're selling your business.' Dean stood above her looking down indulgently. She gestured to a chair and as he sat opposite her, his large hands resting on his knees, she could not help noticing the solid gold signet ring gleaming on his finger.

'That's right,' Mali said and, feeling that she might have sounded a little ungracious, forced herself to smile. 'Are you interested in buying, then?'

'I sure am,' Dean nodded his large head. 'I like to have a finger in as many pies as possible.'

Mali stared at him thoughtfully. While it was true that she did not personally like Dean Sutton, she could not fault him on his loyalty to his workers. He had stood up in court and defended Billy Gray with convincing enthusiasm, swearing that Billy had always been upright and honest during the years he had served as his groom.

'There is one condition,' Mali said, 'but an easy one to fulfil. I want Mary Jenkins to keep her position as overseer at the laundry.' She searched his face, trying to read his expression.

'Mary's been a very good friend to me and I'm sure you'll find she's a fine worker. She knows the laundry inside out and everyone respects Big Mary.' Mali ended on a defensive note, knowing she was babbling nervously but there was something in Dean's manner which made her uneasy. Then the moment was past and he was smiling warmly.

'Anything you say, Mali. The young lady can stay on for just as long as she likes.'

Mali relaxed against the soft cushions of her chair. She must be getting fanciful, she chided herself, but she could have sworn for a moment that the blue eyes twinkling at her now from under heavy brows had held an expression that she could only describe as lustful – he had seemed to light up at the mention of Big Mary.

Sterling rested his hand on her chair in a caressing gesture. 'No need for you to worry about any of the arrangements,' he said, smiling down at her upturned face. 'I'll see to everything.' He turned to Grenville who had strolled across the room to join them, including him in the conversation.

'It's a very poorly kept secret that my wife is expecting another child,' he smiled, 'and so I'm insisting that she takes things easy.'

'Congratulations, both of you!' Grenville took her hand in his with great care, almost as if she might break. 'A woman's place is at her own fireside with her little ones round her skirts, that's what I say. Too many so-called ladies are calling like carrion crows for what they say are their rights, but 'taint proper and I've no time for such nonsense.'

She hid her chagrin, telling herself she must make allowances for an old man's fancies. Grenville was from a different age and from a background where women were reared to sit around and do nothing but stitch samplers all day. She wondered if Grenville knew of her past, of the stink and dirt of Copperman's Row where she'd been born – she doubted it.

Unconsciously she twisted her fingers together in her lap, thinking back to her life before she had married Sterling. She remembered vividly how her mam had gone to her grave in a pine box fashioned by her father's unskilled hands, carried on a cart that stank of fish however hard Mali scrubbed it.

'The matter is settled then?' Dean's smooth voice broke into the thoughts and Mali looked up at him swiftly. 'I'll get my lawyer to see to the papers as soon as possible,' he continued.

Mali felt a twinge of regret. Perhaps she could change her mind even now, she told herself. Then she became aware of Sterling's hand still smoothing her hair, as though he was soothing a frightened animal, and she knew it was too late, much too late.

'I'm delighted you're being sensible about this, Mali,' he said softly. 'I'll be much happier knowing you're at home instead of down at the laundry wearing yourself out labouring over the books.' His eyes were violet and Mali caught her breath, for she loved him so much she could deny him nothing. She clung to his hand as though seeking reassurance and his fingers curled in hers.

She would never forget the time when she had thought him lost to her for ever. It was at the Kilvey Deep just after the explosion, when the dead were being laid out on the dusty earth. Victoria was bending over the still figure of James Cardigan, weeping as though her heart would break and Mali, searching for Sterling, had been dragged down with pain and fear. The moment he had emerged from the chaos of the flooded pit lived with her now and sometimes she was almost afraid to let him out of her sight.

'I do declare you're the finest pair of lovebirds I ever did see,' Dean laughed as he rose to his feet. 'I'll leave you to yourselves now, but don't forget to see to that business for me, Sterling.' Then Dean rested his hand on his father's shoulder and the two men moved away, apparently deep in conversation.

'I hope I'm doing the right thing,' Mali said softly and Sterling made a wry face at her.

'Nothing has ever been proved against Dean,' he reminded her. 'In any case, this is business and his money is as good as anyone's.' His face softened. 'He'll be good to your friends down at the laundry, so don't worry your head about them.'

Mali relaxed in her chair. 'You always did get right to the heart of what's bothering me, Sterling. I swear sometimes that you can read my mind.'

She bit her lip, thinking of Mary – she must let her know that the business was about to change hands. Mary had said more than once that Dean was a fair boss to Billy Gray, so she should not be too upset that he had bought the laundry.

'Come on,' Sterling said gently, 'I think we should mingle with our guests, don't you?'

As Mali moved across the room on her husband's arm she felt light, the white head of a dandelion blowing in the breeze. Her independence was an easy price to pay for all the joy she had as Sterling's wife, she told herself… and yet a small, niggling doubt continued to irk her.

Chapter Four

The sun slanted across the roadway as Mary left the small neat house in Canal Street. A soft breeze lifted a strand of her hair and impatiently she tucked it into place behind her ears. She glanced back anxiously but the windows stared at her like blank eyes behind neat lace curtains.

There was no sign of Heath, although she had thought he might have waved to her or at least watched her leaving. But then, at sixteen years of age her brother was no longer a child, even though to her the soft planes of his face and the fine fluff of hair on his young chin were endearingly childlike.

She hurried smartly along the cobbled roadway, the heels of her shoes clicking as she walked. Outwardly, she knew she must appear composed but inside her there was a raging torrent of anger, for three times she had visited the prison and been turned unceremoniously away. Griffiths was bent on humiliating her, having his revenge because she had dared to speak her mind.

And now she had a new worry to face. Heath was sick, his thin frame racked with bouts of coughing. Mary felt a burning disappointment that her brother would not give up his work in the tinplate but, as he pointed out, the only alternative was the pit.

Nevertheless the job was a gruelling one and Heath returned home at night pale and exhausted, the fumes clinging to his clothing. The sweat on his shirt turned to rust so that the material became hard and unyielding.

Mary wished she could find him something else to do, but anything was better than the coal pits where the miners spent their lives digging in the ground like moles, never seeing sunshine or rain or feeling the softness of the sea breeze.

It seemed strange to be turning into the gates of the Canal Street Laundry knowing that Mali would no longer be seated at her desk, for she had written to say the business had been sold to Dean Sutton. Mary felt he would be fine as a boss, but no one could ever replace Mali.

In the packing room the air was hot but sweet with the scent of clean linen and Mary breathed in the familiar atmosphere with a feeling of satisfaction.

'Guess what's happened while you've been away, Mary?' Sally Benson was staring up from her job of packing sheets with eager eyes. 'The laundry has been sold, there's a shock it was to us all!'

Mary's expression remained bland. 'Mali has told me all about it and she has her reasons.' She was not prepared to explain that Mali was expecting another child.

Sally licked her lips as though savouring the moment. 'Well, you don't know everything, you'll see, Mary Jenkins.'

'Shut your mouth,' Mary said flatly and Sally sank back into her seat, her lips pressed firmly together although nothing could hide the gleam of spite in her eyes.

There was a sudden silence in the packing room as the door opened. Mary glanced up and it was as though she had been suddenly doused in cold water, for Grenville Sutton was coming towards her, his eyes like chips of ice.

'Miss Jenkins,' he said, looking at her with implacable gaze. 'I think you are a little late arriving, especially as this is your first morning back in harness as it were. The job of overseer carries a great deal of responsibility, you know.'

If it had been Mali standing there Mary would have explained at once that her brother was poorly, that Heath had spent the night coughing his young lungs away, but in the face of the old man's hostility she could say nothing.

'No excuses, hah? Well, I sure don't feel I can rely on you to run this laundry properly.' He paused and Mary stared at him bemused, unable to collect her thoughts.

'I thought Mr Dean Sutton was going to be boss.' She spoke woodenly, struggling against the quiver in her lips for she would not let Grenville Sutton see that she was upset.

'Well, you thought wrong then, didn't you?' He paused. 'Tell me, what would you say is the most lowly job in the laundry?'

Mary blinked rapidly, surprised by the sudden turn in the conversation. '*Duw*, stoking the boilers, I suppose, that's the place where most girls start here.'

'That's it then – as a disciplinary measure you will be required to stoke the boilers for one week, Miss Jenkins.'

She felt anger begin to flower within her. 'Mr Sutton, you're being unfair to me. I was only a few minutes late and I have my reasons.'

'I'm not interested in reasons,' he said as he turned away impatiently. 'Either you stoke the boilers or you return to your home – sure I can't put it more plainly than that.'

Mary stood for a long moment trying to regain her composure, conscious of Sally Benson's wide eyes taking in her every move. Then she turned and walked, head high, towards the boiler house. She hurried down the rickety staircase with her heart thumping, anger at the injustice meted out to her like a roaring, rushing tide inside her head.

'Lordy be and what are you doin' here, Mary?' Sarah looked down from her short flight of steps and stopped poking the washing back into the steaming water.

'I'm to stoke the fires,' Mary said evenly. 'That's what the new boss wants me to do and so I'm doing it.' Sarah snapped shut the lid of the boiler and stared at Mary aghast. 'But you're the overseer, for God's sake. You're not exactly dressed proper for carrying coal, are you?'

'Tell Mr Sutton that,' Mary said slowly, aware that her colour was high and that despair was beating like a bird in her chest struggling to be free.

'Well I never!' Sarah gaped like a fish in a bowl. 'Tell him to stick his job, I would, stoking is no job for the likes of you, Mary Jenkins.'

Mary sighed. She was calmer now, thinking of Heath back at home gasping for breath was enough to chase all her anger away. 'I've done it before, I can do it again,' she spoke fiercely. 'I'll show Mr Sutton that I'm made of sterner stuff than he thinks.'

A few of the other women had gathered round, staring at Mary as if she had grown two heads.

'What would Mali Richardson say?' One of the older women pushed the cap back from her hair and wiped the sweat from her brow with the corner of her apron.

Mary shrugged. 'She wouldn't be pleased.' That was an understatement, for Mali would be furious and Mary felt certain that she had known nothing about Grenville Sutton taking over the reins of the business.

Quickly Mary grasped the handle of the coal scuttle, staring around edgily. 'I should get on with your work if I were you, girls. We don't want Mr Sutton coming down heavy on anyone else, do we?'

The job itself was no effort for Mary, since she had worked the boiler-house fires as a young girl and as for lifting the buckets full of coal, she had strength enough to go on doing it all day. It was the injustice that got her, the inner knowledge that old Mr Sutton had a grudge against her and was paying her back for her angry words spoken in the heat of the moment. She had ignited a bitter scene between Dean and Brandon and Mr Sutton did not intend to forget or forgive her for causing the two brothers to quarrel.

At grub-break, Mary sat dispiritedly on an upturned box and rubbed the coal dust from her fingers with a handful of straw.

'Mother of the Blessed Virgin, I heard you were down here but I didn't believe it.' The soft Irish voice was unmistakeable and Mary turned with a smile.

'And what are you doing in the boiler house, Katie Murphy? You'll be getting yourself the sack if you don't look out.'

'That old tyrant, he's only been here five minutes and he's treating you like dirt – well, we won't have it.'

Mary shook her head reprovingly. 'Now don't do anything silly, Katie, you all need your jobs and can't afford to be uppity with the new boss.'

'Uppity, is it? We'll all stop work if he doesn't bring you back up to the packing room and he can put that in his pipe and smoke it!'

Katie sat beside Mary, her long red hair swinging over her shoulders like spun copper in the sunlight. She was no longer the exuberant girl she had been when Mary first met her; Katie had known suffering and had lost the man she loved and that had changed her. And yet there was a new serenity in her eyes now, a way of holding her slim shoulders that spoke of self-confidence.

'Now look, *merchi*, I don't want any fuss, right?' Mary said positively. 'A week the boss man said and a week I'll do – then we'll take it from there, see?'

Katie sighed. 'I'm not happy about it, Mary, not happy at all. Sure an' won't we all be asked to work the boilers next? If he can do it to you, Mary, he can do it to any of us.'

Mary frowned. 'No, this is a personal thing between me and him and I don't want anyone else interfering.'

Katie pushed back her hair and stared at Mary soberly. 'But it was you who always said we must stick up for our rights,' she said softly. 'You told us that we as workers must never be put upon, that we must fight tooth and nail against any injustice from the bosses, am I right?'

'Yes, of course you're right,' Mary conceded, 'but for this once, just leave it be, as a favour to me, will you, girl?'

Katie sighed. 'All right, do your week's penance for whatever it is Mr Sutton thinks you've done, but after that there will be a fuss, believe me.'

She paused and bit her lip. 'Anything to do with Billy, is it, Mary? Now I'm not prying, but if you're being victimised because you have a man who is behind bars, then it's nothing to do with the new boss and I'll be the first to tell him so.'

'I don't want to talk about it,' Mary said evenly. 'It's just something between Mr Sutton and me and we must work it out ourselves. Now go back to the packing room before you get covered in dirt. Oh, and Katie, keep an eye on Rhian, will you? I didn't have a chance to see her when I first came in to work. Shaping up all right, is she?'

Katie paused for a fraction of a second. 'Aye, she'll do fine once she gets used to it; don't worry your head about her, think of yourself for a change.'

As the afternoon shift began, Mary lifted the scuttle and made for the coalhouse where the mounds of fuel stood like eggs laid by black hens. She felt warmed inside, proud of the support offered by her workmates. But she could not allow them to take any action that might rebound on them.

'Hey, wait a minute, Mary, you're wearing the drawers off me! I can't keep up with you.'

Mary turned, smiling, 'It's all right, Doris. I won't do you out of your job as stoker, don't worry – this is a temporary arrangement only. How's that boy of yours, growing like a stick I expect?'

Doris smiled broadly. 'Big as a pea pod about to burst, he is, fine and handsome just like his dad.'

Mary hid a smile. 'Any sign of that man of yours putting a ring on your finger?' she asked and Doris snorted inelegantly.

'Gawd, I'm lucky if he comes home to me half the time. I think he's servicing most of the girls in the neighbourhood – all those that will have him anyway.' She smirked. 'But he always comes back to good old Doris in the end, so I'm keeping my trap shut. Don't want him going off me altogether.'

'Well, watch you don't get your belly full again,' Mary warned, 'One mistake is all right, two is daft, mind.'

'Don't you worry about that,' Doris said smugly. 'I got Mrs Benson to give me something that stops you from clicking for a babba. I won't have any more – can't afford 'em, need my money too much I do. There's no relying on my man to bring anything in.'

Mary eased her back, rubbing it with the palm of her hand. 'Right then, we'd better get on – don't want the boss man breathing down our necks, do we?'

Doris spat deliberately on to the dust of the floor. 'That's what I thinks of 'im for doing this to you, Mary.' Nevertheless, she took her scuttle and hauled it back into the boiler house.

Mary spent the rest of the afternoon deep in thought. She worked without effort, loading coal into the scuttles, feeding the fires, doing three times as much work as Doris. Once Sarah commented on the brilliance of the fire and the busy way her washing was boiling in the steaming water, but Mary simply smiled absent-mindedly.

She wondered apprehensively what would happen at the end of the week, for she could not believe that Mr Sutton would simply reinstate her. She feared that he would keep on pecking at her until she lost all patience and gave up her job.

Mary was shrewd enough to know that Mali would insist that the present staff be kept on at the laundry, so it was doubtful that the new owner would dismiss her out of hand – rather he would do all in his power to make it impossible for her to stay.

And she needed her job, relying on the good wages she earned to pay for the upkeep of her beautiful home.

She had moved to Canal Street about six months ago, renting a fine clean, airy house which she had made her own with the introduction of warm curtains and good second-hand furniture. It was her pride and joy, a symbol of her achievement. From poor beginnings, she had gradually made a better life for herself and for Heath and she would not willingly see it all disappear into the mist.

Her thoughts turned to Mrs Delmai Richardson, who called once a month to collect her rent. Always dressed in finery, she was; ladylike on the outside but with an unsatisfied glow in her dark eyes that betrayed her as a wanton. And who could blame her, married to Rickie Richardson?

He was so different from his brother that the two did not look even remotely alike. Sterling was a golden man, handsome and tall with smiling eyes, while Rickie had a meanness in him that not even good grooming could conceal.

Mary, like everyone else in Sweyn's Eye, had heard the gossip about the Richardson inheritance. Sterling, though born in wedlock, was said to be a by-blow, the result of an illicit passion between Victoria Richardson and James Cardigan. That the story was in all probability true did not bother Mary one little bit. In marrying Mali he had flouted convention, but then Mali was an unusual woman who had made a success of her life against all odds and Mary was proud of her.

When Mali had sold the laundry she had believed that Dean Sutton would be running it himself. She knew that the American had been good to Billy Gray and believed he would be equally kind to Mary. In any event, it was all over and done with now and Mary felt she must make the best of it. Maybe after her week of penance, as Katie had called it, she would find herself back in the packing room as though nothing untoward had happened.

She held her head high as she once more took up the coal scuttle. While she was boiler-house girl, she would do the job well and show Mr Sutton that he could not break her spirit. In spite of herself her lips quivered; she longed to fling the fuel to the seven winds and tell the new boss what he could do with the Canal Street Laundry. Then she thought of Heath, lying in his bed back home, his face pale and his body thin and weary with coughing and with a sigh, she went back to work.

–

The early morning light shone into the small neat kitchen as Heath Jenkins pushed back the sheets and began to dress. He stifled a cough, fearful of waking Mary, for she would be on his back like a virago, telling him to keep to the bed she had made up for him near to the fire. Always mollycodling him, she was, like a mother hen – but she was all right, was his sister.

He grimaced as he thought of Mary's humiliation, for the gossip had spread like wildfire along Canal Street and Heath was soon aware of her demotion to boiler stoker.

He drew on his knee-length flannel drawers and tied the tapes neatly about his legs. His moleskin trousers creaked and cracked as he buttoned them around his thin waist, for they were stiff with sweat and spilled water gone rusty. His flannel shirt, traditional among tinplate men, was short, reaching just below his ribcage which made for coolness in the face of the furnace fire. Around his neck he swung a sweat rag made of soft gauze. Now he looked like the tinworker he was and he was proud of it.

He let himself out of the house and paused in the street to put on his clogs before joining the stream of men making their way to the Beaufort Works.

The stacks of the blast furnaces rose high into the air and on a dark night when the tapping out was done the entire sky was illuminated for miles around. It was not in the iron that Heath spent his time but across the river in the tinplate section of the works.

As yet he was only a behinder, and at his age, lucky to find work in the mill at all. Later he would be promoted to the position of doubler, or ever rollerman. He would be earning high wages then and Mary could give up her job altogether, stay at home the way a woman should do.

'Mornin' boyo, how's that fine sister of yours then?' A man tall and as thin as Heath himself fell into step with him. Heath grinned. 'Well, Ianto, she's just as lovely and just as far away from your grubby hands as ever.'

'Tut tut, will you listen to the boy? There's a nice thing to say to a fellow who is in every respect a gentleman. Not to mention being the best doubler in the business.'

'That's something I do agree with,' Heath said smiling. 'If I get to be half as skilful with the steel as you then I'll be a happy man.'

Ianto swelled with pride. 'A damn orator you'll be, boyo with that silver tongue, or perhaps a member of parliament. Wasted you are in the tinplate anyway.'

The mill was shimmering with heat, the furnaceman having been more than liberal with the coal.

'Got some iron in the oven for you, Ianto,' he said. 'There's a rush on. It seems that Mansion Polish sent in a big order and Mark's been over here screaming for tinbar like it was gold.'

'Let 'em scream, Rees, they don't give you no medals here if you kill yourself.' Ianto shrugged off his coat and drew on a clean duck apron. 'The boss sure as hell won't pay a man for spoiled pieces of eight and that's all that comes of rushing the job. Where's Kenny? Can't start the heat at all without a rollerman.'

Heath tied an apron round his thin frame and over it a piece of sacking. He rolled up his sleeves and wiped his face with his sweat rag, preparing for the long shift that was ahead of him.

His job was to accept the sheets from the rollerman. The razor-sharp steel would come hot and fast through the taw pair, the first of the rolling mills, and Heath would grip the tongs ready to grasp the flexible sheet and swing it back to the rollerman. Once begun, the heat was a never-ending round of activity continuing until all the pieces had been doubled four times.

He grinned to himself, remembering his first shift in the mill. He had been so overcome with the heat and had drunk so much water that his belly had swelled and he had been violently sick.

'Sorry, boys, didn't mean to be late.' The rollerman hurried into the mill tying on his apron, his hair flattened across his forehead. 'My Ida just gave birth again – six we've got now, all boys; she'll kill me if I father another teapot with a spout on it.'

Rees was busy taking the iron from the first of the two furnaces that stood side by side the fires roaring like wounded beasts. He pulled the door open and with long tongs manhandled the hot iron over to the rollerman.

'Not so much talk and more work, is it?' he said dryly.

The thick pieces of iron baulked and banged through the rollers with a bone-shuddering noise but Heath scarcely noticed it. He took a draught of water, thirsty already, the sweat beading his face and catching in the fine hairs of his upper lip.

He fell quickly into the rhythm of the heat. The sheets went from furnace to rollerman and then to him and, deftly, Heath lifted the hot metal over the pair of rollers and when it was returned to him swung it neatly onto the floor.

Ianto wielded the tongs with great skill as, with his clogged foot resting on the hot sheet of metal, he flipped the edges over so that a crease was formed. It appeared as simple as folding a blanket, Heath thought as he watched Ianto manipulate the sheet onto his table.

The piece was returned to Rees, whose fourteen-inch tongs deftly wielded the steel back into the furnace. The heat would continue until the sheets had been folded four times, making pieces of eight.

Heath breathed deeply, sandwiched between the sizzling gusts of air belching from the furnaces in front of him and the growing stack of hot sheets neatly piled behind him. He prayed that his chest would not play him up, for a bout of prolonged coughing would throw the heat right out of balance. He paused to drink some water, his muscles aching and sweat running from the nape of his neck along his spine. The work was gruelling, but it was man's work and Heath was proud of his part in it.

The heat had just finished when Heath became aware of the boss coming across the floor of the mill. The men touched their caps in respect, but Mr Brandon Sutton waved the gesture aside impatiently. He was an American and far more familiar with his men than any of the other bosses in the neighbouring works.

'I want to talk to you,' he said, folding his arms across his chest. He was a fine man, tall and strong with muscles like a navvy. Heath was willing to bet that Mr Sutton would not be above taking off his coat and rolling up his shirtsleeves and joining the men in the heat.

'Talk away, sir, you've chosen your time right, there's a heat just finished.' Rees, as senior man in the mill, spoke up for the others: 'You don't look too cheerful, sir – bad news, is it?'

Brandon Sutton nodded. 'I'm going to have to ask you to accept a cut in wages,' he said. 'I'm speaking bluntly now, man to man, for it's either that or lay some of you off.'

'But I thought Mansion Polish was crying out for tin,' Heath surprised himself by saying forcefully.

Brandon Sutton looked at him levelly. 'While that's true, there are also other considerations. You've doubtless heard that in some steel mills men are striking. I've tried my best to keep your wages fair but without a scale of pay properly set down and recognised by owners, I guess it's a pretty difficult task.'

Heath pondered this a moment. 'But then you said you'd try to implement such a scale; there's talk that you're working on it now.' He was amazed at his own boldness, but Brandon Sutton had a reputation for honesty and fair play and Heath believed they might as well learn the worst from him right now.

'That's right.' The American allowed himself a smile. 'And you can bet your last dollar that I'm making myself mighty unpopular round these parts. So much so that it's affecting trade, I'm being squeezed out you might say.' He shrugged his big shoulders. 'If you men stick by me now, we have a chance of winning through and there's a lot more than my profits at stake.'

The older men had fallen silent and it seemed to Heath that unless he asked questions no one else would.

'I'm willing to accept a cut in wages for a start,' he said firmly. 'But there's something I would like to ask; how would this wages scale work?'

Brandon looked at him with interest. 'You're Heath Jenkins, aren't you?' he asked. 'Mary Jenkins' brother? I guess there's a great family likeness between you.' Heath hid his surprise, for he had had no idea that his boss knew anything about him or his sister. Before he could think of a reply, Brandon was speaking again.

'As it stands now, you only get paid by what comes out at the end of a watch. Any spoiled tinplate, any under the correct weight or cut short by the shearers is wasted time and effort. Apart from that, a man might cut seventy boxes of sheet and find at the weigh-in that half of them are rejects. Is that not so?' He paused, looking round at the men as though trying to gauge their reactions.

'My aim is to have set prices for work done so that no one is cheated at the end of the day.'

'Sounds very grand,' Rees said doubtfully, 'but will it work, sir?'

Brandon Sutton regarded him steadily. 'I don't know, but we can at least give it a try. Now, what do you older men say about a cut in wages? I hope it will be a temporary measure but I can't say for sure. I guess you'll suffer most, Kenny, since you have a large family to support, but some economies must be made and soon.'

'I'm with Heath,' Rees said. 'Things are bad in the valleys, I know that; I don't go round with my eyes shut and if taking a drop in pay now will keep me my job, then I'm all for it.'

'Then I guess everyone is in agreement.' Brandon turned to look at the neat stacked sheets and nodded approvingly. 'That's what I call work well done and I wish I was giving you a raise instead of a reduction in pay, but don't despair – that time might come and sooner than we think.'

Heath watched as the boss strode away. He was strong, a man of principles and Heath admired his guts.

'*Duw*, I don't know what my old woman will say.' Ianto wiped his face with his sweat rag and shook his head slowly. 'Times are getting bad, boys. I sometimes wonder what the world is coming to.'

Rees stared at him levelly. 'Well, we still have a job,' he said reasonably, 'and a boss who knows how much skill goes into the sheets, so things could be much worse, man.'

As another heat began, Heath was deep in thought. He would ask Mary if she knew the boss, for it was strange he should mention her by name. Not that Heath blamed any man for looking at his sister – she was a fine woman, tall and beautiful with thick abundant hair and a gleam of health in her face.

He wondered wryly if he had been the runt of the litter; at sixteen he was still small, though his shoulders were beginning to fill out a little now and the muscles of his arms were hard and strong. Perhaps what Mary had told him was true and the Jenkins family were slow developers, becoming tall only after twenty years of age was reached.

Deftly he swung a hot steel sheet over the pair and smiled at Kenny as he accepted it with his tongs. Kenny winked back. 'Don't work too hard now, boyo, save some of your sap for the girls, is it?'

A picture of Rhian Gray sprang to Heath's mind. She was a pert girl, very full of herself and he felt like taking a pinch out of that pride of hers. Though since Billy's imprisonment she had become a little quiet, grieving for her brother no doubt.

Mary was looking after her well though; she had even managed to find Rhian a job in the laundry. Pretty eyes Rhian had, and a lovely slim body. And it was her resistance that excited him, even thinking about her brought a tingling to his loins.

He suppressed a smile. In one aspect at least he was not lacking, as many a girl from the wash house would readily testify. He sighed and looked up at the small patch of sky that could be seen through an overhead window. Tonight, in spite of Mary's mollycodling, he would be out tomcatting – it was what made all the hard toil of life seem worthwhile.

Chapter Five

'But I didn't want to work in the laundry in the first place!' Rhian Gray sat in the front parlour of the house in Canal Street staring rebelliously at Mary Jenkins. Her small face was set into lines of obstinacy and her large dark eyes flashed with fire. 'And now that that old goat owns it, I want nothing more to do with the place.' She placed her small hands in her lap, folding her fingers together as though that was the end of the matter.

Mary listened to the morning bells ringing from the Church of St Nicholas on the Hill, trying to quell the impatience rising within her.

'That's all you ever do, is complain, Rhian,' she said mildly. 'You grumble that your aunt treats you like a baby and then it's Carrie who's at fault for expecting you to help more around the house. Try to remember that Carrie is good to come in and work every day – you'd be in a fine pickle without her. You can't have everything your own way, you know.'

'I don't see why not.' Rhian flung back her long hair. 'I can't live with Aunt Agnes for ever; I'll need a home of my own before long.'

Mary sighed, knowing that Rhian had the foolish idea that she could coax Heath into marrying her. Little did she know that he was out this very moment with another girl. But Mary tried to make allowances for Rhian; she was young and thoughtless, she didn't mean to hurt anyone with her outspokenness. All the same, she needed putting in her place now and again.

'Your auntie has been like a mother to you, mind,' Mary said quietly. 'She gave you and Billy a home all those years ago when your own mam died. You mustn't think of up and leaving her now that she's getting old and needs you.'

'Our Billy couldn't wait to get out of Auntie's house,' Rhian protested. 'Went into service as groom to Mr Sutton as soon as he was old enough. Why should I be the one to be left behind?'

Mary sighed. 'Well, don't think you're moving in here, my girl. There's enough for me to do without another mouth to feed and another one to fetch and carry for. No, you be patient – stay with your Auntie Agnes and be thankful you have a roof over your head. As for the job at the laundry, that's entirely up to you. I told Billy I'd look after you and I have done as far as possible, but wet-nurse you I shan't.'

Rhian rose to her feet, a rosy flush on her face. 'Well, that Mr Sutton is a horrible old man, mind, he talks to us as if we're daft. I don't think I can stand it another day.'

'Well, just think about this,' Mary said firmly. 'Jobs are scarce around these parts, what with all the strikes and so on, so you bite your tongue until you're sure you can find something else to go to.' She paused, regarding Rhian steadily. 'Listen to me, now, for this is very important; I'm not allowed to visit Billy so you must go, no shirking it, right?'

'I won't forget.' Rhian spoke truculently, then her face brightened. 'I could always work in the tinplate, there's plenty of jobs for picklers or openers.'

Mary shook her head. 'I doubt it, Heath's told me that men are being asked to take a cut in wages. Anyway, have you seen what happens to the girls who work at the pickling? The acid makes their teeth rot and fall from their head; that's not a fairy tale, it's a plain fact. As for the openers, they get more cuts than any of the men. But do as you like, I wash my hands of you.' She moved to the door and opened it. 'Go on off home, I'll see you at the laundry – if you stay.'

Rhian's lip quivered, suddenly she put her arms around Mary's waist and hugged her. 'I didn't mean to moan,' she said. 'I'll work at the laundry and try to settle down with Auntie Agnes, if that's what you want me to do.'

Mary patted her hair absent-mindedly. What she wanted the girl to do was to grow up and stand on her own two feet.

When Rhian had left, Mary felt restless. She stared through the window and felt the softness of the breeze ruffle her long hair which hung loose to her shoulders. She felt suddenly constricted – she must get out into the sunshine, away from her thoughts, all of which seemed unpleasant just now.

Pulling a light shawl over her shoulders, Mary stepped out of the house, leaving the door ajar. Heath would be returning soon, anxious for sleep. He had insisted on going to work though he still coughed most of the night away. She smiled to herself at the thought that even after a long shift he found the strength to go up on the mountain with some girl or other.

As Mary strolled along the cobbled road past the closed gates of the Canal Street Laundry a pain seemed to grip her and she had a sudden vision of the gates being closed to her for ever. But that was surely an absurd fancy? Mr Sutton would recover from his fit of anger and reinstate her; anything else was unthinkable.

She found herself outside the prison and in a spirit of defiance, she knocked on the wooden door. It was Griffiths who answered and his face was like granite. Mary's heart sank. The man did not speak a word, he simply slammed the door in her face and trembling she turned away.

It did not take her long to reach her favourite spot near the docks. From the old quay she could sit and watch the ships lifting and falling with the incoming tide. She breathed in the scent of tar and salt and felt comforted by the familiarity of her surroundings.

It was strange, she mused, that people constantly came to her for help and guidance, leaned on her broad shoulders and looked to her for support. Just because she was tall and strong! No one stopped to consider for even a moment that she might be in need of help herself.

The church bells rang out melodiously over Sweyn's Eye and Mary closed her eyes, leaning back against the warmth of the stone wall, wondering why it was that religion had never drawn her. In that respect she was different from so many of the townspeople, for it was a ritual to attend church or chapel at least three times on the sabbath. But even when revivalists swept through Sweyn's Eye, convincing the backsliders to mend their ways, Mary had never indulged in the mass fervour which faded as soon as the preacher moved to the next village.

Mary became aware of a shadow falling over her and glanced up to see a tall figure whose broad shoulders blocked out the sun. Her heart began to beat swiftly, the blood rushed into her ears and she felt she could hardly breathe.

'So, Mary Jenkins, I find you occupying my favourite spot – are you waiting here to plead for Billy Gray?' Brandon Sutton stood bareheaded, his dark hair curling about the collar of his crisp shirt. He wore no jacket and his riding breeches clung to the strong muscles of his legs; in his hand he held a riding crop and he looked every inch lord and master of all he surveyed. But not of me, Mary told herself as she rose slowly to her feet.

'How dare you even speak to me after what you've done?' She spoke more in surprise than anger.

He took her arm. 'I have done nothing.' He propelled her away from the dock and towards a small grove of trees that clung precariously to the hillside. Mary tried to free herself but his hand held her firmly.

'I don't know what you think you're doing, mind,' she said breathlessly. 'I don't want to talk to you, don't you understand?'

The arch of greenery spread over them, cutting out the heat of the sun. Mary felt as though she had been placed in a bowl of dark glass which closed her in so that there was no escape.

'I want to know why you are following me?'

'I'm not following you!' She glanced up at him. He was so handsome, so masculine, his hair curling crisply around his face. Quickly, Mary looked away from him.

'You are so wrong about Billy,' she said in a low voice. 'You had him put in prison, that's all I know, and he's innocent.'

He stood looking at her, not touching her now, his gaze compelling. Mary met his eyes almost against her will.

'I can't apologise for doing my duty,' he said reasonably. 'How can he be anything but guilty? He was at my brother's house, he had some of my money on him; I had no choice but to send for the constable.'

'Do you know how they treat him in there?' Mary demanded, gesturing along the stretch of golden beach to where the prison stood grey and austere in the shadows. 'They act as if he's a mongrel to be whipped and they kick at his feet. Breaking his spirit they are and he's an innocent man – it's not fair.'

She felt tears come to her eyes and blinked hard; she would not allow this stranger to see her distress.

'I know all that.' His voice seemed to touch her like soft fingers. 'I don't condone barbaric treatment even for a thief, so I shall speak to Griffiths, the man needs putting in his place.'

There was conviction in his tone and Mary felt hope begin to warm her. She glanced up at him and slowly he smiled. They regarded each other steadily for a long moment, both wary like the adversaries they were, then Mary shook her head as though to clear it.

Her feelings were a tumble of confusion. This was the man she thought of as her enemy, yet she could not deny there was an attraction between them, an invisible force that persuaded her to trust him.

Slowly he lifted his hand and held it towards her. 'Come on, Mary, let's talk. I'm not a vindictive man and I'd like to help you in any way I can.'

Without realising it, she placed her fingers in his, she and this stranger seemed suddenly linked together and a power seemed to flow from him. Then she shivered in spite of the warmth of the day and quickly withdrew her hand.

'All right,' she said. 'Let's walk around the hill and away from the town. I don't want to be taken for a loose woman, mind.'

She thought that Brandon was hiding a smile, for there was laughter in his voice when he spoke.

'No one would take you for anything but a lady, Mary.' She glanced at him, but his face was turned away from her and she could not read his expression.

'Tell me, why should Billy want to rob you and why, in God's name, should he attack Twm-Nightwatchman?' She was trembling as though she had been running through the lush grass for hours.

'As I said, Billy had notes from my safe tucked in his pocket. My brother insisted that the Price men were on his property at his express orders, and it seemed that Gerwin Price had seen Billy running up the hill from the direction of my house – reason enough for the attack, I suppose.'

Mary thought over his words in silence for a moment. 'I don't believe any of that foolish story and how can you?' she asked almost pleadingly.

Brandon shook his head. 'You are only fooling yourself, Mary,' he said patiently. 'Of course the man's guilty, it stands out a mile, it's just that you don't want to see it and I admire your loyalty.'

Mary's eyes studied his face, seeing the strength of his lean jaw and the firmness of his mouth, the way his hair curled around his forehead and over the whiteness of his collar. He was awe-inspiring, she thought fearfully and wondered how she dared to stand here talking to him as though they were equals.

'You don't know Billy as I do,' she said, her voice trembling. 'He's kind and honest, he wouldn't steal from anyone – why should he when he had a good job with Mr Sutton? Been his groom for a long time now, you ask your brother what sort of man Billy is.'

Brandon shrugged. 'My brother is the last one I'd listen to,' he said dryly.

Brandon led her through the bracken and took her hand to help her over an outcrop of rocks, then they were facing the Channel and the coast of Devon seemed near enough to touch.

He settled himself on the grass and after a moment's hesitation, Mary sat beside him, placing her skirts neatly around her ankles, wondering if he was ever going to answer her question.

'I have been writing a book,' he said quietly. 'It's a manual of tinplate sizes which would help to bring about a fairer system of wages for the workers. And because of that, it would be in the interests of some local businessmen, my brother included, if the handbook was suppressed. I believe that my brother sent Billy Gray to raid the office and steal my manuscript.'

Mary felt her heart miss a beat. 'You are wrong,' she spoke fiercely. 'It's my opinion that the Price men were the thieves!' He didn't reply and she stared at him questioningly. 'In any case, you're a boss,' she said briefly, 'so why should you care a damn about the men?'

Brandon's voice was dry. 'Just because I'm a boss it doesn't mean I'm some sort of ogre. The fact is that I do care – is that so unusual?'

Mary's eyes were on his face, his eyes were clear turquoise and held an expression she couldn't quite fathom. 'It is around here, Mr Sutton.'

He smiled and Mary's heart seemed to lift; she felt as though she were floating high on a billowing cloud or sinking in the depths of the foaming sea. It was a strange sensation and she was not sure it was one she liked.

She rose to her feet and stood for a moment pressing out the creases of her skirt, uncertain how to take her leave.

'I must get back,' she spoke awkwardly, 'for there's dinner to cook.' She straightened the folds of her skirt, her eyes avoiding his. In a moment he was beside her.

'I guess I'd better walk back to the road with you.' He smiled lazily. 'I wouldn't like to see you cross the fields alone.'

Mary felt absurdly happy and, as the breeze lifted her hair, as though she had suddenly become a free spirit.

'Don't worry about me,' she said. 'No one in Sweyn's Eye would dare set on Big Mary.' Her voice held laughter. 'That's what they call me behind my back, see, but I appreciate your offer of company all the same.'

Brandon looked into her eyes. 'Proud Mary would be a better name for you.' He moved closer and for a moment she stood quite still, afraid that he would touch her and yet disappointed when he didn't.

'Is that an invitation I see in your eyes, Mary?' His words were like a whisper and she felt her colour rising as she shook her head.

'No, it is not.' She tried to speak firmly, but her voice quivered. 'I'm Billy Gray's girl, remember?'

The walk back across the fields was a silent one and it seemed to Mary that Brandon was once again a stranger. As she glanced at him covertly from under her lashes, he was austere, far removed from her and she shivered in spite of the sun on her back.

'Well, goodbye, Miss Jenkins,' he said formally as they reached the dusty ribbon of road that ran like a question mark from the beach to the centre of the town. He moved away quickly, his long strides eating up the distance between them.

Mary's heart was heavy, her step slow as she made her way back to Canal Street. With one word she had broken the friendship that was offered to her by the strangely compelling American. Yet she had been right to remind them both that the reason they were together was to talk about Billy.

It had been only too easy to forget everything but Brandon's turquoise eyes lit with admiration as he looked at her. He was a fine man, she thought, and unusual in his wish to help the men who worked for him. She felt exhilarated by him but that was something she must guard against in future, she told herself sharply.

Heath had returned home when Mary let herself into the house. Sitting near the window, his head back against the anti-macasser his eyes closed, he looked weary.

'Too much tomcatting, boyo!' Mary said sternly, but her brother saw right through her.

'And you don't blame me, do you, *cariad*? Because if I don't do it now, there's no likelihood of me doing it when there's a wife hanging around my neck.' He smiled and Mary's heart contracted with love for her brother. They were very close, with an affinity that bridged the gap of years between them. When her mother had died giving birth to Heath, Mary had taken over the responsibilities of bringing up a baby at a time when she was little more than a child herself.

She ruffled his hair. 'How's that cough, any easier now?'

Heath shook his head. 'Don't worry so much, Mary, there's nothing wrong with me – nothing that doesn't ail any tinman in the Beaufort Works.'

Mary began to set the table. The meat had been in the oven for hours and the aroma of it filled the kitchen.

'Dinner won't be long,' she told him as she leaned over the hob to peer at the simmering potatoes. 'What's your boss like?' she asked casually and Heath looked at her with shrewd eyes.

'Brandon Sutton is a fair man, he thinks of his workers perhaps more than his profits.' He frowned. 'I can't say what it is exactly but he's not the same as the other ironmasters, he's more like one of the boys. Why?'

Mary turned away from him to hide the rich colour that was in her cheeks. 'Well, he was the one responsible for putting my Billy behind bars. Guilty Billy was, so he says.'

Heath frowned. 'The boss has always been straight with me.'

Mary glanced at her brother sharply. 'He's mistaken this time!' She bit her lip, trying to calm herself and went on, 'Mr Sutton is fairly new around these parts – is he trying to make a good impression, do you think?'

'He's been boss for as long as I've been in the mill,' Heath replied. 'True I never saw anything of him when I was in the wash room, but I can only speak as I find and I see him as a good man not concerned about making impressions.'

Mary began to slice the joint of meat with undue vigour. She knew that Billy was innocent, felt it in her bones, yet Brandon Sutton had touched some chord deep within her; she could still feel the tingling awareness of his presence and see the tallness and the beauty of him in her mind's eye.

There was silence in the small kitchen except for the scrape of knife and fork against the plate. Outside the window, an insect droned in the stunted honeysuckle and sunlight patterned the room. Mary wondered at the feelings than ran through her; she was exalted, uplifted, perhaps the way some folk might feel when they had been to church.

An uneasiness gripped her. She must not make up fairy tales in her mind, for it would be absurd for her to find pleasure in the company of a man who was an ironmaster. Brandon was as far removed from her as the moon was from the sun. In any case, she was Billy Gray's woman and she must not forget it.

She loved Billy, hadn't they been promised to each other these five years past? Known each other since childhood and Billy never looking down on her because of her humble beginnings.

Yet neither of them had felt ready to make the commitment of marriage and she wondered now why that was. Had there ever been passion between them? She had certainly never felt with Billy the way she had with Brandon Sutton, as though the world was opening out like a beautiful rainbow before her.

'You're not eating much,' Heath's voice broke into her thoughts. 'There's work again tomorrow and you'd better keep up your strength.'

Mary smiled at him. 'I was thinking about Billy,' she said and at least that was part of the truth. '*Duw*, I wish I could get him out of there, how he must hate being cooped up like an animal.'

Heath shook his head. 'He'll survive,' he said with the certainty of youth, 'Billy is a tough man, they won't break his spirit, you'll see!'

He rose from the table and went to the sink in the corner of the kitchen to splash water over his face and hands.

'I'm off out,' he said. 'It's too nice to sit in by here. See you later on, don't wait up for me if I'm late.' He kissed the top of her head. 'And let's hope that old man Sutton sees sense and puts you back to work as overseer instead of treating you like a slave.'

As the door slammed and a silence fell over the house, Mary put her elbows on the table and sighed deeply. She too hoped that Mr Sutton would have relented by now; she must work, for she needed the money for the upkeep of her home. She looked around her at the gracious house full of light and space, not at all like the hovel in which she had been reared.

But Mrs Delmai Richardson was a woman who liked her rent to be paid in advance and not a day late. Mary would find it hard put to meet her demands on the money a boiler stoker earned.

She washed the dishes and tidied the kitchen and then moved into the front parlour where the air was cooler. As she sat in a soft armchair she saw the elegance of the room with new appreciation heightened by fear of losing it all. It would be unbearable if she had to give it up now, for this was her home. The piano against the wall, polished lovingly and often, which she had saved so hard to buy and the bright carpet which though second-hand was clean and rich, glowing with discreetly blended colours.

The curtains she had sewn herself, spending the long winter evenings sitting under the gas lamp labouring over her task. She was not skilled at needlework for her fingers were too large and clumsy, and she had been proud when she had hung the finished curtains against the long window.

She made up her mind that she would he humble tomorrow, and if Mr Sutton spoke to her she would bridle her tongue and be submissive. Yet her entire being rebelled at the thought, for she had never grovelled in her life and it would be difficult to start now. Yet perhaps he had some grounds for his hostility, for she had gone into his son's house unasked and caused a scene. And it had all been so unnecessary. She had accused Brandon Sutton and in doing so had set the Sutton brothers against each other; perhaps this was what their father could not forgive.

A sound in the kitchen startled her, and she rose to her feet and hurried along the cool corridor. Then she stopped in her tracks, poised in the doorway with her hands on her hips.

'Gerwin Price, what on earth do you think you're doing skulking around my house?' She was surprised as well as angry, for Gerwin had never been a friend of hers even though they were about the same age. He was handsome in a rough sort of way, his thick hair springing up from his head in untidy tufts and his slanting eyes dark and unreadable. He had tormented her as a child, calling her names because of the way she and her family had lived. She hated him then and that hate exploded now within her.

'Out with you, boyo! You're not welcome here. Mixed up in something shady, you are and yet my Billy is the one in prison.' She picked up a broom and brandished it at him but he simply stood his ground.

'There's a way to treat a man who's been bereaved, Mary Jenkins!' he said reprovingly. 'Is there no charity in you, woman?'

She paused in mid-stride, suddenly ashamed of her behaviour, then lowered the broom and shook back her hair from her face.

'Well, what are you doing here, tell me that? There's no good comes out of sneaking into other folks' kitchens.'

'Look Mary,' he held out his hand palm outwards. 'I haven't touched nothing, I came to ask a favour of you, that's all.'

She studied him carefully for a moment, unable to make up her mind. She could not trust him and yet he had been affected by his father's death, the narrowness of his long face told her that.

'All right, sit down by there and I'll make you a cup of tea,' she said, although it was against her better judgement. She saw him glance towards the meat on the large plate with a hungry look in his eyes.

'You might as well have a bite to eat I suppose,' she added grudgingly.

'I'm starved and I'll not deny it,' Gerwin said bleakly.

Mary busied herself cutting bread. She was distinctly uneasy and yet at the same time a little sorry for Gerwin.

He ate heartily and Mary busied herself with the kettle, not wanting to sit down with him; but at last, there was nothing left to be done.

'Things been bad lately, Mary,' he said, wiping the back of his hand across his face. Mary was repulsed by him but she kept her thoughts hidden behind a bland smile.

'Times haven't been exactly easy for Billy or me either,' she said. 'Find yourself a job – you didn't expect your father to keep you for the rest of your life on his nightwatchman's pay, did you?'

'There's the young ones to think of,' Gerwin had a ready reply. 'You know as well as I do, Mary, that I can't leave them to fend for themselves.' He shrugged. 'If my woman hadn't run off and left us things would be different.'

Mary bit her lip. She knew Gerwin was making excuses and yet in a way he was right – who *would* take the responsibility of caring for his brood of children if he wasn't there?

'The babbas are hungry, Mary,' he said. 'I need food for them and clothes. They've got no shoes to put on their feet, it's as bad as that.'

It pained Mary to think of any children growing up in the kind of grinding poverty she herself had known, but the Price family were not her worry she told herself firmly.

'I'll give you some food,' she said briskly, 'and whatever clothes might be of any use but to be honest with you, Gerwin Price, it's not any of my business, is it? Why don't you go up to the toffs on the hill, perhaps Dean Sutton will help you?'

He brushed that aside. 'It is your business in a way,' he said and his dark eyes were narrowed into slits. Mary longed to move away from him but she would not allow him to see that she was uneasy in his company.

'How do you make that out?' Her voice was surprisingly strong and confidant and Gerwin looked away. He was like a wild dog, Mary thought; show him fear and he would pounce.

'If it wasn't for your Billy, my dad would still be alive and we'd have a regular wage coming in through the door, not like now.' He shrugged. 'In time, I might have been able to find a job for myself and let my father look after the little ones, but what am I to do now, Mary?'

She did not like Gerwin Price and indeed could scarcely bear to be in the same room as the man, but she was touched by the plight of his children. She rose to her feet. 'I'll give you what I can,' she said sighing in resignation.

Mary put a parcel together and tied it with string, then from a tin box at the back of the wardrobe took out some coins. She felt instinctively that she was behaving foolishly and yet she didn't have any choice, for she could hardly ignore the fact that the Price children were hungry.

'Here,' she put the money on the table alongside the parcel of clothes. 'I'll give you some food as well, but don't think this is going to be a regular thing. I'm not a soft touch, mind.'

Gerwin nodded. 'All right, Mary, I won't bother you again.' He snatched up the money and thrust it into his pocket before tucking the parcels underneath his arm.

'Right charitable girl you are, Mary. I don't know why we've never got together before this, you and me.'

'We haven't got together, as you put it. I'm just giving you the same bit of help I'd give anyone in your place. It's for the children, mind, not for you – do you understand that, Gerwin? No going down to the Mexico tipping the shillings down your throat in mugs of ale, right?'

He looked offended. 'Now would I do any such thing? You don't understand me at all, Mary, so I don't know why you mark me down as a bad 'un.'

She opened the back door. 'Out you, the same way you came in and don't pester me again, mind, or you'll get the sharp end of my tongue. Now you sort out your worries, I've got enough of my own.'

Mary watched as Gerwin loped off down the path and into the back lane where he turned and raised his hand for a moment before disappearing out of sight. She closed the door with a sigh of relief and slipped the bolt into place; she would make very sure that Gerwin Price would have no way of getting into her house again. In Canal Street, no one ever thought of locking doors but from now on that was one habit she must acquire, Mary thought anxiously.

It was cool in the parlour with a soft breeze blowing in through the window. Mary stood looking out at the clouds billowing across the dying sun, not fluffy white like summer clouds should be, but grey mingling with the dark green fumes from the plethora of works' chimneys dominating the banks of the river Swan.

Mary took a deep breath knowing that in the morning she would have to face old Mr Sutton and that she would need all her courage if she was to humble herself as she had planned.

'*Daro!*' she said aloud. 'What's a bit of humble pie compared to keeping my job?'

She sank into a chair and closed her eyes and, all at once, she was reliving the moments spent in the green glade of trees just above the docks. She felt again the same tingling sensation of lightness and freedom she had experienced that morning in Brandon Sutton's company, and she shivered as she remembered the magnetism of the man. In her mind's eye she saw his tall frame and strong build and the teasing, turquoise eyes looking down into hers.

'There's soft you are, *merchi*,' she whispered, but a smile curved the corners of her mouth and her eyes were suddenly bright.

Chapter Six

The long windows of *Plas Coch* looked out over the softly rolling waters of the Channel, gleaming like eyes in the mellow brickwork of the gracious building. It was the most stately villa on the hillside with the exception of *Plas Rhianfa*, which stood proud above all others.

To the rear of the house was a long garden equipped with brightly painted wooden toys. A rocking horse, eyes staring, moved softly in the breeze as though imbued with life. And a glossy red see-saw pointed arrow-like towards the cloudless skies. But the garden was empty, for there were no children at *Plas Coch*.

Delmai Richardson sat in the drawing room, her sewing idle in her lap, her small fingers plucking restlessly at a knotted flower, twisting and worrying the silk bloom destructively.

She was a beautiful woman with gold hair that shimmered like a new sovereign. Her large, dark eyes were fringed by silky fair lashes and her skin was flawless, her mouth soft and young pouted in discontent.

Her fingers tensed as she heard footsteps in the hall and she eased herself back in her chair and mentally prepared herself for the appearance of her husband.

'Well, isn't this a charming domestic scene?' Rickie came across the carpet slowly, his eyes upon her face and Delmai felt the usual shrinking inside her which she experienced whenever she was in her husband's company.

He kissed her brow and she tried to smile up at him, hoping he did not notice the quivering of her lips. It wasn't that he was ugly or deformed; indeed, Rickie Richardson was a catch – hadn't everyone said so, especially Delmai's mother who remembered the days when the Richardsons virtually owned Sweyn's Eye.

'How are you feeling today, my dear?' Rickie sounded solicitous but there was derision in his eyes. 'Recovered from your vapour of last night, I expect!'

'Yes, thank you.' Her voice was small and apologetic as she looked up and met his eyes defensively. 'I can't help it, truly Rickie, I do try to be a good wife to you.'

He laughed shortly and walked away from her. 'Yet you always seem to develop some mysterious sickness when we are about to go to our bed. Don't you think you should consult Dr Thomas? After all, there is no hope of us having children if we don't consummate the marriage.'

'Oh, no, please don't make me do that,' Delmai said breathlessly. She could just see Marian Thomas the doctor's wife divulging the wonderful titbit of gossip to the ladies who took tea with her. She could imagine the ribald laughter in Marian's voice only too well: 'My dear, they haven't actually done anything yet, if you know what I mean.'

Rickie came to her and laid a hand on her arm. 'Do you really mean it, that you'll try?' His face was anxious now. 'I want a family so badly, Delmai, and only you can give me that. The other I can get from whores.'

Delmai flinched. 'Do you have to be so coarse?' she said sharply and Rickie shook his head at her in despair.

'I'm only trying to save you the embarrassment of thinking up further excuses to reject me,' he retorted. 'I want children and I will have them, but as for pleasure, then I shall find it elsewhere – that's all I'm trying to say.'

He stood near the window, lifting the curtain and Delmai knew he was staring into the garden, looking longingly at the swings.

'Two sons and perhaps a daughter, that's not too much to ask, surely?' He spoke as though thinking aloud. 'There's my brother Sterling with a son by that slut and if what I hear is correct, another child on the way.' He turned and looked so challengingly at Delmai that she shrank back against her silk cushions.

'Is there any justice in this world, Delmai? I took you for my wife because you were from a fine family. The Glynmors are good stock through and through.' His shoulders sagged. 'I just can't understand why you are so reluctant to sleep with me.'

'Give me more time,' Delmai pleaded softly. 'You know how nervous I am and I don't know why. These things can't be explained.'

'You come from farming stock, for God's sake!' Rickie's voice was harsh. 'You must have seen animals breeding more times than you can remember. You've even assisted your father when he wanted one of his stallions to cover a mare, so you can't be that squeamish.'

Delmai bit back an angry retort, for how could she tell her husband of only two months that his very touch repelled her? Perhaps the cold way in which the marriage had been arranged was to blame; in any event, she didn't understand herself, so how could she explain her feelings to anyone else? That her father had handed her over to Rickie along with a big fat dowry and bid him to 'breed some fine young 'uns' didn't help matters. She was being treated just like a mare herself and she hated it.

She had not even been consulted about the marriage – perhaps no one thought she had enough intelligence to decide anything for herself. Her father, a florid-faced hearty man, had always believed that the Glynmors were a race apart. He had been bitterly disappointed when his wife had produced only one child, and a girl at that, though it was rumoured that more than one male Glynmor bastard had been spawned in Sweyn's Eye.

When Rickie Richardson had shown an interest in Delmai, the marriage had been arranged so quickly that she had had no time to accustom herself to the idea. And she had never been instructed in matters of the flesh; her mother avoided the subject like a plague and so Delmai had grown up to believe that there were no feelings attached to the act of procreation.

She had seen the mares hobbled and tied so that the stallion would not be harmed. Conversely, the mare needed her neck protected so that the stallion did not bite her during the mating. It had seemed a painful and joyless experience to Delmai, with the stallion thrashing and thrusting and the mare standing with great frightened rolling eyes as though waiting for the ordeal to be over.

Delmai decided that it was not real marriage she had desired at all. She had wanted a ring on her finger and a pretty white dress and orange blossoms and a fine handsome man at her side. Perhaps she had even wanted children, but not wrenched from her own unwilling flesh.

In a moment of panic she had considered refusing to go through with the wedding at all, not that she had anything personal against Rickie – not then. He was presentable enough and came from one of Sweyn's Eye's leading families, but some deeply hidden instinct warned her that the step she was about to take was wrong.

She was well able to support herself, for her grandmother had left her a clutch of properties which brought in a fair income over the years. Yet it was the thought of being an outcast in society which had forced her to sublimate her own wishes in the end. She knew that otherwise she would become an oddity, a vinegary old maid. Her one consolation now was that she was being invited to social gatherings; she had standing in Sweyn's Eye now that she was Mrs Richardson.

'Are you listening to me, Delmai?' Rickie's voice broke into her thoughts. 'I want you to be ready for me when I come home tonight, I'm not prepared to put up with any more excuses.'

'Oh but...' Her voice faltered in the light of her husband's cold stare.

'Oh but nothing! It's tonight, or I'll pack you up bag and baggage and return you to your father's house. Don't you realise that he's asking me already about an heir? He wants a grandson as much as I want a son. Can you be selfish enough to deny us both?'

Dumbly, Delmai shook her head. 'No,' she said, but the word carried little conviction.

As Rickie came to her and put both his hands on her shoulders, she could feel the warmth of his fingers through the thin material of her dress and with difficulty suppressed a shiver.

'Look, I'm not completely insensitive,' he said and though he spoke softly there was an element of laughter in his voice. 'This sort of thing is probably difficult for any nicely brought-up young lady to cope with.' He paused. 'Not that my mother suffered any lack of the physical urge.' He looked down at her almost curiously. 'What if I promise I won't do anything to hurt you, will that help?'

When she refused to answer, he gripped her more tightly. 'I want you ready for me when I return this evening, no headaches, no vapours, no sickness, do you understand?'

Delmai looked up at him, her hands were clammy as she clasped them together. 'I understand, Rickie,' she said woodenly.

After he had gone, she tossed the scrap of linen she had been embroidering to the far corner of the room. She felt sick already at the thought of submitting to Rickie, yet the alternative was to face the humiliation of being packed off to the farm where she would never hear the end of her father's wrath.

She looked around her desperately. Was there no one to whom she could talk, confide her fears? Not her mother, certainly, Bronwen Glynmor would simply close her ears and frown in horror if her daughter should be indelicate enough to mention anything pertaining to the marriage bed.

Delmai rang for tea. Her throat was parched and her hands were trembling as her mind twisted and turned, exploring endless possibilities for escape. She wondered if she should just pack her trunk and run away, but then she would be leaving herself open to ridicule: the woman who would not consummate her marriage! She put her hands over her face just as the maid entered the room with the tray.

'Oh, Miss Delmai, there's awful to see you cryin', what is it then?' Gwen had been with Delmai for as long as she could remember and, for a moment, she was almost tempted to confide in the girl who had come with her from the Glynmor farm to the hillside above Sweyn's Eye. But it was not politic for a servant, however friendly, to know too much about her betters and so Delmai dried her eyes and forced a smile.

'It's silly, nothing at all really,' she lied glibly. 'I wanted to go out with Mr Richardson and he wasn't able to take me today.'

The maid's expression softened. 'Ah there's lovely to see you so affectionate.' Gwen poured tea into a fragile bone china cup and added a slice of lemon. 'I wish some nice fellow would come courtin' me,' she said wistfully.

'Have you ever had a follower, Gwen?' Delmai knew she was prying, but she was desperate for any scrap of comfort she could get. The girl nodded and a bouncy chestnut curl escaped from under the cap.

'Yes, Miss Delmai, I was keeping company with a fine handsome boy back on the farm.' She looked crestfallen. 'He promised me he'd stay true even though I wouldn't be seeing him every day, but as soon as my back was turned he was up the petticoats of the new young maid.' She put her hand to her mouth. 'Pardon me for talkin' so open like, but you're married now and I suppose you know how a man can make you do things you shouldn't.'

Delmai remained silent, unable to think of anything to say and Gwen's cheeks reddened. 'P'raps it's different for the gentry, though,' she said stiffly and moved towards the door.

'No, wait, tell me about yourself. I'm interested, really I am,' Delmai said quickly. She didn't want to be alone and perhaps she might learn something from the earthy Gwen who seemed to know all about the sins of the flesh. 'Did you love him, your fellow, I mean really love him as a woman does her husband?'

Gwen hesitated. 'Well, my mam would kill me if she knew, but then she's old – there's no hot blood in her veins now. Yes, I did love him truly, Miss Delmai and I let him take me into the barn and... well, you know...'

Delmai felt a sense of shock though she managed to conceal it. She stared covertly at the maid whose face was illuminated, as though she was recalling some kind of spiritual experience. What was lacking in herself, Delmai wondered, that she could not feel the way about Rickie that her maid obviously did about some farm-hand?

'Was it difficult, the first time, I mean?' Delmai hated herself for probing, but she could not stop herself now that she had started.

Gwen looked at her sheepishly. 'It's a bit awkward-like, but you forgets the embarrassment, don't you?' She shrugged. 'I suppose it's because you love the man you're with.' She smiled shyly. 'Is that 'ow it is for you, miss, 'cos you aren't to worry yourself over it. It don't come right first time off, nor the second, either. With me, it took a long time before I really got into the way of it.'

Delmai looked down at her hands; she still didn't quite understand. 'But you wanted him, your fellow, you liked him to touch you and...'

Her voice trailed away and Gwen smiled. '*Duw*, of course I did. It's nature's trap, isn't it, so that there'll be all the more babbas in the world.'

Then she was different from all other women, Delmai thought with a sense of horror, for even Gwen had known love and passion and the warmth of a man's arms holding her close.

When the maid had left the room, Delmai drank her lemon tea and tried to quell the sense of panic that rose within her every time she thought of Rickie's homecoming. She did not dare to make any more protests, he was at the end of his patience with her.

She frittered the afternoon away, arranged and rearranged the flowers in the hallway and then sat at the table trying to write a letter home, but found she had nothing to say. At last, she simply sat at the window in the drawing room and stared out at the rolling waves splashing in on the shore far below.

A cool breeze was blowing in from the water by the time Rickie returned home. He had bought shares in Dean Sutton's business with the dowry he had received from her father, and

Delmai was grateful that the chain of shops at least kept her husband away from her during the day.

He shrugged off his coat and sank into a chair, rubbing his hand wearily across his forehead.

'I hate working in Sutton's office,' he said with unnecessary venom. 'If Sterling hadn't taken what was rightfully mine I would be sitting in clover now.'

It was a story Delmai had heard many times over and she was bored with it. It seemed to her that Rickie did not do too badly, what with an allowance from his mother and the not inconsiderable income he received from the business.

'I'd be a respected copper boss instead of running some fiddling little shops trying to beat down the wholesale merchants on their prices,' he continued.

'Have some tea, Rickie, with a slice of lemon in it just as you like it, I'll ring for Gwen.'

'Sit down and don't fuss!' Rickie snapped at her pettishly. 'There's nothing to stop me ringing for tea myself should I want any, which I don't. Right now I'd prefer something stronger.'

He moved towards the large polished sideboard and poured a stiff measure of brandy, then twirled the glass around watching the amber liquid through half-closed eyes. He was at his most difficult when in this sort of mood, Delmai thought with sinking heart.

'Even my brother has a son.' It was a repetition of what he had said that morning, Delmai thought, trying to stop her hands shaking.

'Sterling gets everything he wants, there's no justice. Everyone in Sweyn's Eye knows he's a bastard and yet they still continue to kowtow to him. I just don't understand it.'

'He's well respected,' Delmai said in a low voice, 'because he's pleasant to people and he doesn't treat everyone else as fools.'

Rickie turned on her angrily. 'And I do, I suppose? Perhaps you should have married my half-brother and I could have done worse than marrying that little slut of his – at least she's not unnatural.'

Delmai flinched at the bitterness in his voice. 'I'm not unnatural,' she replied. 'I'm just a woman who has been taught modesty, is that so wrong?'

'I'm not going to quarrel with you,' Rickie said. 'That would be playing right into your hands, wouldn't it?'

'I don't know what you mean.' Delmai's lips were numb as Rickie came and put his finger under her chin.

'It would give you the chance to turn your back on me yet again, wouldn't it? Well, that won't work, my dear sweet wife. I've been patient, God knows how patient, another man might have given you a good hiding by now.'

'Don't even consider it.' Delmai was growing angry. 'My father would horsewhip you if you so much as laid a finger on me and you know it.'

Rickie helped himself to more brandy. 'I don't think so, not if I told him how you have denied me my marital rights all this time.' He suddenly banged his fist down on the table. 'No more talking! We shall have supper in peace and quiet, then we shall take a turn or two around the garden before we go to bed. That's it, finish! I don't want to hear any more whining.'

Delmai took the opportunity to dress for supper when Rickie was in his room shaving. She quickly drew on a high-necked gown with pearls stitched along the neckline; it was a soft shade of blue, a demure gown and yet it showed the line of her breasts clearly. Not even the corset, tightly laced to give her an hourglass figure, could conceal her shapeliness. But Delmai did not pause to stare at herself in the long mirror; she moved quickly to the door as Rickie came in from his dressing room and stood before her.

He wore only soft linen trousers. His chest was bare, matted with dark hairs and Delmai felt the colour rush into her face.

'I'll wait for you downstairs.' Her voice was light and she felt as though she couldn't breathe.

It was cool in the high-ceilinged dining room, for the French windows stood open to the evening breeze. The long dining table was set with gleaming silver and cut-crystal glasses, most of them taken from *Plas Rhianfa* while Victoria Richardson had still been living there. Rickie had rifled the house unashamedly, telling his mother bitingly that all this should have been his by rights anyway. He had practically dared her to protest and Delmai's heart had gone out to the older woman.

Victoria had become a shadow of her former self over the past years and Delmai wondered if it was the death of James Cardigan which had affected her or the whispers of their outrageous affair that buzzed continually through Sweyn's Eye even now.

Delmai's father, like everyone else, had heard the gossip which had revived after the explosion at the Kilvey Deep which had killed James Cardigan. Since then, he had harboured the hope that Rickie might be declared the legal heir to the Richardson Copper Company. The business was flourishing now under Sterling's capable hands, which in Rickie's view was little more than a quirk of fortune. He maintained loudly and often that the company remained solvent more by luck than judgement.

'I must say you look very fetching tonight. It seems you are at least making some effort to please me.' Rickie had entered the dining room so silently that Delmai was startled. She dropped the napkin she had been pleating between her fingers, almost overturning a glass.

Rickie ignored her clumsiness and poured them both wine from the carafe standing on a silver tray. His eyes gleamed as he looked at her and Delmai felt that he was enjoying her discomfort.

She scarcely touched her food, but she noticed that Rickie ate heartily enough. She picked at a piece of chicken in sauce before pushing it away from her in despair.

Aware of her husband's eyes upon her, she made a pretence of enjoying her peach melba. In any case, she wanted to prolong the meal, knowing that when she rose from the table it would only be a matter of time before Rickie insisted on taking her to bed.

Delmai had never thought of herself as a weak person and yet she was waiting meekly to go like a lamb to the slaughter. As a girl, she had believed in fairy-tale romances with a lover's lips upon her own as the final curtain. She could not imagine even now achieving a union with Rickie and her thoughts took panic-stricken flight – would Rickie hobble her and mount her the way a stallion did a mare, she wondered hysterically.

She rose abruptly from the table. 'I must get some air,' she said quickly. 'It's very warm tonight, don't you think?'

Rickie was at her side in an instant, his hand on her arm. 'We'll go and sit outside in the garden for a while.' He sounded solicitous and a faint hope beat within Delmai's heart as he led her along the edge of the lawn and into the maze where the trees grew thick, hiding them from view. They sat on a small wooden seat and Rickie took her hand in his.

'There is no way out, not this time.' His eyes looked into hers and she felt as if she was a rabbit hypnotised by a snake. He ran his finger along her arm towards her shoulder and caressed her neck softly.

'You may find it very pleasurable after all,' he said in a low voice. 'I'm not that repulsive, not according to the other women I've had.'

Her coolness seemed to excite him and he drew her close, his mouth on hers. To her surprise she felt nothing, neither distaste or pleasure, just nothing. He moved away from her, appearing pleased. 'There, you see, I told you that perhaps you would find me attractive, didn't I?'

Jubilantly he drew her to her feet and without a word led her back to the house. The sun was sinking in a red blaze over the sea, splashing the sky and water with scarlet like blood.

Gwen helped her to undress as she always did and a smile was curving her mouth. 'Master needs an early night, does he, miss?' she giggled. 'It's the hot weather that gets 'em, you know, makes young men randy and old ones sorrowful.'

Delmai quickly slipped her cotton gown over her head and fastened the buttons to the throat. 'Good night, Gwen,' she said evenly, though her heart was beating so fast she thought it would burst from her breast.

Gwen winked knowingly. 'Good night, miss, sleep tight!' The door closed behind the maid and Delmai fell back against the pillows fearing the moment when Rickie would enter from his dressing room. He always spent a long time at his ablutions and usually she managed to feign sleep by the time he joined her beneath the sheets, but she would not get away with such a subterfuge this time.

A soft breeze stirred the curtains at the window and the scent of flowers filled the room. Delmai closed her eyes and wished herself a million miles away from her marriage bed. Why, she asked herself yet again, had she agreed to become Rickie's wife? He had seemed agreeable enough at the start and she thought him sensitive, his long face having the look of a poet about it. But there was a fine point of cruelty in his nature which she had only discovered after the ceremony.

As though on cue, Rickie swaggered into the bedroom. He was wearing a silk dressing gown and the lines of his body could be clearly seen through the softness of the material. Delmai turned her eyes away from the visible evidence of his arousal.

'My dear Delmai, you are packaged up like a parcel there, let me help you.' His hands were on her neck, undoing the buttons of her nightgown and Delmai swallowed hard as his fingers brushed her breasts. She found it embarrassing in the extreme to have her nightdress drawn up over her slender hips but lifted her arms as Rickie pulled the cotton gown free, tossing it carelessly to the floor.

He stared at her, his eyes making an inventory of her body. Delmai felt like shrinking beneath the sheets but she was too afraid to move.

'Don't look so frightened,' Rickie said softly and then his palm was upon her breast, stroking, teasing at her nipple.

'Will you put out the lamp, Rickie?' The darkness might make what was happening more bearable, she thought in despair, but her husband shook his head.

'I want to see the pleasure on your face, Delmai. Don't worry, you'll soon get used to all this – perhaps even learn to enjoy it.'

His hand was on the flat on her stomach, pausing, moving lower, touching, exploring. Suddenly she gasped with shock as he thrust hard, his fingers like knives spearing the softness of her, probing intimately, hurting, violating.

She closed her eyes and let him handle her undisturbed, feeling his mouth cover her nipple as she tried to arch away from the cruel fingers that still pierced her. Then his full weight was upon her and if she thought she had met pain already, then she was wrong. As he plundered thoughtlessly she pressed her hand to her mouth, attempting to suppress her cries. Above her, Rickie breathed harshly.

His hands were gripping her breasts, the fingers plunging deep into the flesh. Pain was all around her, possessing her, filling her mind and body. She heard herself whimpering and tears pressed from under her closed lashes. She wished she could swoon, fall into a darkness where she knew nothing, felt nothing, but her ordeal went on. He was like a demon, she thought wildly, crushing and destroying her.

At last it was over. Rickie fell back onto the bed panting and triumphant while she lay like a discarded flower. Every part of her ached and throbbed and she felt she had lost herself, been swallowed up in his lust.

Without a word he rose and went into his dressing room and Delmai opened her eyes, staring up at the shadowy ceiling, trying not to think or feel.

A little while later, he returned and stood looking down at her. 'Send for one of the maids to change the sheets,' he said coldly and Delmai obediently stumbled from the bed without attempting to cover her nakedness. Rickie knew her body as intimately as she did, he had taken possession and it was no longer hers.

'Don't be too long.' Rickie's voice was light but Delmai felt a prickling of fear as she waited for him to continue. 'One swallow doesn't make a summer, I'm sure you know what I mean.' She closed her eyes, feeling a scream rise in her throat. Was it possible, she wondered, to find the courage to end her life?

Chapter Seven

The early Monday morning haze drifted over the turgid waters of the canal where brown weeds floated like a maiden's hair just below the smooth surface. Mary walked slowly towards the gates of the laundry. She had done her week's stint working at the boilers and now she hoped fervently that there would be no more trouble. Mr Sutton might well be in a kinder frame of mind, but she doubted it. He was at best a crusty old man and well used to being obeyed without question, so he would find no merit in her willingness to stoke boilers.

'Mornin', Mary.' Rhian hurried towards her, curls bouncing, clean apron gleaming in the sunlight. There was a likeness to her brother Billy about Rhian's nose and mouth, Mary decided, and her gaze softened.

'There's nice to see you early for work for a change,' she said, but her smile took the sting of criticism from her words.

'Well, I thought over what you said the other night and I'd much rather work in the laundry than in the tin.' She frowned. 'Though Heath would have looked after me, he said so.'

Mary gave her a stern look. 'You keep clear of our Heath,' she said dryly, 'he's a toerag when it comes to girls. Love 'em and leave 'em, that's his motto, so you just forget him and find yourself a nice steady boy.'

Rhian flushed. 'Heath is very fond of me,' she protested a little too quickly. 'He's told me so himself, mind.'

Mary deliberately ignored Rhian's outburst. Glancing towards the window of the office, her heart turned over as she saw Mr Sutton bent over his desk. He did not look up as the two girls passed and Mary bit her lip, wondering if she was right to go directly to the packing department. But he had said a week, hadn't he? And she'd worked like a slave in the boiler room.

She hesitated for a moment at the foot of the flight of rickety stairs that led upwards. The smell of urine and soap permeated the yard from the wash room, but Mary had grown used to it over the years although Rhian wrinkled up her nose.

'How you could bear to work in that stink beats me,' she said as she flounced up the stairs, the hem of her white petticoat peeping from beneath her flannel skirt. Rhian was small-boned with dainty hands and feet and for a moment Mary found herself envying the younger girl. She sighed and followed Rhian to the packing room; if Mr Sutton wanted her, then he must come and find her.

'In the name of the Blessed Virgin, 'tis you, Mary!' Katie Murphy looked up smiling and flung back her silky hair. 'Good to see you back where you belong, so it is.'

Sheets that had been left neatly stacked at the weekend were ready for packing and Mary set to with a will, finding a sense of comfort in the familiar tasks.

'Have you heard about Mali?' Katie leaned forward confidentially. 'She's havin' another little one, let's hope 'tis a girl this time.'

Mary smiled. 'Yes, I did know, I had a letter a few days ago.' She stared at Katie pensively. 'She comes often to visit you in Market Street, doesn't she?'

Katie smiled. 'Oh, yes, not one to forget her old friends! Brought a basket of shirts and trews for the boys last time she came. My mammy is right proud to dress her sons in the clothes of the gentry, even though they be cast-offs.'

A hum of activity filled the packing room as the girls fell into the rhythm of the work. Mary finished packing the bundle of sheets and then strolled through the long room, chastening any one who fell below her own high standards. Her job was to oversee all aspects of the laundry business and that included starching and pressing as well as checking lists of parcels sent out to customers. She became so immersed in her work that it was a surprise when Mr Sutton sent for her.

As she descended the rickety stairs, Mary's heart was hammering inside her breast. What had she done wrong now, she wondered anxiously. She entered the office with her expression bland and Mr Sutton stared up at her with cold eyes as though he had never seen her before.

'I guess you're not aware that you should knock at the door before entering this office.' His voice was harsh and Mary knew with a sinking of her heart that there was no hope of forgiveness, not from this man.

'I'm sorry,' she spoke as calmly as she could. 'I'm so used to just walking in here that it's become a habit.' The old man sifted through a sheaf of papers on his desk as though he had not heard her and Mary stood still, trying not to fidget and waiting for him to continue. Impatience was like an itch within her, he had her at his mercy and the old autocrat knew it. All the ideas she had had about humbling herself before him vanished like mists before the sun.

'What is it you want of me, Mr Sutton?' she asked quickly. 'I know you don't like me personally and in all truth I can't blame you, but I do my job properly and that's something you can't deny.'

He took a long time to look up at her and his brows were drawn downwards into a frown. 'I don't think you're as competent as you say, miss,' he spoke softly. 'Indeed, I can think of plenty who would do your job as well if not better than you.'

Anger was red-hot now, searing a course through Mary's veins so that her hands trembled. She thought she must step forward at any moment and cry out her rage into the man's hostile face, but controlled herself with difficulty. 'Name me one,' she said evenly.

His smile was fixed and his eyes held no light of humour. 'What about Sally Benson?' he asked, his voice hard.

'You must be crazed by the sun!' Mary said in disbelief. 'Sally Benson couldn't hold down a sheet flapping in the breeze, she would let everything go to pot in no time at all.'

'Ah!' His voice was softer now as though he knew he'd touched her on the raw. 'I was told there was no love lost between you two.'

Mary drew in her breath sharply. 'You're sacking me then, giving me the order of the boot, is that it?' she demanded, caution thrown to the winds. He rose and moved to the window, staring out into the yard, his hands folded behind his back.

'Oh, not me, Miss Jenkins. I gave my word to my son Dean that I would keep you on – for as long as you wanted to stay.' He did not look at her as he continued speaking. 'Some changes will have to be made, for with Sally Benson as overseer you would be working permanently in the boiler house.' He glanced towards her, his eyes alight with triumph. 'Of course, Doris would have to leave us. You see, Miss Jenkins, that I'm keeping my word to the letter.'

Mary clenched her hands together – he was putting her in an impossible situation and he knew it. She wondered for a brief moment if she could call his bluff and stay on, but something in the set of his jaw told her that he meant every word he said.

'Very well, I'll resign. That's what you want, isn't it, Mr Sutton?' she demanded. 'But you don't know the laundry business as I do; everything needs careful checking if it's not to fall into a muddle. Sally, whatever you choose to think, doesn't have the necessary experience for the job.'

Mr Sutton returned to his chair and pushed a clean sheet of paper towards her. 'You will of course express your wish to resign in writing,' he said coolly.

Mary scribbled furiously, her thoughts whirling. What was she going to do now? How could she begin to hope to meet her commitments without a regular wage coming in? But she gave no hint of her feelings as she signed the letter with a flourish.

'I hope you're satisfied, Mr Sutton,' she said coldly.

He looked over the paper carefully and as Mary turned to the door he spoke again. 'Collect your belongings at once, Miss Jenkins,' he said smoothly. 'I'm sure it will be best for all concerned if you quit my premises as soon as possible.'

Mary was blind with rage as she mounted the stairs to the packing room. The familiar scent of hot linen was like a blow; she would never again experience the satisfaction of doing her job well, she thought dismally.

'What's wrong with you, Mary?' Katie was staring up at her wide-eyed. 'You look as if you'd seen a ghost.'

'I'm leaving,' Mary said flatly. She moved towards the cupboard and took out her coat and a spare apron and folded them over her arm. Suddenly the girls were all around her, voices shrill as they questioned her anxiously.

'Has the pig given you the sack?' Rhian asked angrily. 'Let's go down there, girls, and give him an earful.'

Mary felt tears burn her eyes at the chorus of assent from the other women. She held up her hand for silence, swallowing hard, hoping that her voice would not reveal her emotion.

'I've not been sacked, I've resigned,' she said loudly. Silence fell for a moment and then Katie came to her side.

'You'd never give up the job of your own free will, Mary,' she said. 'Tell us the truth now, what's happened?'

Mary shrugged her shoulders. 'If I stay, Sally Benson takes over my job and I work the boilers. That means Doris would be sent packing after all these years.' She could not keep the bitterness of such an injustice from her voice.

'Mary, Jesus and Joseph, we can't let anyone do such a thing!' Katie said indignantly. 'We'll go on strike, like the men do – we'll show Mr Sutton that he can't treat us like dirt.'

'No,' Mary said positively, 'I told you I've resigned, there's nothing any of you can do.' Her tone softened. 'Look, you'd only make it worse for yourselves and how could I work here now, after this – you must see it's impossible.'

In frustrated anger, Mary turned to look at Sally Benson. 'It seems you are the new boss and the girls will be relying on you.' She paused. 'Now, you're not to let things slide, mind. Keep up with the deliveries or we'll lose customers, and see that the boilers are cleaned out regularly; don't want any accidents, do we?'

The girl was truculent, aware of the rising tide of feeling against her. 'Why did he pick on me?' she asked. 'I don't want to be boss girl, I'll tell him so to his face an' all.'

Mary moved towards the door. 'I shouldn't if I were you, otherwise you might find yourself out of the gates too. Look to the more experienced girls for help, then you should make out all right.'

There was silence heavy and brooding in the long room as Mary walked its length, feeling as though she was cutting away part of herself. She knew the laundry inside out, had worked here ever since she was a child. She had made it her life, her career, had even taken on a fine big house feeling that her position was secure. Now it all lay in dust around her feet.

She descended the rickety staircase for the last time and paused under the swaying trees, wondering if she should say goodbye to the women in the boiler house. But the thought of their surprise and the effort of explaining the situation all over again deterred her. Slowly she made her way past the office without even glancing in through the window.

As she walked through the gates and stepped out on to the cobbled street, Mary felt as though there was a dam inside her, longing to burst. Her throat ached with unshed tears and her eyes were misted so that she did not see the tall figure loom up in front of her until it was too late.

'Careful!' She felt a steadying hand on her arm and shook her head dumbly, trying her best to disengage herself before the tears came. Blinking rapidly, she saw turquoise eyes looking into hers. She tried to pull away but she was held fast.

'Let me go,' she said raggedly. 'The last thing I want now is anything to do with you Suttons.'

Brandon ignored her words, leading her quickly away from the laundry gates and past the canal.

'Hush, you can tell me all about it later.' He led her along the winding road, past the shops and down towards the docks.

Mary was slumped against his broadness, uncaring that the wind was disarranging her neatly coiled hair. She felt bowed, as though she carried the weight of the world on her shoulders.

He guided her towards the glade where the sun slanted green through the trees. 'Sit down,' he said firmly. 'Let's talk.'

She sank onto the trunk of a fallen tree and lifting the hem of her skirt, dabbed at her eyes with the frill of her pristine petticoat.

'My father has upset you in some way, how?' Brandon said crisply. Such was her misery that Mary did not even attempt to make a denial.

'I've had to leave my job,' she said at last. 'Your father has taken such a dislike to me that he made it impossible for me to stay.'

'I was going to see him anyway,' Brandon said thoughtfully. 'And when I do, I'll have this matter sorted out, don't worry. He's blaming you for the argument at my brother's house.' He paused. 'Well, you're not going to let him beat you, surely? You seem to me to be a girl who can fight her own battles. Come on, stop crying and see this for what it really is, just a setback in your career.'

Mary gave a hollow laugh. 'A setback? You don't know what you're talking about, it's the ruination of everything I planned.'

Brandon's eyes were unreadable. 'So you were going to be an overseer at the laundry all your life, is that what you're saying?'

Mary was bewildered. 'I don't know.' She shook back her hair. 'Perhaps.'

Coming out of her misery, she was suddenly aware of his hands warm on her shoulders. She rose abruptly to her feet, conscious of the sight she must look with her face blotched by tears.

Suddenly she was angry. 'Anyway, who are you to say what I should do with my life? There's a nerve, when it's you and yours who've put me in such a position.' She rubbed her fingers across her eyes and watched as Brandon moved away from her thrusting his hands deep into his pockets. He was very handsome with the sun bringing redness to the dark of his hair; he stood tall and straight and a pang of something she couldn't quite understand shot through her.

'I see you are determined to blame me for what happened at the laundry as well as for Billy's imprisonment.' He spoke in a tight, hard voice and Mary stared at him, fighting a longing to cling to him and cry out her hurt and misery on his broad shoulders.

'Well then, who should I blame?' She found the words springing from her lips of their own accord, though it was not what she wanted to say at all. He gave her a quick look.

'Billy is guilty, get that into your head, he belongs behind bars.'

Wearily, Mary sank back onto the fallen tree and shook her head. 'I don't know what to think any more, my world has turned topsy-turvy; it's running out of control and I don't seem to be able to stop it.'

He sat beside her but without touching her. 'Mary, you can find another job, you have a good reputation – and more, you have friends who can help you. There's no need to look so despairing.'

Mary stared at him. Here he was, owner of the Beaufort Steel and Tinplate Works, talking about other people offering her help but making sure that he did not help her himself.

'What have I done to you Suttons?' she asked bitterly. 'My life was smooth enough 'till you and your father came on the scene. He's a spiteful, petty man.'

Brandon gripped her shoulders tightly. 'My father is human, he makes mistakes like the rest of us.' Brandon's mouth set into lines of anger as he stopped speaking and Mary felt as though she would like to slap his self-assured face.

'You seem a great family for making mistakes.' Sarcasm rang in her voice and she saw Brandon stiffen with anger. The next minute he was drawing her close, his hand pressed into the small of her back, imprisoning her. His mouth crushed hers in ruthless anger and Mary struggled helplessly against him, her senses reeling.

Then his attitude changed subtly and he held her more gently, his hand caressing her spine, his mouth moving over hers and pushing her lips apart, his tongue probing. Flames seared Mary's body, every nerve seemed to come alive. She clung to him, her hands touching his face, his hair. The moment seemed to stretch on with infinite pleasure as Mary allowed the tide of emotion to carry her away. She did not think, all she could do was feel and the strange sensations seemed to govern her mercilessly.

Brandon moved away from her, standing tall and staring down at her, his hair tangled, his eyes bright like those of a wild animal. The silence was broken only by the shrill calling of a bird and the swish of the leaves on the branches overhead.

He pushed back his hair with rough fingers and turned away from Mary as though he could not bear the sight of her. 'I thought you were Billy Gray's girl,' he said harshly. 'So this is how far your loyalty goes!'

Mary felt suddenly lost. She pushed her skirts around her ankles with shaking hands, as though erasing the creases from the coarse flannel was the most important task in the world. Humiliation swamped her as the meaning of his words sank into her dazed mind. He had been playing with her, demonstrating that she too was fallible. How she hated him in that moment and yet, as she glanced up at him, there was the pain of loss and rejection that was almost impossible to bear.

'You think you're so clever, don't you?' Unbelievably, her voice was cool. 'Trying to pass your own guilt onto my shoulders – how I despise you!'

She turned and ran away from him lifting her skirts, leaping over fallen branches, unaware that her hair was streaming behind her like a mane. All she wanted to do was to put as much distance between Brandon Sutton and herself as possible. Tears constricted her throat as she found herself out on the main street, where she paused and pushed back her hair. It would not do to let the citizens of Sweyn's Eye see her in such a state.

As she hurried along Canal Street, her one thought was to lock herself in her bedroom and cry out all her bewilderment and anger. Since Brandon Sutton and his father had come to the town, they had caused her nothing but trouble, she thought tremulously.

It was cool inside the house and the scent of the freshly-cut flowers permeated the kitchen. Mary leaned against the door breathing heavily; she had escaped from Brandon's presence, but there was no escaping her own thoughts.

In her room she sank on to the patchwork quilt and kicked off her shoes. She lay back closing her eyes and once again could feel the power of Brandon's presence, the thrill of his mouth probing hers and the warmth of his hand pressing into her back and holding her close to him. Why, she wondered, had she never felt like this with Billy? Her response to him had been one of affection and warmth but without the passion of a lover.

'Damn Brandon Sutton to hell!' she said, muffling her tears in the coarse linen of the pillow cover. She would put him out of her mind, he was nothing to her, nothing at all. She must concentrate on her future and in that respect at least, Brandon had spoken sense; she would not wilt away, she would find herself another job. But as what? she thought dismally.

A strange languor seemed to have taken possession of her body as she stretched voluptuously and for the first time in her life knew the pain of desire that could not be assuaged. She wanted Brandon Sutton as she had never wanted any man, but that did not mean she was in love, she told herself fiercely. Lust was a sin of the flesh, or so the good book said. But surely giving yourself to a man in the marriage bed if you did not care for him was more of a sin?

Mary rose after a time and sponged her body in cool refreshing water. She was a grown woman, and though slow to reach her prime, the moment had come now when she felt the need for a mate. She was achingly aware of her own desires and it had been Brandon who had awakened her dormant senses. But she was a woman of strong mind and will, she would not give in to her needs; she would throw herself into a job of work, occupy herself with other matters.

She dressed in fresh clothes and stood at the window staring down at the water of the canal. The second of the shrill sirens from the works rent the air and soon the street was ringing with the stamp of clogs against the cobbles. Mary leaned on the sill and waved to Heath who winked at her as he moved across the road to let himself into the house. Guiltily she hurried downstairs, for she had given no thought to preparing a meal for her brother. He would be starving after a day's work at the tin mill.

'What are you doing home before me?' Heath threw down his sweat rag and, drawing his shirt over his head, moved towards the sink. Mary's heart swelled with pride; her brother was turning into a fine handsome man, his muscles hardening, his jaw growing lean and strong.

'I've left the laundry,' she said bluntly. There was no other way to break the news to him. 'Old Mr Sutton got my rag up and in the end I was forced to give him my resignation.'

Heath divested himself of his trousers and washed his body carefully, his back turned to Mary who was busy at the fireplace cooking bacon and eggs.

'Tell me all about it, later,' he invited. 'There's more to this than meets the eye, isn't there, love?'

When he had rubbed himself dry, he ran lightly on bare feet up the stairs and Mary heard him moving about, opening drawers, and cupboards. She knew he would be out tomcatting again tonight and she shook her head and smiled. Yet she wondered that he found girls so ready and willing to lie with him, thinking ruefully that she must somehow be different. After all, she was not getting any younger. Only three more years to go and she would be thirty and she had never experienced a man's love – never felt desire either until today. She pushed the thought away as Heath returned to the room.

'Now then, what's all this about leaving the laundry? You'd sooner cut off your right arm than pack in your job; I know you too well, Mary.'

'It was either leave or keep working in the boiler house and do Doris out of her job. Mr Sutton has taken a dislike to me, that's all there is to it.'

Heath paused, a forkful of bacon halfway to his mouth. 'Am I hearing right? Is this my sister speaking? How can you give up so easily? Start a union like the men do and fight for your rights, girl!'

Mary smiled. 'It's nice to hear you calling me girl, though I'm fast becoming an old woman, you know.'

'Rubbish! I don't know what's got into you lately. You never used to be self-pitying. Come on, stir yourself and show a bit of the spirit that got us out of that hovel and into a lovely house like this.'

Mary stared at her brother – he was almost repeating the words Brandon Sutton had said, only in a far more outspoken, brotherly way.

'Mr Sutton, our boss, now,' Heath continued almost as though he had read her thoughts, 'he's a man who's all for the workers. Believes in fair play, he does, whatever the other owners might say. If you have faith in something, then you must fight for it, or don't you think that any more, Mary?'

'All these questions!' Mary was aware that she sounded pettish but she could not help herself. 'It's a well-known fact that everyone knows what to do with a kicking cow except the one that's milking it.'

She put out some bacon and eggs and set her plate on the table, but she had never felt less like eating in all her life. She toyed with her food, pushing the bacon around the plate aimlessly.

'Be a suffragette,' Heath said, smiling a little. 'I don't mean to say you must chain yourself to the railings or anything like that, but you could always go round the countryside campaigning for the rights of women workers.'

Mary shook her head. 'No, I wouldn't want to do that. My dream is to open a shop where women can buy on tick and pay when the wages come in. I'd like to have enough money to help them through strikes too, keep the families of the men who are out, give them food and clothing until the men go back to work again. That would be a good way of beating the bosses, for it's when the babbas are starving that the men give in.'

Heath pushed back his chair. 'Well, there's the money you've put away in the jar,' he said. 'That must come to a few guineas by now.'

Mary shook her head. 'No, I'll need that to pay the rent until I find another job again at least.'

Heath moved to the door. 'I'd give you a bit more pay, mind, but Mr Sutton has just docked our wages.' He stood in the doorway looking back at her for a moment, waiting for her to speak.

'We'll be all right, *bachgen*, for a time anyway.' She knew that was what he wanted to hear. She rose to her feet and stood in the window, watching him stride down the road, loving him. And yet a sense of sadness lay heavily upon her. Perhaps she thought, she had been too fussy as a young girl. Had held her chastity as a precious gift to be offered only to one man. It did not seem to bother the girls who lay with Heath so readily that they were throwing away their virginity.

As she washed up the plates, a strange restlessness seized her. She should be writing her weekly letter to Billy, but she couldn't bear to sit indoors. She would go and walk along the beach, stare up at the stars and try to sort out her muddled thoughts.

It was cool at the water's edge, the waves lapped inky blue against a shadowy shore. The pier stretched outward like an arm pointed across the Channel and the lights of a ship coming in to port were waveringly reflected in the water.

Mary sighed and breathed in the salty air as though it was a balm. She felt the sand shift between her toes and, on an impulse, sat on the beach and kicked her feet free of the tightly laced shoes. She laughed as the breeze lifted her hair with loving fingers and then tossed it back across her eyes.

She felt like a child again and absurd tears rose to her eyes. She had never had time to be a child – old before her time she was, and now realised for the first time how much she had missed. She had never gone to Sunday school outings, run in the egg-and-spoon races or splashed shrieking and heedless into the cold of the sea. She had been too busy earning bread to put in her brother's mouth. She wept for the child she had been and yet despised herself for her weakness.

But now she was a woman and Grenville Sutton threatened to rob her of all she had achieved. As for his son, well he had taken something far more precious – her belief in her love for Billy Gray. For now she knew herself to be a passionate woman and had woken as if from a long sleep. Brandon had bred in her a strong desire, but one that must remain for ever unfulfilled. She lay back in the sand and the tears that ran into her mouth were as salt as the ocean.

Chapter Eight

As Delmai Richardson entered the huge grim prison gates her heart was in her mouth and her hands trembled. On her arm hung a basket filled with gifts for the unfortunate men incarcerated behind high grey walls, donated by the Ladies' Charity Guild. It was a duty that Delmai could not in all conscience avoid.

When Bea Sutton had given her the task, pleading sickness as a reason for not attending the prison herself, Delmai had readily agreed for Bea looked too ill to rise from her sickbed; she was painfully thin and so very pale that her eyes stood out like dark lamps in her gaunt flesh. But now the moment had come, Delmai felt the visit was less a recognition of her new status as a married woman than something of an unpleasant chore.

''Day to you, ma'am.' The uniformed warder spoke ingratiatingly and Delmai dragged her thoughts back to the matter in hand.

'Good morning, Officer Griffiths,' she replied. He smiled down at her, but the cynical look in his eyes told Delmai he did not approve of gifts for the prisoners under his care.

'I'd advise you not to linger here today, ma'am; the prisoners are affected by the hot weather, if you know what I mean?'

Delmai looked away from him, her colour rising; she did know what he meant, only too well.

She hurried through the yard and up the steps into the dim hallway. The cells were beyond and she shivered in the sudden cold. Quickly, she distributed cards containing needles, thread and spare buttons, cynically called 'housewives' by the prisoners who received them without enthusiasm.

Billy Gray was picking oakum, teasing the greasy cord between fingers that were rubbed raw. Something in the set of his head and the light in his eyes caught Delmai's attention and she paused. She had heard the story of his arrest, of course, and had discussed with the other women the possibility of his innocence – and even if guilty, to be responsible for the death of another human being must be a dreadful burden.

'Billy Gray, isn't it? Mrs Sutton gave me something special for you.' She held out a bag of apples and a soft woollen jacket and Billy took them without any sign of emotion.

'Don't you like them?' Delmai asked curiously and Billy shrugged. 'Doesn't make any difference if I do, the warders will only take them away as soon as you've gone.'

'But that's awful!' Delmai said softly. There was something in his air of hopeless acceptance that reminded her of herself. He was a handsome man with hair sprouting short and curly all over his head; his eyes were gentle, grey and shadowed as though he suffered a great deal in silence. She felt inexplicably drawn to him.

'Can't you complain to the governor?' she asked in a low voice. 'I know Mr Jones to be a fair-minded man.'

Billy looked into her face and shook his head. 'I wouldn't even get near him,' he replied flatly. 'All I'd get for my pains would be a kicking.'

'Surely not!' Delmai could not conceal her shock. And yet she believed this man, for his eyes met hers squarely with no sign of guilt and she could imagine him in other circumstances being full of life and laughter.

'Come along, ma'am.' Griffiths was at her shoulder and she saw the way he examined the woollen garment as though assessing its value. She smiled at Griffiths, hiding her dislike of him before turning to speak to Billy.

'Take care of that waistcoat,' she said clearly. 'Mrs Sutton will be around to see you next week if her health has improved and she will want to know you've been wearing her gift.'

Griffiths looked as though he had swallowed a sour plum and, hiding a smile, Delmai made her way back through the courtyard towards the gate, a feeling of unexpected warmth rising within her.

Later as she sat in the garden listening to the calling of the birds in the trees that surrounded the house, she remembered Billy's gentle eyes and subdued manner and felt inexplicably sad. The scent of roses was almost overpowering, but the garden was a sweet clean place and it was here that Delmai usually managed to find peace of mind.

She had come to seek privacy, for the house was always bustling with servants especially when, like today, preparations for the arrival of a visitor were in full flood.

Delmai could have sought privacy in her bedroom, but simply being there made her uneasy. Not since that first night when Rickie had virtually raped her had she wept, for tears did nothing but excite her husband. He turned to her often, as though determined to make her fulfil the role of wife and mother and the more he forced himself upon her, the more she hated him.

A gasp of apprehension caught in her throat for Rickie had appeared on the pathway, striding purposefully in her direction. It was too late to move away, for he had seen her and was lifting his hand in greeting. She tried to relax and smile but her face felt frozen and stiff and the beginning of a headache teased the edges of her mind.

'How are you feeling today, Delmai?' Rickie flung himself on the grass at her feet and stared up at her with a penetrating stare. Delmai wished she could tell him she was well and full with his child for then, she believed, he would leave her alone at nights.

She shrugged. 'I'm all right, thank you.' She saw the disappointment on his face and yet could find no twinge of pity within her.

'I see I shall have to try harder with you.' He spoke truculently, as though she had spited him. 'Do you know something, Delmai? Even now there is a whore who has conceived of my child – should I divorce you and marry her instead?'

Delmai stared at him steadily. 'A whore might tell the same story to a dozen men and have them all believing themselves stallions,' she said coldly.

His face turned a dull red and he glared at her as though he would like to slap her. 'Well, if I am disappointed in you yet again this month then we shall have to see what Bryn Thomas has to say,' he retorted. He knew her fear of having their intimate business bandied about and he used that fear as a weapon in his armoury of barbs. Delmai lifted her head and looked him full in the face.

'Your own prowess will be brought into question then, have you thought of that?' She rose to her feet and returned to the house and as she walked away from him, she was gritting her teeth in anger and despair.

Inside the house it was cool and fragrant, bowls full of summer roses perfumed the rooms. Gwen bobbed a curtsey and smiled warmly.

'Everything is ready for our guest, Miss Delmai,' the maid said brightly. 'Mr Glynmor should be pleased with the way you run your household.'

Delmai nodded, but she knew that her father would have only one matter on his mind, would ask the same question Rickie kept repeating – was she yet with child?

'It all looks lovely, Gwen,' she said softly. 'Tell the other servants how pleased I am.'

In her room, she took off her gown and let it slip to the floor, staring hard at her reflection in the mirror. She wondered that her naked flesh still looked the same as before she had married Rickie Richardson. Except for a small bruise on her thigh where he had gripped her with too much enthusiasm, there was nothing in the milky white body to show the suffering she endured at her husband's hands at nights.

'Very lovely.' Rickie had come into the bedroom silently; there was amusement in his voice and something else that made her blood run cold. Hastily she snatched up her underclothes and held her silk chemise against her breasts.

'Such modesty.' He came towards her and deliberately took the garment from her, dropping it slowly back onto the carpet.

'Get on the bed,' he said flatly and Delmai looked at him appealingly, her heart pounding like a caged bird trying to be free.

'But there's no time, I have to prepare…' Her voice trailed away as he reached out and caught her arm.

As he drew her to the bed and pushed her unceremoniously against the pillows, her heartbeats quickened so that she could scarcely breathe.

'Why don't you go to your whore?' she said in desperation.

He smiled as he began to undo his buttons and Delmai's hopes of deterring her husband vanished. But she had to make one last desperate effort.

'Rickie, my father will be here soon. You must let me get ready, we shall have plenty of time later on tonight.'

He knelt on the bed beside her and the sneer was still in his eyes.

'Don't worry, Delmai,' he said softly, 'this won't take long.'

The evening was cool with the promise of rain and the curtains billowed softly against the windows. The long table gleamed with crystal glass and polished silver and Delmai sat beside her husband for all the world as if she was truly his beloved wife.

She watched her father push his plate away and toy with his brandy glass and she knew that the inquisition was about to begin.

'Now my boy…' He ignored Delmai and addressed his remarks to Rickie; she felt degraded, as though she was simply a chattel which was the way her father always made her feel. 'Is there any sign of a child yet?'

Rickie lit a cigar and stared at his wife accusingly. 'I'm doing my best in that direction, sir,' he said evenly. 'But I am beginning to wonder if my wife is barren.'

Delmai saw her father's face redden. 'A Glynmor, barren? Rubbish!'

Feeling like a bone between two dogs, she rose to her feet in a swift movement and stared at her father and her husband with fierce anger, wondering which one she hated the most. She suddenly thought of Billy Gray, held against his will behind the high walls of the prison; there was nothing he could do except endure his fate, but she had a free choice. Was she willing for this to be her way of life for evermore? Not if she could help it, she told herself firmly.

'Enough!' She spoke loudly, her voice echoing through the long room. Both men stared at her startled by her tone. 'This is not a cattle market we are discussing but a marriage.' She moved away from the table, noting with satisfaction that Rickie was for once at a loss for words. She stared at him defiantly.

'I shall sleep in the spare room for the time being, but as soon as I find a suitable house, I shall move into it bag and baggage.'

She stared at her husband; his face was suddenly pale and she felt a savage sense of satisfaction. As with all bullies, she thought, he simply wilted when the opposition was strong. She lingered in the doorway, staring at him with burning eyes.

'If you lay a finger on me again, I will kill you,' she said quietly. 'Don't think I'm not capable of it – ask my dear father there, he will tell you I can shoot as well as any man.'

A heavy silence fell over the dining room as Delmai swept out and hurried up the stairs. She took a pistol from the bottom of her trunk and weighed it in her hands almost lovingly. 'I mean it,' she said loud.

She rang the bell and Gwen came bustling into the room, her face flushed from hurrying. Delmai guessed that the servants had heard raised voices and were agog with curiosity.

'Move my belongings into the room at the end of the corridor, please, Gwen,' Delmai said firmly.

The maid scurried to do her bidding, her wide eyes asking questions she dared not utter aloud. Delmai followed her more slowly and sat on the bed kicking off her soft pumps, resting against the pillows, suddenly aware that she was filled with a sense of power.

How easy it had been to assert herself, she thought in satisfaction, and what could Rickie or her father do about it? Bluster and threats carried no weight, not when she had a pistol tucked away under her pillow. Just let her husband try to force his will on her again and he would see the business end of the firearm. Why, she asked herself, had she put up with her husband's badgering and cruelty for so long?

She undressed and lay back in bed, her eyes closed. It was still daylight outside the window and the birds were singing in the trees. But Delmai was deep in thought, making a mental inventory of her property and wondering which house she could afford to run on the allowance she had been left from her grandmother's estate.

There were two large imposing buildings high up on the hill, but both would need a considerable staff and she simply could not afford it. The house in Canal Street now, that might be suitable. On consideration it was her only option. True it was near to the laundry, but the house itself was large enough and comfortable, only a stone's throw away from the sea.

Canal Street had once been a respectable area with owners of local industries occupying the tall houses. Mr Waddington, proprietor of the Canal Street Laundry, had once lived there, but lately it had become run down and the houses had gone to seed a little.

At the moment the house was occupied by Mary Jenkins who lately had been a little slow in paying her rent. Excuse enough for asking her to leave, Delmai thought, though it was a task she did not relish. Still, her overriding need was to get away from Rickie before she either went mad or did him a violence.

She sighed as Gwen brought her clothes into the room and began to hang them in the large cupboard.

'Put out only enough for a few days,' she said firmly. 'The rest you can pack away in my trunk, for I'll be moving from here in a week or two.'

She knew that the servants' quarters would be buzzing with speculation as soon as Gwen went below stairs. The gossip would spread like wildfire to servants in other houses in the district, and perhaps people like Marian Thomas would speculate on Rickie's failure as a husband. As she snuggled down into her bed, the thought of Rickie's shame gave her an intense feeling of satisfaction.

Chapter Nine

The afternoon sun was shining in through the bedroom window, sending motes of dust drifting slowly downwards in a shaft to light. The bed was rumpled, the patchwork quilt had slipped to the floor and under the remaining sheets, Heath Jenkins tossed and turned – his fair hair darkened by sweat, his face unnaturally flushed.

Mary stared down at her brother in dismay. She had been worried when he had failed to get up for work this morning, but to stay in bed until this hour was unheard of.

She had gone into town to fetch some groceries, expecting to see him sitting at the kitchen table with a mug of tea in his hand when she returned, but the fire had fallen low in the grate and the kettle had gone off the boil. Even from the doorway where she stood, Mary could hear Heath's laboured breathing and it was quite clear that he was very sick. She went to him and rested her palm on his forehead; his skin was hot and clammy and Mary's heart plummeted in fear. He needed attention, but she paused at his bedside a moment, reluctant to leave him.

Sally Benson's mother lived just a few doors away; she was a nurse and used to sickness and whatever Mary felt about Sally herself, she could not allow her pride to prevent her asking for Mrs Benson's help. With a last distracted look in the direction of the bed, she hurried down the stairs and out into the sun-splashed street. Her heart was in her throat as she knocked at the plainly varnished door of the Benson household.

Heath had made too free, she told herself, as she waited on the step; he had caught a chill which had gone to his chest, but still he insisted on working in the gruelling heat of the mill. And he had spent his nights with some girl or other, courting on the high slopes of Kilvey Hill. Well, now the boy was suffering for it.

'Mary Jenkins! *Duw*, what are you doing here, my Sally hasn't taken sick at the laundry, has she?' The nurse was plump-cheeked, her gown dark and neat, her hair coiled cleanly away from her face.

Mary shook her head. 'No, it's nothing like that, I don't work at the laundry any more. It's my brother, Mrs Benson,' Mary swallowed hard. 'He's sick and I don't know what to do for him.'

Mrs Benson looked at her for a moment in silence, reading the desperation in Mary's eyes. 'Right, I'll get my things and come along with you at once,' she said briskly.

As Mary hurried back to the house, Mrs Benson had difficulty keeping up with her. 'An old midwife I am, mind,' she gasped, 'not a young chit of a thing like you. Ah, here we are, let's have a look at the boy.'

Mary watched as Mrs Benson wrapped her ample form in a crisp clean apron. Even as she tied the belt around her waist she was staring down at Heath with experienced eyes.

She bent over him and lifted his hand and Mary turned away biting her lip, dreading to hear what the woman would say, hopeful and yet deeply troubled.

'It's his lungs,' Mrs Benson said at last. 'Rattling like a bottle of pop, he is, poor boy!' She shook her head. 'The fever it is, got it bad too but we'll see what we can do then.'

She rolled up her sleeves. 'Know how to make a bread poultice, do you? He'll need one put on his poor chest every hour or so; then once it cools, change it. Can't give the boy no medicine, got none handy, but I'll stay by here with him while you run to the chemist.'

Mary nodded her thanks and hurried down the stairs. She took her purse from the back of the kitchen drawer and let herself quietly out of the house. Heath was sick, very sick. The gravity of Mrs Benson's expression as she looked down at the boy confirmed

Mary's worst fears. Well, if he did not respond to the nurse's ministrations, Mary would simply have to send for Dr Thomas. She knew his bills were steep, but she would use the rent money to pay them if necessary; all that mattered to her now was that Heath should get well.

The chemist shop had a smell all of its own, a mingling of methylated spirits and petroleum. 'George, I need something for my brother,' Mary said quickly. 'It's his lungs, Mrs Benson says he's got the fever.'

'*Duw*, there's sorry I am to hear that, Mary.' The chemist stood before shelves filled with bottles and chewed his lip thoughtfully. 'I'll mix up a linctus, combined with an expectorant. It should ease the boy a bit.' He moved about the shelves selecting bottles apparently at random while Mary waited in trepidation.

'Terrible thing, the fever,' George said softly. 'There's no telling which way it will go. But then, Heath is young and strong and he should pull through, so don't look so worried, *merchi*.'

When Mary returned to the house she hurried upstairs to find that Mrs Benson had already spread Heath's chest with poultice and had covered it with a piece of old red flannel.

'He seems a bit better already,' the nurse spoke encouragingly. 'Fetch a bowl of steaming water, gel, I'll give you some mentholated crystals to put in it. Hold the bowl beneath his nose and let him breathe in the fumes, and the congestion should ease.'

Mary hurried downstairs, glad to have something to occupy her mind. When she returned with the water, Heath seemed a little less flushed but his eyes were closed and his breathing still loud and harsh. Mary touched his cheek softly; it was burning hot as though he had sat in the sun too long.

She shook her head. 'I'm not happy about him, Mrs Benson,' she said. 'I'm sure you're doing your best but he looks so sick.'

Mrs Benson folded her apron meticulously, easing it back into the original creases.

'These things take time,' she said slowly, 'but I tell you what, wait until nightfall and if Heath is worse, then get the doctor.'

Mary gave the midwife a few shillings and when the coins had disappeared into a deep pocket, Mrs Benson smiled.

'Now don't forget to call me if there's anything more I can do.' She paused on the step. 'There's a strangeness about fevers I can't explain,' she said pensively. 'Sometimes they move away by themselves, there's just no telling.'

Mary watched Mrs Benson as she bustled away along the street and then hurried back up the stairs. Heath was tossing and turning, his face puffy, his hands restlessly plucking at the edge of the sheets. He opened his eyes and they stared at her as though seeing a thousand demons.

'Water!' he said in a hoarse whisper and as Mary held a glass to his lips, he drank thirstily. She wrung out a cloth and placed it upon his forehead and though he seemed calmer, his breathing was still uneven. Mary dragged the old rocking chair nearer to the bed and sank into it wearily. Her shoulders ached and her eyes were so heavy she simply must close them just for a moment.

A knock on the door startled her and she sat up with her heart pounding. It was dark in the room and hurriedly she lit the lamp. Heath was quieter and he seemed to be sleeping more easily.

Mary hurried downstairs as the knocking became louder and more insistent. She lifted the latch and froze for a moment, then remembering her manners, she stepped back and opened the door wider.

'Mr Sutton,' she said, stumbling over the name. 'What are you doing here?' Mary was aware that she must sound ungracious but her heart had begun to beat uncomfortably fast at the sight of Brandon standing on the step.

'I heard from one of the men that Heath was sick,' he replied. 'I've come to see if there's anything I can do.'

Mary stood behind a chair, her hands gripping the wooden back so tightly that her knuckles showed white. 'Heath's bad,' she said despairingly, 'there's a fever inside him and it's burning him up.'

She hoped he would not touch her, for she would make a fool of herself by bursting into tears at any sign of softness.

'I guess it's all right if I see him?' Brandon asked and Mary nodded dumbly towards the stairs.

She waited in the kitchen, half afraid of what Brandon might say and yet filled with relief that there was someone she could rely on to give her guidance. She sat down and clenched her hands in her lap and waited stoically for him to return. When he did, his face was grave.

'You must send for the doctor.' He spoke decisively. 'I realise there's some expense involved, but if I may be allowed to help?'

Mary shook her head. 'It's not the money.' She spoke through stiff lips. 'I have enough to pay Dr Thomas, but I just didn't know what to do for the best.'

Brandon shook his head. 'I shouldn't worry too much.' He stood near Mary but without touching her. 'Fevers usually seem worse during the night.' She longed to lean against his broad shoulder, to find comfort in his strength.

'I'll fetch Bryn Thomas, I won't be long.' He paused, waiting for her to speak and after a moment she nodded.

'Yes, thank you.' She went slowly up the stairs and sat beside Heath, leaning over him and watching him intently as if she could banish the sickness from him by sheer strength of will.

The doctor's examination of Heath was thorough and after a time, he stood back sighing softly. 'Keep him cool, Mary, sponge him with cold water at least once an hour. Open all the windows and persuade your brother to drink plenty of boiled water.' He took a small packet from his pocket and smiled ruefully. 'Here's something else you might try.' He gave her the pouch and it lay lightly in the palm of her hand. 'It is an old remedy for the fever,' Dr Thomas continued.

Mary peered into the linen bag and saw what looked like dried yellow flowers. 'What is it?' she asked and the doctor smiled.

'It's a herb called bugloss and I want you to make a cordial of it, do you understand?' He paused. 'It's said that it protects the heart and takes away the heat of fevers.' He smiled somewhat wryly. 'I've found it very useful, but then I'm old-fashioned. In any event, try it, my dear; it certainly won't do any harm and it might do some good.'

He moved to the top of the stairs. 'I'll call again tomorrow, Mary. Now take care of yourself, it won't help matters if you become overtired.'

Brandon did not leave with the doctor as Mary expected. Instead, he filled a bowl with water and carried it up the stairs to the bedroom.

'I'll sponge Heath down while you make up that potion.' He gave her a quick look. 'I guess I could use a little refreshment, so could you by the look of it.'

'There's only lime water or tea,' she said apologetically.

He smiled at her and she trembled. 'Lime water sounds fine and dandy,' he said.

The night hours passed as slowly as if every minute was an hour, made bearable only by the presence of Brandon Sutton. He and Mary took it in turns to watch over Heath as he moved restlessly between the sheets, battling for every breath.

Even when Mary sank on to her bed and tried to rest, she was conscious of Heath lying near to exhaustion in the next room and of Brandon caring for him as though he was his brother.

She heard the church bell strike every hour and at five o'clock when the grey of dawn was streaking the sky, she rose and pulled a shawl around her shoulders, ready to take her place at her brother's side once more. As she opened the door, Brandon was standing over Heath, a glass of water in his hand. He stared at Mary in the dim light and beckoned her forward.

'Look!' His voice was filled with elation. 'The crisis has passed, Heath is sleeping peacefully.'

Mary felt her throat thicken with tears. She knelt beside Heath and touched his face with her fingers; his skin was cool and dry. 'We've done it,' she said in wonder. 'Between us, we've done it!'

She was warm with relief and gratitude and almost unthinkingly she made a move forward. Then she was in Brandon's arms and he was holding her close. She wept silently, her tears falling against the crisp cotton of his shirt.

'Come, you can sleep now.' He led her into the adjoining bedroom and with his arm still around her shoulders, stared down at her in the dim morning light. Neither of them spoke, but Mary felt as though a spring of tension had been released within her. Slowly, Brandon lifted her chin and then his mouth was on hers and she clung to him, feeling the silkiness of his hair under her fingers as they locked around his neck. 'It's all right now,' he whispered, 'everything is going to be just fine.'

His arms held her closer, his body was hard and firm against hers and Mary was suddenly plunging into an abyss of emotion where there was nothing but joy and desire. She felt his hand linger on her breast and like a wanton she was pressing against him. His tongue was probing hers and she shuddered with longing, wanting the bliss to go on and never cease. She might have lain upon the bed and let him take her, except that Heath moaned softly in the other room and the spell was broken.

She drew herself sharply away from Brandon and stared at him with anguished eyes.

'It would be better if you went now,' she said raggedly 'But thank you.'

Without a word, he picked up his jacket and left the room and as she heard his footsteps hurrying away down the stairs she felt as though he was taking part of her with him.

Chapter Ten

The summer sun was warm, patterning the cobbled roadway, shimmering on the water of the canal so that it shone molten gold. The soft breezes that drifted over Sweyn's Eye were fragrant with the scent of honeysuckle growing wild in the hedges.

Mary sat in the window seat, staring out through the lace curtains but seeing nothing except the words on the piece of paper that had fallen to the floor. She bit her lips, her mind searching for a way out of her dilemma, but there seemed to be no solution. Delmai Richardson was asking for the rent arrears to be paid in full and Mary simply did not have the money. Too proud to allow Brandon Sutton to help, she had paid the doctor herself.

But at least Heath had improved a hundredfold. He was looking well and strong now, with a good colour to his cheeks and the strength returning to his slender young frame. He had grown like a weed in the two weeks he had been in his bed, and his hair had become long and curly so that he had the look of a bard about him. Mary's face softened in to a smile – a bard indeed, her brother a poet. This was certainly not likely, he was too much a man of action for that.

She rose restlessly to her feet. Heath had left the house early, before she was out of bed, and she saw with misgivings that his working clothes were missing. She knew deep in her bones that he had returned to the mill because of the letter lying discarded on the floor. He had read it yesterday when a young maid from the Richardson household had delivered it and his frown told Mary that he was as worried as she. But she had not wanted him to go back to the gruelling work and the blistering heat of the tinplate – not yet, not ever if the truth be told.

She sighed and rose to her feet, since there was bread to be baked and potatoes to be scrubbed and nothing at all would be accomplished by sitting around dreaming the hours away.

Mary pushed the dreadful empty feeling of panic to one side. She still had no job and the town seemed full to bursting with folks looking for work. But she must not despair, she told herself, nor did it do any good to brood on the problem of the arrears. Yet the spectre of the hovel in which she had been brought up had never ceased to haunt her. Again she felt the weight of the coarse blankets against her limbs, recoiled from the bite of vermin that clung to the weave of the bedding, heard the scurry of rats in the corners of the dark foetid room where her father lay sick and dying and his wife sucking on her bottle of gin, stretched out next to him. But she would never live like that again, Mary vowed; she would do anything rather than return to such squalor.

She threw all her energies into her household chores, kneading the dough with vigour as though the physical effort could ease her worries, but the possibility of losing the home was like a weight inside her.

When Heath returned home, his face was shadowed with fatigue and the healthy colour had fled, leaving his cheeks drawn and pale. He threw down his grub-sack and sank into a chair sighing heavily.

As Mary poured him a cup of fragrant tea and pushed it towards him, he smiled and her heart went out to him.

'I'll have good wages this week, Mary,' he said proudly. 'We had some fine heats today, not many rejects in the tinplate.' He sipped the tea. 'You can pay off some of the rent then, and ask Mrs Richardson can you catch up with the rest when you've got a job of your own again.' He lay back and closed his eyes, appearing very young and vulnerable yet with the beginnings of a moustache above his firm mouth.

Suddenly the future didn't seem so bleak and Mary smiled, 'You're right enough, boyo.' She rested her hand on his shoulder. 'There's daft I am to sit here worrying when I should be out searching the town for something to do. The Canal Street Laundry isn't the only place to work, is it? There's always the tin, in the last resort.'

Heath stared at her thoughtfully. 'I don't fancy you working the tinplate, Mary,' he said slowly. 'But the boss did say he could find you a place at the Beaufort.'

Mary refilled Heath's cup, her hand suddenly trembling as she settled herself opposite him. 'Not too proud to do anything, me.' She smiled. 'But separating the sheets is a skilled job, those slices of tinplate are like razors.'

Heath nodded. 'I've seen the cuts for myself, women slashed across the knees and ankles when a sheet has slipped. You're too clever to waste your life doing that sort of work.'

Mary leaned forward and ruffled his hair. 'Needs must when the devil drives, Heath,' she said wryly.

In the silence she thought about Brandon's offer to work and felt warm inside. So he did care a little, after all.

Mary served Heath his meal and then hurried upstairs to her room. She changed from her rough flannel dress and faded pinafore into a neat serge coat and skirt and a high-necked lace-trimmed blouse.

Heath was still sipping his tea, hunched wearily over the table, and her heart contracted with anxiety. She rested her hand on his shoulder. 'I shan't be long.' She moved to the door and stood there a moment staring back at him. 'Now, if you must go out tomcatting tonight, get a little bit of shut-eye first, mind.' He grinned and waved her words away airily, but he did not speak and with a sigh, Mary left the house.

The air was fresher now with the coming of evening and as Mary made her way towards the tram terminus, she wondered if she was choosing the right time to visit Mrs Delmai Richardson. But then what time would be right? Her task was a difficult one and nothing would change that fact.

The tram was crowded and Mary jostled aboard staring unseeingly at the bright advertisement for Ogden's cigarettes. She sank into a seat and tried to frame the right words in her mind, words that hopefully would give her time to find the money she owed Mrs Richardson.

Up on the hill the air was balmy and sweet as wine. The breeze carried with it a hint of salt blowing in from the sea that spread out like a vista of dull blue glass, as pure and unruffled as the surface of a mirror. Mary paused, looking around, her heart beating swiftly. Brandon Sutton lived in one of the fine houses overlooking the bay and overwhelmingly she felt the gulf between them, even though sometimes he acted as though he and she were equals.

She wondered what he would think if he knew of her dreadful background. The poverty and misery of her past was a sickness she hoped she had left behind, but at times like this when she was worried it rose up again to confront her like a gaunt threatening spectre.

Almost without thinking, Mary had walked up the driveway and knocked on the door of the gracious Richardson household. She was admitted almost at once and stared around her in wonder. The interior of the building was beautiful, the tasteful curtains that matched the cushions on the sofa and chairs were soft to the touch. Mary sat stiffly on a high-backed chair, shoulders straight and hands clasped in her lap.

'Miss Jenkins, sorry to keep you waiting.' Delmai Richardson entered the room with the air of someone wasting valuable time. She was dressed in a fine silk gown which fell away to reveal white skin and slender arms decorated with thick gold bracelets. Her eyes were misty, as though her feelings were well hidden from prying eyes. She seated herself and lifted her head, remaining silent as she waited for Mary to begin.

The tension in the room was almost tangible and Mary realised with a sinking of her heart that Mrs Richardson did not intend to make the interview easy for her. She took a deep breath and smiled pleasantly, but there was no answering response from the other woman.

'It's about the arrears,' she began haltingly. 'I'm sorry, but this is the first time I have fallen behind with the rent as you know. It's entirely due to unforeseen circumstances.'

Delmai Richardson looked at her coldly. 'I believe you have lost your position as overseer at the Canal Street Laundry.' Her words fell like stones into a pond and Mary's confidence began to melt away.

'Yes, but it was through no fault of my own,' she explained hurriedly. 'The laundry is under new ownership and my services were no longer required.'

Delmai Richardson waved her hand, dismissing Mary's words. 'That is none of my concern.' She spoke quickly, as though dealing with a matter that was distasteful to her. 'I'm afraid, Miss Jenkins, that I shall have to ask you to vacate the property as soon as possible. I'm sorry.' She twitched her skirt into place, folding out the creases in the fine silk as though she had nothing more important to occupy her mind.

Mary's mouth was dry. Fear grew black and threatening, beating at her like wings. 'Can't you give me a little more time?' she asked, her voice quivering in desperation. The other woman rose and moved towards the window, staring outwards as though forgetting Mary's presence but with every line of her body rigid and unbending.

Mary rose to her feet. 'Thank you for your time.' She spoke calmly as she walked slowly towards the door, hoping even now for some softening in the other woman's attitude but Mrs Richardson did not even turn to look at her.

Mary left the house and walked blindly down the drive. She could not think or feel; she was numb inside and in spite of the warmth of the evening, her hands were icy cold.

She heard a rush of sound and wondered if it was in her own head, then looked up quickly and was startled to see an automobile bearing down upon her.

'Hell and damnation!' The voice was heavy with an American accent, and for a moment Mary thought it was Brandon Sutton leaping out of the driving seat and hurrying towards her, but it was Dean who took her by the shoulders and stared down into her face.

'What are you trying to do, honey?' he asked in agitation. 'You almost caused a nasty accident just then. Come and sit down for a minute, you look properly shaken up.'

Mary allowed herself to be led towards the car and she sank gratefully into the seat, realising that she was trembling.

'Good thing I always slow down at that corner leading to Rickie Richardson's house,' he said more gently. 'Otherwise I might have done you a real injury. Come on, you can stop shaking now, it's all right.'

She found his arm around her shoulder strangely comforting. Dean Sutton was a generously proportioned man, his bulk reassuring against her arm. And he had been a good employer to Billy, even visiting him at the prison. Apparently he was doing all he could to get Billy a pardon and for that much at least Mary felt she owed him a debt of gratitude.

That there was no love lost between Brandon and his brother Dean was none of her business, since family squabbles were best left to those concerned. She became aware that Dean was studying her closely.

'Are you all right, not hurt at all, are you honey?'

Mary sighed, knowing that she must confide in someone. 'I've lost my job,' she said. 'But then I expect you know that. Your father gave me the sack – well at least he made it impossible for me to stay.' She shrugged. 'Now I'm in arrears with my rent and Mrs Richardson wants me to pay up or get out. I don't know what to do.'

His arm tightened around her shoulders and he leaned towards her, his eyes unreadable in the dimness of the twilight.

'The devil he has! I'm the owner, not my father, and if you want to be reinstated, just say the word.' He smiled slowly. 'But nothing is ever as bad as it seems,' he said softly. 'As a matter of fact, I can offer you a better position right now.'

Mary looked up at him, not daring to hope. Could her problems be solved this easily? 'What would you want me to do?' she asked quickly. 'I'm not experienced at anything but the laundry, mind.'

He laughed. 'It's as easy as pie! All you have to do is just take complete charge of Sutton's drapery store in Wind Street. You will be expected to see that the girls do the repairs correctly and be pleasant to my customers. That wouldn't be too difficult, would it? And the wages will be better than at the laundry, I'll warrant.'

Mary could scarcely believe her luck. She shook back a strand of hair that had come free from the pins and her heart was warm with thankfulness. 'Well, I don't know why you should be so kind,' she said unevenly, 'but if you think I'd be suitable for the job, then I can't say no.'

Dean laughed in triumph. 'That's the spirit! I knew I could count on you.' His hand began to caress her shoulder and Mary moved a little uneasily.

'Your problems are all solved,' he said. 'You now have a job and a new home, all in one fell swoop. Isn't that just fine?'

'A new home? I don't quite know what you mean.' Mary was bewildered and she tried to move away from him, but Dean held her fast. He put his hand beneath her chin and tilted her face up to his.

'Shop assistants have to live in, surely you know that, Mary? There are quarters above the Wind Street store where my girls are housed, but you, as a more special employee, would be required to live at my own home.' His hand had slipped to her waist, he was drawing her closer to him and his breath was hot on her cheek.

'Come on, Mary, you must see what I'm getting at. You're all grown-up now. I've always admired you, so big and robust, so beautiful.'

Mary's heart sank as she saw only too clearly exactly what Dean Sutton was offering her. 'You want me to be your mistress, in other words,' she said flatly and Dean did not flinch.

'Is that so bad, honey? After all, Billy is behind prison walls; you must feel the lack of a man in your life and I would be so good to you.'

Mary climbed down from the seat of the car. 'No trade, Mr Sutton,' she said flatly and then she was running down the hill, like a caged bird suddenly set free, exultant and yet frightened all at the same time. Below her were the lights of the town twinkling like fallen stars and overhead the sky was huge, a deep indigo bowl; Mary felt insignificant as she ran towards the safety of her home.

-

It was cool in the kitchen, with the back door opening out into the softness of the night. Mary sat with her mending idle in her lap, wondering at the way the men of the Sutton family were influencing her life. She could not help but feel angry with Dean, he had been so confident that she would accept his offer without hesitation. True, he was a big handsome man, rich and powerful, and in other circumstances she might have found his attentions flattering.

She had no false illusions about herself. Chaste she was, but that was an act of providence and not one of will. She felt the colour rise to her cheeks as she thought of her response to Brandon's touch – her defences were down when he held her close in his arms.

She remembered with a sense of pleasure the night when Brandon had helped her look after Heath. She had experienced joy and delight as potent as heady wine when she realised that Heath would live. And Brandon had shared it with her. She had almost succumbed to him then; he had reached out and touched her and she was aflame with desire for him.

She sighed restlessly, aware that she needed something more from life. She knew deep within her that she wanted love and the joy of a relationship built on solid foundations.

'Fool!' she said softly. 'All you need is a good strong man to bed you.' She had never realised except perhaps in the dimness of her dreams how moved she could be by a man's caresses. But not just any man, she told herself firmly – not by Dean Sutton! It was his brother Brandon who had the power to stir her desires.

She heard a sudden noise and startled, rose to her feet. Her heart began to pound and as she stared at the figure in the doorway her eyes widened in surprise.

He was standing in her kitchen then, as though he owned the place, tall and proud. His dark hair curled around his face and his eyes were alight as they met hers. It was as if she had drawn him to her with the strength of her thoughts.

'Brandon.' The name was like a sigh leaving her lips. He stepped further into the room and the glow of the lamp fell upon his face. His cheeks had a sculptured look, his head was held high and his manner autocratic; for the first time, Mary realised that he was angry.

'I don't know what game you think you're playing.' He spoke in a clipped hard voice and Mary fell back a step, her hand going to her bodice as though to still the beating of her heart.

'What's wrong, I don't understand...' Her voice faltered into silence as he stepped closer to her.

'You certainly had me fooled, I could have sworn you really wanted me.' He laughed shortly. 'I believed when I took you in my arms that your passion was for me alone. I should have known that honesty in a woman in a rare jewel.'

Mary shook her head in bewilderment. 'I still don't know what you're talking about, there's no sense in what you say. What have I done?'

Brandon shook his head. 'I saw you with my brother, he was holding you in his arms and making you a pretty proposition, I don't doubt.'

Hot colour flooded into Mary's cheeks. She could not look at Brandon – his words were so near the truth, so how could she deny them?

'At least you have the grace not to lie to me,' he said. He stood aloof from her, his face averted and Mary was so aware of his presence that it was as though a great light filled her being. She longed to throw herself into his arms, to beg him to understand that what he had seen was none of her doing, but his firm jawline and the coldness of his eyes as he turned to look at her was unnerving.

'It wasn't like that,' she tried to explain. 'Mr Sutton was offering me a job.'

'As what, his kept whore?' Brandon said in a low voice and suddenly Mary was as angry as he was.

'All right, you have made up your mind that I'm a floosie,' she said briskly, the hurt within her almost unbearable. 'So what are you doing standing here in my kitchen?'

He looked surprised as though he expected her to make further protestations of her innocence, but Mary pressed her lips firmly together, unwilling to let him see the depths of her pain.

'Heath told me something of your problems,' he said briefly. 'I came to offer help – an advance on Heath's wages, let's call it.' He reached in his pocket and drew out a bag of money, laying it carelessly on the table.

Mary stared down at it. Pride was thick in her throat and yet she needed the house in Canal Street. It was more to her than bricks or mortar, it was a haven from memories of her past.

Brandon had described the money as an advance on Heath's wages and for a moment she was tempted to accept the offer. As she glanced up at him their eyes met and she felt as though she was suddenly drowning in a turquoise sea.

He took her in his arms so suddenly that she could not move. His lips crushed hers but there was no tenderness, only passion and anger. For a long second of time Mary remained motionless, savouring his mouth upon hers, then his hand touched her breast and pain surged upwards bursting from her in a torrent of resentment.

'No!' She pushed him away fiercely. She picked up the money and threw it towards him, and the purse fell to the floor scattering coins in every direction.

'Get out of here and leave me alone!' she said more quietly. He shrugged and turned to the door, his look one of scorn. Mary scooped up the money and pressed it into his hand.

'At least your brother was honest with me,' she said, her voice shaking. 'He told me he would give me a job, but that I would become his mistress for which service he would pay me well and keep me in comfort. You come along with your thirty pieces of silver and expect a quick tumble on the mat by the fire as though I were a doxy. Who is the worst devil, I ask you?'

Brandon smiled but there was no humour reflected in his eyes. 'I don't need to pay for what you would have given me freely,' he said harshly and then he had gone, striding away into the darkness and leaving Mary alone with her humiliation.

She closed the door sharply and paced restlessly around the small kitchen, her mind a kaleidoscope of thoughts that whirled blackly, merging into despair as she sank at last into her chair. And from it all, one painful fact emerged: Brandon thought of her as a floosie, a woman who would give her love freely to any man. Tears rose in her throat, her eyes burned but she would not cry.

She was riddling the ashes in the fire, preparing for bed, when Heath returned home. He looked better now with a healthy bloom of colour in his face and the old gleam was in his eye once more.

'There's a silly grin splitting your face,' she said, staring at him. 'Been out courting, have you?'

He nodded. 'I have that and I think I'm falling for her,' he said softly. 'She's a beautiful girl and good too, Mary, and there's not many like that around these days, believe me!'

What was it in men that they put women into brackets of good or bad, according to whether they gave in to a man or not, Mary wondered. She folded her arms across her breasts. 'Well, what's her name? Do I know her?' She tried to speak pleasantly, though the mood of black despair still hung over her.

'It's Rhian – I'm surprised you didn't cotton on before now,' Heath said gently. Mary unpinned her hair and it fell long and flowing down her back. She had been blind, so wrapped up in herself and her problems that she'd had no idea what was happening to her brother.

'Well, she's a bit spoiled, of course, and wilful, but I expect a man of character could handle her,' she said at last.

Heath smiled. 'Oh, I can handle Rhian all right,' he said confidently. He perched on the edge of the table. 'I'm going over to stay with her auntie for a few days next week – is that all right with you?'

Mary nodded. 'Of course it's all right, *cariad*, you've got your own life to live. You are not tied to me by any apron strings, mind.'

He leaned over and brushed the hair back from her forehead. 'Mary, I am tied to you by so many bonds. You've been wonderful to me, taken the place of our mam; you've brought me up, fed me and clothed me and loved me. What more could I ask? Mary, I'm trying to say thank you!'

She reached up and hugged him, hot tears pressing against her closed lids. 'Sounds as if you're saying goodbye, boyo. Not thinking of marriage so soon, are you?' She paused. 'You're young yet, only sixteen, there's a lot you should do before you settle down.'

'I'm going on seventeen, Mary,' he said as he held her shoulders and looked into her face. 'I've lived a lot and worked like a man and nearly died. What more do I need do know?' He smiled ruefully.

'Rhian's aunt will take us in with her. I'll be the breadwinner, it's true, but one day the house will be Rhian's and mine and so I suppose it's only fair that I pay towards it while I'm young.'

He touched her cheek lightly. 'Only one thing worries me, what's to become of you?'

Mary rose to her feet and stared down into the greyness of the dead fire. Billy was gone from her, enclosed behind prison bars, and now Heath was about to leave. Her life was changing. Like a rushing tide that could not be stopped it was carrying her hither and thither, a twig upon a wave. But self-pity was something that did no good, she had learned that lesson early. She smiled and turned to her brother.

'Well, when is this wedding going to be?' she asked brightly. 'There's plenty of sewing for me to do if I'm to send you off properly.'

Heath pushed himself away from the table edge and Mary noticed afresh how tall he had grown. 'The autumn, we thought, end of September or beginning of October. But how will you pay the rent without my wages coming in?'

She smiled brightly. 'Well, it so happens that I might be moving anyway.' She took a brush from the drawer and began to tidy her hair. 'I've been offered a job, a good one but it means living in.'

Heath's smile betrayed his relief and Mary turned away so that he would not see the darkness of her fear.

'That's lovely then. Who will you be working for? Tell me all about it, Mary, it sounds exciting.'

She shrugged. 'It's all right. Working in Sutton's Drapers down in Wind Street, it is, supervisor over all the girls. Good wages too.'

Heath sighed. 'Well, that seems to solve all our problems. I'm so happy for you, you don't know how bad I felt telling you I meant to leave.'

'Remember this, *cariad*,' Mary said softly, 'that you can't live another person's life for them. You must be the master of your own destiny. I've been around a lot longer than you and so I know what I'm talking about.' Heath moved towards the door. 'Well, I'll sleep with an easy mind tonight.' He smiled. 'You're a clever girl, Mary. How could I doubt that you'd find a job?'

Mary sat alone in the kitchen for a long time, knowing that her path was clear before her. She was alone now without a man to work for her or a roof over her head. She must make what she could of her own future. Tomorrow she would go to Dean Sutton, tell him that if he still wanted her she would accept his offer. She held herself unconsciously straight as she rose to put out the lamp.

'I'll be a damn good shopkeeper,' she said out loud and then grimaced a little. 'What's more, I'll make sure I'm the best damn whore Sweyn's Eye has ever seen!'

Chapter Eleven

Delmai Richardson paced the hallway, waiting impatiently for the groom to bring the carriage round to the front entrance. Rickie had left the house early without speaking to her and she had felt nothing but relief as the door closed behind him.

Since the evening of her father's visit, when she had caused a scene, she had managed to stave off all his attempts to ingratiate himself with her. One night when he had entered her room, she had threatened to scream and call the servants if he so much as laid a finger on her.

The firearm was safely tucked under her pillow as an extra precaution, but it was Rickie's innate fear of ridicule that kept him away from her. Just the same, the sooner she was out from under his roof and installed in her own house the better she would be pleased.

A slight movement attracted her attention and Delmai became aware of the maid bobbing her a curtsey. 'Kent is outside, Miss Delmai, he's ready for you.'

'Thank you, Gwen.' Delmai moved across the hall with a sigh of relief, for it would be good to be outdoors riding along in the warmth of the sunshine. She was nervous but at the same time exultant, knowing she was taking the first step to freedom for she intended to speak to Mary Jenkins and tell her that she must leave her house in Canal Street at once.

The brougham, though old-fashioned, gleamed with the care the groom showered on it. Kent helped Delmai into her seat with respectful diffidence and Delmai, scarcely noticing him, glanced towards the gardens which were rich and full of blooms glowing in the summer sun.

Perhaps this was what she would miss, she decided, for the house in Canal Street had no garden to speak of, just a pocket-handkerchief square of lawn to the rear of the building. But her peace of mind was a more important concern than a few flowers, she told herself sharply as she sank back in her seat, feeling she was taking the only course of action open to her.

The gentle clip-clop of the horse's hooves lulled her, a fat-bodied insect droned around her head and a breeze fanned her hot cheeks. She sighed and twisted her hands in her lap. It was not going to be easy to face Mary Jenkins.

Delmai allowed herself a few minutes to think of the woman to whom she would be dealing an unkind cut. Mary Jenkins had kept the house in Canal Street pristine and fresh and until recently had paid her rent without a day's delay. In fact she had been an ideal tenant and to evict her now seemed shabby treatment meted out when times were hard for the woman. But then Mary Jenkins by all accounts was used to hardship and as she was strong she would doubtless survive such a temporary setback.

Delmai was not completely insensitive. She felt sad that the woman was to lose her home, but there was no alternative. She shuddered, for nothing on earth would induce her to live with her husband a moment longer than necessary. It was clear that her own need was the greater and Mary Jenkins would just have to solve her own problems.

Nevertheless, when Delmai stepped out of the carriage and stood outside the door of the neat little house, her heart began to beat a little more swiftly and her hands trembled.

Her knock was answered at once and Mary stared down at her, giving Delmai the irritating impression that she was small and helpless by comparison.

'Good afternoon,' she said briskly, making her way uninvited into the neat parlour. She did not sit in one of the highly polished chairs but stood with hands folded across the smooth fine linen of her skirt and stared at Mary unflinchingly.

'I'm afraid I have to ask you to give up the tenancy of my house by the end of the week.' She spoke loudly, uncertain how to react to Mary who was conducting herself like a grand duchess. There was no sign of servitude and certainly no indication of the tearful pleas Delmai had half-expected.

'I see.' Mary's voice was calm, light with a warm trace of a Welsh accent but without the tiresome sing-song quality that was often heard in the streets of Sweyn's Eye.

The silence dragged on endlessly as Delmai waited for Mary to make some protestations, berate her even, but the woman lifted a strand of thick dark hair and patted it into place, outwardly at least quite composed.

'I have to move into the house myself,' Delmai said quickly. 'I need to be alone and Canal Street is the ideal situation for me.' She did not know why she was babbling so inanely, but something in Mary's deep eyes unnerved her.

'You may think me harsh, but in any other circumstances I would give you time to make good the arrears.' She shrugged. 'As it is, I must ask you to leave the property as soon as possible.'

Mary inclined her head graciously in acknowledgement. 'I understand and it's all right. I have packed up my belongings.'

Delmai was bewildered by Mary's apparent control of the situation. Here she was being put out of her home, a home she kept in excellent order, yet she did not show by even so much as a flicker of an eyelash that she was disturbed. But these people were stoics, Delmai reasoned; they were born and bred to face difficulties, so how could they be expected to have sensitive nerves as she did. She made a slight movement towards the door, feeling absurdly as though she was intruding.

'I'm sorry.' Her words fell into the silence, cold like chips of ice, a gesture but nothing more and Mary recognised them as such.

How would Mary Jenkins have dealt with a man like Rickie, Delmai wondered. Sharply, no doubt, but then Mary was tall and statuesque, strong in character as well as frame; she would be a fighter, a she-wolf.

Delmai sighed. 'I'd better go,' she said bleakly, but suddenly the room seemed dark and she stumbled a little, feeling suddenly ill.

Mary Jenkins held out a steadying hand. 'Would you like some tea?' She spoke kindly as though to a child and to her surprise, Delmai found herself nodding. She lifted her hand to her head and allowed herself to be guided towards a comfortable armchair.

She looked around her as Mary left the room, noticing that there was not a speck of dust to be seen. The piano stood against one wall, the wood shining so brightly that she could see her reflection in the mirror-like surface. The curtains hung soft and fresh to the floor and the inevitable lace covered the body of the window, preventing the curious from staring inside the little room. Delmai felt as though she was intruding on the woman's privacy and looked quickly down at her hands.

Mary brought a tray and placed it on the table. It was surprisingly well appointed, with thin china crockery and a silver teapot. The more Delmai saw of Mary Jenkins, the more of an enigma she became and she found she was watching her curiously. Mary had been Billy Gray's sweetheart before his arrest, but Delmai could not envisage the relationship being a successful one. Mary was too strong, too superior for Billy who was a sensitive being and needed gentleness not strength.

'I really am sorry, you know.' Delmai was feeling better already. She took her cup and sipped the tea that contained milk instead of lemon, but found that it was refreshing. Also it gave her time to study Mary more closely.

'What can't be cured must be endured,' Mary said with such an air of resignation that Delmai felt for the first time that she was really depriving her of her home.

'I don't get on very well with my husband,' she said, surprising herself with her confession, but once started she seemed unable to stop. 'I suppose I did not know what to expect of marriage.' She stared at Mary more closely. 'Why have you remained a spinster so long?'

Mary's eyes met hers coolly and Delmai found herself colouring with embarrassment. 'That was rude of me,' she said quickly, but Mary smiled.

'It's all right, I suppose the answer is that Billy and me never felt passionate enough about each other to set the date for the wedding.'

Her words gave Delmai a glow of happiness, though she did not care to examine the reason for it. The chinking of cups against saucers seemed unnaturally loud in the sudden silence and she felt the need to speak again.

'Marriage is not romance and roses as I was led to expect – it's a trap.' Her words tumbled from her lips and Delmai could not check them. 'I was not so much a wife as a piece of breeding stock, used cruelly and without feeling. I suppose I was enchanted with the prospect of being married without considering what the role demanded.'

Mary's gaze had softened as though she sympathised, but she didn't speak. Delmai wished suddenly that she could make friends with Mary Jenkins; she was an unusual woman, beautiful in a big-boned almost peasant way and yet with a sort of regal dignity that Delmai found impressive.

'Have you been able to see much of Billy?' she asked and her heart was beating uncomfortably fast as she waited for a reply. At last Mary shook her head.

'Only once.' She stared down at her hands as though the memory was painful to her. 'There was a nasty incident, Billy was hurt and the warder stopped me from going again.'

'Do you love him very much?' Delmai hated herself for prying and yet she waited eagerly for Mary's reply.

Mary sighed. 'I think I love Billy as a brother.' Her shrewd eyes rested on Delmai in a disconcerting way. She did not enlarge on her statement and Delmai could not bring herself to dig any further into what was really none of her business.

'I visit the prison regularly,' she said brightly. 'If you would like me to take anything in to Billy…' Her voice trailed away as

Mary shook her head. 'Well, I really must be going.' She rose to her feet. 'Thank you.' She did not know why exactly she was thanking Mary Jenkins, but she couldn't take her leave without some kind of gesture of apology.

As she rode home in the carriage, Delmai felt strangely exultant, knowing she would be happy in the little house on Canal Street. As soon as Mary Jenkins moved out, she would have the whole building refurbished; there would be new, softer, richer carpets, curtains and covers of her own choice. She would have the front door painted and replace the tarnished knocker with a bright new one. Feeling more confident and happy than she had done for a long time, she wondered again to herself at her apathy in remaining with Rickie when he had made her life so miserable.

She would take Gwen with her to Canal Street, of course, and she would need to hire a cook and a kitchen maid. Her staff would be very small, for there was no room for a retinue of servants. She would live quietly, contenting herself with good works, she told herself a little smugly. There was the prison visiting, which had become entirely her province now that Bea Sutton was too sick to leave her bed. Delmai smiled, because it was a task that she had accepted gladly since it meant she could meet with and talk to Billy Gray each week.

Rickie was at home when she returned and Delmai felt the usual shrinking feeling inside her whenever she was in his company. She seated herself quietly in a chair, hoping he would not notice her, but after a long moment of silence he looked at her sourly from over the top of his newspaper. She tensed, waiting for some reproof or other, preparing a reply that would make him more amenable. But when he spoke his criticism was not, for once, directed at her.

'That stupid American doesn't know what he's doing.' Rickie's brows were drawn together in a frown. 'Trying to bring out a handbook for the tinplate men indeed what rubbish! Only an American could be so namby-pamby. There are bosses and workers and both can't be on the same side, but try telling that to Brandon Sutton.'

'Is the prospect of the handbook being published so bad?' Delmai said mildly, happy that her husband's mind was on other matters and that he had not thought to question her absence from the house.

'Bad? It's downright absurd!' Rickie replied fiercely. 'The workforce must be kept in their place, otherwise they strut around talking of strikes. This fool American is encouraging them. Drummed out of the Employers' Association, that's what he should be.'

'I don't understand.' Delmai was not in the least interested in the subject, but it diverted Rickie's attention from herself. 'What is this book you're talking about, what harm will it do?'

'It will give men ideas above their station.' Rickie was agitated, his face flushed as he shook the newspaper violently. 'Letting them think they can have fair wages for all, and the owners footing the bill.'

He paused, his brows drawn together in a frown. 'If there are spoiled sheets the workers are at fault, but Brandon Sutton wants the men to be paid for the hours they put in and not for the end results.' Rickie sighed and shook his head. 'Pay the men by the box, he says, whatever size of sheets are worked. The fool American doesn't know what he's talking about, he'll soon be bankrupt and where will his workers be then?'

Delmai rose slowly to her feet. Looking at Rickie's flushed faced, she wondered how she could ever have brought herself to marry him. The scales had dropped from her eyes now and with a vengeance.

'I'm going upstairs,' she said softly – so softly that Rickie, shrunk once more behind his newspaper, did not hear her which was exactly what she wanted.

In her room, she sat on the bed, staring out into the gardens below.

The grounds were rich and lush – a riot of colours with huge rhododendrons and beds of geraniums set among green lawns. But she would be happy in her new home, she told herself. Small it might be, but it was what she wanted. She shivered, for Rickie would rant and rave when he saw that she really meant to leave him, but nothing would stop her now. She smiled happily to herself, for in the meantime – while she was preparing the move – there was always the prison visiting to keep her spirits high. As she lay back on the softness of her bed and closed her eyes, the image of the gentle face of Billy Gray was suddenly very clear in her mind.

Chapter Twelve

The blast furnaces were being tapped out and the sky above the tall iron-clad stacks was illuminated with a yellowish molten glare. Clouds of smoke thrust heavenward, blotting out the rays of the sun so that the day seemed shadowed and overcast.

Brandon, standing on the banks of the river Swan, glanced upwards wondering at the mighty spectacle which never failed to impress him. He felt a glow of pride that he owned the works; he had sunk all his money into the venture, but at moments like this the risk seemed well justified.

He could imagine the heat inside the works, almost feel the sweat breaking out on his brow. The men in the sheds worked like donkeys and determination rose within him to see that they were given fair play.

Mark came hurrying across the uneven ground, a newspaper in his hand.

'Look at this, sir!' he said breathlessly. 'We've been given headlines on the front page – got the date we intend to publish, they have, God knows know.'

'Damnation!' Brandon thrust his hands into his pockets, his face grim. 'Where do these reporters get their information from? It looks as though someone inside the works is feeding them this stuff, otherwise the facts wouldn't be so accurate.' He shrugged. 'I suppose there's nothing we can do about it now.'

Mark kicked at a stone and it bounced into the river, sending ripples working outwards in ever widening circles.

'All the same, I'd like to know who the songbird is, I'd teach him to be a *bradwr* to his workmates.' Mark grinned as he saw

Brandon's eyebrows lift questioningly. 'Traitor, I mean, sir. I always fall back into the Welsh when I'm angry!'

Brandon began to move along the bank towards the small bridge that joined the two sections of the Beaufort Works. 'I'm going down to the press tonight, care to join me?' He saw Mark smile sheepishly and correctly interpreted his expression.

'I guess you're going out courting? Katie must be a mighty fine girl.'

Mark nodded. 'Aye, lovely she is, but she keeps hinting at a wedding ring and that frightens me to death.'

'Don't let any woman tie you down, Mark.' Brandon stepped off the wooden planking of the bridge onto earth soft with rain and looked back at his manager. 'The old saying that a man travels fastest alone is very true.'

Mark was silent for a moment and as Brandon watched the changing expressions on his face, he could hazard a guess at the conflict in the younger man's mind. On the one hand the need for a woman was strong, yet Mark was level-headed enough to know that he could go far if he had no ties to clutter his life.

'I wonder if Heath Jenkins would be prepared to help me.' Brandon changed the subject, turning to stare across the turgid waters at the yellow glare dying now from the skies. 'He's bright enough and willing and the boy has guts.' He was aware of Mark looking at him in surprise. 'You don't agree?' he asked.

'Don't know about that, sir, but the boy is very young. Someone with a silver tongue could work on him, convince him of anything. Perhaps it would be best to let him mature for a few more years and then he'll be ripe for reforming, the way all we Welsh are.' Mark grinned: 'Preachers we are to a man!'

'You may be right,' Brandon agreed. 'Heath probably needs a little more time to grow up.' He sighed. 'But I must see Evo tonight or that handbook will never be published.'

'Evo's willing to work the press I suppose?' Mark asked and Brandon nodded.

'Very reluctantly though, took quite a bit of convincing that it was all in his best interests.'

'Aye, well he would. Evo is good at being backward, knows that it pays him in the end. Is the book nearly ready?'

Brandon nodded. 'Yes, it's almost finished.' He smiled to himself in anticipation. 'I guess it will cause quite a storm when it finally hits the streets, the owners of the steelworks will be rocked to their boots.'

'Aye and you'd better look out then, sir. There'll be more than one big shot after your hide and they have some sneaky ways of dealing with those they don't like.'

'I'll take that risk,' Brandon said evenly, 'though I confess I'd like to be a fly on the wall when they get a special delivery of the handbook on their doormats.'

He moved away from the river and towards the mill. 'I'm going to look at the new furnaces,' he said, then turned to Mark. 'In the meantime, I'd like you to do a check on the steam hammers; they should be working fine now but it does no harm to keep an eye on things.'

The mill was humid, the oven-like furnaces going full blast. A heat was in progress and Brandon marvelled at the skill of these men who had worked the tinplate for much of their lives. He saw the furnaceman swing a piece of plate to the rollerman, who wielded it deftly with the tongs that were as much a part of him as his own fingers. The steel jerked and bumped through the rollers and then the metal was transferred to the doubler. Brandon was fascinated by the way the man trod on the hot shimmering piece of steel and, with a twist of his arm, folded it as though it was nothing heavier than a linen handkerchief.

Behind the rolls, Heath Jenkins was working as hard as the other three men. He was last in line, as yet unskilled, but if he remained in the mill he would work his way through the grades, becoming at last a highly paid furnaceman.

Brandon moved away, unwilling to disturb the silk-like flow of the activities centred around the furnaces. The steel would be folded and heated and refolded until it was a piece of eight. It was a man's job, well crafted and yet needing muscle to wield the razor-edged sheets with safety.

In the tinning house the air was alive with the chatter of women. The acrid smell of acid filled the room and the bosh set into the floor steamed as each plate was swung into the liquid.

The openers sat a little distance away from the pickling area, lifting the pieces of eight, slamming them down onto the bench, curling an edge so that the sheets would separate like the pages of a book.

Brandon stood unnoticed, watching the efforts of the women as they neatly packed the opened plates. The women filled up to sixty boxes a day and yet still found time to laugh and chatter as they toiled.

'Morning, Jessie, how's your boy doing? Not finding the work too hard, is he?' The plump woman, her face wrinkled like a dried-up apple, smiled at him revealing blackened teeth.

'Love it by here, he do. Adding acid to the bosh is all our Robbie 'as to do all day long. Money for old rope, it is.'

A sharp cry suddenly rent the air, changing to an animal howl of fear. Brandon turned quickly, reasoning that the sound came from the area of the acid bath. No one moved, then Jessie screamed aloud in terror. 'Jesus! It's my boy, he's fallen into bosh!'

Brandon moved forward swiftly, taking in the situation at a glance. The boy had been standing on the edge of the bosh and had slipped, falling feet first into the acid. He was slowly disappearing into the murky liquid, his young face grey with fear and his eyes starting from his head.

Brandon stepped forward and yanked at the rough flannel of the boy's shirt, lifting him upwards. Swiftly he covered the distance between the acid and the water and plunged the boy in head first.

'Keep still boy, the water will wash the acid away. You'll be all right, just don't struggle or you'll end up drowning us both.' Carefully Brandon lifted him, the water running in rivulets from the boy's flannel clothing as he laid him on a piece of sacking that one of the women had thrown to the ground. It was fortunate that the boy had been wearing good strong boots, for the acid had eaten them away into ribbons of steaming leather.

'My son! Jesus, Mary and Joseph, what's happened to my son!' Jessie flung herself onto the ground beside the dripping boy, her eyes wide with horror.

'He's all right' Brandon spoke reassuringly. 'But take him home, Jessie, and give him a bath.'

Jessie studied her son's feet and legs minutely. 'Yes, he's all right. Get up boy, see if you can stand.'

Shakily the boy got to his feet and Jessie slapped him across the face. 'That will teach you to take care, boyo, don't you frighten your mam like that again!'

As the young boy snivelled Jessie hugged him to her, looking up imploringly at Brandon. 'I can't afford to go home, boss, I haven't reached my number of sheets yet.'

'Go on home.' Brandon rested his hand on her shoulder and felt the coarseness of the material turned rusty in the acid atmosphere. Jessie smiled at him, her teeth rotting in her head.

'I'll see you have your pay and your son's too,' Brandon said quietly. 'Now take him home and feed him a good meal; he looks very sorry for himself.'

'Thank you, boss,' Jessie, her arm around her son's shoulder, moved away and Brandon knew by her attitude that far from appreciating his gesture, she thought him soft.

He left the mill and retraced his footsteps to the melting shop. The open-hearth furnaces were heaving and roaring like beasts from Hades, spitting as the slag was racked from the chimneys.

It was difficult to believe that from the reducing of the ore to pig iron through the processes of refining, annealing and pickling, fine tinplate would eventually emerge. And then the loads would be shipped to many ports to become containers for Mansion Polish or Skippers Sardines.

Brandon ran his fingers through his hair. He would inspect the furnaces, talk to one or two of the men and then get off home. He would need rest if he was to be up most of the night working on the handbook.

It was much later when he made his way to the small printing premises nestling in the corner of a dingy court in the heart of

Sweyn's Eye. He could see a dim light shining through the cracked glass of the window and he felt a sense of satisfaction knowing that Evo had kept his word, however reluctantly.

Yet he had an instinct that the man was not to be trusted; his eyes were shifty and he lied as easily as he drew breath. Brandon had worked very hard to convince him to print the manuscript, and even with the offer of a large sum of money as recompense the man's acceptance had been lukewarm. But at last he had agreed and that was all Brandon required of him. He did not need Evo's undying devotion – which was just as well, he thought dryly, for he certainly was not about to get it.

The door was locked and barred and it took the printer interminable minutes to open it. He peered outside suspiciously, his waxed moustache dipping at the corners as he sniffed nervously. 'Come in, Mr Sutton, I'm almost finished here.'

Brandon stepped into what seemed a snowstorm of loose papers; pages littered every surface and Brandon frowned, knowing that many hours yet would need to be spent on the book.

Evo apparently read his mind. 'Don't worry, sir, I'll soon have the pages fastened together. The hardest part is setting up the type. After that it's all work a child could do.'

Brandon sat at a table and began to put the pages in order. It was as easy as Evo had claimed, but laborious and slow. 'We'll have to get some help with this,' he said as he threw down a crumpled page in disgust, 'it will take us a month of Sundays to complete one handbook.'

Evo shook his head. '*Duw*, a couple of youngsters would make short work of it, Mr Sutton. You are not used to the job, that's what it is.'

Brandon rose to his feet impatiently. 'Is there anyone you can trust to help out for a couple of hours?' He thrust his hands into his pockets, staring round the lamplit room; the job was going to be more difficult than he had imagined.

'My two daughters work for me normally, but for a job like this I'm not too keen.' Evo rubbed his ink-stained hands against his canvas apron. 'There's an awful lot of blabbing goes on between young girls and I'm not putting my head on a chopping-block for anyone.'

Brandon moved towards the door. 'Very well, I'll see to it myself,' he said evenly. It was cool outside, the silvery moon throwing an eerie light over the narrow court along which he was walking. He glimpsed a shadowy figure and his muscles tensed, his hands bunching into fists. The footsteps behind him were stealthy and uneven and Brandon strove to hear from which direction they were coming.

As he came into the light of the main street, the shadowy figure following him seemed to dissolve and he wondered if he had been imagining things. He rubbed his hand across his eyes, wishing now that he had ridden his horse and buggy to the press instead of walking. Perhaps it was time he bought himself an automobile, but then he could hardly spare the money – all he owned was invested in the steel and tinplate works.

He turned into Canal Street and the lights from the houses spilled onto the pavement and danced in the smooth waters of the canal. He thought suddenly of Mary Jenkins, seeing her tall, shapely figure in his mind's eye. She was lovely and intelligent, with a temper like a viper's sting.

His mouth curved into a smile. He would enjoy an encounter with Mary, he decided. He needed a woman, for he had done nothing but work of late, concentrating on building up trade as well as striving to get the tinplate handbook published. It was time he relaxed, found a diversion so that he could forget business for a while.

Yet Mary Jenkins was not really the answer to his problem. She was passionate enough, but she would demand more perhaps than he was prepared to give. In any event, he did not feel predisposed to share her with Dean.

Suddenly the door to her house opened and Mary was standing on the step staring at him. She looked beautiful in the moonlight, her hair loose, dark shimmering waves hanging to her waist. He paused in mid-stride and they eyed each other like adversaries.

'Have you been snooping round my house?' she demanded, her hands on her hips. He moved so that the light from the doorway fell on to his face.

'Why should I snoop around, as you put it? If there is anything I want of you, I'll come right out and say so.'

Colour suffused her face as she stepped away from him. 'Well, someone was in my back yard, and then I heard footsteps outside my window.' She spoke angrily, as though she did not believe his denial. Before he could reply she had closed the door and he cursed himself for a fool; he could have stepped into the bright neat little parlour and perhaps whiled away an hour.

On an impulse, he moved to the back of the row of buildings. The lane was dark and gloomy in the shadow of the tall houses and as he moved forward, a burly figure rushed past him almost knocking him off his feet. In spite of the darkness, Brandon was sure he recognised the broad shoulders and tufted untidy hair of the man. It was Gerwin Price.

Chapter Thirteen

The smell of the clean linen permeated the long room, the dreaming summer silence broken only by the rustle of brown paper. Rhian folded a sheet with meticulous care before passing it to the girl who stood next to her tying parcels with strong twine. At first, Rhian had rebelled at the thought of working in the Canal Street Laundry, and had considered Mary Jenkins an interfering busybody for insisting on finding her a job.

'Just because you were courting our Billy don't mean you have to boss me around.' She could hear her words even now and would have liked to bite them back, but it was too late for that now that Mary had lost her own place in the laundry, dismissed by the new owner's father, Mr Grenville Sutton.

Sally Benson, chosen to replace Mary as overseer, was a witch of a girl, plain as sin and jealous of anyone with passing good looks. She never missed a chance to speak spitefully about Mary.

For a time, Rhian had tolerated the girl's company, her own irritation relieved by Sally's frank dislike of Mary. But things were different now that Rhian recognised herself as being in love with Heath.

Her hands fell to smoothing the sheets in a caressing movement as she imagined herself in his arms, his lips warm, his strong young body straining against hers. Sometimes she was almost as frightened as she was thrilled by Heath's passion.

She was well aware that so far she had made all the running. But lately, Heath had stopped thinking of her as a little girl and was beginning to take her seriously.

'Dreamin' again, sure and don't you take the biscuit for going off into a trance!' Katie Murphy placed a fresh pile of sheets beside

Rhian. 'These have to be folded, so come on and help me or we'll be here till past midnight, sure enough.'

Rhian smiled. She liked the Irish girl, who was always friendly and not given to moods of sulkiness. Yet there was a sadness deep in her blue eyes that even her smile could not quite conceal. Rhian had heard, along with everyone else, the story of how Katie had lost her lover in an explosion at the Kilvey Deep. The tragedy had a romantic pathos about it that appealed to Rhian's sympathy.

'Don't tell me, you were thinkin' about your young man again,' Katie said softly. 'I know the signs, sure I do, for wasn't I in love myself once?'

Rhian took the end of a sheet and heard the crack of linen as Katie shook out the folds.

'Love can be a painful thing,' Katie continued. Her face fell into lines of sadness and her deep eyes seemed haunted with inner despair; but then she smiled and the effect was like a sudden glow of lamplight.

'Sure and aren't I a moaning minnie, then? And you so young with all your life before you.' She brushed back her red-gold hair impatiently.

'How is Big Mary faring these days? I suppose you see her often, you walking out with her brother?'

'I see quite a lot of Mary, it's true,' Rhian said slowly, 'but it's as if there's a wall around her that no one can break through.'

'I know what you mean. Mary was always the dignified one, lovely as the morning sun but not one to make friends over-easily.' Katie put the folded sheet on the table. 'I must go and see Mary soon, for 'tis on my conscience that I've not visited her since she left the laundry.'

'You'd best hurry up, then,' Rhian said, 'otherwise you won't see her at all.' She saw the Irish girl's eyes widen in astonishment.

'What on earth can you mean?' Katie's hands rubbed at her apron and her brow was creased into a frown of anxiety. Rhian savoured the moment, realising that she had not only Katie's attention but also that of the other girls sitting around the room too.

'Being put out of her house in Canal Street, she is, at the end of the week,' Rhian said slowly.

Katie sank down on to the long bench. 'Jesus, Mary and Joseph, that can't be true, can it?' She spoke in a low voice. 'Why, Mary loves that place, she's worked like a tiger to make it her home.'

'It is true,' Rhian said hotly. 'Heath told me so himself, worried sick about his sister he was when I spoke to him last.'

Katie fanned her hot cheeks with her hand. 'I don't know what to say and that's for sure. Mary out in the street, after all this time! Poor girl, her lucky star must have fallen from the skies.'

'Serves her right.' Sally Benson stopped at the end of the long table, staring down at Katie with her eyes alight with mischief. 'Always was uppity, wasn't she? Thought herself better than the rest of us, looked down her toffee-nose at us, she did, just because she was friends with Mali Richardson.'

'Sure, that's all nonsense!' Katie rose to her feet angrily. 'And you shut your mouth about all this, do you hear? If there's any gossip outside this laundry, then I'll know who to look for.'

There was a murmur of agreement from the other girls and with a sniff, Sally Benson moved away. 'Get on with your work, all of you,' she called back over her shoulder. 'There's enough to be done without wasting time talking about Mary Jenkins.'

As Rhian settled into the routine of folding sheets once more, she wondered if she had been wise to speak of Mary's affairs so openly. Sally Benson, for one, would make the most of such a titbit of gossip. Rhian shivered, for Mary could be frightening in her anger; she was a fair-minded woman, but her tongue could be sharp when the occasion called for it. She put the unpleasant thought out of her mind, remembering that she had persuaded Heath to meet her later. They would walk hand in hand beneath the trees, he would kiss her and tell her he loved her and she would be warm with happiness.

The afternoon passed quickly, for Rhian was busy with her thoughts. It was almost time to put on her coat and go home when suddenly the room bristled with anticipation.

'Mr Sutton is on his way upstairs,' Katie whispered and the long line of girls fell to working as though their very lives depended on it.

He was an imposing man, Rhian thought, as the boss of the laundry entered the packing room. He stood at least six feet tall, his broad shoulders straight in spite of his advanced age. His collar was white and stiff around his throat and a thin brightly coloured tie hung down to his waistcoat.

'There have been complaints,' he began, his voice echoing through the long room. 'Some of the customers have been receiving laundry not up to the usual standard of cleanliness.' His heavy American accent made it difficult to understand him and Rhian found herself straining to make sense of his words.

'Other customers complain of having the wrong items of washing and of late deliveries.' He paused for the effect of his words to sink in, his hands thrust into his pockets and his eyes scanning the room as though to winkle out the culprits. 'It seems that there is a decline, ladies, in the entire laundry standards and this I shall not tolerate – do I make myself clear?' He moved further into the room. 'Now where's the girl who's in charge?'

Rhian watched as Sally Benson moved forward, her lip jutting out mutinously. 'I am sir, but you can't blame me. I've only taken over in the last few weeks, so whatever's wrong it's Big Mary's fault.'

Mr Sutton eyed her in silence for a moment. 'I don't like to hear blame laid at another's door, young woman, but in this case I'm inclined to accept what you say. All the same, if matters do not improve – and quickly – heads will roll, is that understood?'

He was all set to retreat and Rhian breathed a sigh of relief – for a moment she had worried about being late meeting Heath. Then Katie Murphy was on her feet.

'Just a minute, Mr Sutton.' The Irish girl was flushed, her eyes bright with anger. 'You can't blame Mary Jenkins for what's going wrong here now. The laundry has to operate week by week, so if washing has got mislaid in the last few days, how can Mary be at fault when she's not even been here?'

Mr Sutton paused in mid-stride and turned to look at Katie, his grey brows drawn together in a frown. 'I've said my piece and I don't want to hear another word on the matter,' he said flatly. 'What I want now is results, not excuses.'

He left the room and Rhian rose to her feet nervously. 'Come on, we can't do anything now, let's all get off home, shall we?' She moved to the window and stared into the sunlit street, straining her eyes to see if Heath was standing near the laundry gates.

'Well, I think it's rotten to put the blame on Mary, but that's just like you, Sally Benson!' Katie's voice was raised. 'You couldn't run a wheel-barrow, let alone a laundry, and the boss is going to find that out sure enough.'

'Hold your tongue, Katie Murphy,' Sally retorted, 'or I'll tell the boss that it's you who's making the mistakes.'

'Jesus, Mary and Joseph!' Katie rose angrily to her feet, her hands resting on her hips. 'We all know who is making the mistakes, now don't we, and as I just said, there's no hiding such things. You might fool the boss for a little while, Sally Benson, but your sins will find you out, never fear.'

Rhian eased her way past the crush of girls and hurried down the steps into the fresh summer air. She stared up and down the street but there was no sign of Heath and she leaned against the laundry wall, biting her lip impatiently. She had wanted to show off Heath to the other girls, see their glances of envy, bask in their admiration at her cleverness in catching a man as handsome as he was.

Her heart lightened, her eyes grew wide as she saw him turn the corner and enter Canal Street. He was growing taller by the day and his hair was shining in the sunlight. She waited for him to come up to her and flushed with pleasure as he put his hands on her shoulders and kissed her in full view of the girls streaming through the laundry gates.

'Come on, Heath.' She took his hand. 'Auntie will have our tea ready for us.'

Heath smiled down at her. 'Who wants food when my girl is pretty enough to eat?'

'There's a tease you are, Heath Jenkins,' Rhian said softly. 'You know as well as I do that you'll eat a plateful of Auntie's *tiesen lap*.'

'Aye, well, she's a good cook isn't she, and I hope she teaches you to make flat cake the way she does, otherwise I might start taking her out courting instead of you.'

Rhian became aware of footsteps hurrying behind her and turned to see Katie Murphy waving to her.

'Wait a minute, you two, I want a word with Heath Jenkins if he can take his eyes off you for five minutes, Rhian Gray.'

Rhian clung to Heath's hand, waiting for Katie to speak again. 'Could you give Mary a message for me, Heath?' Katie was breathless, her cheeks flushed, her eyes bright, her red-gold hair hanging down her shoulders as though she was a young girl, Rhian thought with a sudden stab of jealousy.

'There's a daft question.' Health laughed, his smile charming and Katie rested her hand on his arm.

'A man you are now, Heath Jenkins – nearly seventeen you're sure to be, fine and handsome too, like your sister and if you have half her guts you'll be all right.'

'Come on, Katie,' Heath said sheepishly. 'Stop all this blarney and tell me what you want me to tell our Mary.'

'Ask her if she's coming with me to the fair tomorrow. I'm taking no excuses and so she'd better be ready, 'cos I'll sit on her doorstep until she agrees.'

Heath rested his hand on Katie's shoulder. 'That's good of you, mind,' he said soberly. 'It's just what Mary needs, a day out, a little time to forget all the bad things that have been happening lately. I'll try to persuade her to go with you, don't worry.'

Rhian tugged at his arm impatiently. 'Come on, Heath, Auntie will be mad with us if we're late, you know how she is.' She was not going to let Katie Murphy with her beautiful sad eyes take up too much of Heath's time, she thought angrily. Older than Heath, Katie was, but anyone would jump at a catch like him.

'I won't keep you talkin' any longer for sure.' Katie's eyes held amusement, but Rhian chose to look the other way. 'Go on off to your auntie's house then, and don't do anything I wouldn't do.'

Katie's laughter echoed on the soft air and Rhian pressed her lips together, suppressing the hot words that longed to be spoken. However, she didn't want Heath to think her ill-tempered or jealous and after a moment, she forced herself to smile.

'I suppose Katie and your Mary are good friends, aren't they?' she said, continuing to speak without waiting for an answer. 'They get on so well because they're both so much older than we are.' She glanced sideways and though Heath's expression didn't change, Rhian had the uncomfortable feeling that he was laughing at her.

–

Mary sat waiting for Katie in the sun-splashed front parlour of the house in Canal Street. She stared around at the high-ceilinged room decorated with heavy flock wall covering with despair eating at her heart. She couldn't really believe that she would soon be leaving this all behind her and panic beat at her with dark wings as she wondered for the hundredth time where she would go. And yet deep within her, she knew the answer. It was plain and clear – an unmistakeable landmark in her life. Mr Dean Sutton had offered her a position in his shop and she must accept on his terms.

She had no worries about Heath, for he could move in with Rhian Gray's aunt any time he chose. The maiden household ached to have a man in residence and Rhian was determined enough to see that Heath filled the role.

Mary could not blame the girl, she only wished that her own life was as clear-cut and simple. Could she have gone after the man she loved with such obstinacy, she wondered.

Uncomfortably, the image of Brandon Sutton sprang to her mind. She felt the vitality of his presence, saw the handsome eyes so prone to laughing at her and felt the thrill of his mouth capturing hers. But that was not love.

Brandon was a man like any other, she told herself unhappily. At least Dean was forthright about his intentions, he didn't attempt to veil his desires.

Mary forced herself to see sense. Thinking about Brandon did her no good at all; he wanted to bed her just as his brother did and a quick tumble was all she could ever be to him. Well, if to be a whore was her fate then she would be a good one, selling herself to the highest bidder. Dean Sutton at least offered her security and a place to live. In return, she would make sure that the Sutton draper's shop flourished under her care. She had gone without a decent house and food to put in her belly as a child and she didn't intend to ever be in that position again.

The clock on the wall seemed to tick loudly as she looked up at the long pointed hands and rose impatiently from her chair. Soon Katie would arrive and together they would walk to the recreation ground where they would enjoy the warmth of the sun, be part of the noise and bustle of the fair. Mary would throw hoops, eat candyfloss and swing on the boats that hung from steel rods and lifted the riders high in the air so that the beach looked like a nail paring and the sea a blue glistening surface. They would enjoy the sunshine while it lasted, for summer was dying and autumn preparing to take up its mantle of reds and russets and falling leaves.

'Hey, are you in there, have you gone deaf or somethin'?' The voice of Katie Murphy startled Mary from her reverie. She took up her light knitted shawl and made for the door, unconsciously squaring her shoulders. She would forget all her worries just for today, she promised herself.

'So there you are!' Katie said. 'Jesus, Mary and Joseph, ye must have got a lover in there, you're as hard to prise loose as a snail from its shell.'

Mary smiled and allowed Katie to link arms with her. The two girls had always been friends, but never close until Mali Llewellyn had left the laundry and then they had discovered in each other a kindred spirit.

'You look very smart, mind.' Mary looked down at the Irish girl, who was wearing a white crisp cotton skirt and a blouse pleated and tucked and decorated with soft baby-blue bows. Katie's smile was warm. 'You don't look too bad yourself for an old girl!'

Mary glanced down at her finely woven flannel skirt and the plain dark blouse. 'I'm not very festive, I'll admit, but there's no need to make me sound like somebody's grannie.'

'Here, bend down, let me tie a bow in your hair.' Katie smiled. 'Now I won't have any refusals, this is a day out at the fair. We are going to have fun and I'm determined we're going to catch ourselves a man.

'I'm tired of being on me own, Mary, and that's God's truth. I don't know if Mark is serious about me or not, got no faith in myself any more.' Suddenly she brightened. 'Come on now, let me loosen that lovely dark hair of yours, that's right. Jesus, Mary and Joseph but you're tall. There!' She stood back: 'You don't look so much as if you're goin' to a wake now!'

Mary suddenly felt light-hearted. The sun was shining as though to prove it still had some strength and the breeze was soft and salt with the tang and tar to give it bite. 'I'm going to enjoy myself if it kills me, mind,' Mary said ruefully and Katie laughed softly.

'Tell me, Mary, have you ever had a roll in the hay with a man? Now don't go sayin' me it's none of my business, for today is a special day when we can all do what we wish, right?'

Mary paused for a moment before replying, 'All right then and the answer is no, I haven't had a roll in the hay with any man. Why, have you?'

Katie smiled softly. 'To be sure I have! There was my William, sweet as a flower yet strong as an ox but since he...' Her words trailed away and Mary broke the silence quickly.

'Well, there's a lot of men here for us to take our pick from, Katie. See, over there, sailors – must be a boat in the docks from Sweden by the look of those golden curls.'

'Let's go and talk to them!' Katie said at once, 'and find out how much English they speak.' She laughed. 'Their attempts can't be any worse than yours, Mary Jenkins, 'cos you murder the language so you do.'

Mary smiled. 'Look who's talking!' She followed Katie across the drying patchy grass and paused, unwilling to admit to her shyness as Katie with wide-eyed innocence asked one of the sailors for change of a shilling. 'I want to try roll the penny,' she said, 'but I can't until I've got some pennies to roll.'

Both girls were immediately surrounded and Mary felt her colour rising as she was jostled between two amazingly tall Swedish sailors.

'Mother of God, this is awful!' Katie gasped. 'They're like hungry wolves, poor men. I talked about a roll in the hay, but I'm being made into a human sandwich here!'

Laughing, Katie pushed her way through the crowd of men and Mary followed her quickly, brushing the hair from her face as she saw the Irish girl begin to run towards the coconut shys.

'That wasn't a very good idea, was it?' Mary said when she had recovered her breath. 'I think I'll forget about finding a man and just concentrate on having a good time on the shows.'

'Don't give up so easily,' Katie said. 'I've got the divil in me today and I'm not content with my humdrum life any more. Change is what I want and sure as shamrocks come from Ireland I'm going to make things happen.'

Mary laughed, infected by Katie's high spirits. The merry-go-round was blaring out a distorted tune, the brightly painted horses rising and falling, great wooden monsters with frozen leers on gaudy faces.

'Let's have a ride.' Katie took Mary's arm and as the music and movement stopped, hurried Mary up the wooden steps.

The soft breeze lifted Mary's hair, tugging it free from the ribbons. She felt young, perhaps younger than she'd ever been. She glanced at Katie and saw that the Irish girl was talking animatedly to a young man at her side. He took her hand just as the wooden mount rose higher, carved hooves appearing to paw the air. Katie smiled up at him and her eyes were bright with merriment.

Dishevelled, Mary climbed unsteadily down from the wooden platform and glanced behind her. Katie was brushing back her hair, laughing happily, the young man at her heels.

'This is Mark,' Katie said. 'He's manager for Mr Brandon Sutton at the steel and tin works.'

Mary shook hands formally and inwardly chastised herself for the way her hands trembled at the mention of Brandon's name.

'Mark's going to bring us a drink of cordial.' Katie moved towards the edge of the fair where the grass was deeper and softer and flung herself down, leaning against the rough bark of a tree.

'Did you know that Mark was going to be here?' Mary asked with mock severity and Katie blushed rosily.

'Saints be praised, there's a suspicious mind you have, Mary Jenkins!' But Katie couldn't keep a smile from turning up the corners of her mouth. 'He's a fine young man, had my eye on him for some time now but it don't do to be too eager.' She gave Mary a hard look. 'Now don't you go lettin' on that I like him, for he's got a head the size of Burrows Rock with all the girls in work chasin' after him.'

'A blabbermouth I've never been, mind,' Mary said quickly and put her finger to her lips as Mark came across the grass towards them.

It was clear that Mark admired Katie more than a little. His eyes drank in every detail of her face and once he reached out and brushed back a strand of red-gold hair that had blown across her forehead. Mary envied them both, for they were falling in love and it was beautiful to see.

As though aware that Mary was becoming excluded from the conversation, Katie turned to her. 'The Canal Street Laundry is goin' to the dogs, sure it is,' she said. 'That Sally Benson can't do the job of overseer like you, Mary. Lettin' everything slide, she is, and old Mr Sutton is going to find her out one of these fine days.'

Mary shrugged, pretending indifference, though it troubled her to think of the high standards she had set falling by the wayside.

'It's none of my business now,' she replied quietly. 'Mr Sutton wanted me out as quickly as possible and so he must take the consequences.'

'Mr Sutton?' Mark spoke questioningly. 'That's Grenville Sutton isn't it? He's my boss's father.'

Katie nodded. 'That's right, and I don't know about your boss but ours is a hard-nosed old man who won't listen to reason. Pity he had to take over the place at all; I know Mali thought it would be run by Dean Sutton, otherwise I doubt she'd have sold the laundry at all.'

Mark shook his head. 'Well, Brandon Sutton is one of the best, I admire him. You know he's written a book, trying to get fairer wages for the men? All the local bigwigs are against him, including his own brother, but nothing will stop Mr Sutton from getting what he wants. I'd back him any time.' Mark laughed suddenly. 'Sorry, you've got me at preaching now and we're all here to have a bit of fun. Come on, ladies, let's enjoy the fair, shall we?'

Mary found herself longing to speak to Mark about Brandon's plans. She was like a bird, she thought ruefully, pecking at crumbs – yet anything to do with Brandon Sutton immediately caught her interest. She opened her mouth to question Mark but he was bending over Katie, taking her hand and helping her to her feet.

'Let's go see the bearded lady,' Katie said, smiling over her shoulder at Mary. 'I always feel like pulling at the hair to see if it's stuck on.'

'You go ahead,' Mary said brightly. 'I think I'll get another drink and I'll catch up with you later.'

Katie hesitated but Mark was tugging at her arm eagerly. Mary winked and with a quick smile, Katie allowed herself to be drawn away.

Mary wandered aimlessly between the stalls, watching idly as a group of children ran pennies along chutes screaming as the coins spun around before falling on to a board covered in numbered squares.

Once or twice she had a distinct feeling that she was being followed, but when she looked over her shoulder, there was never anyone behind her. She told herself she was becoming nervous and tetchy as a proper old maid. In a few more years, she would be thirty yet until just the other day she had never been really kissed. Well, that wasn't quite true. Billy had kissed her but never with any real passion.

Brandon was the man who had aroused in her the knowledge of her own sensuality. She had responded instinctively to his touch, wanted him as she'd never wanted anything in her life. But he was false, a man who wanted a tumble with a working wench but lacking the honesty to say so.

She looked around her but could see no sign of Katie. The air was growing chill now, the dying sun streaking the sky with red. Mary drew her shawl closer around her shoulders, deciding that she would make her own way home. Katie would probably not even miss her, she thought dryly.

As she left the recreation ground, she once more had the feeling she was being followed. She sensed a shadowy figure moving behind the trees, and wondered if it could be one of the sailors Katie had teased earlier. She shivered a little. 'There's soft you are, Mary Jenkins!' she scolded herself out loud. 'Who would want to follow you?'

And yet as she made her way through the streets of Sweyn's Eye, she could not shake off the feeling that someone was watching her every move.

Brandon stood on the curve of the bay staring out to sea. Lights from the pier reflected in the dark shimmering water and red from the sunset lay like liquid fire on the rippling surface. He felt strangely restless. Perhaps he thought, it was the smallness of the town which gave him his sudden feeling of claustrophobia.

America was big and open and Brandon had travelled the land from south to north. Here, in Sweyn's Eye, the streets and houses huddled together as though for warmth, courts were narrow and dark, the cobbled roads barely wide enough to allow a pony and trap to pass.

The hills rose on either side of the town, overshadowing the string of iron and copper works that lay along the banks of the river Swan.

It was only here, near the sea, that he felt any sensation of space. He breathed deeply of the salt air and front out in the bay heard the mournful sound of a tug boat guiding home a steam packet with the incoming tide.

Brandon moved away from his view of the ocean and stood on the dunes looking across at the lights from the fairground. Music brazen and brash shattered the silence of the evening and crowds of people thronged between the brightly lit sideshows. Men in caps and scarves were showing off to their womenfolk whose long skirts swept the dusty ground.

Brandon's senses were suddenly alert as he caught sight of Mary Jenkins. She was alone, an unmistakeable figure, tall and stately, her head held high as she walked along the lush grass of the recreation ground. But what concerned Brandon was the man at her heels who hurried from tree to tree watching Mary's progress. He was careful to keep out of her sight whenever she glanced over her shoulder and as the last rays of the fading sun struggled through the clouds, Brandon's suspicions were confirmed. The man following Mary was Gerwin Price. The question was, did she know of his presence? She turned often to look behind her as though expecting to see someone, and there was no telling the workings of a woman's mind. Brandon slowly moved from the dunes and into the roadway, his steps measured, his hands thrust into his pockets. It might be just as well, he reasoned, to find out exactly what was going on between Gerwin Price and Mary Jenkins.

Chapter Fourteen

Darkness slivered through the passageways and a cold easterly wind rattled the windows as Mary let herself into the house on Canal Street. Suddenly the sky was overcast, darts of spiteful rain beating up off the cobbled roadway. No one would believe that the fairground had been washed with sunlight only a short time ago.

Mary shivered and hurried into the kitchen, bending over the dying embers behind the black-leaded bars of the grate. She pushed rolled paper into the greying coals, endeavouring to fan the flames into life once more, and was rewarded by a small spark.

The evening stretched ahead of her long and empty and on an impulse Mary decided that she would bring in the zinc bath which was hanging on the back door and put it before the fire which would soon grow into a cheerful blaze.

Later, after bathing, she would wash her best petticoat and camisole so as not to waste the hot water. She lifted her skirt and grimaced as she saw that the dust from the fairground had stained the hem of her petticoat.

She was wearing her best underclothes, finely stitched and highly decorated with drawn threadwork. Mary was proud of the quality of her linen, which was a symbol of the success she had made of her life.

The soft cotton and pale ribbon were a far cry from the unbleached calico she had worn as a child. She clearly remembered how her underclothes had been tattered and grubby, hanging loosely from her shoulders, for she had been painfully thin.

Mary brushed the thoughts aside and went out into the yard. The lawn beyond was full of shadows and she shuddered, quickly lifting the bath from its hook and carrying it indoors.

It took her some time to boil enough kettles of hot water to half-fill the zinc bath. Adding cold water, she stood for a moment breathing in the steam and anticipating the comfort of the water on her limbs.

Then she carefully removed her clothes, slipping open the linen-covered buttons of her camisole and letting it fall from her shoulders. With a sigh, she stepped into the bath; she was tired now and low in spirits, knowing that this would be the last time she would use the house in Canal Street as her home.

The water lapped warmly over her body as Mary soaped her skin and tried to relax. She hoped she would not be awake half the night thinking of the plans she must make, the clothing she must pack and all the difficulties of moving. She had not yet spoken to Dean Sutton and she shivered, wondering if his offer was still open or even if she wanted it to be.

The fire threw a red-gold glow over her bare breasts, the warmth was soothing and gradually she began to feel more cheerful. She would make herself some hot milk and then go to bed early, leaving her problems until the morning.

When she heard a scraping noise outside the back door she froze for a moment, listening intently, but the sound was not repeated. She was becoming over-imaginative, she told herself; she was worried and tired and her nerves were strained. All the same, the bath no longer seemed as soothing as it had been.

She stepped from the water on to a rug, noticing a chink between the curtains where it would be easy for someone to peer in at her. But that was absurd, she told herself; she had bathed this way all her life, so why should she suddenly be self-conscious now?

There was a sudden crash and Mary screamed as the door burst open. She reached frantically for a towel with which to cover herself, conscious of another presence in the small kitchen. A shadowy figure moved slowly into the light and Mary trembled, gasping in fear, for Gerwin Price was staring at her with a greedy expression in his eyes.

'Get out of here, what do you think you're doing?' she said loudly. For a moment he wavered as though he might meekly go away; he half turned towards the door and Mary held her breath.

'I only came to ask you for more food, Mary, and a few shillings if you can spare them. I mean no harm.' He shuffled from one foot to the other, his eyes dark and frightening as he scrutinised her.

'Don't treat me like I was dirt under your feet, I'm human just like you after all.' He stared at her as though he could see through the soft material of the towel, his tongue running over his lips as though he had a great thirst. His hair stood up from his head in tufts, his attitude menacing even though his tone was conciliatory. He moved forward and Mary, reading his intentions, backed away. Her feet slipped on the wet floor and as she fell, she screamed in terror.

Afterwards she could never recollect exactly what happened. All she knew was that Gerwin was suddenly thrown against the wall, his face was bloody and he was whimpering with fear. His hand rubbed the blood from his face and he looked like a trapped animal.

'Get out of here, Price, while you're still alive!' The voice spoke over Mary's head and dimly she recognised it as belonging to Brandon Sutton. He stood over her, his fists bunched, his face a mask of anger.

Gerwin scurried to the door, calling threats over his shoulder until his voice died away into the silence of the night. Mary found herself being lifted to her feet then and harsh sobs racked her body.

'Don't cry.' Brandon's voice was gentle now. 'You're all right, I'm here.'

She stared up in bewilderment at the strong-boned face so near her own. 'Brandon.' She could scarcely believe that he was really standing there in her kitchen, holding her in his arms.

Mary drew a ragged breath as she clung to him, glad of his strength for her legs were trembling so badly she wondered if they would support her.

'Come on, I think you'd be better off in bed.'

Brandon lifted her into his arms and made his way up the curving staircase as though her weight was nothing at all. In her bedroom, he set her down lightly and drew the covers over her nakedness.

She was still trembling as she clung to his hand and he hushed her softly. 'Don't be afraid. I'll stay with you for a while.'

Mary felt exhausted emotionally as well as physically. She curled beneath the sheets, aware of him lying above the blankets, his warmth and nearness comforting. Her head was pounding and she doubted that she would ever sleep, yet a great weariness drew her slowly downward into a warm welcoming darkness.

It was dawn when she awoke and she was immediately aware of a soft breathing on the pillow beside her. Carefully she raised herself on to her elbow and stared down in the dimness of the morning light.

'Brandon.' She whispered his name and then his eyes were open and he was staring at her in a way that made her heart pound. He was so close to her that she could feel his breath against her face.

'Mary,' he said softly and the sound of her name on his lips was like a caress.

His finger traced a line across her shoulder and down to the tip of her breast and she shivered, sensations she had never experienced before running through her so that she felt weak.

'You're very beautiful.' His mouth was above hers and Mary waited breathlessly for his kiss. When his lips touched hers, flames of desire ran through her and she felt as if she was being washed by a sea of warmth and passion. Her arms crept around his neck as if of their own volition and she clung to him desperately.

She wanted him with all of her being and at the core of her desire was the knowledge that she loved him as a woman can only love one man. However impossible the idea might be, she was Brandon's woman. He had come to her in the darkness like a knight in shining armour and was holding her now with such gentleness that he must surely love her a little in return?

Brandon's hands moved to her breasts, caressing, teasing, rousing emotions that Mary had never known existed. She stared at him in the pale light of morning and he was magnificent, strong, his shoulders muscular and broad. Now he was drawing the sheets away from her and as they touched, his skin felt like silk beneath her fingers.

Mary was past reasoning now. All she knew was the exquisite swamping of her senses, a rush of emotion as they lay side by side, breast to breast and thigh to thigh. His hands were moving over her back, caressing the nape of her neck, moving lower and tracing the firm line of her spine.

His tongue probed her mouth and she pressed herself against him, drinking in his nearness, wanting to become part of him. She longed to cry her love out loud but she merely whimpered as he continued to arouse her.

He kissed her breasts, his mouth like flame on her proud flesh. Her thoughts and feelings became a kaleidoscope, whirling and turning. He was above her, within her, around her, possessing and delving until they were one flesh.

She thought that she cried out in a mixture of pain and joy, but she could not be sure. She was drowning in sensation, giving herself completely into his care – trusting him, loving him, wanting only to belong to him utterly.

When it was over, they lay side by side and Brandon's hand caressed her hair, brushing the strands away from her damp brow. They lay silent and yet together for a long time, but when the sun crept into the room warming it into life, Brandon stirred. Mary watched as he left her bed, wanting him to say he loved her, but his back was turned and his broad shoulders bent as he drew on his clothing. She wished she had the courage to beg him to come back to bed and take her once more, but she was tongue-tied and shy and was possessed by an overwhelming desire to cry.

He came and sat beside her, staring down at her almost with wonder in his eyes. 'I didn't expect that,' he said softly and Mary shook her head, not trusting herself to speak. Brandon kissed her mouth softly. 'It hadn't occurred to me that I would be the first, I'm sorry.'

Mary tried to make sense of his words, an emptiness growing inside her as she stared up at him. 'There's a strange thing to say.' Her voice trembled. 'Did you think I was a whore, then?'

He didn't reply and Mary's heart sank. Clearly the experience they had just shared did not mean as much to Brandon as it had to her. Anger began to blossom inside her. She sat up straight, her languor vanished, and held the sheets around her body in a protective gesture that did not escape his notice.

'You thought I'd been with Billy, didn't you? And perhaps with other men as well? All this night meant to you was a means of relief from your urges. Any woman would have served the same purpose – it's true, isn't it?' Her voice rose and Brandon turned away from her, thrusting his hands in his pockets.

He spoke slowly, his voice devoid of emotion. 'You wanted me as much as I wanted you.' His eyebrows lifted, almost as though he was making fun of her and Mary felt the rich colour flood into her cheeks. She avoided his eyes, for her own were full of tears as he leaned over and touched her shoulder gently.

'It was good for both of us, but let's not make it out to be more than it was. You are more suited to Billy Gray, we both know that. You're missing him and it's perfectly natural that you should turn to another man for comfort.'

Mary shook her head dumbly, too overwhelmed with misery to say anything. If she had allowed herself to speak, she might have blurted out the truth, that she loved Brandon as she had loved no other human being in all her born days.

The events of the night had changed her irrevocably and she could not even consider becoming Billy's wife now. If she was honest with herself, she would be bound to admit that she had already come to believe there had never been anything but friendship between them. And now Brandon Sutton had taken her life and broken it between his fingers as surely as if he had held her throat and squeezed until she was dead.

He was fully dressed now, standing looking down at her with his hands thrust into his pockets in a gesture that was characteristic of him. He looked so handsome, so sensual still with his eyes dark and unfathomable that her heart contracted in pain.

Then a cold anger began to bring her strength. She threw back the bedclothes and rose with as much dignity as she could muster, unaware of her beauty as she drew a chemise over her head.

'Is it true you have to leave Canal Street?' Brandon was speaking to her politely as though she was a stranger and Mary looked over her shoulder at him, her eyes narrowed.

'Yes, that's right.' Her voice was clipped and hard, but Brandon appeared not to notice.

'Where will you go?' he asked and she turned to face him, her hands clenched at her sides.

'Why?' she said harshly. 'Thinking of having your way with me again are you, hoping I'll play the whore whenever you want a woman?' Anger was like a flame inside her now as the full import of what had happened sunk in.

Brandon gave her a quick look, his face hard. 'If you're trying to say I deflowered you against your will, it's not true. The first man to come along would have had just what I did. You're a plum ready for picking, honey, and I just happened to be the one to catch the windfall.'

Mary wanted to hit him, to keep battering at his face until the derision was wiped away. Instead, she drew herself up proudly and stared at him as though she had no further interest in him.

'Well, to answer your question about where I shall be going, my future is all mapped out.' Her voice was calm. 'If you're really interested, then I'll tell you – I'm going to become your brother's mistress.'

She saw his eyes widen and with a surge of savage satisfaction saw that her jibe had struck harder than any physical blow.

'Dean's *mistress*?' He echoed her words disbelievingly. 'But I thought you were above that sort of thing. If I had known you wished to be a kept woman, perhaps I would have made you an offer.'

He stared at her, a smile beginning to curve his lips though his eyes were like ice. 'Dean would be surprised to know that I'd pipped him at the post, don't you think?'

Mary lifted her chin defiantly. 'I don't think he'd believe you.' She smiled bitterly. 'Anyway, I'm taking up residence in his house as from next week and I shall manage his shop in Wind Street; it's all arranged.'

Brandon walked to the door and stared back at her for a long moment. 'Well, I'll say this much for you, Mary Jenkins,' his voice was deceptively soft, 'you'll make a damn good whore.'

As she listened to his footsteps hurrying down the stairs, Mary felt as though her world was crumbling around her. She sank down on to the bed and put a shaking hand to her face, feeling the tears run down her cheeks and into her mouth.

She felt utterly weary as though she had been running for a long time without stopping. Her body ached and a pain crushed her spirit. Lying with Brandon had been the greatest experience of her life and then he had had to go and tarnish the beauty of it. Well, he had made his position more than plain, he could not put it more clearly; he wanted a tumble, he was attracted to her, nothing more. It was a great pity, she thought bitterly, that Brandon had wanted only her body when she was prepared to give him her soul. She would not be taken in again, she promised herself.

Finally Mary rose wearily from the bed and went downstairs into the kitchen to wash in the cold bathwater. Mechanically she tidied up the room, putting away towels and then hanging the zinc bath outside on the door.

She did not shiver in the early morning breeze that drifted in from the sea, for she already felt numb and lost and the coldness within her was worse than anything that could touch her body.

She paused in the doorway for a moment, staring out across the row of backyards that nestled close together as though for comfort; soon she would leave Canal Street behind her for good, and perhaps it was just as well.

She would lie down on her back for Dean Sutton and she would build up a store of money so that, one day, she could be her own woman and beholden to no man. She realised that she had never really believed she would accept Dean Sutton's offer, but now in her bitterness she wanted to reach out and hurt anyone who came within her grasp.

Mary returned indoors and sank into a chair before the cold grey ashes of the fire and then the tears came, hot and angry. 'Brandon,' she whispered his name into the silence of the morning. 'Oh, Brandon, why couldn't you have loved me?'

Chapter Fifteen

It seemed as though the whole of Canal Street came out to see Mary Jenkins' humiliation. The sun shone across the cobbles, the shadows soft in the pale early morning sunshine. The lamplighter had finished his round extinguishing the flames and he stood now with hands thrust into shabby coat pockets, his eyes narrowed as though he still looked into the white glare of the gaslight.

On the doorstep of one of the houses was Mrs Benson, her white nurse's apron crisp and fresh, crackling with cleanliness, the starched folds glittering like icing sugar. On the low wall that separated the canal from the roadway, children gathered to stare, sucking fingers, eyes wide in pale faces.

Mary lifted the grandfather clock on to the cart, looking at the growing pile of her belongings with pain but determined not to shed the tears that burned her eyes. *Eviction* – the word was ugly and harsh and even though she was moving before the bailiffs had been sent in, Mary was aware that the entire neighbourhood knew of her shame.

'To be sure, haven't folk anything better to do than stand and gawp?' Katie Murphy had come to Mary's side, her soft voice filled with indignation. Mary straightened her shoulders in an involuntary movement.

'Curious, that's all they are so don't be too hard on them,' she said quietly. 'I think that's all now, and the house looks as though I'd never set foot inside it, let alone spent part of my life there.'

'Me dad's coming out the back way,' Katie said softly. 'He's carryin' your tin bath under one arm and a chamber pot in the other.'

Mary's face relaxed into a smile as Tom Murphy staggered round the corner and made his way to the cart. The big horse moved restlessly between the shafts and Tom called to him impatiently.

'Hang on there, Jim! Don't want to shed the load before we've left the street.'

Mary stood as tall as the Irishman, thinking he was not a man to inspire great friendship. His eyes were narrow beneath the ginger shelf of brows and his mouth was weak, but for all that he had come to her aid when she had needed him.

'Thank you, Tom Murphy.' Mary pressed some coins into his hand and he touched the brim of his cap.

'That's all right, miss, I'll see that your bits and pieces get safely put away in the shed at the back of my house.'

Even as Mary nodded her head, she was thinking it ironic that all her possessions amounted to nothing more than what Tom considered 'bits and pieces'. Then she became aware that Katie's hand was resting on her arm.

'Come on home with me, have a cup of tea and a bite to eat for by the name of the Blessed Virgin, you're as white as the sheets I pack all day at the laundry.'

Mary shook her head. 'No, I'd better get along to Mr Sutton. I want to find out how I stand straight away.'

Katie stared at her for such a long moment in silence that Mary felt uncomfortable. 'Are you sure you're doin' the right thing, now?' Katie's soft Irish voice was filled with sympathy. 'There's still time to change your mind.'

Mary shook her head firmly. 'Working in the drapers will suit me,' she said. 'There's no other way out for me. Mr Sutton is offering me a job and a roof over my head, don't you understand?'

Katie shook back her fine red-gold hair. 'I understand more than you give me credit for,' she said as she moved away. 'But sure an' you're big enough to know what you're about when all's said an' done.'

As Mary hurried away from Canal Street she felt almost ill, overwhelmed by the misgivings she had denied feeling. It was one thing to lie with a man because of love and quite another to take a cold-blooded decision to be a kept woman.

Her one comfort was the way Dean Sutton had reacted when she had gone to see him at *Ty Mawr*. His face had become wreathed in smiles as she falteringly told him she was accepting his offer of help and he had placed a large hand on her shoulders, squeezing gently.

'You realise all the implications, don't you honey?' His voice had been soft, his eyes warm.

Mary's gaze did not waver. 'It's all right, Mr Sutton.' Her tone had been level. 'I know perfectly well what I'm doing, so there's no need for you to worry.'

A tram came rattling along the street and shuddered to a stop and Mary climbed on board, seating herself near the doorway, her eyes straining to see the house where she had been so happy. But all that was visible now was the uneven slate roofs of the tall houses and, running alongside like a ribbon, the waters of the canal.

How much her life had changed in the last few months, she thought in bewilderment. It seemed that the coming into her life of the men of the Sutton family had created a maelstrom, totally disrupting the even tenor of her life.

There was no going back, she reasoned. She was a different woman now from the one who had sat in the courthouse with heavy heart and listened to the life sentence imposed upon Billy Gray.

He had been everything to her then, or so she had believed – yet how easily had she forgotten him as she had lain in Brandon's arms.

She had made every attempt to visit him and had even tried to approach the governor and ask him to override Griffiths' orders. But she had been baulked by a wall of silence; Griffiths, it seemed, had the upper hand. Perhaps she could speak to Dean, she thought guiltily, and ask him to ease the situation for Billy. There were soft options even behind prison walls.

As Mary stepped off the tram, a chill autumn wind was drifting over the hilltop. The trees waved gold and red leaves over her head and the spiky gorse bushes gleamed with yellow blooms. Her steps slowed as she reached the imposing gates of *Ty Mawr*, feeling as though she, like Billy, was entering a prison from which there would be no escape. She moved round to the back of the house, where she was obviously expected for the door stood open.

'Come in, Mary Jenkins, there's no use standing out there staring.' The maid was crisply dressed in a dark gown and a clean white apron that was decorative rather than functional, made of lace and ribbons and daintily sewn seams. 'I'm Bertha, and I'm to welcome you and show you where you're to stay.'

Mary entered the long passageway and gazed through the open door to her right. The kitchen was the largest she had ever seen, with a huge range dominating the room and a long table at which worked two young girls.

'Mr Dean is away on business and Mrs Sutton is too sick to see you, so you'll have to put up with me.' Bertha's tone was hostile and as Mary followed her up the dark back stairs, she sighed softly. It seemed that even here she was not welcome.

Her room was at the top of the house, little more than an attic but well-furnished and with a cheerful fire glowing in the grate. 'Sorry you're put right away from the rest of the servants,' Bertha remarked as she paused inside the door with one hand on the polished knob. 'But Mr Dean wanted you to be somewhere quiet.'

It was clear from the way she spoke that the maid knew exactly what Mary's position in the household was to be. Mary stared at her levelly, unwilling to apologise for her role.

'I understand your loyalty to your mistress,' she said crisply, 'but I don't like the way you pass judgement on me without waiting to learn my character.'

Bertha appeared a trifle put out by Mary's bluntness but she soon recovered her composure. 'It's not my place to pass judgement,' she protested, 'but I do not want my mistress upset. She's very sick, but then I suppose you know that.'

Mary shook her head. 'I guessed as much, but I am not a threat to Mrs Sutton – there's no fear of me wanting to take her place, now, is there?'

After a moment, Bertha nodded. 'We'll call a truce then, and we'll see what happens when Mr Sutton comes home, but I warn you now that everyone from the cook to the kitchen maid knows you're really here to warm the master's bed.'

'That is no one's business but my own.' Mary lifted her head high and stared down at Bertha, and the maid moved back a pace with a new respect in her eyes.

'Some food will be sent up on a tray,' she said, her tone practical now. 'Later this evening you may like to come below stairs and eat with the rest of us. And I wish you luck.' She allowed herself the glimmer of a smile.

Bertha's eyes suddenly had a faraway look. 'Mr Sutton always wanted a son, but Miss Bea couldn't oblige him, her being sick an' all.' She shook her head as though seeing things that troubled her mind, then blinked rapidly as her gaze rested on Mary. 'You're big and strong, a fine woman, you could give Mr Sutton the boy he's set his heart on.'

Mary's thoughts were tumbling over each other in confusion. 'There will be no son,' she said fiercely and turned away, the set of her shoulders indicating that the conversation was at an end.

When Bertha had gone, Mary turned to look at the closed door, standing quite still in the centre of the room and trying hard not to let the burning tears slide down her cheeks. She was in an unfamiliar world now, a hostile world where her position was tenuous, depending upon the whims of a man she hardly knew.

After a moment she removed her hat, set it down carefully on the washstand and moved to the window, pushing aside the curtain. Far below the sea washed against the shore, the white lip of the waves curving round the bay like the smile on the face of a clown. What if Dean Sutton did get her with child? It was a sobering thought and one she had never considered. Indeed, she had not thought beyond moving into his house. The idea of going to Dean's bed had been one she had kept at bay on the fringes of her mind.

Now she sat in a chair and leaned her head back against the antimacassar, her eyes closed. Dean might possess her body any time he chose but he would never possess her soul, would never even know the inner being that was Mary Jenkins.

Panic beating dark and suffocating within her, she rose abruptly to her feet. She paced the length of the room, turning, retracing her steps, hands clasped together.

'Be calm,' she told herself as she paused before the window once more, hearing the tiny whimper of surf on the golden shore below. At least she had a reprieve, the opportunity to think things out, since Dean was gone away on business. She would give herself time to recover from the events of the last few days and perhaps find there was an alternative open to her.

She lifted a strand of hair from her hot brow, deciding to unpack only the clothes she would need right away, so that if she decided to leave she could do so without delay.

A knock on the door startled her. 'Come in!' she said quickly and a thin young maid entered the room, carrying a silver tray which appeared to be much too heavy for her. Mary took it and set it down on the table beside the bed.

'Cook is asking, would you like lamb for supper?' The girl's eyes were large in a pale face and Mary smiled reassuringly.

'Lamb is my favourite meat,' she said gently. 'Don't look so frightened, I'm not an ogre whatever you might have heard.'

After a moment's hesitation, the maid smiled. 'I'm Muriel, miss. I do odd jobs, mostly sewing, I hope you like it here,' she said hurriedly. 'Can I be excused now? Cook will fetch me a blinder if I don't get straight back to the kitchen.'

Mary sighed as the door closed quietly behind the girl. It seemed as though the tone had been set and the domestic staff at *Ty Mawr* were going to treat her like an outsider. Well, so be it, it would take more than a few servants to frighten her off.

She sat down on the bed and stared at the tea tray set with fragile china resting on an immaculate linen cloth. She had a difficult role to play in the Sutton household and no one, not even Dean Sutton himself, would dictate to her just how she should play it.

It was early Monday morning when Mary met Bea Sutton. The sun was shining with a mellow autumnal glow slanting across the wide bed so that the figure beneath the sheets appeared small and at first glance insignificant. But on closer inspection, Mary saw that Dean's wife had fine eyes and a noble cast to her forehead, the only remaining evidence of the beauty she had once enjoyed.

'Good morning, Miss Jenkins.' Bea smiled and her face was illuminated. Mary wanted to look away, but the direct, honest gaze of the woman in the bed did not waver.

'Good morning, Mrs Sutton,' Mary replied, her even tones betraying nothing of the turmoil within her. The instinct to turn and run was very strong, but she forced herself to remain where she was.

'Here are the keys of the shop, my dear.' Bea spoke slowly, her voice trembling as though she was a very old woman. 'Take them and look after the business well, my husband too.' There seemed to be a double meaning behind the lightly spoken words which Mary chose to ignore.

'I shall do my best, though as I explained to Mr Sutton I'm not experienced in drapery work.'

Bea allowed herself a brief smile. 'I'm sure you are a very quick learner. Just keep your patience and above all, bide your time.' Her eyes met Mary's and it was clear to see that Bea Sutton knew her days were numbered. Mary searched her mind for something to say, but the words would not come. Bea lifted her hand in a gesture of dismissal. 'Go now, we shall doubtless talk again some time.'

As Mary left the bedchamber that reeked of sickness, her heart was heavy. Mrs Sutton was a fine woman, full of strength and character and it was almost certain that she knew the true purpose of Mary's presence in the house.

Mary pushed the unpleasant thoughts aside, uncertain still as to what she would do when Dean returned home. A small hope flickered within her that once she was established in the shop, he would find her invaluable as an employee and would put aside any idea of making her his mistress. She hurried back to her attic room and sat near the window, her hands clasped in her lap, the silence enveloping her. It was very peaceful at *Ty Mawr*, but it was that very peace which gave her time to think and to remember the joy she had found in Brandon's arms. She sighed. The sun was rising from behind the mists; soon she would put on her coat and leave the house to take up the reins of the drapery business. A faint feeling of hope and optimism grew within her as she left her seat near the window and picked up her coat from the bed.

Her first day at the shop was one that was to leave an indelible imprint on Mary's mind. As soon as she stepped inside from the cobbled roadway of Wind Street, she became aware that she was in another world. Bales of cloth were stacked on shelves from ceiling to floor, a headless dressmaker's dummy stood in one corner, swathed in a bolt of organdie, fluffed and befrilled, giving the appearance of a ballgown. Cards bright with ribbon lay strewn untidily over the polished wooden counter and threads of cotton covered the marble floor.

As Mary clipped the bunch of keys to her belt she heard the ticking of a large clock in the silence of the room which should, by now, have been bustling with activity. She moved to the closed door behind the counter and unlocked it. Facing her was a kitchen, untidy and smelling of grease. To her left was a shadowy staircase and Mary moved upwards to the room above.

In the large front bedroom two young girls lay heavily asleep, neither of them so much as stirring as Mary stared down at them. In the smaller back room, in a narrow single bed, a plump grey-haired woman lifted her head to stare at her with sleepy eyes. Mary sighed.

'When the cat's away the mice will play,' she said loudly. Then she lifted a large tray from the chest of drawers and banged it boldly against the wall. The effect was startling and screams rent the stillness of the morning as the girls appeared on the landing.

'I'm Mary Jenkins,' she said with heavy authority. 'This is the first and the last time I want to find you abed when I arrive in the mornings. Is that understood?'

The silence lengthened and the hostility was almost tangible but Mary was not perturbed. 'I don't care a shirt-button if you like me or not,' she continued to talk loudly. 'But I will have your obedience or it's out on the street with you.' She moved towards the stairs. 'I shall expect you down in the shop fully dressed and ready for work in five minutes.'

'But what about breakfast?' One of the girls scrambled for her clothing. 'I'm Nerys Beynon, vicar's daughter, you can't boss me about as though I was a servant. I don't do anything 'till I've had my breakfast – I have a weak constitution, you see.'

Mary looked at her steadily and the girl's eyes wavered. She turned to her companion, a mutinous look on her face. 'Come on, Joanie, speak up for yourself. There's soft you look with your mouth hanging open like that.' However, her words were greeted with a heavy silence.

Mary shook her head. 'Save your breath, it's downstairs in five minutes or I'll personally put you out in the street, bag and baggage, understood?'

She returned to the shop and removed her coat, hanging it on a peg behind the door. She smiled to herself as she heard the clatter of feet on the stairs – it seemed she had won the first round.

'We'll have the place cleaned up a bit this morning,' Mary said quietly. 'You, Nerys, can tidy the cards of ribbon; find a board and pin them on it so that the colours can be seen at a glance. And you, Joanie, can get the floor cleaned up. The place is a shambles.'

She turned to the older woman who was watching her with wary, hostile eyes. 'Perhaps you would like to go into the kitchen and make us all a cup of tea?' Mary smiled and the woman after a moment responded.

'There's sorry I am for oversleeping,' she said in a light breathless voice. 'It's the fault of them girls, gave me a glass or two of wine, they did. Can't take it, getting old I am, see.' Her smile broadened. 'I'm Mrs Greenaway, it's my job to look after the girls.' She grimaced. 'Didn't do very well last night, did I?'

Mary shook her head. 'The two of them are like playful puppies. They need a firm hand, Mrs Greenaway, but I shouldn't worry about it if I were you.' The woman nodded and Mary felt as though she had made an ally if not a friend.

It was an hour later before the first customer arrived and it was obvious to Mary that the late opening time had become a custom rather than an occasional lapse. She stepped forward as the bell on the door pinged and it was with difficulty that she hid her embarrassment as Delmai Richardson, her young maid in attendance, walked into the shop.

'Can I help you?' Mary spoke civilly enough but Delmai's eyes slid away and she plucked at a bolt of cloth nervously.

'I didn't realise you were working for the Suttons,' she said casually, though her colour was high. 'I'm looking for some good velvet for window drapes. What can you show me?'

Mary held her head high, concealing the pain she felt as she imagined Delmai Richardson refurbishing the house in Canal Street, changing all that Mary had done, marking the rooms with her own personality.

'Nerys, show Mrs Richardson our best velvet,' she said with such quiet authority that the girl hurried forward, bobbing a curtsey.

Mary made a show of busying herself tidying a tray of buttons. Her back was ramrod straight and her senses alert as the conversation between Delmai Richardson and Nerys Beynon washed around her.

'Mrs Richardson will take the green velvet, Miss Jenkins.' the young girl said haughtily. Mary glanced at her questioningly and a small smile appeared on Nerys's face.

'You have to work out the price, Miss Jenkins,' she said triumphantly. 'Mr Sutton always does it himself, so I can't do it.'

Mary felt panic just for a moment. She could not begin to gauge the price of the material when she had no idea how much a yard it should be.

'That's all right, Nerys,' she said firmly. 'Just cut the cloth and the bill will be sent on to Mrs Richardson later.'

Nerys pressed her lips together, obviously annoyed at Mary's deft sidestepping of the problem.

'Have the girls help Gwen to carry the velvet to the hansom cab,' Delmai Richardson said quickly and Mary looked at her, knowing that dislike was growing between them, gaining ground each time they came in contact with each other.

As soon as Delmai Richardson had gone, Mary searched for the stock books that must be kept somewhere on the premises. There had to be a price list of the bales of cloth somewhere and she did not intend to be caught unawares again. The next customer might be a copper worker's wife, who would wish to take with her a piece of unbleached calico or some coarse linen and pay on the spot.

Mary found the books at last beneath the counter; they were covered in dust and obviously not used very often.

'How does Mr Sutton tell the prices?' Mary asked Nerys and the girl shook back her curls.

'Don't know, 'spect he keeps it all in his head,' she replied unwillingly. Flicking through the pages, Mary could see that the figures before her were at least a year out of date. It was no wonder Dean did such a booming trade, for his prices must be the cheapest in Sweyn's Eye. While it might be a good idea to keep them low, Mary felt that some alterations must be made and she would do them herself without delay.

'Fetch me a pen and some thick paper please.' She glanced over her shoulder and when neither of the girls made a move, she raised her voice. 'Now!'

Nerys scurried into the back room, reappearing a few minutes later, her face red and angry.

Mary drew a chair towards the counter and sat down, studying the figures before her and writing prices neatly on squares of paper.

'Take this and pin it to the velvet,' she instructed, permitting herself a smile as she saw the chagrin on Nerys Beynon's young face. 'Then put the prices on all the other bales of cloth, understand?'

By noon when it was time to close the shop for dinner, the place was almost unrecognisable. The bolts of cloth were neatly labelled and rearranged in order of price on the freshly dusted shelves. The floor gleamed with polish and the room was fragrant with the scent of beeswax.

'Now we ought to see about something to eat,' Mary said, realising suddenly how hungry she was. 'What do you usually have?'

Nerys, who seemed the only one not afraid to speak to her, moved forward.

'Mr Sutton sometimes treats us to hot pies from the baker's two doors down,' she volunteered. 'I'll run and fetch them if you like.'

Mary nodded. 'Yes, all right but just for today.' She nodded towards the door behind the counter: 'There's a kitchen back there and we'll get it cleaned up this afternoon so that we can cook our own food.' She ignored the look of outrage Nerys gave her; she was not here to be popular, all she wanted to do was to learn as much about shopkeeping as she could.

Perhaps then Dean might accept her as simply a valuable employee. In any case she was finding the business fascinating. Already she enjoyed the feel of the cloth beneath her fingers. She had watched the girls carefully as they cut, slipping one blade of the scissors beneath the material and sliding it along in one liquid movement, slicing instead of cutting.

It gave her a sense of excitement to make a sale. She was finding that she had a glib tongue and could convince even a difficult customer that to buy at Sutton's was to save valuable pennies.

By the time she was ready to close up the shop, Mary's feet ached as though they didn't belong to her. As she sat on a chair and eased off her shoe, Mrs Greenaway stared down at her sympathetically.

'Soaking in salt, that will harden your feet up just fine,' she said, tucking a piece of grey hair back into place. 'And soft shoes. Comfort is what you want in by here, not style.'

Mary nodded. 'I'm just finding that out to my cost. I'll wear something more sensible tomorrow.' She shrugged her coat around her shoulders and picked up her bag. 'Now be sure to lock the doors carefully behind me and remember, Mrs Greenaway, no more wine.' Mary turned to the two girls who were making for the kitchen.

'I shall expect you to be in the shop early, mind. If I can travel from *Ty Mawr* and be here on time, then you can surely get out of your beds and be ready to serve when I arrive.'

Nerys gave her a quick look. 'Perhaps you won't be here so early once Mr Sutton gets back.' Her tone was low but Mary caught the gist of her words. She regarded the girl steadily and it was Nerys who looked away first.

Mary held her head high as she moved along the darkening street towards the tram terminus. Her cheeks were flushed and she was glad of the cool breeze blowing in off the sea. So everyone knew the role she was to play in Dean Sutton's life; even the girls in the shop were aware of the situation.

As she boarded the tram, her thoughts were in a turmoil. She had believed herself ready to do anything Dean wanted, to be his mistress as well as overseer in his shop. What had happened to her brave resolutions? Was it the words spoken by Bertha who was loyal to Bea Sutton, or was it something more, some perverse pride that jibbed at being recognised by all and sundry as a whore? She sighed softly and stared out into the indigo night as if somewhere in the vast emptiness of the sky she could find an answer.

Chapter Sixteen

Leaves drifted down from the trees, the rioting colours dulled now by the teeming rain. In the distance, the sea was a mist-covered strip of water, still and motionless under a leaden sky.

Delmai Richardson stood at her window and trembled as she rehearsed in her mind the words of farewell she would say to her husband. Her trunk was already packed and though it was filled to the brim with winter clothes, this represented only a small part of Delmai's wardrobe. But she would have to send Gwen to the house for anything else she might need, Delmai thought, for once she walked out through the front door she would never return.

The door of her bedroom opened and Delmai tensed as she saw Rickie peering in at her, his face creased into a frown, his eyes narrow as they took in her appearance.

'Why are you dressed to go out?' he asked and Delmai noted with scorn how like a petulant child he sounded. She took a deep breath. The time had come for her to tell him the truth, there could be no prevaricating.

'I'm leaving you.' The words fell like chips of ice into the silence of the room. Rickie stared at her as if he had not understood her words and so she repeated them, 'I'm leaving you.'

'You must be mad!' Rickie's voice was strangled, his face had turned almost grey and his nostrils quivered as he moved closer. 'If you think I'll let you make a fool of me in front of the whole town, then think again, you bitch!'

'I'll stop at nothing to get away from you,' Delmai said breathlessly. 'I'll kill you if I have to.'

Rickie slumped against the wall. 'You are quite crazy, out of your mind.' He blinked rapidly, consumed with self-pity. 'I never should have married you, too much interbreeding has ruined your bloodline.'

'Then you won't be sorry to see me go.' Delmai moved past him but suddenly he was pinning her against the door.

'You can't do this to me, I'll be a laughing stock. Think about it for a day or two, Delmai, I promise I'll change my ways. I'll be good to you.' He was whining now and Delmai felt sick with loathing. She pushed him away and began to descend the stairs.

'All right, get out of my house then, you filthy whore!' His voice was frenzied. 'I'm throwing you out, do you understand? I want no truck with you, you're frigid and unnatural and I'll be well rid of you!'

Delmai held her head high as she stepped outside into the pouring rain. The hansom cab was waiting, the driver slumped into his seat with coat collar turned up against the weather and hat pulled low on his forehead.

'Canal Street,' Delmai said quickly as she climbed inside and sank back gratefully into the creaking leather seat.

She did not even look back; there was nothing to hold her, now or ever. She had sent Gwen ahead to light the fires and make the house in Canal Street cheerful. Now her spirits lifted and she sighed with relief as she stared out of the window into the rain-dulled landscape.

The rugged hilltop was being left behind now and the warmer air of the valley drifted upwards carrying with it the scent of the town. It was a mingling of odours that could belong nowhere else but Sweyn's Eye.

The stench of the copper works hung heavy on the air trapped under the lowering clouds. But as the cab turned into Canal Street Delmai smiled. She could bear the strange smells of the copper and of the laundry situated a few hundred yards away from her house, she would learn to love her new home for it offered her freedom and release from her husband's petty tyranny.

Gwen held the door open, her faced wreathed in welcoming smiles. Delmai paid the cab fare and watched as the driver manhandled her box into the narrow passageway of the house.

'Home!' she said softly and looked around her joyfully, seeing the rooms transformed by rich carpets and heavy curtains and solid, highly polished furniture.

'Go and sit near the fire, Miss Delmai,' Gwen said with concern. 'You look cold and wet, in need of a hot drink.'

Delmai slipped off her coat and unpinned the large hat, shaking her hair free.

'You've done well, Gwen,' she said gently. 'Everything looks beautiful, just as I expected.' She sank down into a low rocking chair and closed her eyes. 'We'll be happy here, won't we?' she spoke wistfully and Gwen pushed the kettle on to the bright new stove with eager quick movements.

'Yes, of course we will, but you shouldn't mix with your neighbours too much, miss, there's common some of them are. Some are not so bad, there's a nurse a few doors down, a Mrs Benson, proper clean and sparkling she looks, a nice enough body, might come in useful if there's any sickness.' She paused only to draw breath. 'Noisy it is sometimes, too, when the girls are coming out of the laundry after finishing time. The sound of their voices and the clatter of their boots on the cobbles is enough to give you a bad headache.'

'I think I can put up with all of that, Gwen,' Delmai sat forward in her chair. 'I've got my freedom and that's all that counts.'

Gwen looked at her mistress with an unspoken question in her eyes. Delmai sighed. 'I can't expect you to understand,' she said softly. 'But Mr Richardson and I… we just couldn't live together. I suppose it's my fault.'

'No, never your fault, Miss Delmai,' Gwen said stoutly. 'I heard Mr Richardson shouting at you sometimes, made you cry he did too. You did right to get away from him and damn what anybody else says.'

Delmai's stomach turned over. 'Do you think there'll be much gossip?' she asked, imagining already the speculation and sly innuendos that would be passed around s all over the town.

'Bound to be, miss.' Gwen busied herself setting out china on the damask tray cloth. 'People round here just love to have something to talk about but a nine-day-wonder, that's all it will be – you mark my words.'

Delmai settled herself back in her chair, sipping the fragrant tea gratefully. She had always dreaded being the subject of idle chatter and yet now it didn't seem to be important. She sighed contentedly. This was the beginning of a new life for her and she meant to make every moment of it count.

A watery sun greeted Delmai when she woke the next morning and she sat up in bed with the feeling that something pleasant was going to happen. Then she remembered that she was to visit the prison later on that day. She rose from bed, drew off her silk nightgown and stared at her reflection in the long wardrobe mirror.

She was shapely enough, she decided, though perhaps a little more fullness of breast and hip might be flattering. There were no marks on her white flesh now and it was as if Rickie Richardson had never touched her. But would she ever be able to respond to a man's desire with love and joyfulness, she wondered sadly. She shook back her tangled hair and stared at her face, as yet young and unlined. Perhaps she would spend her life doing good works, finding solace from what Rickie had called her unnaturalness in helping others.

When later she went downstairs into the kitchen, she sniffed appreciatively. 'Something smells good!' She moved to the range and watched as Gwen broke an egg cleanly into a large pan already containing several rashers of bacon.

'Got to feed you up.' Gwen's eyes twinkled. 'Eat like a sparrow you do; and you're as thin as a bird too.'

Delmai smiled. Gwen, though only a year or two older than she was, treated her like a child.

'Do you want your breakfast served in the dining room, miss, or will you have it here in the kitchen?'

Delmai stood considering the question for a moment or two. Was it important to keep up the conventions of a lifetime, she wondered. Only servants took their meals in the kitchen, yet the cosy warmth from the range made the prospect inviting. In any event, she was breaking all other conventions, so why not do just as she liked?

'I'll eat in here,' she said firmly. 'Along with you, Gwen.'

The maid looked at her and there was a smile in the depths of her eyes. 'Your daddy wouldn't approve of such behaviour, mind,' she said gently and Delmai shook her head. 'No, he wouldn't, which is reason enough for doing it.'

The day passed at a leisurely pace as Delmai wrote letters and amused herself with some embroidery but at the back of her mind, like a ray of sunshine, was the thought of seeing Billy Gray once more. At last, when she could dally no longer, she began to dress with care, choosing a gown that was high-necked and restrained in design yet in a soft pastel shade of rose which was most becoming to her pale complexion.

She set out early, a basket on her arm containing freshly baked buns and a slice of fruit cake. Billy always appeared half-starved, his young face long and thin, his strong jaw lantern-like beneath his cropped hair. Her heart skipped a beat as she made her way along the road, breathing in the scent of the breeze salt and tangy coming in off the sea. The mists and rain of yesterday had vanished and a soft autumn sunshine lit the cobbled roadway.

Griffiths greeted her, opening the small door with reluctance, but Delmai was ready for him.

'Good morning, Mr Griffiths,' she said brightly. 'Would you like to try one of my cakes?' She lifted the cloth and the warden sniffed disapprovingly.

'Not supposed to take nothin' from visitors,' he said sourly. 'Get me into trouble you will, Mrs Richardson.'

Delmai smiled most charmingly and pointed to the basket. 'Look more closely, this is a very special cake.'

Griffiths leaned forward, curious now, and his eyes brightened as he saw the folded roll of five-pound notes. With a quick look around him, he dipped his hand into the basket and swiftly pocketed the money.

'What is it you want, Mrs Richardson?' He still sounded surly, but there was a looseness in his stance which suggested he would be receptive to her requests.

'It's Billy Gray,' she said shyly. 'He seems such a nice young man. I'd like to see him made more comfortable; I'm sure someone like you could arrange such a small detail?'

Griffiths blinked rapidly for a moment but he did not speak and Delmai's heart sank. 'I'm very generous to those who please me,' she said, allowing herself to smile though she felt more like slapping the warder's set face. He nodded at last and she sighed with relief.

She moved about the prison with Griffiths continually behind her, keeping the visit to Billy until the very last. She wondered at her own feelings, knowing that she was taking far more than a casual interest in the young man who was locked away behind bars accused of murder. Yet when she finally entered his cell she knew deep within her that Billy, with his gentle eyes staring at her, could harm no one.

'Good morning, Billy,' she said lightly. 'I've brought you some fresh cakes. I hope you have a sweet tooth.'

He looked up, a small light kindling in his face as Delmai seated herself on the solitary wooden chair and placed her basket on the table.

'I believe I left my coat in the last cell, Mr Griffiths,' she said archly and the warder tugged at his moustache thoughtfully.

'It's against the rules for me to leave you alone with a prisoner, ma'am,' he said uncertainly, but Delmai turned the full battery of her smile in his direction. 'I shall be perfectly all right, I promise,' she said quickly.

'Very well, but I'll only be a few minutes away should you need me.'

There was silence in the small cell after Griffiths had gone. 'This is silly,' Delmai said, her voice cracking. She leaned forward and touched Billy's hand, her fingers gently stroking his. 'Look, things should be better for you in here now. I've bribed Griffiths to make you more comfortable. It's all I can do for now, but I'm going to start a campaign to get you out of here. I know you're not guilty of any crime and I'm going to try to make the rest of the town understand that an injustice has been done.'

Billy looked at her without hope. 'Save your breath,' he said, his voice dull. 'I'm shut away here for good. Anyway, why should you care? I'm nothing to you!'

'I don't know the reason,' Delmai answered truthfully, 'but care I do.' She stared at Billy for a long moment and he returned her look with surprise.

'Don't waste your time on me, Mrs Richardson.' He emphasised her name and looked pointedly at her hand resting on his.

Delmai spoke quickly, breathlessly. 'I know it's wrong to be talking like this, but meeting you has changed my life in some inexplicable way.'

She leaned closer, staring at him appealingly and with a sigh Billy covered her fingers with his own. 'I'm not a free man, not in any way,' he said in despair. Delmai bit her lip, knowing he was alluding to his relationship with Mary Jenkins. She paused, wondering how far she could go.

'I'm sorry to be the one to tell you this,' she said awkwardly, 'but Mary is not the woman you left behind. She has moved into the household of Dean Sutton.' Delmai lowered her lids, unable to look at him. 'The talk is that she's more than just an employee. I'm sorry.'

Billy glanced at her quickly. Colour rose to his thin cheeks and the pain in his eyes was hard for Delmai to bear.

'Please don't be hurt,' she said gently. 'Some women are not born to be faithful. I'm sure she thinks no less of you, it's just that she needs someone to lean on. We all do,' she added wistfully.

'Mary and me, we've been promised to each other for years, I love her.'

'Do you?' Delmai managed to speak evenly though her heart was pounding swiftly and her mouth felt dry. 'Or is it simply that she had become a habit?'

Billy frowned. 'If I hadn't been shut inside here we'd be married by now, I'm sure of it.'

Delmai's hand curled within his. 'But Billy, neither of you was in a hurry to be tied, else why are you not married with a brood of children by now? One of you must have had doubts?'

'Well, it wasn't me.' Billy seemed bewildered. 'I love my Mary and I can't believe that she would change in a few months from a respectable girl into a floosie.'

Delmai strove for patience, pushing the pain of his loyalty to Mary into the recesses of her mind. It showed that Billy was a man of character that he defended the woman so forcefully.

'I'm afraid a great deal has happened to her in the last few months,' Delmai said. 'She seems to have changed her character entirely. Old Mr Sutton was forced to let her go, dismiss her from her job at the laundry.'

Delmai looked down at her fingers entwined with his and there was a warmth inside her. 'And she didn't pay her rent either. No, Billy, Mary is not the same person as the woman you gave your promises to. I'm sorry to be the one to tell you all this, but there is no way of softening the blow.'

Billy rubbed his hand over his eyes. 'I must get out of here,' he said harshly, 'I can't bear to be shut away like this unable to help Mary.'

'Be patient just a little while longer, Billy,' Delmai urged earnestly. 'I promise that I'll have you freed before too long. But you must put Mary out of your mind, she's no good to you.'

He looked at her and the trust in his eyes made Delmai tremble with the enormity of what she was saying. Yet she was jubilant, she had risked his anger and it seemed she had succeeded in her persuasions for Billy was turning to her for salvation.

'Excuse me, Mrs Richardson,' Griffiths had returned to the cell, the keys at his waist jangling. 'I can't find any coat. Are you sure you brought it with you?' Delmai smiled warmly at the warder. 'How silly of me, I've got it here all the time! I'm so sorry for causing you so much trouble.' She rose to her feet and with a quick glance in Billy's direction left the cell.

She heard the door clang behind her with a sound of dreadful finality and her courage wavered. Could she keep her promise to free Billy? She clasped her hands together tightly, gripping the basket until her knuckles gleamed white.

'Thank you for your help, Mr Griffiths, and do remember our little talk, won't you?' She had to be content with a grunt from the surly warder as he opened the gate to allow her to pass through the courtyard. Then she was standing facing the beach and the creaking old gallows that should have been burned to the ground long ago. She held her head high as she walked along the street and there was a softness within her that she dimly recognised as the beginnings of love.

–

The late afternoon had brought a glimmer of sunshine to wash the cold streets and Mary walked slowly away from the prison breathing in the scent of salt and tar that drifted on the breeze from the docks. Yet again she had been turned away from the big gate and had watched bitterly as Delmai Richardson strode past her with a triumphant lift to her head. With a sigh she returned to the shop, glancing up at the clock and shaking her head impatiently as she realised that Nerys and Joanie must have persuaded Mrs Greenaway to spend the afternoon in town.

But after all, it was only once a month that the staff were free to spend a day just as they chose, and in the two weeks since Mary had been in charge of the store the girls had been transformed from undisciplined children to able, capable assistants.

Mary left the door on the latch and went into the kitchen where she sank into a chair, closing her eyes wearily, pushing her disappointment at not seeing Billy to the back of her mind. She thought with pride of her own progress in the shop – she knew all the prices now and could cut cloth with as much skill as any of the girls. She could run the shop with her eyes closed and deep within her an ambition was growing.

She wanted her own store, but not just for selling drapery. She would like a shop that sold everything from bacon to long woollen drawers. She smiled to herself – it was nothing but a dream, yet one day she would make it come true.

Her heart dipped with fear as she thought of Dean Sutton. She had been delighted to learn that his business trip had had to be extended and as yet she had not come face to face with him.

Meanwhile his wife grew visibly weaker and Mary found herself greatly admiring Mrs Sutton's stoicism. She sighed softly. Any day now Dean would return, indeed his wife's sickness demanded his presence. And then would come Mary's day of reckoning. She moved restlessly from her chair, unable to relax, wishing that the girls would return to take her mind from her own problems with their noisy ways and constant arguments.

It was with relief that she heard the bell clanging on the door, but when she looked into the shop her heart almost stopped beating as she recognised the tall figure standing near the counter.

'Can I help you?' She sounded stiff and formal, but her mouth trembled and her hands were clasped together tightly as she fought for control.

Brandon said nothing but moved towards her with such purpose that she could not mistake his intention. She stepped back a pace and he followed her into the kitchen, deftly slipping the small bolt into place.

'Mary!' His voice was gentle and when he held out his arms, she found herself going into them, closing her eyes in ecstasy at the feel of his broad shoulders under her hands and the litheness of him against her body. His mouth was on hers and there seemed no need for words as his tongue devoured hers and he held her close as though she was a precious piece of porcelain.

Mary clung to him, giving herself up to his touch. She did not stop to question his presence for fear she might spoil the magic of the moment. It seemed only that he had come to her as if in answer to an unspoken prayer, and she wanted nothing more than to drown in the sensation of his nearness.

She was aware of him laying her back on the long couch and of his hands moving over her, bringing her thrill after thrill of delight. It was as though she had drunk some potent wine that removed her inhibitions and left her pliant, responding to Brandon with every part of her being. At the back of her mind she told herself that he had come to claim her as his own, that he would lie with her, giving her his love, and then he would take her away from the shop and from all the implications of working for Dean Sutton.

When he came to her, she gasped with joy and pleasure, tears of happiness misted her eyes and her fingers caressed the crisp dark hair that curled around his face. They were one flesh, she was his and his alone and there could be no other man, no other love for her ever again. She cried out his name and clung to the broadness of his back, pressing him closer, wanting to possess him body and soul. If she had thought the first time with him was beautiful, then she had not plumbed the depths of the man. He weaved a spell of desire and of passion that coupled with a blinding brilliant love was all the glories of life rolled into one experience.

There was a silence in the room like the calm after a storm as Mary lay within Brandon's arms, her eyes closed, her hair wild and tangled over her naked shoulders. She felt replete as though she had enjoyed a great banquet – and so she had, she told herself, only this was a feast of love and wonder and delight.

Brandon sighed and moved her gently away and as he dressed she watched him, her eyes devouring him. She longed to reach out and touch the warmth of his skin, to have his breath mingling with hers once more, but she was suddenly shy and aware of her own nakedness.

When they were both dressed, Mary stood waiting in breathless silence, expecting she knew not what. Brandon came to her and took her face between his hands and his mouth was tender now, lacking passion but sweet all the same. She held him close, pressing her face against his shoulder, but neither of them spoke. It was as though the silence was a fragile bubble that might burst and destroy everything.

She watched him go with a light heart. He had spoken nothing of love or possession, yet she knew in her bones that he felt for her as much as she did for him. Her eyes drank in his lithe walk and the square proud set of his shoulders and she stood in the doorway of the shop until he was out of sight.

Then she tidied the room and placed the kettle on the hob ready for boiling. She no longer felt lonely, she felt loved and cherished and her heart was beating swiftly, filled with happiness and joy.

By the time the girls returned, Mary had brushed and repinned her hair and was standing over the stove cooking a rabbit stew as though nothing had happened to disturb the quietness of the afternoon. And yet Nerys looked at her suspiciously, her eyes narrowing, her mouth pursed.

'You seem different,' she said at last. 'You look as if you've lost a penny and found a sovereign.'

Mary laughed lightly. 'Perhaps I have!' She gestured towards the dresser. 'Bring out some dishes, the stew's just about ready.'

Mrs Greenaway sank into a chair, her face red from exertion. 'There's a job I've got looking after these two girls,' she grumbled good-naturedly. 'Like naughty babbas they are, running off just when you think you've got them to heel.' She eased her feet out of her shoes and rubbed at her toes, sighing with relief. 'Glad I am that there's only one day a month they've got off; couldn't put up with them for any more than that, they'd have me six-foot deep they would.'

'Come and eat, you'll feel better then.' Mary smiled and sat at the table. 'Here, pass me the bread, Nerys, I'll cut a few slices myself before you turn it into a heap of crumbs!'

The girl readily obeyed, taking up her spoon and tasting the strew. 'There's lovely,' she said appreciatively. 'I wish you lived down by here with us instead of up at the Big House.' Mary looked at her levelly, though her stomach turned over at the thought of returning to *Ty Mawr*.

'So do I,' she said lightly. 'We'll see what can be arranged.'

'Will you ask Mr Sutton tonight then?' Mrs Greenaway's eyes were shrewd as they rested on Mary.

'You know as well as I do that he's away on business,' Mary said, her voice unnecessarily sharp. 'I don't know when he's expected back.'

The girls fell silent, glancing uneasily at each other and it was left to Mrs Greenaway to speak.

'He's returned already. Saw him with my own eyes driving up Canal Street, going home to *Ty Mawr*. It's all the gossip that Mrs Sutton's taken a turn for the worse and the master had to be sent for. Didn't you know?'

Mary pushed away her plate, suddenly she did not feel hungry. 'No, I didn't know.' She heard her own voice, but it seemed not to belong to her. She rose to her feet and took her coat from the peg on the back of the door.

'I'd best get up there.' She spoke evenly now, concealing the turmoil of emotions within her. 'I might be needed.'

Mrs Greenaway stared at her with something like pity in her eyes. 'Yes, it's the only thing to do. Don't worry, I'll look after everything here.'

The twilight glow of early evening should have had a soothing effect on Mary, but she was too mixed-up and emotional to notice how the dying sun-splashed sea and sky with scarlet and gold. She walked along the edge of the beach, trying to gain enough courage to make for the tram terminus.

At last, reality forced itself upon her chaotic thoughts and she paused for a moment, taking a deep breath of the tangy sea air before turning back to the roadway. One thing was clear, she could not become Dean's mistress – not now, not ever. She was Brandon's woman – he had put his mark on her and she couldn't bring herself to lie in another man's bed, not even if it meant that she was out in the street with no job and no roof over her head.

Brandon had made her no promises, none at all and perhaps he never would. But she would take the crumbs he offered her with selfish joy, holding each experience close to her heart like a precious gem.

Her mind made up, she walked purposefully now, each step bringing her nearer to where the tram waited to carry her out of the town and up on to the hill. She lifted her head and saw the glory of the night sky and a smile curved the corners of her mouth.

Chapter Seventeen

The windows of *Ty Mawr* were ablaze with lights by the time Mary arrived. The front door under the stone porch stood open, the glare from the hallway spilling onto the drive. A carriage stood in front of the house, the horse pulling impatiently between the shafts.

As Mary approached the doorway, Dr Thomas was walking slowly through the hall. His shoulders were stooped and his black bag hung down at his side; his appearance was one of complete dejection.

He paused in the lighted porch and turned to look at the tall man looming behind him whose large frame cast a great shadow onto the pathway.

'The improvement will just be a temporary one.' The doctor spoke softly, but Mary was close enough to catch the gist of what he said. Dean Sutton acknowledged the doctor's words with a slight inclination of his great head.

'You know there is nothing more I can do but make her comfortable. She has at best another month and after that her life is in the lap of the gods.'

The big American rested his hand on the doctor's thin shoulder. 'I'm grateful, Bryn, for all you've done. Thank you for coming up here so promptly and for spending so much time with Bea.'

'It's the least I can do.' Dr Thomas's voice was muffled. 'I brought the girl into the world, it's sad to see her reduced to a shadow of her former self. Bonny and lovely she was as a child. With great fat glossy curls and laughing eyes, always laughing they were.' The old doctor shook his head. 'But then life must go on as they say.'

Mary waited until the doctor climbed into his carriage and then made her way round to the back of the house. In the kitchen Bertha was seated at the white scrubbed table, her head buried in her apron. Awkwardly, Mary sat beside the maid and touched her arm lightly.

'I'm so sorry about Mrs Sutton,' Mary spoke quietly. 'Is there anything I can do to help?'

Bertha looked up at once, her eyes red and puffy through weeping. Her face was deathly pale and her hair dishevelled.

'There's nothing anyone can do. She's dying, my beloved mistress is going to her great sleep and I don't know how I'll manage without her.'

Mary put her arm around Bertha's shoulder, patting her back as though she was a child.

'Now listen to me,' Mary said sternly, 'Mrs Sutton may live for some weeks yet. I heard the doctor telling Mr Sutton, so you must be brave. Go wash away your tears and smarten yourself up a bit, you can't let your mistress see you looking like this otherwise she'll know something is very wrong.' She helped Bertha to her feet. 'Now, come on, cold water works wonders and so does a smattering of wet tea leaves wrapped in a linen handkerchief and placed on the eyes.'

Bertha stared at her gratefully. 'Will you take up her tray, just this once? Tell Miss Bea I'm busy in the kitchen, what with the cook off visiting her sister an' all.'

Mary watched as Bertha went over to the sink in the corner of the room and washed her face, allowing the cold water to trickle between her fingers. But by the way her back heaved, it was clear that she was still distressed. Mary set the tray with reluctant fingers. She meant it when she had offered her help, but for all that, she knew it was going to be an ordeal to face Mrs Sutton.

'What am I to take up to her?' Mary asked and Bertha broke into a fresh spasm of weeping, tears running down her cheeks even as she served a piece of boiled fish and spread it with butter.

'This is Miss Bea's favourite meal,' Bertha gasped. 'I've tried to give her proper food and look after her, thinking she'd be cured, but she's never been the same since she had her babba taken away from her.'

Mary had heard the story of Bea's suspicious visit to Mrs Benson on Canal Street. No one knew at the time the full facts of the case, but speculation had been rife. Some believed the father of the child to be Sterling Richardson, but Mary had given little credence to that story.

'I expect you think my mistress was bad to do what she did.' Bertha rubbed at her eyes with the corner of her apron. 'But no one knew how much she was hurting inside. Loved her man she did, but couldn't have him. Blood of her own blood he turned out to be. A punishment, my mistress said, but she didn't deserve fate to be so hard on her.'

'I'd better go up with the tray before the food is cold,' Mary said practically. 'Now dry your eyes, there's a good girl, then later you can sit with your mistress for a while.'

The long wide staircase was filled with shadows, the scent of beeswax permeated the air and through the stained-glass windows the silver of the moon shed a diffused light on to the portraits on the wall. Mary was not given to being fanciful, but she could almost believe that the eyes of the people in the paintings followed her as she moved up towards Mrs Sutton's room.

'What is it?' Bea's voice was light, insubstantial, as though she had already departed this world, Mary thought with a shiver.

'I've brought you something to eat.' Mary crossed the room and set the tray down on the small side table. 'It's your favourite, so Bertha tells me, and she's very anxious that you should eat and recover your strength.'

Bea allowed Mary to help her into a sitting position but she shook her head when Mary made to lift the tray.

'I'm not hungry and tell Bertha not to fool herself. I shall not get better, not this time.'

Mary stood uncertainly beside the bed at a loss, not knowing what to say in view of Bea's frankness.

'Sometimes miracles happen,' she ventured at last. Bea smiled and gestured for Mary to take a seat.

'Miracles have happened for me, for I found happiness with Dean Sutton in spite of a great many difficulties. But now my share of luck has run out and I can't say I'm sorry. I'm tired, so very tired.'

Mary was forced to lean forward in order to catch the softly spoken words. 'You shouldn't be trying to talk,' she said in concern. 'Try to conserve your strength, won't you?'

Bea lifted thin fingers and brushed back a stray piece of hair from her face. After a moment her pale, limp hand fell back onto the counterpane as though even such a small effort had drained her.

'I know why Dean brought you here,' she said. 'And please don't think I'm blaming you. He needs a woman, a strong healthy woman and I give you both my blessing.'

Mary turned away so that Bea would not see the expression in her eyes. In her heart and mind she had rejected Dean's proposition, but now was not the time to say so.

Bea closed her eyes. 'I think the medicine Dr Thomas prescribed is making me sleepy.' She sighed heavily. 'He's a good friend and he has promised not to let me suffer. What more can I ask?'

Mary moved silently out of the room and closed the door behind her. She felt trapped, a spider caught in a web of silken thread. No one was holding her by force, yet she could not find it in her to deny Bea Sutton her peace of mind.

As she passed the library she saw Dean sitting near the fire, his head lowered. She felt a sense of pity for him wash over her and impulsively went to him, placing her hand on his shoulder. He took it, looking up at her gratefully and pressing her fingers to his lips suddenly and with such desperation that Mary could not draw away.

Dean spoke slowly. 'Help me, Mary! Stay with me tonight, please.'

Mary fought a battle with herself and lost. She could not bring herself to ignore the pain in Dean's eyes. She sat down gingerly and watched as he poured himself a whisky, the liquid glowing amber in the light from the fire.

'Dean, we must talk.' She settled herself more comfortably against the scroll-backed sofa, rearranging her skirt around her ankles, trying to find words that would not hurt and wound.

'What is it?' He spoke almost absently, tipping the glass up to his mouth and swallowing the liquor in one quick movement.

'I can't be your mistress.' She spoke hurriedly, the words tumbling out like pebbles into a pool and sending small whirls of emotion across the room. Dean stared at her dully as though uncomprehending and Mary took a deep breath.

'I must tell you the truth. I'm in love with your brother; I can never give myself to you or any man, not now.'

Dean brushed a hand through his springy hair that was touched at the temples with grey. Then he gave a hollow laugh and poured himself another glass of whisky before crossing the room to sit beside her.

'So my brother is finally revenged.' His words were spoken softly without anger and Mary tensed.

'What do you mean?' she asked anxiously, the blood pounding in her ears.

'It's a long story.' Dean's face had fallen into lines of sadness. He twirled the glass between thick fingers, staring down into the whisky as though seeing something beyond.

'We were living in America, both of us very young, rivals we were always. Never had brotherly love for each other, can't say why. At each other's throats all the time, each trying to be top dog.'

Dean paused and stared at Mary pityingly. 'Brandon is still playing the same game, can't you see that? By taking you he is simply paying me back an old score.'

Mary's mouth was suddenly dry. 'Paying you back, but for what?'

He shook his head. 'I don't want to hurt you, Mary but a long time ago I took Brandon's fiancée away from him. Her name was Mary, too: Mary Anne Bloomfield. The affair caused quite a stir in our little town, me getting Brandon's girl with child and then leaving her in the lurch. That's the reason I was packed off to Britain, honey – the black sheep of the family, that's me.'

Mary felt as though a darkness was beating at her brain. Surely there must be some mistake, Dean's words could not be true? And yet they were, it was written in the clearness of his eyes and the timbre of his voice.

'I know it must be a blow to you, Mary,' he continued, 'but it's only your pride that's hurt, you must see that.' He took her hands and held them between his own. 'I have been honest with you from the first time we talked, I've told you exactly what I want of you, no punches pulled.'

Mary held back her tears with difficulty. She was reliving her happiness of the afternoon when she had lain in Brandon's arms and thought she held the whole world on her grasp.

And all the time he was taking his revenge upon his brother! He had spoken no words of love and she realised now that she had been a fool to believe he felt anything at all for her.

'I can see you're upset,' Dean said sympathetically. 'And I don't blame you. My brother has a tongue of silk and words to charm the birds from the trees when necessary.' He put a casual arm around her shoulders. 'Put it down to experience, Mary, and remember that we all make fools of ourselves at some time in our lives – it's inevitable.'

Yes, she'd been a fool, she thought bitterly. She had given herself heart and soul to a man who cared nothing for anyone but himself. Would she never learn that all men wanted but one thing from a woman of her station?

'And you, Dean?' Mary moved away from him, her hands clenched at her sides. 'What do you want of me? Am I to be just a floosie, or is it something else you have in mind for me?'

Dean looked up at her, his eyes shadowed. 'I just want a woman to love, Mary, is that so bad?'

The silence was suddenly shattered by a terrified scream and Dean dropped his glass so that the amber liquid spread in a stain over the carpet. He rose to his feet, his face suddenly white, then bounded away from Mary and hurried towards the stairs, taking them two at a time. Mary followed him, her heart in her throat.

In the bedroom Bertha was cowering against the wall, her hands covering her mouth, her eyes anguished pools of misery. She pointed speechlessly and as Mary stepped into the room behind Dean, she saw that Bea was lying half out of the bed, an empty bottle just out of reach of her slim white fingers.

It was Dean who lifted the dead woman back into the bed, resting her gently against the pillows and closing the wide, empty eyes. He drew up a sheet and covered Bea's face while the sounds of Bertha's harsh laboured weeping filled the room.

Mary moved to the window and drew the curtains, shutting out the paleness of the moon and the denseness of the star-studded night. She turned to Dean but he did not see her. His shoulders were slumped and his tread heavy as he made his way out of the room.

-

Mary stayed at *Tŷ Mawr* for the next few days promising herself that once the funeral was over she would leave Dean's house and make a life of her own. Perhaps she would even move away from Sweyn's Eye altogether, start afresh in a new town.

During the daytime she worked hard at the shop, dusting and re-dusting the shelves, scrubbing the floor until the marble glowed with colour. To Mary it seemed as though she had fallen into a black abyss where there was no hope or light. From the moment Dean had told her about Brandon's wish for revenge to the time when she had gone into the bedroom and seen Bea Sutton's dead white face, she had been feeling as though she was living in a nightmare. It was Mrs Greenaway who pulled her up sharply.

'You're never doin' those blasted shelves again, are you?' The old woman stood firmly in the doorway leading from the kitchen to the shop and behind her Mary could see the two girls staring at her as though she had gone mad. And perhaps she had for a little while, she thought in surprise.

'Kill yourself, that's what you'll do if you go on like this.' Mrs Greenaway's voice held sympathy but a reproof too and Mary sank down on to the high-backed chair placed near the counter for the use of customers. The duster fell idle in her lap and she sighed heavily.

'Mrs Sutton is being buried today, just at this moment I suppose.' Her eyes went to the large clock on the wall.

'So what?' Mrs Greenaway said bluntly. 'We're all sorry for the poor lady, but there's nothing any of us can do; she's been dying for years, no one expected her to last this long if the truth be told. Now, come on, Mary Jenkins, pull yourself together before you make yourself ill.'

Mrs Greenaway rested a hand on Mary's shoulder and her pale blue eyes looked down with as much censure in them as sympathy.

'Can't go living other people's woes for them, can you?' she said. 'Oh, I know it must have been awful for you finding the poor lady as you did, but now you must put it all out of your mind, see?'

Mary nodded, feeling suddenly weary. She put her head in her hands and closed her eyes.

'Look, why not go up and lie on my bed for an hour? It will do you good to have a sleep if you ask me.'

She nodded again, allowing herself to be drawn to her feet. Then slowly Mary climbed the stairs, her footsteps heavy. She lay down on the bright patchwork quilt and faced the wall. Her very bones seemed to ache with tiredness and her mind refused to function properly. She could not decide if it was the death of Bea

Sutton or the knowledge of Brandon's betrayal that was affecting her so badly.

However, she must have drifted off to sleep because it was dark in the small room when she opened her eyes again. The moon was a silver orb shining in through the small window and the stars seemed close enough to touch. Mary sat up and brushed back her long hair, realising that she felt alive again. The torpor which had held her in its grip had vanished and she was tinglingly alive. She felt pain, felt it deeply whenever she thought of the events of the past few days, but at least she could come to terms with herself now.

When she went downstairs, the shop was in darkness and a light glowed from the kitchen shining through the stained glass of the door. The scene inside was one of peace and tranquillity: Joanie was stitching a tear in the petticoat and Nerys was reading by the light of the gas lamp. Of Mrs Greenaway there was no sign.

'Hello, Mary, would you like a cup of tea or something?' Nerys put down her book. 'The kettle is on the boil, it won't take a minute to brew up.' She was being treated as though she was an invalid, Mary thought ruefully, which was a clear indication of the way she had been acting recently.

'I'd love some tea,' she said gratefully, settling herself in the low rocking chair and brushing back her hair. She must look a sight, she thought, staring down at her crumpled skirt, trying vainly to smooth out the creases with her hands.

'Where's Mrs Greenaway?' Mary asked and Joanie looked up from her sewing.

'Gone to get some gin, I expect,' she said in a matter-of-fact tone that did not fool Mary for one instant.

'Come on, you'd better tell me, she's gone to fetch someone to see me, hasn't she? The doctor, is it?'

The two girls fell silent, looking at each other with scared eyes, afraid to answer and yet fearful of remaining silent. 'She's fetching Mr Sutton,' Nerys said at last.

Just then the outer door opened and the two girls exchanged relieved glances. 'There's Mrs Greenaway now.' Nerys rose to her feet in a fluid movement, opening the shop door and standing back a little, her eyes wide. Dean was suddenly filling the small kitchen with his presence. 'Come on, honey,' he said slowly. 'I'm taking you home to *Tŷ Mawr*.'

'I'm all right,' Mary protested. 'Whatever Mrs Greenaway has been telling you, there's nothing wrong with me.'

Dean took her arm, staring down at her dishevelled appearance, his eyes full of concern.

'You could have fooled me, Mary,' he said gently and his grasp on her arm was firm.

It was chilly out in the night air and she shivered a little. Dean put out his hand to help her into the hansom cab and then sat beside her. It was as though he already owned her, she thought with a dart of dismay.

'How's Bertha?' She forced herself to speak normally and Dean shook his head.

'Taking it badly, but then Bea was a very lovable woman. I cared for her more than anyone will ever know.' His voice broke and Mary put her hand over his. As they clung together she felt suddenly strong. But then all her life people had leaned on her; she had needed strength to raise herself and Heath from the mire of their childhood.

It would be wonderful to have someone strong so that *she* could do a bit of leaning for a change, she thought bitterly. She had believed she had found that strength in Brandon, but it had just been an illusion. When he held her close, he had taken her soul as well as her body. She grimaced to think how quickly he had cast her aside.

–

It was little more than two weeks after the funeral when Dean stealthily entered Mary's room. She heard his soft tread on the carpet, felt the weight of him as he sank onto the bed and in her half-dreaming state, she imagined for a second that he was Brandon. She clung to his broad shoulders for a long moment, sighing softly, and she must have spoken Brandon's name for suddenly her arms were empty.

Dean lit the gas and stared down at her, his face white in the sudden glare.

'Forget him, Mary,' he said softly, his eyes drinking in the nakedness of her creamy skin. He leaned close to her. 'I'll be good to you, you'll never lack for anything. Don't turn me away, Mary!'

She tried to clear her thoughts, for she was still half asleep, confused but becoming angry.

'How dare you come to me now?' she whispered. 'Without at least allowing a time for mourning.'

His face became hard as he pressed her back against the pillows.

'What I want of you is nothing to do with my dead wife,' he said savagely. 'I just want to use you, as my brother did.'

Mary's colour rose. 'I hate you Suttons, you've brought me nothing but misery! I hate the entire Sutton family, do you understand?'

Dean's face grew pale with rage.

'How dare you speak to me like that, you little hoyden!' He dragged her from the bed. 'You're a little slut, get back onto the streets where you belong!' His hand caught her a blow across her cheek and she reeled away from him.

As she fumbled for her clothes, drawing a skirt over her nightgown, she felt tears blind her eyes and her mind was reeling with bitter thoughts.

Dean thrust a coat at her. 'Go on, get out! I don't want you under my roof one moment longer. You'd be a whore for my brother, but not for me. You're a fool, Mary Jenkins.'

Mary buttoned her coat with trembling fingers, unable to speak, then she moved to the door. As she stood on the landing she could see lights blazing below and could imagine how the servants were savouring this moment, with the possible exception of Bertha who had come to have a kind of guarded respect for her. She hurried down the stairs and as she strode out into the sharpness of the autumn night, she heard a dog howl somewhere to the rear of *Ty Mawr.*

She stared around her and the night closed in, shadows covering her path so that she stumbled over a boulder, almost falling to her knees. Then the moon slid from behind the clouds, lighting her way, and she lifted her head. A little way above her, standing out against the sky, was the turreted rooftop of *Plas Rhianfa*. Fresh hope filled Mary as she began to stumble up the hill. Mali would take her in and would ask no awkward questions.

Yet as she neared the imposing house, her steps faltered, Mali was Mrs Sterling Richardson now – would she be embarrassed by Mary's plight? She hesitated on the step and almost turned away but then it began to rain, light specks at first like the spitting of a cat but then growing harder, more spiteful.

Mary lifted the handle shaped like a lion's mouth and let it fall. It echoed loudly through the silent house. For a long time nothing moved behind the dark elegant front of the huge building and she almost turned away, thinking of seeking shelter in one of the outbuildings. Then a light spilled suddenly from the stained-glass window over the door and Mary paused, her mouth dry, her heart pounding, knowing only that she had never felt so ashamed in all her life.

Chapter Eighteen

Market Street was unspectacular, a row of plain-fronted houses. The only saving grace was in the large windows superimposed upon the old buildings and giving them the dubious respectability of being described as shops. The street led directly off Copperman's Row, where the low flat cottages housed copper workers and had done so for over a hundred years.

Mary hoisted her bag on her shoulder and passed along Copperman's Row into Market Street, where she knocked at the door of Murphy's Fresh Fish Shop.

It opened at once and Katie stood with a child in her arms, her face wreathed in smiles.

'Come in, Mary, and sure you're more than welcome. Me Mammy's got a room ready for ye.' She grinned. 'Well, part of my room it is really, but there's a curtain put between the beds so you should have some privacy.'

Mary swallowed hard. Why was it that those with very little to give were the most open-handed?

'There's kind of your mother! I shan't be staying long, mind, only until I find somewhere of my own.'

Katie took the bag from Mary's arm. 'Hush, now, sure isn't this your home for as long as you need it?'

Tom Murphy was nowhere to be seen and Mary felt a sense of relief. He was kindly enough and yet there was something about his pale eyes that repelled her.

'Would you like a cup of tea or something stronger?' Mrs Murphy was sitting before the fire, her sons playing at her feet, quarrelling like young puppies over a slice of bread and butter.

She scolded one of them and without rancour the boy stared up at her with mouth open.

'Tea, please,' Mary replied quickly. The smell of gin permeated the room and the fumes were sickly-sweet, mingling badly with the odour of fish from the shop at the front of the house.

'Sure and Mary can take her things upstairs first, Mammy,' Katie said firmly. 'Come on, this way!'

Katie showed her upstairs and then retreated. Mary was grateful, knowing that her friend was giving her time to get her bearings.

She sat down on the narrow bed and looked around her. The room was not overly large, but Katie had given Mary the half that boasted a window. Below there was little to be seen but a tangle of gardens, ill kept for the copper dust killed everything in its path except (it seemed) the most ferocious weeds.

Mary sighed. At least she had a resting place, an oasis of time where she could stop running scared and take stock of her life. She had left her home in Canal Street and moved in to Dean Sutton's house and now, here she was in Market Street with a half-formed plan running round in her brain.

She thought with bitterness of the night Dean had turned her out into the darkness. He had no right to think she should fall into his arms just when he wanted her to. He might have bought her services in the shop and she had to admit that she had led him to believe she would be his mistress, but he had allowed so little time to elapse since his wife's death and he flatly refused to listen to reason.

She had turned to Mali for help that night and had received a warm response. Mali had begged Mary to stay with her at *Plas Rhianfa* for as long as she liked but Mary could not settle there, could not intrude on a life that was not of her making. But she had taken the loan of money Mali pressed upon her. It was only what was due to her, Mali had said.

'After all the years of looking after the affairs of the laundry so well, it's the least I could do for you.' Mali's face had been warm and sweet. 'And it's my fault, indirectly, that you are without a job.' She sighed. 'I had no idea that Dean wanted his father to run the business or that there was any dissension between the old man and you.'

Mary had grimaced. 'I'm afraid I caused quite a barney between the Sutton men, I don't suppose I'll ever be forgiven for that.' She squared her shoulders. 'Never mind, when I make my fortune I'll pay you back.' Mary had spoken solemnly, meaning what she said and after a time Mali had nodded her agreement.

Mary leaned against the windowpane, which was cold beneath her cheek. Staring out along the row, she could hear the faint sound of music and smiled to herself. That would be Dai-End-House, she had heard Mali talk about him many times.

She stared broodingly out at the dullness of the day, recognising that she had come down in the world suddenly. But she was nowhere near the bottom where she had begun. To her as a child, a cottage in Market Street would have seemed like a palace, born and bred as she was in the poorest part of the town. In the slums rats were bedfellows and rain poured in through holes in the roof. No one owned anything, not even the house they lived in, for when one family died or moved away others would take their place without causing a ripple.

Mary pushed the thoughts aside and turned to sit on the bed. Then she heard footsteps coming up the stairs and knew that Katie was bringing her some tea.

The Irish girl placed the cup beside Mary and retreated to the door. 'Shall we walk along Market Street for a while afterwards, then I can show you round the place?'

Mary nodded. 'That would be lovely, *merchi*.'

Katie smiled. 'Something in you reminds me of Mali when you speak like that.'

Mary gave a short laugh. 'Except that I'm three times as big as her and not half the lady she is.'

Katie rubbed at her forehead. 'I know all that, and yet it's somethin' in your spirit. Aw, it's daft I'm talkin', take no notice.

See you in a few minutes then, and bring your shawl, it's turned cold outside.'

The air was freezing as, later, Mary walked down Market Street beside Katie. The trees, losing their colour now, moaned and twisted in the biting wind coming in from the sea, filling the valley as though it was a bowl, scurrying the leaves along pavements and lifting the skirts of women shoppers.

Market Street led downhill, a long narrow road which at the bottom branched out into a wide square. Mary stopped and looked around her, staring at the scene with a strange sensation of excitement.

There were about twenty market stalls set in a chaotic pattern that somehow added up to a scene of colourful disorder. Butchers' stalls vied for room among a riot of vegetables and bakery counters, and just to add spice some of the stalls were selling woollen blankets and Welsh shawls that would warm a body even in the coldest weather.

This Mary felt was her new lifeline. She would start to build her dream here and to hell with the men of the Sutton family! She would not be beaten by any of them, least of all by Brandon who had taught her the meaning of love and then discarded her.

'You look as if you're in church standing before the Blessed Virgin,' Katie spoke softly at her side and Mary glanced down at her. 'Perhaps in my own way, I am,' she replied.

Katie shook back her red-gold hair, her face puzzled and Mary rested a hand on her shoulder. 'Would you mind if I went off alone for a while, though it's kind of you to come down here with me, mind.'

'You're not a little girl in a pinny, and I don't have to look after you,' Katie said. 'In any case, I want to get some shopping done, me mammy's asked for something special for supper tonight, in your honour.' She grimaced. 'We're all getting to be tired of fish everlasting.'

Mary wandered through the crowds with an almost magical sense of belonging. She breathed in the scents and sounds of the marketplace, knowing in her bones that her ambitions had lain dormant for too long. Now born of necessity, the time was come to move into a new way of life.

Suddenly she felt as though she was drowning in a whirlpool of emotions. Like a shaft of lightning she was tinglingly aware that she was not meant for marriage and children. She could not envisage belonging to Billy Gray, not now or ever, or being the chattel of any man come to that. She would forget about love and emotion, she told herself firmly, put everything of herself – her heart, her mind and her passions – into the building of a business.

She looked round her, wondering who she could approach for information. She would need a stall and some stock, but what was she going to sell? The answer came at once: she would have a stall that sold anything and everything! She would run more than one stall – why not? she thought in jubilation.

It took some time to find the owner of the plot of land on which the market stood. At first the stallholders had looked at her with suspicion and then she had explained that she was staying at Tom Murphy's Fresh Fish Shop and tongues were loosened. Folk felt that her association with a local trader, however tenuous, entitled her to a place in the market.

Mrs Evans was more like a farmer's wife than a businesswoman. She lived in a good stout house at the bottom of the hill, a comfortable existence brought about by the fact that her late husband had left her some land and she had had enough innate sense to make the best use of the property. She looked up at Mary from her rocking chair in the corner of her comfortable parlour and pursed her lips.

'You want room for two stalls?' she asked curiously, 'Do you know anything about the business of buying and selling, *merchi*?'

Mary shook her head. 'Only a little, but that is not your problem, Mrs Evans. I have the money and it's up to me to make a success of the business. Either way, you can't lose.'

'Quite right, too.' The woman nodded her head and drew her shawl more closely around her shoulders.

'All I rent is the land, you understand that? You must get your own stall or table or whatever you mean to show your wares on. You will have stiff competition; there's Jake Zimmerman my bailiff for one; hates newcomers, he does. And don't forget that customers are fickle; they will come to you at first just to see if they can get you to make a mistake in the change or give them a bargain out of ignorance. They're mad dogs, are customers, they will savage you any time they can so have no illusions, Mary Jenkins.'

'Then you'll rent me some land?' Mary asked quietly and after a moment Mrs Evans nodded.

Mary moved to the door and the old woman stopped her. 'Just one piece of advice I will give you because I admire your courage – join the Cooperative Movement, my girl, the customers like to think they're getting a divvy, even if they're not. In any case, soon the Cooperative will take over everything and those who do not belong will be left behind.' Mrs Evans smiled, revealing rotten stumps of teeth.

'Don't bother to thank me, *merchi*, you'll be perhaps blaming me when all your money and all your stock is gone and you haven't made yourself a fortune. Why don't you marry a man with money, that's the quickest way to get rich!'

Mary shook her head as she opened the door. 'See you tomorrow,' she said and let herself out into the roughness of the afternoon.

The wind had dropped, the trees no longer swayed and moaned overhead but the few remaining leaves rustled like children whispering.

Mary moved down the hill and stared out towards the sea which was topped by white foam like milk come straight from the cows. Her heart was filled with hope. She would get a carpenter to make her stalls. They would be different from the others in the market, because these stalls would have sides that Mary could close and lock. In that way, her stock could remain in place overnight and she would save herself the task of setting up the stall and taking it down every day. She was prepared for opposition, she expected it, but soon she would be accepted. Once the strangeness of seeing her in the square wore off, she would be recognised as one of the traders.

With a feeling of excitement running through her veins she made her way back through the town, avoiding Canal Street and making once more for the market. She walked around the stalls, summing up what goods were being displayed, her mind constantly working on what would be the best items to sell.

There didn't seem to be many children's clothes on display. There was only one stall as far as Mary could see, and that was poorly stocked. She watched a cobbler mending shoes as he sat before his bench, which seemed to her the ideal way to work. Not a minute of his time was wasted and he even tapped a pair of boots while the owner stood barefoot and self-conscious in the street.

Mary pursed her lips in thought. What if she hired a girl to do some sewing, bought a machine that would run up hems in a few moments? Alterations while you wait, big brother's trews cut down and fitted on the spot.

She could have someone at work on one stall while she stocked food on the other. Bacon was a good seller – salted, it would keep for days. And potatoes, gathered fresh from the farmer, perhaps even picked by herself from the ground. Her thoughts whirled as she stood in the bustle of the market square and hope blossomed within her.

At last she turned away and walked down the road towards the docks. A sailing ship bobbed restlessly on the water, sails unfurling, cracking in the wind as the vessel prepared to go out with the tide. Mary perched on the low wall and stared out to sea; she had the plans for her future sorted out and she felt happier than she had done for weeks.

Crisp hard footsteps caught her attention and she looked up quickly, knowing the walk. Her heart began to beat uncomfortably fast, though outwardly she appeared composed. The last person she expected to see now was Brandon. He stopped before her, thrusting his hands into his pockets in a gesture she had come to know well. He smiled arrogantly, looking down at her, his eyes dark and unreadable.

'I hear you were taken up to *Ty Mawr* only to be thrown out on your ear.' He spoke brutally. 'Didn't you please my brother?'

Mary glared at him furiously. 'Mind your own business.' She made to rise and walk away but he barred her way. 'Let me pass, I don't have to answer to you for anything, mind.' She spoke desperately, her eyes refusing to meet his; she longed to press herself close to him, to lay her head upon his shoulder and beg him to love her. But he would only laugh in her face.

She held her head erect and stared past him at the bobbing sails of the ship in the harbour, wishing herself a thousand miles away from Brandon Sutton. Her hands were clenched at her sides even as he caught her shoulders, his hands caressing. He drew her nearer and she stared up at him angrily.

'Mary,' his voice whispered softly in her ear. She closed her eyes and breathed in the scent of him, love flowing from every pore of her body.

'What do you want of me?' she asked, trying desperately to cling to her image of herself as a businesswoman doing no man's bidding.

'I just want to talk to you, Mary,' he said reasonably and she stared up at him, her eyes hard.

'Go ahead,' she said harshly. 'I'm listening.'

'Not here.' He took her arm. 'Come with me, Mary and stop behaving like a spoiled child.'

Although her thoughts were in a confusion of anger, she allowed him to lead her away from the docks and into the narrow streets of the town. He kept her in the shelter of his arm and she could think of nothing to say. She was a fool, she told herself, she never had nor never would love anyone the way she loved him, and he simply was not worthy.

In silence they walked arm in arm, like lovers. The air was tingling fresh as Mary breathed, the sky was darkening now and the first of the stars beginning to shine. She wondered where Brandon was leading her but she went with him trustingly. He took her through the entrance of the Mackworth Arms where a plethora of plants stood in jardinières and the pile of the carpet was softer than grass.

In the foyer, he left her for a moment and spoke to the man at the desk in hushed tones; then he was leading her up the staircase into a room that had russet curtains on the windows and a matching quilt on the large bed which dominated the room.

'Mary, sweet Mary!' He took her in his arms and kissed her mouth and even as his hand deliberately opened the bodice of her blouse, Mary's thoughts were racing. She drew away from him suddenly, her heartbeats uneven.

'What's this place?' She looked round her at the grand wash-stand covered in green marble, the high ornate gaslights and the dark tones of the wall coverings.

'It's a hotel room, silly.' Brandon took off his coat and cast it aside and it lay discarded, one sleeve turned inside out, the shot-silk lining glowing before Mary's eyes.

'Why have you brought me here?' Her voice cracked and Brandon drew her towards him, his mouth going to her throat and then moving with tantalising slowness to the open neck of her blouse. She leaned back, trying to draw away from him but his mouth had captured her nipple and flames of sheer joy ran through her veins. Mary felt his hair crisp beneath her fingers, and she closed her eyes in an involuntary movement, her breathing ragged.

'I brought you here to do this to you, Mary… and this.' Brandon kissed her breasts in turn and then his mouth was on hers, his tongue quick, sending shivers through her body, yet warning bells were ringing in Mary's mind. Brandon had not seen fit to take her to his house but had brought her instead to an hotel room. She pushed him away suddenly, shame drawing the colour from her face as she held her bodice over her breasts and stared at him, her eyes hot with unshed tears.

'You're treating me like a floosie!' she accused. 'You've brought me here just to to...' Her words trailed away and Brandon smiled.

'To make love to you, Mary, is that so wrong? I want you, I desire you greatly, you're very beautiful – but then you know that, you've been told it many times before, I daresay.'

Mary backed away from him, pain slowly filling her until she thought she must scream out loud with it. 'And then, when it was over,' she panted the words, 'were you going to leave me a shilling for my pains?'

Brandon's eyes were cold. They roved over her and she put up her hand, trying vainly to tidy the fall of long thick hair.

'I had no intention of offering you money.' His voice was hard like stones that hurt and wounded. 'I assumed you did this sort of thing with all and sundry for the sheer love of it. You're a sensual woman, Mary, you have needs and I am not averse to catering for them from time to time.'

She could scarcely believe she was hearing him properly. 'How dare you talk to me like that?' she said, buttoning her blouse with shaking fingers. 'I'm not the bad woman you make me out to be, mind.'

He folded his arms across his chest and put his head on one side as though summing her up. 'No, not bad at all, I'd say you were very good.'

Colour rushed into Mary's face as his meaning became clear and she moved towards the door, her legs almost failing to carry her. He caught her wrist and stared down into her face, his mouth twisted into an angry smile.

'You certainly gave my brother as much as he could take,' he said after a long silence in which Mary thought she might break down and cry. 'He took great pains to tell me about you – the white of your shoulders and the way you look with your hair loose – oh, he was quite graphic in his descriptions!'

'But Dean doesn't know anything about me!' Mary gasped. 'It's not true, believe me, it isn't true! Dean has never touched me in that way, never!'

Brandon caught her face in his hands and his fingers bruised her flesh.

'He shared your bed, Mary, that's why you spent all that time at *Ty Mawr.* Need I say more?'

Suddenly Mary lashed out with her fist. 'It's not true! I never let him sleep with me, he's lied to you and like a fool you believe him.'

'Then convince me, Mary,' Brandon said harshly. She shook her head in defeat, remembering suddenly and with sharp clarity the moment when Dean had come into her room while she was still half asleep. He had seen her then, had lit the gaslight, stared at her as though she was a hated stranger. She put her hand to her mouth and turned away and Brandon drew in his breath sharply.

'So you've remembered my brother bedding you?' He spoke with heavy sarcasm. 'I don't think Dean would take kindly to your casual attitude to him.'

Mary stared at Brandon appealingly. 'All right, Dean did come to my room, to my bed, I was half sleep, I...' She stumbled to a halt, knowing by the look on Brandon's face that he believed the worst of her.

He pushed her back gently but determinedly on to the bed. Mary covered her face with her hands. This could not be happening, it must be a nightmare from which she would soon awake.

He took her quickly, and when he was done he took out a handful of coins and threw them at her.

Without sparing her so much as a glance, he turned and picked up his coat and then the door closed quietly behind him. Mary lay where she was unmoving for a long time, tears coursing down her cheeks and running into her hair. She felt dead inside as though she had no more emotions, no more love or hate, just a nothingness where her heart had been.

She roused herself at last and washed in the water from the jug on the ornate marble stand. Then she brushed at her hair with her fingers and turned to look around her desperately, wondering how she would find her way out of the hotel alone.

The corridor seemed never-ending and brightly lit and Mary prayed she would meet no one. The stairs fell away towards the stained-glass doorway and she attempted to keep in the shadow of the potted plants as she passed the desk. But the porter looked at her without interest as she let herself out into the street; doubtless he saw a great many comings and goings and turned a blind eye to it all.

Out in the roadway, Mary felt the cool evening air on her cheeks with a sensation of relief. She hurried away from the noisy streets where the taverns spilled light and men out onto the pavements and up the hill towards Market Street, her breathing laboured, her heart heavy and her limbs seized with a trembling she could not control.

Only Katie was still up, sitting in the kitchen and drying her hair before the dying flames of the fire. She looked at Mary, her eyes suddenly concerned.

'Jesus, Mary and Joseph!' She rose to her feet. 'Can I get you anything, you look awful.'

Mary sank into a chair near the table and covered her face with her hands. 'Don't ask me any questions, now, please,' she said in a cracked voice. She felt Katie's hand brush her shoulder.

'Go on up to bed and rest yourself, have a little while alone while I dry my hair.'

Gratefully Mary stumbled upstairs and sank onto the bed behind the curtain. She stared for a long time out into the darkness of the night, her hands clenched into fists as she thought of what had happened to her that night.

'I hate you, Brandon Sutton,' she whispered to the stars but they seemed to mock her as at last she lay down and closed her eyes, knowing in her heart that she lied.

–

Mary quickly put her business plans into action. She paid a carpenter to make the stalls to her own requirements and saw the amazed curiosity on the faces of the other traders with a dry amusement. Next she needed to find a girl, someone who could sew, and in that instant she thought of Muriel who worked for Dean Sutton. It would do no harm if she stole away the young maid; indeed, it would go a little way to paying Dean back for his cavalier treatment of her. She did not trust herself to go up to the Big House in person, fearing that her anger might just get the better of her. Instead she gave a shilling to one of the Murphy boys, telling him to give Muriel a message. As it turned out, the girl was more than happy to do some work for Mary in her spare time. Mary smiled to herself; now she would have the use of the sewing machine belonging to the Big House as well as Muriel's expertise.

She spent the early hours of the next morning walking to and from the abattoir carrying sides of beef across her shoulders, until her whole body ached. But at last she had one stall set up and by the time the sun was rising into the sky she was ready to do business.

Instead of waiting patiently beside her stall as did the other people around her, Mary began to call out loudly: 'Fresh meat, killed today, take some home and salt it and it will keep for weeks. Lower price than any you'll find in Sweyn's Eye!'

Soon she was doing a brisk trade. People gathered just to watch and most of them stopped to buy. Mary found she was enjoying herself hugely; she took money briskly, thrusting it into the large pocket in her apron and cut up her meat with more zeal than skill. But the customers didn't seem to mind, they laughed along with her at her mistakes and she felt warmly that she was winning them over.

She ate a hot pie for her dinner, sitting alone at her stall. It seemed that the other traders were giving her a wide berth. Soon she was back at work and it was much later in the afternoon when she looked up to find Muriel standing staring at her almost in awe. Mary smiled and beckoned to the girl to come nearer.

'I know I must look a sight with my apron covered in blood, but I'm quite harmless really.' She smiled and Muriel, relaxing, drew nearer to the stall.

'Think you can run me up some undergarments on that sewing machine of yours?' she asked briefly, and when Muriel looked at her blankly Mary explained in more detail.

'I'll buy the material and you make the goods and we might both have ourselves a good profit, mind.'

Muriel looked doubtful. 'But what if Mr Sutton found out? Cook is so nosey, she would worm out of me what I was doing and then run to the master with it as soon as she could.'

Mary thought quickly. 'Well, what if I send Cook a nice piece of beef now and again and you make her a new apron or a blouse occasionally? Do you think that would keep her sweet?'

'I think so, but you'd have to put it to her,' Muriel said slowly.

'Right then,' Mary nodded, 'I'll take care of it, you just be ready to start sewing when I give you the word.' As Muriel disappeared into the crowd Mary smiled to herself. She had the girl interested and that was a good enough start. Cook would be no problem – she would take the beef and charge it to Dean Sutton, pocketing the money with no qualms at all.

By the time Mary returned to Market Street, her back ached fit to break and her shoulders felt as though they were still weighted down with a side of beef. Mrs Murphy took one look at her bloodstained clothing and shook her head ruefully. 'Sure and doesn't the meat stink just as bad as the fish, why couldn't you do something ladylike, Mary?'

Mary laughed. 'There are too many down there doing that and no butcher in sight. I've sold all I bought this morning and made a good enough profit. Tomorrow, if things go as well, I'll be very pleased.'

'Away with you now out into the back and have a bath,' Mrs Murphy said, holding her nose. 'And put them clothes in water to soak after you've finished.' Mary boiled just enough water so that she could stand in the zinc bath and soap herself all over. She would have muscles like a man at this rate, she thought ruefully as she rubbed her aching shoulders. But soon she would have more than enough money to pay Mali back what she owed her.

Mary ate her food with eyes half-shut and then climbed up the stairs to bed, glad that Katie was still out and she wouldn't have to talk. She fell asleep immediately, only to dream about Brandon and awake before sunrise with tears on her cheeks.

In the market square, the stallholders were already setting up. Mary opened up the locks and dropped the flaps and her stall was ready for business.

She laid papers out over the wooden cutting slab before wrapping a stiff canvas apron around her waist. So preoccupied was she that she didn't notice a man standing before her, waiting to catch her eye.

When she did look up, he smiled and doffed his hat and his lips were thin beneath the sparse line of his moustache.

'Good morning, Miss Jenkins,' he said. 'I'm Alfred Phillpot from the Sweyn's Eye Cooperative Movement.'

Chapter Nineteen

Brandon rode his horse with almost brutal energy. He forced the animal onwards across the dew-wet fields and the pounding of hooves echoed in his brain.

'Whoa, King' he panted, hauling on the reins and leaning forward to pat the stallion's heaving flanks. 'Good boy, that's enough for today.' He turned the animal around and headed for home at a more leisurely pace.

The sky above him was blue and it was one of those autumnal days when summer paid a brief return visit, lightening the earth and turning the rolling seas into an unbelievable blue.

But Brandon's thoughts were dark, his brow was furrowed as he thought of Mary Jenkins. He had tried to erase her from his mind and yet the image of the pain on her beautiful face as he had taken her so savagely haunted his imagination.

He had no right to be angry with her; what she did with her life was her own business and no affair of his. Why had he reacted so violently to the knowledge that his brother had made love to her? Was it the memory of Dean stealing Mary Anne Bloomfield from under his nose? His pride had taken a tumble then as it had now.

Mary Anne had been young and impressionable, but Mary Jenkins was a different kettle of fish. She was a woman of strength, she knew her own mind; had she not told him to his face that she would become Dean's mistress? She had dared him to condemn her and she was right, blast her! But the thought of his brother or any man possessing that sweet body set Brandon's teeth on edge.

But what was he making all the fuss about? he asked himself impatiently. 'Dog in the manger!' he said out loud and the words were carried away on the breeze. But it was true. He did not want Mary for himself – not as a permanent feature in his life, anyway – and yet he begrudged her finding pleasure elsewhere. He could have sworn that she had fallen in love with him, but then he had always been an egotistical bastard where women were concerned.

The sun was rising higher in the sky as Brandon rode King into the paddock behind the house. He entered the hallway glancing up at the clock, cursing himself for being a fool. Now he would be late for work and any sign of slackness on his part would be to set the men a bad example.

The atmosphere was as hot as Hades when later he walked across the floor of the mill where the men were working a heat. Once the round of heating, rolling, doubling and trimming began there could be no stopping. It was a continuous process, requiring coordination and concentrated effort. Brandon watched the men with respect as the tinbar was hauled and rolled and eventually forced into shape. He waited until the end of the heat, when the men could relax for a few minutes, before approaching them. Heath Jenkins was wiping his streaming face with his sweat cloth, his shirt jerking up to reveal a thin wiry torso.

'Come to see me at the office when your shift is finished,' he said and the boy nodded, his eyes filled with curiosity. As Brandon moved away, he smiled to himself. Heath was a good worker despite his youth and he deserved a rise in pay. The wish indirectly to benefit Mary was not a small factor in his decision, Brandon realised wryly.

In the office, Mark was leafing through the books. He glanced up as Brandon entered the small room and brushed back a lock of hair that had fallen across his eyes.

'Plenty of orders here, boss,' he said genially. 'Both Mansion Polish and Trubeys Salmon are calling out for tinbar. You've enough work here to keep you going for months.'

Brandon nodded, peering over Mark's shoulder. 'Things are looking up,' he agreed. 'I guess we're building ourselves a good reputation.' He studied the books, frowning. 'The first shipment should reach the railway before morning.' He paused. 'There's been a lot of talk against me and my handbook; there could be a demonstration outside the gates, so we'll ship the tin tonight.'

A movement at the doorway caught Brandon's eye and he looked up quickly. Rees was standing just outside the office, gripping a finger from which blood was slowly dripping.

'Nothing serious, sir,' Rees said heartily. 'Better get off home, though, get my old girl to bandage it for me, all right?'

Brandon nodded. 'Get on off with you then, and tell your wife to wash the wound clean.'

'She'll do that all right, sir,' Rees said. 'My old girl is a dab hand with herbs and potions – you remember that if you ever get the bellyache.'

Brandon watched Rees make his way out of the gates. 'We'll have to get another man over to the mill,' he said thoughtfully. 'Who do you suggest?'

Mark considered. 'I think Heath Jenkins could work the furnace for today and we could put on a boy from the wash room as a behinder. Best we can do for the moment.'

'I guess that will be fine. See to it, will you Mark.' Brandon was well pleased with his manager's suggestion, which would be a good enough reason for giving Heath a rise. Perhaps if the boy worked out well, he could be promoted permanently before long. Rees was not getting any younger and would soon need a lighter job. It was strange the way boys started in the steel at the easier jobs, then worked their way through the tough, back-breaking processes of tin making only to end their days demoted to the same tasks they had started with. It seemed an insult to offer a man boy's work, but the alternative was nothing at all.

Later when Heath arrived at the office, his face sweat-stained, lines of fatigue around his mouth and eyes, Brandon stared at him levelly.

'Mark tells me you've done well on the furnaces. I'm glad to hear it.'

Heath smiled. 'It's a bit like being a juggler with a load of tin going to fall on your head, boss. But rewarding it is, moving the plates about the oven, getting them all at a regular heat, enjoyed it I did.'

'How would you like to keep the job?' Brandon said casually, watching the boy's face light up with a sense of satisfaction. Heath rubbed at his neck with his sweat rag and grinned.

'I'd stand on my head in the corner and sing "Rule Britannia" for a proper man's job.' He paused, adding, 'with a man's wages behind it, mind.'

Brandon nodded. 'Oh, yes, there'll be that, all right.' He thrust his hands into his pockets. 'By the way, what's happening to your sister these days? I haven't seen her about lately, all right is she?'

Heath sighed. 'Had to get out of the house,' he said. 'Rented it was, see, and Mary loved it like it was her baby. That home meant everything to her. Lodging with the Murphys in Market Street she is now. Got her own stall in the square as well. Won't keep a girl like my sister down for long, be a rich woman she will in a few years.'

Brandon nodded as though he wasn't really interested. 'I guess I'm glad to hear that she's making out well enough.' He wondered how much Mary would have told Heath; she did not seem the sort to confide her personal life to anyone, not even her brother. If she had, Brandon thought wryly, Heath would hardly stand in the office looking so affable.

'Carries great pieces of beef on her shoulders, she does,' Heath said proudly. 'Strong woman she is, mind, but I told her she must get a pony and trap, it's no life for a woman humping sides of meat.'

Brandon shook his head as if to clear it. What Mary did was no concern of his, he told himself sharply; she was responsible for her own fate, she was a grown woman and he certainly owed her nothing.

'About the job,' he said smoothly, 'give it a few days, so that I can break it to Rees that he's getting moved.'

Heath moved towards the door. 'Right then, boss and thanks.' As Heath made to leave, Brandon held up his hand.

'Wait a minute, how would you like a job for tonight?' he asked. 'Mark and I will be taking some loads of tinplate to the railway station. Care to come along, ride shotgun as it were?'

Heath's face brightened. 'Sound like a good idea. What time and where?'

Brandon spoke quietly. 'At the gates, eight o'clock. I shouldn't think anyone would be expecting us to move at that time of day.'

'I'll be there, don't you worry about that, boss.'

After Heath had gone, striding through the gates as though for all the world he had not just completed a full shift, Brandon settled back in his chair. He stared down at the books open on the desk – things were looking good and if only he could meet the demands for tinbar, the business would be paying dividends before long.

He closed the ledger with a snap, irritated with the way Mary Jenkins kept intruding into his thoughts. He wished now that he had not vented his anger upon her; he should have kept her sweet so that he might continue the affair.

He could not deny that Mary had a strange, almost hypnotic appeal for him. Her ripe breasts and firm silky thighs haunted his dreams. She was a woman full of warmth and strength and there was a clear look in her eyes that became clouded only in passion.

Perhaps, he mused, he might wander down to the market square later in the afternoon and see how she was getting on. It might just be to his advantage to keep her sweet. He felt the throb of desire low in his groin, he wanted a woman, and badly, and for the moment at least Mary Jenkins had the power to assuage the hunger that had eaten away at him ever since he had lost Mary Anne Bloomfield.

The afternoon was still and dull, the clouds of pent-up rain crouching over the huddled town. Brandon strode out towards the market, feeling the need to take an hour or so off work. The wheels were turning well at the moment and the place could run without him for a little while. For now, he had other things beside tinplate on his mind.

He saw her at once. Mary was standing at her stall fastening up the shutters, snapping the locks into place. Brandon moved up behind her, admiring the slimness of her waist beneath the flannel skirt, imagining her body naked and beautiful. God, but he was in need of a woman.

Mary spun round at his approach as though she recognised his footsteps, her face closing up and her mouth becoming a thin line which was quite unbecoming to her. She put both her hands on her hips and stared at him with her head flung back, the white column of her throat running silkily to her breasts which had become partly exposed during her exertions.

'What do you want?' she demanded. 'You can't throw my skirts over my head and rape me right here, can you?'

He smiled lazily, ignoring her angry sarcasm. 'Now how did you know that was exactly what I had in mind?' he said softly. She stared at him as though bewildered as he moved towards her.

'I want to talk to you,' he said more seriously. She jerked backwards as though his eyes were fingers probing beneath her clothing.

'And what if I don't want to talk to you?' she said, but her voice was trembling. She was as keen for a tumble as he was, Brandon thought in triumph and his entire body seemed bathed in heat.

'It's about your brother.' He spoke soberly, sensing that she would need an excuse to go with him, anything to save her pride. She glanced at him quickly.

'Heath, he's not hurt is he?' Her eyes widened and the colour drained from her face.

'I guess that was clumsy of me,' he said, taking her arm. 'No, he's just fine and dandy, but I want to talk to you about him, it is important.'

Mary pocketed the keys to her stall and swung a leather pouch more securely over her arm. She had taken the bait, Brandon told himself in satisfaction.

'I've got a job for him tonight,' Brandon said. 'It will pay well enough and once I know he can handle it, he'll get more of the same.'

'What job is that?' Mary allowed him to lead her away from the market square and down into the main street of the town. He took her past the soft waters of the river and into a patch of ground that was thick with trees and shrubs.

'It's nothing very demanding,' he said gently. The sun pierced the branches, throwing a mellow light upon the drying grass. 'And my manager will be along, so will I incidentally. It's just a matter of seeing some tinbar safely on to the railway.'

Mary sighed softly. Brandon was actually talking to her as though she was a thinking human being instead of simply a woman to tumble whenever the mood took him.

Her eyes searched his face. 'Brandon, I know my brother will be willing to help you in any way he can. Heath thinks highly of you.'

'And you, Mary, what do you think of me?' He stared down at her for a long moment and the silence seemed heavy around them. 'I know I've treated you badly,' he whispered, 'but you're a fine woman, you deserve only the best.' His voice faded as he watched the changing expressions on her face.

Mary turned away from him, her head bowed, and he wondered what she was thinking. He had been a fool to treat her so casually. Mary Jenkins was a special woman, she had strength and character and he wondered how she had ever tolerated him.

'Mary, you're so beautiful,' he said and his hand rested on her shoulder. She glanced up at him and he stepped back a pace, knowing that any advance he might make would be rejected. Then she sighed softly and moved away from him and as he watched the curve of her cheek and the soft flutter of her lashes, something stirred a chord within him. He no longer thought of Mary as a woman to roll in the hay with, he was slowly but surely falling in love with her.

'Lovely Mary, so proud so beautiful,' he murmured softly but she didn't seem to hear him. She was staring through the trees as though beyond his reach, so far removed from him that he might have lost her forever by his careless use of her.

But he was realising all these things too late, he told himself. Mary must be thoroughly disillusioned with him by now, thinking of him as an animal with needs but no finer emotions.

'You think Heath will come along and help tonight then, do you, honey?' he asked as though he had nothing more important on his mind. Mary nodded her head and a wisp of silky hair came free of the pins, drifting across her face in a soft caress.

'Oh, yes, he'll help.' She looked at him steadily. 'If that's all you want to say, don't you think we'd better make our way back?'

As he took her home, walking through the mean streets, passing Copperman's Row he heard the haunting sound of music playing in the soft dimness of the twilight.

Mary looked up at him, her face shadowed, her eyes those of a woman who kept her own counsel. He no longer felt sure of himself, he did not know this new strong Mary who stood before him.

'I'll see you, Mary, soon?' He spoke softly without touching her and then, turning, left her outside the door of the shop where she was lodging.

Why hadn't he taken her more seriously from the beginning, he mused as he strode away down the street. She was a beautiful, passionate woman and she had the gift of making him feel he was the only man in the world.

Did she use the same tactics on Dean? he wondered heavily and yet he could have been wrong about her all this time. Had he underestimated Mary's strength of character?

Brandon took his watch from his pocket and glanced at it, frowning. He would have no time to return home, he would go straight down to the steelworks and wait for Mark and Heath Jenkins to show up.

In the office, he lit the gas lamp and sat down in the leather chair, feet up and resting on the top of the stove that was still warm. He had plenty of time to think about Mary and yet it was the last thing he wanted to do. He closed his eyes and her image was before him, haunting and beautiful.

Mark was the first to appear, smiling jauntily. The young manager had a white silk scarf around his neck and he seemed to be in good spirits.

'Not missing your courting too much, then?' Brandon said dryly.

'Not missing it at all, sir, just postponing it 'till later.'

Brandon smiled good-naturedly and Mark raised his eyebrows.

'I don't see you going without a woman for much longer,' he said quickly. 'Got the looks that the girls go for, I'd say – dark and brooding, like.'

Brandon was saved from answering by the appearance of Heath. He was slim and handsome and with a strength about him that reminded Brandon of Mary.

'Well, come on, let's get rolling.' Brandon rose to his feet. 'The sooner we see this delivery of tinplate safely at the railway yard, the better I'll be pleased.'

It was a dark night with little moon and the night shift was tapping out the blast furnaces. The glow tore the sky asunder, sparks flying upward with a sound as though the end of the world had come. The spectacular scene never failed to excite Brandon and he breathed in the acrid smell of the works with satisfaction. He was on his way to success; there must be no hitches, not now.

'*Duw!*' Mark stopped dead in his tracks. 'What in God's name is going on?'

Brandon moved forward, his teeth gritted together in anger. The gateway to the works was blocked with heavy timbers, it would take hours to clear it.

'Get any of the men we can spare from the foundry,' Brandon said briskly and Mark hurried away into the darkness.

'Come on, Heath, I guess we'd better make a start.' Together they lifted one of the heavy beams of wood. 'Just throw it to one side,' Brandon panted. 'If I could only get the bastard who has done this, I'd string him up.' He paused, pushing his hand through his hair. 'Who in God's name is giving out the information? Only you, Mark and I knew of the plan for tonight.'

Heath rubbed at his face. 'Well, it wasn't me, boss,' he said quickly. 'I was never one for cutting off my nose to spite my face.'

That made sense, Brandon thought and then a chill came over him. There was one other person who knew about the moving of the tin and that was Mary. The bitch! he thought in fury. She must have gone straight away and blabbed to Dean. What a fool he had been to think she was anything more than a cheap floosie.

The delay cost them an hour and Brandon finally brushed the dust from his hands, looking in Mark's direction. 'Not as bad as it could have been,' he said. 'In fact, the effort it cost to put the timber across the gate doesn't seem worthwhile. We'd better keep our eyes peeled on the journey though, in case anything else happens.'

But nothing did. The roadway leading to the railway was silent under the gas lamp and not even a rat stirred in the shadows. 'Very strange.' Brandon said. 'Something's going on, I'm sure of it.'

When he returned to the works, Joe Phillips was waiting for him. The man was off duty, wearing a cap and a rough jacket instead of his moleskin trousers and sweat shirt.

'Been a fire, Mr Sutton, sir,' he said without preliminary. 'Old Evo sent me to tell you – the press is ablaze, sir, don't seem as anything inside will be saved.' Brandon stared at Mark. 'So that's what the bastards were up to! Blocking the gate was just a diversion. Come on, we'd better get over to the press right away.'

By the time Brandon arrived on the scene the fire was raging. Flames issued out of the roof and the heat was almost unbearable. Thick choking fumes hung in the air and charred fragments of paper littered the ground. Evo's face was blackened by smoke, his eyes red and watering.

'My building and machinery all gone up in flames, Mr Sutton,' he said in despair. 'I was only out an hour and by the time I got back it was too late.'

Brandon stared at the flames, a great bitterness and anger filling him. He had spent long hours of study working out prices, gauging hours of work involved in the making of tinplate. Both in Philadelphia and here in Wales he had worked on it, and what had come out of it all but this terrible scene of destruction.

Evo shook his head. 'Your book is finished. Every copy available was in there, nothing left of it now.'

Brandon gazed up at the billowing flames. There was one copy, the one he kept for himself.

'We'll have to start again,' he said harshly. 'I'm damned if I'll give up now.'

The fire raged for hours and by the time the last flame flickered and died, Brandon could taste and smell charred paper. He moved among the ashes, kicking at the curls of paper with anger burning within him. Something caught his eye and he bent and retrieved a button from amid the dirt. He cursed for the object was hot, but he could detect the sign of an eagle in the blackened metal. He frowned, he had seen it somewhere before but where?

'*Duw*, there's a mess,' Heath said in an awed voice. 'Someone must hate you real bad. Mr Sutton.'

Brandon pocketed the amulet and strode away from the ruins of the press building which had been little more than a shed. 'Aye, that's for sure,' he replied. And he knew just who hated him that badly, he thought angrily. But he could hardly tell Heath that his sister Mary must have gone running off to Dean at the earliest opportunity, bent on betraying one brother to the other.

'There's nothing more to be done here tonight,' he said. 'We might just as well go home.' He took one backward look at the still smoking ruins and bitterness filled his mouth like bile. But he would not accept defeat. He would start again and one day soon the handbook would see the light of day in spite of everything.

Dean Sutton sat in the bar of the Cape Horner and mused on the old days. Once before he had sat here in the same place, planning with Rickie Richardson to destroy Rickie's brother Sterling. Now, two years later, Dean was working against Brandon, his own brother. It was strange how history had a habit of repeating itself. He considered communicating the thought to Gerwin Price who sat alongside him, but the man was a moron. His hair stuck up in tufts on his head, he had a button missing from his coat and his chin and jaw jutted like those of bulldog. All in all, he was perhaps the meanest man Dean had ever seen.

When Rickie entered the bar he had beside him an older man, his face like leather, his hands gnarled. This then must be the one feeding the information to Rickie about the Beaufort Steel and Tinplate Company.

'Are we late?' Rickie said with a smug smile.

'No, I guess I was early,' Dean replied affably, tipping back his hat, his narrowed eyes missing nothing.

'This is the furnaceman I told you about,' Rickie said. 'Rees has no reason to be friendly to Brandon Sutton.'

The man had perched on a stool. 'There's never a truer word been spoken,' he said. 'Going to chuck me out on the scrapheap they are! I heard them talking, hear more than they give me credit for, been on the cards for some time now that I'd be shoved off into the wash house.'

Dean ignored the man. He seemed the sort who would bear anyone a grudge if the price was right.

'Is it over?' he asked Rickie. The other man nodded.

'Of course. The press is burned to the ground. A very unfortunate accident, can't think how the fire started.' He exchanged a look with Gerwin Price. 'A place like that, made of wood and filled with paper, didn't stand a snowball's chance in hell.' He laughed. 'All I'm sorry about is that I didn't see Brandon's face when he arrived on the scene. Silly sod, trying to make fair wages for the workers indeed, he must be mad.'

'He is, I guess,' Dean agreed laconically.

Rickie grinned. 'Not so daft though. I saw him with a big busty wench going into the woods; only one thing on his mind and something no man can be blamed for, I'd say.'

Dean felt as though he had been thrown into a cold river. He knew that Rickie was describing Mary and it still rankled that Brandon had got to the girl first.

'Nothing's more stupid than trying to bring out a book for the workers when most of them are too ignorant to read it,' Dean said harshly.

The furnaceman was shifting uncomfortably in his seat and Dean pinned him with a stare. 'I suppose, being one of the workers concerned, you don't agree,' he said flatly.

The man shook his head. 'No, I don't.'

Dean felt vicious. He longed to hit out at someone and this furnaceman who was now superfluous would do very nicely.

'Then get out of here and forget the money you were going to earn from me.' If he had expected the man to beg, he could not have been more wrong.

'To the blazes with you and your money then!' Rees rose to his feet and stared down at Dean with fierce brown eyes. 'Stuff your money right up your arse and don't ask anything of me again.'

Dean watched him go and slowly lit a cigar. 'I think you should arrange for the man to have a little accident, Gerwin,' he said thoughtfully. 'We don't want anyone who can point a finger at us.'

Gerwin immediately rose to his feet, violence being something he understood very well. He loped out of the bar like some wild animal set free and Rickie shook his head.

'Don't trust Gerwin. I know he works well but he has no intelligence, moves on instinct like a big cat. I think he'd cut his own granny's throat for a shilling.'

Dean shrugged his broad shoulders. 'I'm not asking you to like him,' he said. 'Can't say I care for him overly much myself, but he serves his purpose well enough. Come on, get some drinks in. Rickie, it's your turn to pay.'

-

The finding of Rees the furnaceman's body was a nine-day-wonder in the town, for Sweyn's Eye was not used to murder. On the body was a black substance – carbon, some said, as though the man had been in a fire. But Rees had been battered to death in a vicious attack which left him bleeding in a gutter not a stone's throw from the bright lights of the Cape Horner.

A restless feeling prevailed over the streets for almost two weeks, but after that the doxies began to reappear, slinking along the alleyways like cats, plying their trade as carelessly as ever. Only three men knew the truth of what had happened that night and they were not about to reveal the secret to anyone.

Chapter Twenty

It was Sunday and the church bells rang out all over the sleeping town. Slowly, Sweyn's Eye came alive to the misty November morning. Smoke began to rise from the chimneys, lights went on in gloomy kitchens, back doors opened and the pattern of the day was set.

Mary still lay in her bed behind the curtain, listening to the running footsteps of the Murphy children, hearing their laughter and the calling voices with a dismal sense of being an outsider, belonging nowhere and to no one. Soon she must make a move, find a small house to rent; she could not presume upon Mrs Murphy's good nature for much longer.

She rose from her bed and shivered in the cold air. Down below in the backyard, she could see Katie, her face numb with sleepiness, filling the huge kettle with water from the pump.

Mary sighed and climbed back under the bedclothes, hugging their warmth to her chilled limbs. She lay back against the pillows and behind her closed eyelids came a picture of Brandon. He had been gentle and loving last time they had met. He had not punished her with his body as he had done on their previous encounter. He had wooed her, beguiled her, made her cry with passion – yet in the week that had followed, there had been no word from him.

But then she knew he was greatly troubled. Heath had come to see her, told her about the handbook and how when it was almost ready for distribution the work of months had been destroyed by fire. Mary had been concerned for Brandon, longing to see him again, wanting him in her arms so badly that she ached and yet he had not come to her.

She sighed softly. She must put Brandon out of her thoughts, for she had problems enough of her own. Tomorrow she was to go before a board of officials from the Cooperative Movement; Alfred Phillpot had been adamant about it.

'No one trades in the streets of Sweyn's Eye without our approval,' he had told her in a smooth officious manner.

'Top of the mornin' to you, Mary! I've brought you a nice hot cup of tea.' Katie stood peering round the curtain and Mary smiled gratefully.

'It's cold enough to freeze the balls off a brass monkey, sure it is!' Katie sat on the edge of the bed and shivered and Mary took the cup from her with a rueful smile.

'Thanks, though I'd rather it was in the cup than spilled all over me.' She sipped the tea appreciatively. 'It is a cold morning, I just put my toes out of bed and then decided to get back under the blankets again.'

'There's a good fire blazing downstairs,' Katie said. 'The trouble is that you can't get near it for my gaggle of brothers. Me mam is sitting with her knees practically against the bars.'

She smiled. 'Sundays are usually quiet, for all the family goes to mass, but we slept late this morning and you'll have to put up with our noise.'

Mary made no reply. She was thinking of Canal Street and how the sabbath had been a day of pure enjoyment for her, a time when she could dust and clean the house until the furniture shone. One day she would buy her own house and then no one would be able to take it away from her.

'Jesus, Mary and Joseph, you're not listening to a word and me pouring my heart out here!'

'I'm sorry, Katie,' Mary said quickly. 'I'm still half asleep, go on with what you were saying.'

'Be sure to listen then! I was tellin' you about Mark; asked me out again, so he has, gettin' very keen if I read the signs right.'

Mary looked at the Irish girl attentively now. 'Mark seems a fine man from the little I've seen of him, and Heath has a great deal of respect for him. He must be special to be manager of the Beaufort Works and him so young. But what do you think of him, Katie, that's what's important?'

Katie put her head on one side consideringly. 'I'm not sure. I like him well enough, but do I love him, can I love anyone again?' She shook back her red-gold hair. 'I just don't know.'

'There's something I know, you're not going to spend the rest of your life alone, you're too much of a born mother for that. I've seen you with your baby brother; you enjoy bathing and feeding him, I can see it in your eyes.'

'Maybe, but a girl can't marry a man just to have his baby.' Katie rose from the bed and took Mary's empty cup. 'Come downstairs when you're ready and I'll cook you a bit of breakfast.'

Mary listened to Katie's footsteps hurrying down the uncarpeted stairs and then she got out of bed and dressed quickly. She was not looking forward to washing at the pump in the yard, but Katie's house did not boast an indoor sink with running water. Spoiled, she'd been, Mary told herself; living in Canal Street had made her take so much for granted.

By the afternoon, a weak sun had penetrated the clouds. Mary pulled a shawl around her shoulders and left the house in Market Street, thankful to be alone with her thoughts. The Murphys were kindness itself, but the noise of the three young boys and the continual shouting of Tom Murphy as he attempted to quieten them was giving Mary a headache.

She wandered past the market square and stood for a moment looking at her own lock-up stalls with a feeling of pride. She had made a good start with her foodstuffs, selling cheeses now as well as bacon and fresh meat.

The clothes stall had progressed a little more slowly, with Muriel fearful at first of using the sewing machine at *Ty Mawr*. But this last week she had gained courage and had turned out a sizeable number of undergarments which went from the stall almost as soon as they were set out. Everything had been fine until Mr Alfred Phillpot had come along with his grim eyes and his long face and persisted in complicating matters.

But nothing would stop her now, Mary thought with determination. She knew she was supplying goods and food at prices the workers could afford. Even those on strike were able to buy from her, for she never quibbled however small the sale.

She found herself walking past the docks and towards the snaking line of the river Swan. The sun turned the brackish water into gold and the last flare of autumn leaves patterned the swiftly running surface like jewels.

The hill was before her and up there in one of the houses with windows gleaming in the bright afternoon air, Brandon would be living and breathing and perhaps thinking about her.

On an impulse, Mary decided to walk up the hill and see if she could catch a glimpse of him. Her heart beat rapidly with the daring of her thoughts. But she told herself that she and Brandon were lovers, real lovers now; he wanted her as much as she wanted him, didn't he? Yet when she neared the house that stood elegant and unfamiliar in the soft sunshine, Mary's mouth was dry with fear.

She knew she could never pluck up courage to knock on the ornate door and face some cheeky maid who would doubtless ask embarrassing questions. So she watched from a distance, longing by sheer effort of will to bring Brandon to her side. She ached to be in his arms, to look up into his turquoise eyes and see them misted with emotion.

How long she stood staring in the direction of the house she could not afterwards remember, but she was reluctant to leave without at least a glimpse of Brandon's tall handsome frame.

She leaned against the dry bark of a tree. Above her the branches were partly stripped of their leaves, reaching skyward like skeleton fingers.

Mary sighed. She might as well begin the homeward journey, for she was not going to see Brandon today. For a moment she was angry with him, how could he be so casual? Did he not feel the need for her in every pulse of his body? For that was the way she felt about him.

She left the small wooded copse and caught a tram down into town, with a sense of having lost something precious which remained with her for the rest of the day.

–

Mr Alfred Phillpot met Mary in the doorway of the hall, where the body of officials sat waiting to hear her speak. She stared around her, seeing men in starched shirts and one or two women in high-necked serge gowns – heavy and dark as befitted the weather.

Outside a heavy rain was falling and as Mary had walked past the market square, she had seen stallholders shivering in the downpour. Her own stalls were unaffected, closed in, the stock dry and secure, and she congratulated herself on her innovative ideas.

Mr Phillpot greeted her sombrely and led her forward into the body of the hall. It was chilly and damp and rain ran along the outside of the windows, dropping like tears onto the ledges.

'We just want to ask you some questions.' Alfred Phillpot didn't smile, he settled himself opposite her so that she was alone, facing the people of the Cooperative Movement as though she was a criminal and they about to pass judgement on her.

'Why have you not approached us?' he began his attack at once. 'New traders in the area have a moral duty to join the Cooperative Movement. We are for the people against the bosses who force their workers to trade in company shops.' He paused dramatically. 'We do not need freeloaders in Sweyn's Eye, we need to stand together and become strong.'

Mary stared at him, her eyebrows raised. 'This is the first time I've heard of your existence, mind,' she said unperturbed. 'If you want people to join you, then I suggest you go about it in a more friendly fashion. I feel as though I'm being condemned by you for starting out on my own. I wasn't aware that I had to ask the permission of the Cooperative.'

She knew she was saying all the wrong things. Of course it was better for the traders to work together, but the high-handed way in which Alfred Phillpot had spoken was not calculated to gain her support.

Staring at the row of uncompromising faces before her, she felt that not one of the people present in the hall looked as though they knew what a day's honest work was all about.

'Tell me,' she said as she moved towards a woman who was seated near the centre of the group, 'what sort of job do you have?' There was silence for a moment and then Alfred Phillpot spoke up.

'Mrs Asquith is the owner of the Asquith Arms. I'm sure you must have heard of that fine hotel.'

'What I want to know is, have you been out selling goods yourself, Mrs Asquith, or do you merely own shares in the Cooperative?' No one spoke and Mary put her hands on her hips, facing the people who thought fit to put her on trial.

'I know what it's like to come home after stoking boilers for ten hours, sometimes twelve hours a day,' she said evenly. 'I have no servants to clean, fetch and carry for me and no fancy hotel to fall back on. I'm a street trader, nothing else and so I resent the way I have been summoned here as though I were a criminal.'

Mrs Asquith rose to her feet, placing a handkerchief to her nose and sniffing derisively. 'I think we have made an error of judgement,' she said haughtily. 'Obviously, Miss Jenkins is not a suitable person for us to deal with.'

Mary made for the door, drawing her shawl around her shoulders. 'That's quite all right by me,' she said, her voice flat and hard with anger. 'I don't think you're suitable for me either.'

Outside she breathed deeply, trying to calm her anger. Mr Phillpot was right behind her, his face even longer, his eyes those of a mournful dog.

'You've made a bad mistake, Miss Jenkins,' he said softly. 'I think you will find yourself unable to trade in Sweyn's Eye after this.'

Mary stared at him in silence for a long moment. 'Are you making threats, Mr Phillpot?' she asked quietly. He shook his head at once.

'Oh, no, Miss Jenkins, I'm simply trying to warn you.' He turned away and disappeared back into the hall and Mary shook her head in bewilderment.

Why couldn't they just leave her alone? She wanted nothing but to make a living, which reminded her that she should get to the square and open her stall as soon as possible – she had some fresh beef to sell and it would not keep another day.

She did a brisk trade as usual and by the time she was packing up her stall for the night, the foodstuffs had sold out. There were still a few garments on her second stall and Mary covered them with paper before locking up. She knew that she must get more stocks in for the morning and it seemed only sensible to go for them now while she was in her stained apron and heavy working boots. But she felt tired and chilled as she went towards the Murphy household. She had lately taken to borrowing the fish cart, for with Big Jim to take the strain she could transport her stock much more efficiently.

Tom Murphy had been about to give the huge horse a rubbing down, but he handed Mary the reins at once, a broad smile on his face.

'Have the animal by all means, Mary, but you'll be responsible for seein' to the creature when you return.' She nodded, a feeling of tiredness almost overwhelming her. Then she sighed and clucked her tongue and Big Jim ambled forward good-naturedly.

The warehouse stood long and full of shadows, sacks of oatmeal lying around the floor in shapeless humps. Against the far wall stood chests of tea and further along were boxes full of tins of sardines. Mary had quickly learned that the plain foodstuffs were the quick sellers.

A man loomed out of the shadows so suddenly that she was startled. 'Oh, Jake, I just wanted a few things for the stall. I'm not too late, am I?'

His glance slid away from her. 'Can't serve you, Miss Jenkins,' he said flatly. He began to draw the big heavy doors together and Mary frowned, puzzled by his attitude.

'What do you mean, Jake, there's mysterious you're being, why can't you serve me?'

Jake came forward into the light and glanced round furtively. 'You know this is my full-time job here in the warehouse. I couldn't live on the money Mrs Evans pays me to be her bailiff.' He paused for a moment. 'It's Mr Phillpot, you see, he's been here from the Cooperative, says if I sell to you all the Coop shops won't buy from my warehouses any more.' He shrugged. 'I can't be expected to give up big orders like that, especially for a Johnnie-come-lately like you.'

Mary felt anger run through her like quicksilver. She put her hands on her hips and Jake took a step backwards as though in mortal fear of her.

'I'm sorry, but there you are, missus. I've got me livelihood to think of. You can't blame me for looking after what's my own.'

'There's only one person I blame and that is Alfred Phillpot,' Mary said fiercely. Her arms dropped to her sides. 'And if I go elsewhere, I'll hear the same story, I suppose,' she said in resignation. Jake nodded his grizzled head.

''Fraid so, no one will sell to you, not unless you travel outside the borough, that is. I don't think Mr Phillpot's influence is felt so far as Skewen or Neath, though.'

For a moment hope flickered in Mary's heart, only to die as quickly as it had come. It would be pointless travelling such distances, not unless she found herself some transport.

She clucked her tongue at Big Jim and the horse ambled forward. 'You'd be no good to me, boyo, willing though you are.' As she stroked the animal's rough mane Mary's eyes were hard and dry and there was a tight knot of pain and anger in her throat. But one thing she was determined on: Alfred Phillpot would not have the last word. And what's more, in the not-too-distant future, the Cooperative Movement would be begging her to join them.

'Come on, Jim,' Mary whispered, guiding the big horse towards the road. 'We might as well go home.'

–

The laundry was hotter than ever, Katie thought as she pulled at the string that bound the brown paper parcel of sheets. She pushed back her red-gold hair and stared out of the window for a moment, not seeing the rainswept November landscape. Her face softened as she thought of Mark, for he was becoming more important to her with every day that passed.

Mark was forceful, ardent, handsome, everything she could want in a man and yet Katie was reluctant to commit herself to him. She bit her lip, remembering with a sense of pain how much she had been in love with William.

But that was a long time ago. He had been killed near the Kilvey Deep – not, strangely enough, in the explosion that flooded a string of pits but in an accident, falling from a moving car. In any case he had been a bad one, Katie's mother had always said so.

'Taking you to his bed doesn't bind a man to you, beast gives as much to beast.' Katie could hear her mother's words even now and she shivered suddenly.

'Goose walked over your grave?' Sally Benson was standing staring at Katie, her eyes as always hostile, though her tone was amiable enough.

'You could say that.' Katie had no intention of confiding her innermost thoughts to Sally. She was an insensitive woman; she seemed to grow older but no wiser and she was still as ugly as sin.

The door to the long room opened and without waiting to be announced, Mr Sutton was striding down the length of the packing room with an angry expression on his face.

'This really will not do!' He held a letter in his hand and he shook it in Sally Benson's face. 'Complaints, complaints, that's all I ever seem to get from my customers these days. I guess something is going wrong here and I want to know the reason why.'

There was a long silence and then Katie spoke up. 'Well, one thing's for sure, you can't blame Mary Jenkins for what's happening now. Wrong it was to get rid of her, best overseer the Canal Street Laundry ever had, so she was.'

'Shut your mouth!' Sally Benson flashed her a look of pure hatred. 'It's the workers, Mr Sutton, lazy idle lot they are, won't take to be told, slacking all the time.'

Katie pushed the parcel she had been tying to one side. 'Jesus, Mary and Joseph!' she exploded. 'If you'll believe that, Mr Sutton, then you're as green as an Irish shamrock, so you are.'

'Don't be insolent, girl.' The old man looked at her, his face growing red. Sally wasn't slow to take advantage of his irritation.

'She's one of the idlest girls here, is that Katie Murphy.' She spoke with spiteful sharpness. 'Just caught her daydreaming, I did. No wonder the work don't get done around here, I have to be chasing them all the time.'

'You are a liar, Sally Benson,' Katie said hotly. 'You always have been and always will be.'

'Enough!' Mr Sutton glared at Katie. 'You are a friend of Mary Jenkins, I presume? Well, then, perhaps you'd like to leave the laundry since you think it's not well-run in her absence?'

Katie took off her apron with shaking fingers. 'Right then, so be it, but you'll be sorry, Mr Sutton, and that's for sure. Getting rid of fine workers and keeping on the bad 'uns is not doing the laundry any good. Facts speak for themselves and there were no complaints when Mary ran the place, so put that in your pipe and smoke it!'

She left the laundry with head high and marched down the rickety staircase and out into the yard. At the gates, she turned back and stared at the old building for a long moment. It had been part of her life since her childhood and a great emptiness filled her at the thought of leaving behind so many happy memories. Tears misted her eyes, but Katie brushed them aside impatiently.

''Tis daft you are, Katie Murphy!' she told herself briskly. Yet she stood in the gloom of the November evening, watching the lights go on in the laundry and it was as though she was a child again and excluded from a birthday party. At last she turned and walked slowly along Canal Street, her footsteps heavy.

She could not help but glance into the window of the house where Mary had lived. She saw new and richer curtains at the windows now and white fluffy net across the glass for privacy. So much was changing and Katie felt as though she were being swept away by a tide of events over which she had no control.

As she neared Market Street, she began to worry what her mammy would say about her getting the sack. Tom Murphy would not blame his daughter for one moment; he was a strange man, harsh in many ways and overfond of his booze, but he was fair-minded and Katie knew that he loved her best out of all his children.

Just the same, as she opened the door into the house her heart was heavy. She was not looking forward to telling her parents that she was no longer a working girl.

Chapter Twenty-One

As the frosty fingers of winter touched Sweyn's Eye, the town retreated into itself. Doors no longer stood open but were firmly closed, with the smoke from a myriad chimneys telling the tale of roaring fires behind black-leaded grates. Mary, shivering inside her boxlike stall in the market, found the call was for winter clothes cheap and enduring and she made her plans accordingly. She had been virtually cut off from buying foodstuffs and so had been forced to direct her attention to the only other line open to her, that of making clothing.

She had taken a trip to the woollen mills outside the bounds of Sweyn's Eye and had managed to bring back with her a respectable stock of shawls and woollen undergarments, carrying them on the cart with Katie driving Big Jim. The prices were low as she collected the purchases herself direct from the manufacturer, and so she could undercut most of the large stores in town, including those belonging to the Cooperative Movement. Meanwhile Muriel continued to sew linen and coarse calico garments and between the two lines Mary found that she was more than making a fair living.

But it was cold and bleak and during the worst of the bitter weather few customers ventured into the market. Mary stood now rubbing her chilled hands, drawing her thick shawl closer round her shoulders, stamping her feet to keep the circulation moving.

She caught sight of a man with a shaven head a little distance away and her thoughts turned to Billy. She could remember every line of the letter he had sent her. It was a desolate cry for help, begging her to write and tell him she was still faithful and she wondered uneasily if he had learned of her affair with Brandon. She had made yet another attempt to see him, only to be turned away once more from the huge hostile prison doors.

Now she pushed the unwelcome thoughts aside, dreaming with nostalgia of the laundry hot and steamy with the scent of clean linen permeating the long, peaceful room. She had been sorry to leave and yet, in a strange way, Grenville Sutton had done her a favour, for now she was her own woman and she would not change that for the world.

'Mary, I've been talking to you for a solid five minutes and you haven't heard a word I've said!'

Mary looked up, startled. 'Jake! I didn't hear you, I was miles away. There's soft you must think me.' She stared at him curiously. 'Have you come to tell me that I can buy food from you after all?' Jake shook his head and there was such a hangdog expression on his face that she felt sorry for him.

'No, I haven't, Mary, sorry I am about that, mind. I've come to ask you can I buy that.' He gestured to the locked-up stall. 'It's only standing idle after all, isn't it?'

She considered his question for a moment, her hands on her hips. 'Let me get this right – you won't sell me goods, yet you want my stall so that you can have the trade, am I right?'

Jake rubbed his hand against the roughness of the stubble on his chin.

'Well, seeing that you're not able to sell sardines and bacon and tea and such, I don't see any harm in me doing it instead. Good idea of yours, Mary Jenkins, too good to let it waste.'

'What about Alfred Phillpot?' Mary asked flatly. 'Aren't you afraid of crossing him?'

Jake had the grace to look ashamed. 'Well, he won't say anything so long as I support the Coop, see. I'd give you a good price though, Mary. Just think – you could put the money into buying more stock. Stick to clothes and you'll be all right.'

Mary's first instinct was to refuse and send Jake away with a flea in his ear, but she paused. The money would be useful, there was no doubt about that. She was still lodging with the Murphy family and dearly wanted a place to rent where she could be alone. And Jake was right in one thing, the stall was doing her no good standing closed-up and idle.

'Come on,' Jake wheedled. 'You don't need two stalls, not now, you might as well sell.'

'All right,' Mary said at last. 'But I'm going to put the stall up for auction and if you want it, Jake, you'll just have to bid in competition with everyone else.'

He looked at her as though she had suddenly grown two heads. 'You can't do that,' he blustered and Mary smiled.

'Why not? It's my stall isn't it?'

'There's a hard woman you've become, Mary Jenkins,' Jake said with something like admiration in his voice. 'Be taking on the Coop and beating the lot of 'em soon, I'll wager.'

Mary grinned at him. 'Good luck in the bidding and thanks for giving me the idea, Jake.'

That night the Murphy household was a hive of activity. Everyone except the youngest of the boys was engaged in making posters that boldly proclaimed a 'Grand Auction' to take place on Saturday next at three o'clock prompt.

'This will shake 'em all up for sure.' Katie pushed back her silky hair, her eyes bright with mischief. ''Tis glad I am that I left the laundry. Fun it is working for you, Mary Jenkins.'

Mary made a face. 'Aye, but there's very little money in it as yet. As soon as matters improve you'll have a proper wage, don't you worry.'

Katie leaped to her feet as there was a sudden knocking on the door. 'That'll be Mark, I'll bring him in and he can help us.'

Mary exchanged glances with Mrs Murphy. The woman smiled in satisfaction, her pale eyes warm.

'She's with a good 'un now,' Mrs Murphy said as she pushed the last of the posters away from her with a sigh. 'A great deal different he is from that waster William Owen.' She made the sign of the cross. 'Not that I should speak ill of the dead, but hurt my girl that's all he did, used her and gave her pain. I only hope she handles this one with more wisdom.'

'Katie is all right,' Mary replied reassuringly. 'She has her head screwed on the right way and she won't do anything foolish.' She spoke the words with well-meaning conviction, but even as they left her lips she was thinking how little sense had to do with feelings. She who had given herself wholeheartedly to Brandon Sutton had allowed desire to overrule her senses.

But then Katie might well be different. Once bitten, twice shy as the saying went, yet as the Irish girl came into the room at Mark's side her face was flushed, her eyes shining and she had the distinct look of someone who has just been kissed.

'Evening to you.' Mark's voice was pleasant and yet strong. He had a good look about him, Mary decided, and he would make Katie an excellent husband.

'What this?' Mark picked up one of the posters and a chorus of eager voices answered him. Laughing, he held up his hand. 'You're like a crowd of parrots for heaven's sake. Mary, you tell me – it seems to be your doing.'

'It is,' Mary agreed. 'I'm auctioning one of my lock-up stalls. Unusual they are, you see, everyone else having open tables so that they have to take away the stock each night and set it all up again in the morning.'

Mark smiled. 'Enterprising you certainly are, Mary.' They smiled at each other in genuine liking and Mary felt that she had found an ally. She admitted to herself that at first she had been drawn to Mark because of his association with Brandon, but now she felt he would become a valued friend.

'Well, then, let's get this show on the road,' Mark said cheerfully. 'If this is going to be an auction, let us make sure it's a good one and get these bills posted.'

Mary felt an air of excitement as she stepped out into Market Street. She would show the Cooperative Movement and Alfred Phillpot that she could manage very nicely without them, thank you!

The day of the auction turned out to be bright with a pale sun washing over the square. Mary wondered if it was the novelty of the event that brought out the sightseers or the kindly weather.

Auctions were usually reserved for copper and steel owners and their kind, held in the comfort of the Mackworth Arms. Here in Market Square were gathered a motley crowd of the town's inhabitants. Men with stiff Sunday collars and good suits stood alongside fellows in working clothes who had come straight from the copper or the tin, sweat still streaking their faces.

There were women present too and Mary glimpsed Delmai Richardson in the crowd, standing cheek by jowl with a cockle-woman who wore a flat basket hat and dark checked shawl and a black and white apron.

Mary was relieved that Mark had agreed to take over the job of conducting the bidding, for she found that her knees were trembling now that the moment had come. She felt Katie catch her arm and smiled at the enthusiasm on the Irish girl's face.

''Tis exciting, to be sure!' Katie sounded breathless and though Mary was outwardly composed, she too felt a surge of exhilaration.

The bidding began briskly and Mary's head whirled with the sound of voices ringing across the square. Mark was in total command of the situation, his manner firm and confident, his mind quickly grasping the possibilities almost before they presented themselves.

'This is not just a flat table you're bidding for, remember,' he said clearly. 'This is a new idea, a revolutionary method of stall holding whereby you can lock up your stock and leave it here while you go off home. And of course the patent is pending, so don't any of you think of going away and copying the idea because you won't get away with it.'

Mary gasped and whispered excitedly in Katie's ear. 'That's the first I've heard of any patent! There's a cheek your Mark's got, but he's clever, mind.'

Eventually the stall was knocked down to Jake Zimmerman whose face was flushed and triumphant as he handed the purse of money to Mark. 'Got it after all, Mary Jenkins,' Jake said with smug satisfaction and Mary stared at him feeling a small dart of uneasiness.

'Paid a high enough price for it too,' she replied. 'Perhaps that will teach you not to cross Big Mary.'

'Teach me, is it? Well, we'll see and don't worry, it's no price at all for me to pay, *merchi*.' Jake smiled enigmatically. 'I'm well satisfied with today's work, though I daresay you'll not be too pleased once the stall is opened. But then you'll have to wait until Monday morning to see the meaning behind my words.' He lifted his hat. 'Good day to you, Mary Jenkins.'

Mary shook her head, determined not to let Jake with his mysterious words put a damper on her high spirits.

'You must both come back to my house for a meal.' Mark put his arm around Mary's shoulders in a friendly gesture at the same time as he hugged Katie's slim young frame against him.

Mary smiled at him. 'You've been the one to do all the work so far,' she said. 'I think we should be treating you to a meal.'

'Oh, come on, Mary!' Katie pleaded. 'Me mammy can't say nothin' if you come with us.' She made a face. 'You know how she'll nag if I go off alone.'

Mary capitulated. 'All right, why not?' As she turned to leave Market Square behind her, she was determined to put all feelings of uneasiness out of her mind. She would talk to Mark about Brandon and perhaps learn how the business of the handbook was faring. A warm glow ran through her; it seemed so long since she had actually been in Brandon's arms that he had become almost like a dream lover, a man of her clouded sleepy thoughts rather than one of flesh and blood. Just to speak of him would make him a reality once more.

Mark's house was small and neat, a cottage tucked away in the fold of the hills. Below, the river shaped like a horseshoe, seemed spun gold in the pale sunlight.

Mary was aware of Katie softly touching the smooth satin wood of the polished table, the silk of the furnishings and guessed what she was thinking, that one day she might come here as mistress of the house. In that moment, Mary envied Katie so much that it was like a pain throbbing within her.

She would never be wife to any man, she was convinced of it. Mistress, perhaps – and indeed, she supposed that would be her title now if anyone knew of her relationship with Brandon. But perhaps the name given her would not be so kind, she thought ruefully. She would more likely be described as a floosie, a hoyden, a woman who gave herself without the respectability of marriage or even the tenuous status of a kept woman.

'Make yourselves comfortable.' Mark said and his eyes were resting upon Katie's face bright and glowing with happiness. There was a softness in the way he spoke that told Mary he was in love, yet perhaps he didn't even know it himself yet.

She seated herself near the window and stared down into the valley. It was beautiful to see, with soft folding hills running down and to the south the sea laving a long sweeping golden shore. And yet Sweyn's Eye had another face; the gaunt features of industry.

In some places the ground was barren and ugly where the copper and steel had left their scars. Great stacks rose skywards, shooting flames and poisons into the clouds. But all that was hidden from sight here and Mary sighed softly, her chin resting in her hands, her eyes almost closed in dreamy contemplation.

Then she was alert, for a tall figure was coming up the hill riding high in the saddle of a black horse. Mary knew at once that it was Brandon and her mouth was dry, her hands shaking even as she told herself not to behave like a foolish girl.

'Mark!' She had to raise her voice, for he and Katie had disappeared into the kitchen. 'You have another visitor.'

Her blushing cheeks went unnoticed in the flurry of greetings as Brandon entered the cottage. Mark quickly told him about the auction and by the time he turned towards her, Mary had her feelings under control. No one would have guessed that she was anything but a casual stranger to Brandon Sutton.

‘Good for you, Miss Jenkins,’ he said blandly, his face lacking any emotion, his turquoise eyes unreadable. ‘I’m pleased to hear you’re doing well.’

Mary moved away from him, wondering desperately how she could escape. His presence seemed to fill the small cottage so that the very walls appeared to vibrate with the force of his energy.

She sank into a chair. She would rather be anywhere than here, she thought desperately. How could she sit so still, knowing Brandon was so near that she could reach out and touch him. She watched him covertly as he talked easily with his manager, Mark’s regard for his boss being plain to see in the eagerness of his expression and the positive way he spoke.

Mary’s heart seemed to be pounding so loudly that she wondered that no one else appeared to notice. Her hands trembled even as she strove to appear calm. She studied every turn of Brandon’s head and listened to the intonations of his voice. Though he treated her casually, she knew that her love for him was strong and deep-rooted. And as hopeless as it was, she could no more deny her feelings than she could leap from the mountain into the river below.

Mark’s seating arrangements were destined to throw Mary into a fresh wave of panic, for she was on Brandon’s right hand, so close that his knee accidentally touched hers. She felt colour flooding into her cheeks and bent her head praying that no one would notice her confusion. She was unaware of what she ate and her face ached with the effort of smiling politely whenever anyone spoke to her. When the meal was finished, Mark rose to his feet, catching Katie round her waist and lifting her bodily from her chair.

‘Come with me, my lady, you’re going to help me wash the dishes,’ he said forcefully. His eyes met Katie’s and she looked away, her colour high. Mary envied them for the unconscious simplicity of their love. Between them stood no barriers, they could marry tomorrow if they wished.

'You've been very silent.' Brandon's voice startled her and Mary turned to him, trying not to look too closely into the expressive blue eyes.

'And you've scarcely looked at me.' She lifted her chin defiantly, determined not to make matters easy for him.

'If I look too hard, I might feel like ravishing you,' he said, but his voice was cold. 'Perhaps such experiences are commonplace events in your life.' His tone was insulting, his eyes running over as though she was a floosie on sale to any man. She drew a quick breath, feeling pain sharp and searing within her. Whatever she had expected from Brandon, it was not his cold cynicism.

Before she knew what she was doing Mary's hand had lashed out, catching Brandon a blow across his cheek. His response was immediate: he caught her wrists and held them fast with one hand while the other traced a line along her cheekbone, slowly moving to her throat and then, deliberately, he outlined her breast. Mary gasped as though cold water had been thrown over her.

'Stop it!' she said in a low, furious voice. 'I'm not a piece of meat to be touched and inspected by the likes of you.' She struggled to move away but he held her fast. Deftly he undid the small buttons on her bodice – his mouth was warm, giving her excruciating pleasure, his tongue teasing her nipple. Warring against the desire running through her was the fear that someone would walk in and see what they were doing.

'Please, don't do that!' she whispered urgently and then his mouth had captured hers, his lips powerful and demanding.

Suddenly he released her and, shivering, she buttoned her bodice. She glanced up at him but he seemed to have lost interest in her entirely. He moved to the door, pausing in mid-stride to call out to Mark, 'I'm going now.'

Mark reappeared from the kitchen. 'Sorry, sir, didn't mean to neglect my visitors.' He smiled. 'My attention was distracted by the lovely Katie and no one would blame me, I'd wager half my pay on that. My girl is the most beautiful in all of Sweyn's Eye.' His eyes were alight and his voice shook with pride.

'I'm sure,' Brandon said dryly. 'Be down at the press tomorrow at seven o'clock prompt – there's plenty to do.' He glanced at Mary, his gaze penetrating. 'And don't go running to my brother this time, Miss Jenkins. It won't do any good, because we keep the press guarded since the unfortunate fire that destroyed almost a year's work.'

Mary rose to her feet, anger lending her strength. 'I don't know what you're talking about,' she said fiercely. 'It's not my habit to carry tales, mind, not to anybody.'

Brandon ignored her as he went outside and she could hear the low murmur of the men's voices but not the words they were saying. She imagined that she might be the subject of their conversation and clenched her hands into fists at her sides. How could Brandon believe that she would talk to his brother about him? What had she ever done to make him distrust her so, she wondered miserably.

'Sure and don't you look like you lost a guinea and found a farthing! What's wrong, Mary?' Katie was drying her hands as she entered the room from the kitchen. She looked concerned and Mary closed her eyes for a moment, unable to frame a reply.

'What is it, Mary, not feeling ill, are you?' Katie came to her side and rested the back of her hand against Mary's forehead. 'You're very hot, so you are.'

'I'm all right,' Mary protested. 'Just a slight headache, that's all. It's nothing, so don't go looking so worried.' She forced herself to smile. 'Perhaps I'll put the blame on the meal I just ate, the cook's attention was not entirely on the food.'

Katie returned Mary's smile. 'I'll tell Mark about you, so I will and him working hard in the kitchen an' all. Ah, here he is now.'

Mark appeared uneasy and Mary knew with a sinking feeling that Brandon had instructed him to say nothing about their plans in her hearing. She looked at him levelly.

'Whatever Mr Sutton says, I've never once been a cleck,' she said firmly. 'I've repeated nothing, told no one anything at all, you must believe me.'

Mark looked embarrassed. 'I'm sure the boss just thinks that the less anyone knows, the better it'll be for us all. It was a bitter blow to him to have all that work destroyed in the fire and he means to make sure it doesn't happen again.'

The joy seemed to have gone from the day. Even the elation at the result of the auction had disappeared and Mary wasn't sorry when Katie looked at the clock ticking on the mantelpiece and said it was time they were going home.

'I'll come with you,' Mark said at once and Katie gave him a soft loving smile.

Mary made a point of walking on ahead, but she was acutely aware of Mark and Katie, hand in hand behind. She had never felt so alone in her life and though she begrudged Katie nothing, the Irish girl's happiness served to highlight her own misery.

She was forced to hang around outside the Murphy household, waiting for the couple to say their good nights, and she looked up at the crispness of the sky, clear for once of the pall of smoke from the works. The wind was dry, driving westwards, with the result that the stars were clear and bright in the heavens. From down the end of Copperman's Row came the sound of Dai-End-House playing his accordion and Mary felt her eyes mist with tears as the plaintive sounds of the music filled the air.

In bed, she lay awake for a long time, her mind twirling like a leaf caught in the current of a fast-moving stream. She could see Brandon plainly in her mind's eye; she knew every line of his face, every curve of his body like a lesson learned by heart. She ached to hold him in her arms, to put her head on his shoulder and have him smooth her hair with affection. His passion he had given her, but never his love.

'Mary, are you awake?' Katie's voice was little more than a whisper. Mary turned over in the darkness and the bedclothes rustled around her like leaves swept along in the wind.

'Yes, I'm awake,' she replied. 'Is everything all right?'

There was a soft sigh from the other side of the room and then the pad of feet against bare floorboards. Katie pushed aside the curtain, holding a candle that shimmered in the breeze.

'I've got to tell someone or I shall burst with excitement.' She sat on the edge of the bed, tucking her feet up under her nightgown. 'Mark has asked me to marry him!' Her eyes shone in the candlelight and her skin was translucent as though the happiness within her radiated outwards like the rays of the sun.

'I'm very pleased for you, but not at all surprised,' Mary said gently. She leaned forward in an uncharacteristic gesture and kissed Katie's cheek. 'I know you'll be happy, he's a good man,' she whispered. 'Now go to bed and let's get some sleep, is it?'

But long after Katie was slumbering softly, her breathing regular and even, Mary lay awake staring into the darkness, her heart aching at the injustice of Brandon's accusations.

–

Monday was clear and bright but with frost rimming the edges of the windows and drawing patterns on the glass. Mary dressed warmly, knowing that she would be standing in the marketplace for the best part of the day. She hardly had time to speak to the Murphys except to remind Katie to take more calico up to Muriel at *Ty Mawr* and to do all she could to help.

'How are you at buttonholes?' Mary paused in the doorway, bracing herself to meet the full blast of the cold morning air.

'I'm fine, sure I am, but don't ask me to work one of them sewing machines, have me fingers off so I would.'

'Well, you tell Muriel to leave all the hand sewing to you and concentrate on the seams and such.'

It was as cold as Mary feared and she hugged her shawl around her as she walked down Market Street, her head bent against the wind. She felt heavy-eyed and still out of sorts, for most of Sunday had been spent working on her accounts. The results were enormously cheering and yet in her present mood she sometimes wondered if the struggle was worth it.

The square was already alive with people and Mary stared around her in surprise. It was unusual in such bitter weather for customers to be abroad so early. As she moved towards her own stall, she suddenly saw the reason for the press of people and her heart almost stopped beating. The stall that she had sold to Jake Zimmerman was open for business, but what drew Mary's gaze was the lines of calico petticoats and the piles of woollen undergarments – all at slightly lower prices than her own stock.

'Jake Zimmerman, you low-down schemer, how could you do this to me?' Mary said desperately. The man shook his head, covering his face with his handkerchief, his eyes watering with the cold. As if from nowhere the slight frame of Alfred Phillpot emerged, his long face full of triumph.

'You see, Miss Jenkins,' he spoke with false joviality, 'no one gets the better of the Cooperative Movement, or of me.'

Mary longed to lash out at the sneering face before her, but she forced herself to quietly open her stall and set out her goods for display. She must be calm, she told herself, and think matters out very carefully indeed.

'I see your prices are a little high.' Alfred Phillpot was behind her, his thin fingers lifting one of the calico garments with disdain. 'We big traders can afford to cut prices, Miss Jenkins. Now perhaps you'll see the error of your ways.'

Mary turned on him fiercely, unable to curb her temper any longer. 'And you'll see the business end of my boot if you don't get out of my way, you little cockroach!' She spoke so fiercely that the man paled visibly. He backed away and the expression on his face would have been funny if Mary had not been so angry and upset.

She did little trade that morning and once noon had come and gone she put up the shutters, locking away her stock securely.

'Giving up, are you?' Alfred Phillpot called from the safety of the stall. 'Quite right too, the competition is too much for you, dear lady!'

'Shut your mouth!' Mary said and the man smirked.

'Shut-my mouth, indeed, what a way for a lady to talk.' He watched as she pocketed her keys and then turned to serve a customer, a sneer on his thin face.

Mary walked towards the dock, breathing deeply, trying to think out her problem without anger clouding her mind. She would never give in to the man Phillpot or to his Cooperative Movement, she decided fiercely.

At the water's edge, she felt calmer. She stared down into the pewter grey sea as it rolled inwards and sighed softly. There seemed no answer – she could hardly cut her prices any lower or there would be no profit in the business at all. And yet she was determined she would sell her goods even if she had to hawk them from door to door.

'Any why not?' she said aloud. A seagull rose high in the sky, calling out a mournful protest at the sudden noise. Mary watched the bird in flight, a smile turning up the corners of her mouth.

She would buy herself a horse-drawn van, that was the answer. Excitement mingled with fear raged within her, but she would do it, she vowed. She would learn to handle a horse quickly enough, especially if the animal was as docile as Big Jim. And then she would go round to all the outlying districts, selling her goods to the people who could not make the journey into Sweyn's Eye.

Yet how much would a large vehicle cost, she wondered? True she had quite a bit of money from the sale of the stall, but would it be enough?

An imp of mischief lit her eyes with merriment. She could always sell the remaining stall to another trader in clothes and see what the Coop made of that! As she moved away from the docks her step was light. She had a fight on her hands and Alfred Phillpot and his accomplice Jake Zimmerman could both look out.

Chapter Twenty-Two

The winter winds sighed mournfully in the branches of the trees, whining round the cottage that stood alone, small and yet solid in a garden stripped of verdure by the fumes from the copper works. But inside the house was bright, the gas lamps glowing white, the fires roaring in the gates. It was a comfortable house and one day, Rhian thought in satisfaction, it would be hers.

'Come along, Auntie, it's time you were in bed,' she said gently as the old lady sat, head dropped onto her meagre breast, cap bobbing over her eyes, knitting fallen idle in her lap. She jerked into wakefulness and glanced at the clock and suddenly she was fully alert, her needles beating a tattoo, her eyes bright.

'Nonsense, dear, there's plenty of time for me to sleep when I'm in my grave,' she said and Rhian sighed impatiently. Her aunt was just like a cat, napping one moment and full of life the next.

'Would you like me to make you a cup of cocoa, then?' Rhian asked, but her aunt shook her head emphatically.

'No, I don't want anything. Don't fuss, dear. I'll just sit here with you until Heath gets home.' Aunt Agnes smiled. 'Fine young man that, a pity he seems to blow hot and cold. One minute he seems to want you and the next...' There was more than a hint of malice in her aunt's voice, Rhian thought angrily. She knew how to wound with words. Just because she was a vinegary old spinster herself, she wanted everyone to share the same fate.

Rhian's mood of impatience grew, for she had hoped to have the old lady tucked up fast asleep in bed by the time Heath came home – had wanted to snatch some time alone with him so that they could talk.

Unhappiness quivered inside her at the thought of him meeting another woman and yet that was the spectre that rose to haunt her each time she saw Heath preparing to leave the house. He would shave carefully with the long razor, making clean sweeps at the soapy lather with the gleaming blade, and then he would wash at the sink and the water would run down his well-muscled arms, over the strong column of his throat and down his bare chest.

Rhian had never been on such intimate terms with a man before, not ever. To her all the accoutrements of masculinity were unfamiliar and fascinating. Yet Heath continued to treat her in an offhand manner, rather as though she was a dog to be petted and pushed aside at the master's whim.

She heard the latch on the back door lift and glanced quickly at her aunt, but the old lady had heard nothing and was nodding over her knitting once more. Silently, Rhian left the parlour and tiptoed down the passage into the kitchen.

'Still up?' Heath was taking off his coat and his white silk scarf and hanging them on the peg at the back of the door. 'Little girls should be fast asleep by now. You'll never be a beauty if you don't get your rest.'

'Want a cup of cocoa?' Rhian disregarded his words, her eyes running over him as though she might find evidence of where he had been and with whom he had spent the evening. He shook his head and a curl fell on to his forehead. Rhian resisted the urge to push it back with tender fingers.

'Nothing for me, thanks, I'm going up now. I've got to work in the morning and so have you, my lady.'

'Don't speak to me as though I was a little child,' Rhian protested. 'Look at me, Heath, I'm grown-up.' She turned around in front of him and his eyes warmed as they travelled over her slim figure.

'You sure are,' he said with a smile in his voice, 'outwardly at least.' He tapped his head. 'It's just up here that you've remained a little girl.'

'It's not true!' Rhian said angrily. 'I'm as mature as you are.'

Heath came towards her and took her in his arms, his body pressed against her and she felt the hardness of him and was afraid. She tried to disengage herself but he held her fast. He kissed her soundly and after a moment, her arms crept around his neck. She heard his breathing quicken and knew he was aroused. The thought gave her pleasure, but it was not a physical one. She liked the feeling of power that his passion gave her, yet strangely she could not respond to it. After a moment Heath released her, his hands hanging at his sides. 'You see?' he said and it was as though he had proved a point.

'I don't see anything.' Rhian was angry. 'I thought we were walking out together, you used to come and meet me from the laundry every day, now you hardly ever come at all.' Tears filled her eyes and ran down her cheeks and Heath caught her in his arms, smoothing her hair and hushing her, his tone gentle.

'Look, sit down by here, there's a good girl,' he said patiently. 'I'm a man and I have needs and I've been used to satisfying them.' He shrugged. 'Mary didn't keep tabs on me, she was always good like that though she knew full well I was out tomcatting as she called it.'

He paused. 'I can't change my ways, Rhian, not even to please you.' He rose to his feet. 'But I'm waiting for you to be ready and then perhaps we'll see us walking up the aisle together.' His tone had lightened and Rhian had no way of knowing if he was joking with her or not. She stared at him from under her lashes, trying to picture him with another girl, but the image would not come. No, Heath was drinking down at the Mexico Fountain, he couldn't have a woman – not him.

'Now, let's get your auntie up to bed, is it?' Heath said with a smile. 'You know what a performance that always is with me having to practically carry her up the stairs. After me, she is – you know that, don't you?' He smiled again and Rhian sighed with relief.

'There's a one for the jokes you are, Heath Jenkins,' she admonished and for a fleeting moment thought she saw a look of irritation in his eyes. Then he was hurrying her to the door and she knew she had imagined something that hadn't been there.

When she lay in bed, Rhian wondered again about Heath's nightly excursions. He could not be up on the hill with a girl, not in this bitter weather, she thought positively. And Heath was not one to pay a floosie for her services, he was far too fussy for that. No, he had no one else; he loved her, of course he did, it was just that he was a man and needed to be in the company of other men. She sighed and closed her eyes and fell into a dreaming sleep wherein she was clothed in white lace and Heath was slipping a gold band on to her finger and everyone was happy.

In the morning, she rose late and had to rush to be ready for the laundry. She did not see Heath. He had already left the house, which spoiled her day for a start.

'Haven't you got that fire started yet, Carrie?' She pushed past the woman who came every day to look after Aunt Agnes without as much as glancing at her and pulled her shawl around her shoulders, feeling at odds with the world.

'Everyone is rushing about like hens with their heads chopped off this morning,' Carry grumbled. 'Don't know why I bother to come to this house, there's nothing but sulks to greet me. Your aunt's tea was not ready first thing and now she's in a bad mood. I think I'll go home and go back to my bed.'

Rhian was contrite. How would she ever manage without Carrie to do the bulk of the hard work around the house? For as long as she could remember Carrie had been there, picking up after her, pandering to her, but lately she seemed a bit more waspish.

'I didn't mean to moan,' Rhian said quickly. 'Take no notice, we'd all be lost without you.'

'Aye, I know that,' Carrie said, thrusting paper into the fire and puffing on it trying to get a blaze going. She straightened. 'Got choir practice tonight, haven't you, girl?' Her eyes were narrowed and Rhian stared at her in surprise.

'You know I have, why do you ask?'

Carrie shook her head. 'No reason. Get off with you now, or you'll be late for work – and from what I've heard of that new boss, you'll be out on your arse before you know it.'

Rhian frowned. Carrie could be so coarse on times, but then what could you expect? She had been a widow for years and with no man to look after her she'd grown hard; she was to be pitied not condemned.

Rhian left the house and hurried along the cold damp street. A light rain was falling, made bitter by the driving wind that howled around corners, bending trees almost double and scurrying papers along the gutters of the streets.

But it would be comfortable in the laundry. The packing room was warm and pleasant, not smelling of urine like the boiler house – how anyone could work in those conditions, Rhian could not understand. As she entered the gates, Sally Benson was peering out through one of the windows. Trust Sally to catch her out on the one day she was late, Rhian thought miserably. The girl pounced as soon as Rhian entered the packing room. She was standing, arms akimbo, her eyes aglow with spiteful glee.

'Late this morning, aren't we?' she said briskly. 'And the boss has been around already, so there's no hiding it.'

'This is the first time I've ever arrived after everyone else,' Rhian said defiantly. 'I don't think Mr Sutton would be unreasonable about that.'

'I'm overseer of this laundry, or have you forgotten?'

Sally's face was flushed and Rhian knew with a sinking of her heart that she had said the wrong thing.

She remained silent, waiting for Sally to make the next move, for whatever Rhian said now she would only make matters worse.

'I think you'd better spend a day down in the boiler house,' Sally said after a long silence. 'Your boyfriend's sister did it and I can't see why you shouldn't have a taste of what it's like to work hard.' She caught one of Rhian's hands and stared down at the slim white fingers in disgust. 'Never had to get these hands dirty, have you? Well, it's about time you did.'

'I'm not working down there,' Rhian said flatly. 'I'll go and see Mr Sutton first. Too big for your boots you're getting, Sally Benson. Think you're a little tin god, don't you? Well, I won't put up with your bullying, I'm going to see the boss myself.'

Rhian walked away, pleased with the look of sheer panic which had crossed Sally's face at her words. She was being unreasonable and she knew Mr Sutton would not thank her for allowing one of the workers to pester him.

'Wait a minute!' Sally said. 'Perhaps I was a little bit hasty. I'll forget it this time so long as it doesn't happen again.'

But Rhian was already hurrying down the rickety stairs, her white apron flapping in the breeze. She wrinkled her nose as she reached the door of the boiler house, for the stink was intolerable. She could never work in such surroundings, she would rather give up the job altogether. After all, she didn't really need to work – Aunt Agnes was not a poor woman, she had more than enough to keep the house going without the pittance Rhian brought home from the laundry.

Mr Sutton was not in the office and Rhian guessed that he must be in the boiler house, for last night there had been a bit of a fuss over one of the boilers being clogged. She made for the door and swung it open and stared uncertainly into the long room. She had never been into the boiler house before and at first glance it was like a taste of hell. Huge boilers rose up from the floor with fires flaring beneath them.

As Rhian watched, Doris opened one of the doors and thrust a mountain of coal inside. Thick choking smoke gushed forth, along with flames that were like dragons' breath.

Rhian was not aware that anything was amiss until she heard some of the women screaming. Events seemed to move with incredible slowness then. Rhian saw Mr Sutton's tall figure hurrying towards the boiler; at the same time he was calling to the women to leave the room, his arms waving like the struts of a windmill.

The boiler gushed into a deafening roar. It appeared to lift right off the ground, scattering hot coals over Doris who screamed like a banshee. A hail of metal and boiling water swept downwards over the terrified women and one of them fell, clutching at her eyes. Rhian felt a stinging sensation on her arm and then she was joining in the screams that were drowned by the roar of the flames devouring the room.

She fell outward into the yard and alongside her crawled a woman who was unrecognisable. Her hair was enveloped in flames and her face blackened by smoke. Rhian looked over her shoulder and lying only a few feet away from her was the remains of a human arm. Blackness rose up before her eyes, engulfing her, and she knew she was going to be violently sick.

–

The aftermath of the explosion was something that rocked Sweyn's Eye for a few days and then died away into obscurity, a nine-days-wonder to be forgotten by all but those who were affected by the accident. Rhian's arm was badly scalded and she would bear the scar for life but she was one of the lucky ones.

It was Mary who came to see her and explain what had happened. 'The boilers need to be kept cleaned out,' she said, 'or else the dust and coke chokes the flues.'

Rhian stared at her from the comfort of her bed and bit her lip worriedly. 'Was anyone killed?' she asked in a small voice.

Mary looked down at her hands. 'Old Mr Sutton died in the infirmary. They say he was very brave, warning the women to get clear. Old Sarah is dead and most of the women are injured.' She paused, swallowing hard.

'It will take some time to rebuild the boiler house, the fire gutted it. All the girls from the packing room got out all right, as they managed to run down the steps before the fire really took hold.'

'I feel ashamed that I fainted,' Rhian admitted miserably. 'Perhaps there was something I could have done.'

Mary took Rhian's uninjured hand in her own. 'It was lucky you hadn't gone into the room, or you might have been killed,' she said gently. 'No need to blame yourself. It's pointless laying the blame at anyone's door, the mischief's been done now and there's no undoing it.'

'Well, I wouldn't go back to work there any more,' Rhian said positively. 'Not with Sally Benson in charge of the laundry, no fear!' She shivered and the pain in her arm grew more intense. 'What will happen to her now – Sally, I mean?'

Mary shook her head. 'I don't know. The devastation is so great that it's unlikely the laundry will ever open again. In any case, Sally wouldn't be trusted with so much as a shovel of coal from now on.'

'Serves her right,' Rhian said quickly. 'Treated us like pigs, she did, she was so uppity about taking your job and all. Rubbing it in to me, she was, that my boyfriend is your brother as though it was a crime.' Rhian became aware of Mary's eyes upon her and she lifted her head defiantly, 'She's got no one to blame but herself, so don't go giving me funny looks, Mary.'

'I feel sorry for the girl,' Mary replied quietly. 'She's got a lot on her conscience, mind.'

'But Mary, it was all Sally Benson's fault. If she had done her job properly none of it would have happened.'

'I know,' Mary sighed, 'but she has my pity all the same.'

Heath entered the room, dressed to go out as usual. Rhian pouted up at him.

'I thought you might have kept me company this evening,' she said as he sat on the edge of the bed. He leaned forward and patted her head before giving Mary an affectionate kiss.

'Me, I'm off out, playing nursemaid isn't a game that appeals to me. Anyway, you've got Mary here with you, so don't grumble, girl.'

Before Rhian could speak Mary had risen to her feet. 'Don't bring me into this. I'm off home, there's a lot for me to do before morning.'

Heath was taller than Mary now and a strong handsome man, the contours of his face losing their boyishness.

'Still at the Murphys?' he asked and when Mary nodded, he shook his head.

'Get out of there. Find a place of your own even if it's one room in an attic. You're the sort who needs independence as others need air to breathe.'

'You're right.' Mary pulled on her gloves. 'And I keep meaning to look round, but there never seems to be enough time.' She turned to Rhian. 'I'll be back to see you in a day or two. Meanwhile try to rest, it's the only way that the body can heal itself.'

Brother and sister left the room together and Rhian punched at her pillow in anger. Heath could have stayed in with her just this once, it wouldn't have hurt him. On an impulse, she got out of bed and began to dress. Anything, even sitting with her aunt, was better than the boredom of lying in bed.

Downstairs, she peered round the door of the parlour, hoping that Heath wouldn't have left yet, but her aunt was sitting alone, nodding before the fire as usual. She opened her eyes when Rhian came into the room.

'Oh! It's you,' she said and her voice sounded strange, almost as though she was standing at the end of a tunnel. She lifted her hand to her head and her face was very pale.

'I'm not well, Rhian,' she said and held out her hand imploringly. Her skin was dry and burning and Rhian realised that for once her aunt wasn't simply asking for sympathy, she really was sick.

'What can I get you, Auntie?' Rhian asked. 'Would you like me to help you into bed?'

Aunt Agnes shook her head. 'I think you should go down the road and fetch Carrie, she'll know what's best.'

Rhian bit her lip. She didn't want to leave her aunt alone and yet there seemed no alternative, so she pulled a shawl around her shoulders and paused in the doorway.

'Now don't you move from there, Auntie. I won't be more than a few minutes.'

Ignoring the pain of her arm, Rhian hurried along the pavement, her heart beating swiftly. Auntie Agnes might be a moaner, but she had never admitted to being ill before.

The door was on the latch and Rhian let herself into Carrie's house with the ease of long practice. The kitchen was empty, though the gaslight burned brightly and a healthy fire roared in the grate.

Rhian looked round fearfully, wondering if Carrie could be out visiting one of her neighbours. She stood still staring at the clock ticking on the mantelpiece, looking at her reflection in the oval mirror high above the fireplace without really seeing herself. She was about to leave the house when a small sound from upstairs caught her attention.

Silently she moved to the long passageway that was full of shadows and hurried up the carpeted stairs. A strip of light showed from under one of the doors and Rhian thankfully pushed it open.

She had been about to spill out her fears, but the words died on her lips at the picture before her. She stood in the shadows of the doorway, unobserved by the figures in the room. They moved in the bed as though spun in a half-light from a dream. It was Carrie... but not the Carrie she had always known. This Carrie was naked with hair streaming down her shoulders, her eyes closed, her thighs moving rhythmically to meet the thrust of the man above her. He was long and lean and his body seemed coiled over the woman like a spring. His hair was crisp around a strong face and it was several moments before Rhian realised who it was.

'Heath!' The name was like a cry of anguish and then she was forcing back the feelings of rage that washed through her.

Heath was on his feet, staring mutely towards her, unaware of his nakedness. 'I thought you were *my* man!' Rhian's voice was harsh. 'You don't belong with a woman like Carrie, she's old!' Rhian paused, trying to clear her thoughts – she couldn't run away because her aunt might be truly sick. She took a deep breath, trying not to see the pale figure in the bed, mouth open and staring at her. 'Carrie, you must come at once, Auntie is ill.' Her voice was faint, like the whisper of the wind.

It was Heath who replied, 'Rhian, go back to your aunt, we'll be with you in a few minutes. Try to keep calm.'

As Rhian let herself into the house, tears were gushing down her cheeks, sobs choking her throat. 'How could you betray me, Heath?' she murmured in anguish. She forced her mind to return to her aunt's plight and half fearfully, she opened the parlour door. Her aunt was slumped back in her chair, her eyes closed, her hand to her breast. Rhian moved forward, hearing with a sense of relief the small gasp of breath stealing between her aunt's lips.

In a surprisingly short time, Carrie and Heath were in the house, taking control with Carrie holding the old lady's hand and feeling for her pulse.

'Put on the kettle, Rhian,' she said in a matter-of-fact manner. 'We'll mix up some hot water and brandy. Nothing too wrong here, just a little faint I'd say – it's to be expected at her age. Now don't look so pale and lost, everything is going to be all right.'

Rhian filled the kettle and pushed it on to the hob, her movements those of a sleepwalker. She knew that she would never again look at Carrie without seeing her wrapped naked in Heath Jenkins' arms. She wanted to scream and cry and hurt and smash, but she knew it would do no good. She fetched the brandy out of the cupboard and set it on the table, scarcely glancing up as Heath stood beside her...

'It'll be all right, don't worry,' he said, and as Rhian lifted her eyes to look at him she wondered if anything would be all right ever again.

Chapter Twenty-Three

The Camel Top Van dominated the whole of Market Street. It stood high and imposing against the backdrop of shops; a vehicle several years old, bumped and dented but freshly painted now and proud in the winter sunlight.

Mary walked around the van, seeing with a feeling of achievement her name emblazoned on the side in large black lettering. All that remained now was for her to learn to drive the van, to handle the horse drooping between the shafts – and then she was in business. At her side, Mark stood with arms folded, a look on his face akin to that of a father surveying his first child.

'*Duw*, she looks fine now, don't you think, Mary? No one would recognise her as the battered old bakers' van I bought from a bankrupt firm.' He grinned. 'I wouldn't show her to you before, not with all the mud and scrapes and dinginess about her. Now you are seeing old Bessie in all her glory, she'll do you proud.'

Mary pushed back her hair with a feeling of excitement. She allowed Mark to help her into the driving seat and stared around, seeing Market Street from the view of a bird perched on the branch of a tree. It was a terrifying experience and she wondered if she would ever get used to the feeling of sitting on top of the world.

'Where's Katie gone?' Mark said suddenly and Mary shook her head in bewilderment.

'I don't know. I haven't seen her this past hour, but then I've been so busy opening and shutting doors and marvelling at the room inside the van that I've noticed nothing else.'

Mark shook his head. 'She's a mystery, that one. You never know when you've got her and when you've not.'

Mary smiled down at him as he rested his foot on the fender of the bus. 'Ah, but that's where the attraction lies, isn't it, boyo?'

Mark refrained from answering. Instead, he climbed into the driving seat and flicked the reins, startling the horse into movement.

'What do I do if I want to stop?' she asked in panic as the wheels rolled smoothly forward.

'There's a brake at your side and you give old Duke here instructions and he'll take you anywhere in Sweyn's Eye.' Mark smiled. 'Don't look as if someone's stepped on your pet corn, Mary; the van won't bite, you know.'

Mary gripped the reins until her knuckles gleamed white. The wind hissed through her hair and she chewed her lip in concentration. She was worried lest the large vehicle rolling along the road was about to run away with her. Past the Mexico Fountain she drove and down towards the river, her stomach doing somersaults.

'I'll never handle this thing properly,' she said through gritted teeth as she negotiated a corner and Mark laughed.

'That's a daft thing to say. Who do you think is doing the driving now?' He pulled at her shoulders. 'Come on, now, no need to crouch over like that, you're not going to fall off. Back straight, try to relax, that's it, you're doing fine.'

'There's easy it's going to be for me to get round the valleys,' Mary said, manoeuvring the van more deftly round a bend in the road. 'As long as old Duke doesn't stop to chew grass, that is,' Mark replied, smiling.

There was a group of sightseers waiting in Market Street for Mary's return. None of the small local traders had owned anything like the Camel Top Van; anything more than a simple cart with two wheels was a luxury. As she alighted from the driving seat, there was a burst of clapping and she swallowed hard, touchingly aware of the admiration on the faces of the people standing watching her.

'Let your friends and families know that Big Mary will be doing her rounds as of tomorrow,' she said loudly. 'I'll be selling everything from pins to undergarments and all at the best prices in town.'

Mark hustled her into the house and Mrs Murphy moved back from the lace curtains at the window, her pale face flushed.

'I want you to know that we're proud of you, so we are,' she said, her pale eyes glowing. 'And I'm proud to have you beneath my roof – and I'm not a soul who gives voice to my thoughts very often.'

As Mary sat at the table, unable to speak, the door opened and Katie came into the room carrying a cake high above her head.

'Close your eyes, hold out your hands and see what God sends you,' she said playfully. Mary obeyed and felt the coldness of the plate touch her fingers. The cake that Katie set so proudly on the table was a triumph of invention: baked in the shape of a van with Mary's name piped across the top.

'There's clever of you, Katie.' Mary found it difficult to speak. 'I can't cut it, it's too beautiful.'

Mrs Murphy gave a short laugh. 'Don't you say that, girl, otherwise me boys will be right put down. Been waiting ages for you to give them all a piece, so they have.'

Mary's eyes were blurred with tears as she pressed the knife home. It was a wonderful thing to have friends. And then, unbidden, came the thought of Billy, who had once been her love and was now locked away behind bars. She had almost forgotten his existence of late. Suddenly the happiness of the day evaporated and Mary felt sadness envelop her like a cloak.

–

The prison was grey, the yard windswept, the walls thick and unyielding. Billy Gray had finished his walk in the dullness of the afternoon and was being returned to the confines of his cell. Griffiths jangled the keys, his eyes speculative as they rested on him. There was no privacy here, Billy thought mutinously. Perhaps that was one of the worst aspects of prison life, that you could not even call your thoughts your own.

'Lady here to see you,' Griffiths said, a sly grin stretching his mean mouth. And yet unaccountably the warder's attitude to Billy had been subtly altered of late. He was not kind – such a term in connection with Griffiths would have been absurd – but he was tolerable.

'Mary Jenkins, is it?' Billy asked with a faint hope lighting his heart. She had come to say that she still cared, that anything he might hear was just gossip. The hope died away as Griffiths shook his head.

'No, I mean a real lady; Mrs Richardson, her that brings you such a lot of goodies. What is it you got to offer her, boy, have you got a big John Thomas?'

Billy was embarrassed by the man's coarseness. He turned his head away and refrained from answering.

'Well, I take my hat off to you, I do, the only prisoner on the block to get private visits from a member of the fairer sex, you lucky bastard!' He moved aside quickly as Delmai came into sight along the corridor. 'Begging your pardon, Mrs Richardson, didn't see you then.'

He bowed himself away and closed the door and Delmai paused, smiling at Billy, her cheeks flushed, carrying with her the scent of the outdoors.

Suddenly Billy longed to take her in his arms and rest his head upon her breast. He felt he needed the warmth of a woman and instinctively, he held out his arms.

To his amazement Delmai came to him and rested her cheek against his. It was not a sensual gesture, but one that Billy found immensely touching. He had begun to feel like an outcast from civilisation, unclean. Delmai made him believe he was human again and he was grateful.

They remained locked together for what seemed an age. Billy breathed in the fresh woman smell of her, felt her slight breasts resting against him and the slimness of her waist beneath his hand. His manhood stirred and embarrassed, he moved away.

'I'm sorry,' he mumbled sitting on his bed and looking down at his hands. She came and sat beside him, her fingers stroking his arms.

'For what, holding me like that? I liked it, I like you Billy.'

He would not look at her. She was sweet and innocent and even though she was married she was a lady and doubtless misunderstood his apology. She took his face between her hands and forced him to look up at her.

'Billy, you wanted me. I'm flattered. There's nothing for you to be ashamed of.' He did not speak and after a moment she sighed softly.

'Billy, don't allow your hopes to be raised too high, but I think I might be able to get you out of here before too long.' She paused and half fearfully he looked into her face, wondering if she could be jesting with him. But her eyes were sincere and after a moment she nodded her head.

'I've got a petition and lots of people have signed it, Billy. You see, I'm not the only one who thinks you were wrongly imprisoned.'

Hope grew like the flame of a candle until it suffused him, engulfed him. He felt he would burst with hope and Delmai read something of his feelings, for she leaned forward suddenly and pressed her lips to his. It was a chaste kiss, that of a friend... at first, and then, subtly, it altered.

Billy was aware of Delmai's breathing, quick and shallow. Her lips grew warm and her hands held on to his neck as though he was something very precious.

She drew away, but her face was still very close to his as she looked into his eyes. 'Billy, I think I'm falling in love with you!'

He could find no words to speak; he felt in that moment that he loved her too, but there was a bewilderment in him. He had always been Mary's man and she his woman. It was true she had never kissed him the way Delmai had, yet how could he shake off the habits of a lifetime?

'Billy, do you feel anything at all for me?' she asked wistfully and he looked into her eyes, knowing that her need for love and caring was as great as his. He nodded slowly and she touched his lips with her fingers.

'Then you need say nothing. I am content.' She rose to her feet and placed the parcel of food she had brought him on the table at the side of his bed.

'I must go, but I'm working always for your release Billy. Just you remember that and don't despair.'

After she had gone, Billy sat and stared at the wall. He was still bewildered – even if he felt desire and something more for Delmai Richardson, what good could come of it? She was married and what's more she was far above his station in life. His mind was a chaos of emotions all vying with each other – hope and trust that Delmai would succeed in freeing him and apprehension about what would happen once he walked through the prison gates.

Griffiths peered in through the slit in the doorway and Billy winced as he heard the warder's guffaw of laughter.

'Been stirring things up, has that little lady,' he said in amusement. 'Or is that a cosh I see down your pants, boy? Well, make the most of it for it won't last.'

Billy felt a stab of fear. He knew he was rising to the bait, but he couldn't prevent himself from asking the question.

'What do you mean?' His throat was dry and Griffiths took his time, enjoying the feeling of power.

'Governor is stopping all women coming here to visit – causes a disruptive influence on the inmates.' He sniggered. 'I can see what he means now, boyo, and you'll have to take yourself in hand.' He laughed yet again at his own crudity.

'Your lady love won't be visiting again. They're sending a clergyman around, and I don't think your tastes have got around to that sort of thing just yet. Give it another few years and you'll doubtless be as man-randy as the rest of them here.'

He strode away, his footsteps ringing against the concrete of the passageway. Billy put his hands over his face and suddenly his feelings became crystallised. Rightly or wrongly he wanted and needed Delmai Richardson, and if she couldn't free him he would hang himself from the highest tree in the yard.

Mary's forays into the valleys always caused something of a sensation. On her arrival she would sound the horn loudly and by the time she reined Duke to a halt, there would be a crowd of eager women waiting to examine her wares.

The van had been set out in the fashion of a mobile shop, with box shelves running the length of it. The villagers could select goods just as they would have done in any store.

Stout undergarments sold well, Mary found, and calico chemises and stiff linen petticoats were always in demand. But sturdy trousers and shirts in good Welsh flannel seemed one of the best lines to carry and she sold out of them almost as soon as she could stock the shelves.

'Hey, Mary, where's the Welsh shawl you promised me for wrapping my baby in?' Flo Lloyd was a tall, raw-boned woman, her eyes bright and black like the coal that was the life-blood of Clyne valley.

'I haven't forgotten.' Mary reached under her seat and took out a parcel. 'This one is a present from me, it isn't every day that a thirteenth son is born.'

Flo flushed with pride. 'Well, I didn't expect that,' she said softly. 'There's lovely, just look at the thickness of that wool, won't you?'

She discarded the washed-out shawl she had been using and wound the new one around herself, tucking one end under the softly sleeping body of her son and the other under her arm. The shawl became a support for the child, taking most of the weight on the woman's back and leaving one hand free.

'Suits you,' Mary said cheerfully. 'Now come on and look round the van and see what else it is you need for that family of yours.'

Mary's money-pocket set into her apron became heavy and by the time she climbed back into the driving seat, ready to move away, most of her stock had been sold. As she waved goodbye to the women of the valley, she sighed with relief. It was about time that she returned home, for she was tired of urging Duke to go forward and the horse seemed to be limping, she thought uneasily. But at least she could be well satisfied with the takings: she had done better than usual today, because she had coincided her visit with payday in the valleys. She brushed back her hair, which was slipping loose from the pins, and stared ahead into the growing darkness, her mind almost numb with fatigue.

She was only a short distance from Sweyn's Eye when she hit a bump in the road. The van jerked and shuddered and Duke whinnied sadly into the darkness. With a sigh, Mary climbed down from her seat. On inspecting the underside of the van, she found that a large boulder had jammed beneath the wheel. Even exerting all her strength, she could not budge it. She stared around the silent roadway and recognised that help would not be coming. She freed Duke from the shafts and patted the animal's flank.

'Go and eat some grass then, boyo, but not too far away mind.'

There was very little stock left in the van and Mary stood for a few moments debating whether to carry the clothing back into town or trust to luck and leave it where it was.

She looked up, feeling the touch of rain in the air and seeing the clouds scudding across the moon. She decided to leave well alone; it was doubtful that anyone would come along the lonely road at this time of night and even if they did, there was not very much left to steal.

Fortunately the van had shuddered to a stop close to the towering wall of the cliff, allowing enough passage for anyone travelling the road in the morning. In any case, she could have some men out at first light to bring the van in and for now there was nothing for her to do but start walking.

Mary whistled softly to Duke and realised with growing irritation that the horse had disappeared. Well, the animal would come to no harm until morning, she decided wearily.

The pocket of money hung heavily from her waist and she drew her shawl close around her shoulders, covering the apron. She did not want to invite attack from footpads, especially as she was walking the dockland area where sailors of all nationalities threaded in and out of public bars, a continuous chain of human activity.

As she crossed the bridge over the river, the water was fast-moving, dark in the faint light of the moon that peeped between scudding clouds. She hurried along, suddenly feeling nervous though she could not say why. Then she became aware of footsteps – heavier than her own, more measured – and glanced over her shoulder, the hair on the back of her neck standing on end.

'Don't be a fool!' She spoke the words out loud and they fell eerily into the darkness of the night. But she was a strong woman, she could fend for herself if needs be. Against a cudgel at the back of the head? her inner self asked.

She saw the lights shining from the press building – renewed now, the wood new and strong and the roof felted and pitched. She was almost running as she neared the doorway, her heart thumping madly and her breathing ragged.

Brandon Sutton opened the door to her frantic knocking and stood there tall and imposing, his head held at a proud angle, his shoulders with a lift that was so characteristic of him. Such was Mary's shock at seeing him that she was speechless, unable to tell him why she was there at such an hour.

At last she found her tongue. 'Oh, it's you, there's sorry I am to hear of your father's death.' She blurted out the words in embarrassment and he raised an eyebrow.

'It's kind of you to say so,' he replied shortly. 'But to what do we owe the honour of your company?'

He stood back, inviting her in, curiosity clear to read in the turquoise of his eyes.

'Make yourself at home,' he said dryly as she hurried past him. She glanced back into the darkness and Brandon's face was suddenly alert.

'Well, what's wrong?' he asked and Mary shook her head.

'I don't know,' she replied. 'I think I was being followed. I could hear footsteps heavy and slow and yet I could see no one.'

He went outside and Mary moved to a stool, sitting down gratefully with her hands clasped in her lap. A little later, Brandon returned.

'There's no one about now,' he said. 'Perhaps you imagined it?' The implication in his words was clear and she stared up at him, her colour rising.

'If you think I came here deliberately to look for you, then think again, Mr Sutton.' Her voice was full of sarcasm. 'I wouldn't cross the road to give you the time of day, so don't go getting all conceited.'

He came towards her and caught her arms, drawing her to her feet. 'All I know is that tales are told behind my back,' he said roughly. 'I'd like to believe your innocent eyes, Mary Jenkins, but I can't.'

She struggled to free herself from the iron grip of his hands but he was too strong for her.

'I haven't come here to spy on you, if that's what you think,' she protested. 'My van hit a stone and Duke strayed away, so I had to walk home,' She was aware of babbling and of how absurd her words sounded. 'If you don't believe me, look – here are my takings for today. I'd scarcely carry money on me if I was out to do a bit of nosey parkering, would I?'

His hands slid round her waist as he drew her closer and smiled down into her eyes. 'Then I can flatter myself that it was me you came looking for when you were in trouble?' he said, his tone heavy with irony. Before she could move away, he bent until his mouth was above hers and she drew a shuddering breath, knowing that he was weaving his usual spell over her.

'Let me go,' she said, but her voice lacked conviction. He took no notice, but held her closer and it seemed an age before his lips claimed hers. She leaned against him, loving him so much that it hurt deep inside her. She had tried to put him out of her mind, but she had failed dismally. Not a day had passed, she realised now, without her thinking of him, holding to herself the knowledge of her love. Even if he never returned her love, it did not diminish her own feelings. She must have sighed softly, for Brandon was holding her away from him, an enigmatic expression on his face.

'You are a strange woman, Mary Jenkins,' he said. 'Beautiful, capable of great strength and yet…' He put her away from him and suddenly she felt cold, wanting to go back into the shelter of his arms, to hear his heart beating against her body, to breathe in the scent of him. Instead she looked away, afraid of revealing her feelings.

'I don't know what you mean.' The words were spoken almost coldly and Brandon stared at her as though seeing her for the first time.

'I admire you, Mary,' he said. 'You go your own way, letting no one hinder you.' He smiled. 'I've seen you drive that monster of a van like another Queen Boadicea and very lovely you looked too.'

Mary felt her colour rising and was uncertain if he was laughing at her or not. She remained silent, waiting for him to continue, but he suddenly seemed bored with her presence, turned away from her and moved to the door at the far end of the room.

'If you'll wait until I finish here, I'll see you back to your home. I wouldn't want to be responsible for allowing someone to rob you.'

She was alone then and she sank back onto the stool, staring at the wooden boards of the floor, seeing every knot, every piece of grain, studying the nail heads as though they were the most important thing in her life.

She heard masculine voices from beyond the door and she ached with a great emptiness. She was a fool, she told herself. All Brandon had to do was to take her in his arms, pay her a few compliments and she would fall at his feet worshipping. She was confused, wanting him and yet knowing within herself that nothing could come of such an emotion but heartache.

It was all very well for Brandon Sutton; she was a plaything to him, a release from his tensions, a ready doxy willing to lift her skirts at the crook of his little finger. And knowing all this, she still longed to be in his arms.

It seemed an age before Brandon returned to the room. By now Mary's head was swimming with weariness and disappointment, all she wanted to do was crawl away into bed and hide from the world. He smiled at her but his eyes were unreadable.

'Mark's told me he's searching for some property for you,' he said conversationally. 'I understand he's just found a place for you to rent.'

Mary stared at him numbly. 'Mark has said nothing to me.' Her lips were stiff and the words sounded stilted and she was aware of Brandon's eyes studying her closely.

'Then I've jumped the gun, I'm sorry,' he said briskly. 'Come on, I'll see you home, you look awful. Good night, Evo!' He called loudly over his shoulder and was met with a faint answering response from the other room.

Mary did not even have the heart to respond to his jibes. She got to her feet and followed him meekly outside into the cold darkness of the night. He took her arm and led her across the uneven ground and she leaned against him for support, tears trembling on her lashes as she thought of what might have been had this man been of her own kind. But he was Brandon Sutton, a man on his own, not fitting into any mould. He was a rarity in the world of Sweyn's Eye, where it had always been worker and boss and never the twain should meet.

Somehow he had breached that gap, had become one of the men while still retaining his own strength of personality. He was a man she could love and respect and Mary knew that no one would ever take his place in her heart.

In silence they walked up the hill towards Market Street. The gaslights shimmered down on the icy pavements, yet Mary didn't feel the cold. She could have walked with Brandon at her side across the whole world.

At the door to the Murphys' house, Brandon halted. He stared down at Mary for a long moment in silence and then, without touching her with his hands, he leaned forward and kissed her.

'Look after yourself, Mary Jenkins,' he said softly and then he was striding away, disappearing into the darkness. Mary watched him go, and could not help feeling that in some strange way he had been saying goodbye to her. She closed her eyes and clung on to the memory of his nearness for a moment, before turning to go indoors.

Chapter Twenty-Four

The bar of the Cape Horner was steamy and damp. Outside, the rain streamed down the windows like tears running in swift eddies along the gutters. Gerwin Price sat inside the bar, his dark eyes darting expectantly to the door every time it opened.

He shifted uneasily in his seat. He had done his part and for that he had yet to be paid, but he wasn't sure that he trusted Sutton the American, or Rickie Richardson if it came to that. He had taken all the risks so it seemed, since he was the one actually to set fire to the press. Had he been caught it would have been prison for him and he dreaded what would happen should he find himself caged up with Billy Gray.

By now Billy would have caught on to the fact that he'd been framed, and it wouldn't take him very long to figure out who was responsible for the break-in at the offices of Brandon Sutton. Billy had never been stupid, but on the night of the robbery he had taken the blame for everything.

Gerwin had watched as Dean Sutton slipped a package of notes into Billy's pockets. Now he frowned at the recollection; you couldn't trust a man like Sutton, not an inch. Gerwin's hands clenched into fists – it burned in his gut to think of the way his old man had died, falling screaming into the black cavern to smash his skull on the rocks below. The old man didn't deserve that. He had worked hard, sweated his guts out, spending the dark hours of the night as watchman instead of being asleep in his bed. Damn and blast Billy Gray for being there at the wrong moment!

His thoughts were interrupted by the swinging open of the double doors and the sudden inrush of wind and rain. He shivered as Rickie Richardson sat down beside him, his collar turned up against the cold.

'You did well.' Rickie eased himself back in the chair. 'Blast this rain, it gets in everywhere.' He shook his trouser leg impatiently, staring down at the sodden material. 'Good job you did on the press, made sure you weren't seen, I suppose?'

Gerwin shook his head. 'Nobody there to watch what I was about, see, didn't expect no trouble, like.' He was uneasy – where was Mr Sutton who was supposed to be bringing the money with him tonight? He looked at Rickie Richardson and the question stuck in his throat. These men weren't his sort, they were clever dicks and had plenty of money to boot. He must be careful, otherwise he could lose out altogether. It didn't do to offend the gentry.

'Mr Sutton can't come himself,' Rickie said casually, 'but he asked me to give you this.' He placed a packet on the table and Gerwin transferred it to his pocket in one slick movement. He smiled, feeling happier now with the money resting against his side. He drank some of the thick dark ale and rubbed the back of his hand across his mouth.

Gerwin Price was not a pleasant sight, Rickie thought in distaste. The man's hair stood up like bundles of hay in a field and his jaw was slack. Why Dean had any truck with the fellow Rickie didn't know. The man was not over-bright by any standards, and his very unpleasantness was enough to draw attention to the fellow. Well, he'd done his bit now and Rickie felt he could leave. He rose to his feet, nodded at the man and left the bar without another word.

Gerwin stared after him. 'Uppity sod!' he muttered. He knew they all looked down their noses at him, but he didn't care a twopenny toss for that. So long as they paid him good money, they could give themselves all the airs and graces in the world.

He ordered another pint of ale and sipped it slowly, savouring the thought of the moment when he would tip out the money and count it at his leisure. The wind outside rattled the trees and pointed branches tapped against the glass panes like skeletal fingers. Gerwin wondered what he should do next; perhaps he could buy himself a floosie, someone nice and not too old. It was a long time since he'd had a woman, a tidy one that was. The idea grew in his mind and lodged there and after a few more drinks, Gerwin pushed back his seat and made for the door.

The rain had abated a little and the wind had dropped, but the cold hand of winter lay over the shadowed streets, frosting the rooftops with silver and turning the hills into fairy-tale islands, the tops lost in the mists.

Gerwin lumbered towards his home, his tread slow and measured. He never did anything quickly, his every action was deliberate, his body as slow-moving as his mind. But he had done a good job on the fire, he told himself with satisfaction; he had enjoyed seeing the flames leaping skywards like the tapping out of the blast furnaces at the works.

The cottage stood on the edge of the Sutton estate. It was small and dingy and since the death of his father, the conditions in which Gerwin lived had become steadily worse, the younger members of the family had long since been taken off to the workhouse and now Gerwin lived alone.

'Like a pig in shit!' he said aloud as the smell greeted him when he opened the creaking front door. The stench from the kitchen was enough to make him heave and he wrinkled up his nose as he bent to put a match to the fire. He must get the place a bit more tidy, if he meant to bring some floosie home for the night. Whores they might be, but they were women and liked a bit of niceness around them.

His idea of clearing away was to dump all the stale pieces of bread and bacon rind into a sack, along with empty tins and potato peelings. He threw cold water over the floor and rubbed at the accumulation of grease with a broom in a futile attempt to clean the slates.

Later, he washed himself down at the pump in the yard, shivering at the coldness of the night air. He stared up into the heavens, wondering why he was alone in life and depending on the paid services of a whore for comfort instead of coming home to a sweet young wife as other men did. He brushed back his hair, trying vainly to suppress the springy tufts. If he took great care with his appearançe, might he not find himself a nice respectable girl, he thought with sudden hope – he had money now.

When he was ready, he stared at himself in the cracked mirror over the mantelpiece. 'Not 'arf bad,' he said slowly. He had found a shirt that once belonged to his father. It was one used for weddings and funerals and though the collar was a little tight for Gerwin, it was crisp and clean and looked better than his own shirts which were ingrained now with filth.

The sky was clearer, the mists dispelled by the sharp breeze coming in from the sea as Gerwin walked with his usual measured tread down towards the lights of the town. They glittered at him like jewels and his spirits rose. There was no need for a well set-up young chap to be without a woman, he told himself. He had a house and some money in his pocket, which was quite a lot to offer a girl in his opinion.

He went towards the lighted windows of the Mexico Fountain and stood for a moment looking inside. There were women there of course, but floosies all of them with floured faces and red lips and over-bright hair. Perhaps he would have one of them first, just to take the edge off his appetite, then he could start looking round for a respectable girl.

It was warm and cosy in the public bar with the resonant sounds of male laughter and the happy chatter of the women making an accompaniment to the swish of beer as it ran into the waiting mugs. Gerwin tried to see a floosie on her own, but every one of them seemed taken up with some fellow or other. He attached himself to the fringe of one of the crowds, hanging on to his mug of ale like grim death, his mouth dry.

'Bad day it's been, hasn't it?' He spoke too loudly and curious stares were fixed upon him. 'But it's not raining now,' he continued desperately, 'cold though and windy.'

He heard a sweep of laughter and then someone in the crowd muttered something that sounded like 'windbag yourself, man' and he felt the colour rise hot and red to his face. He swilled down the ale, spilling some of it over his clean shirt which caused even more amusement.

Quickly he left the bar, feeling pain and anger surge through him as he stood outside, his big hands hanging at his sides. He was like a friendly dog that had been kicked and suddenly his fist lashed out, hitting the hard stone of the wall. He sucked the blood from his knuckles and moved away from the lighted windows.

'Scum!' He spoke angrily. 'Whores and pimps, the lot of you!' He walked down the hill towards the chapel at *Pentre Estyll.* Pausing, he noticed that the windows gleamed like beacons in the darkness, proclaiming that there was a meeting being conducted behind the thick stone walls.

He leaned against the rough bark of a tree; the ground was sodden beneath his feet, but he did not notice. As he heard the sound of singing rising sweetly on the silent night air, clean and good, Gerwin felt tears come into his eyes.

He wasn't a bad man, not really; he only did harm to those who deserved it. He was misunderstood – no one seemed prepared to talk to him and listen to what he wanted to say.

When the singing finished, there was a stir from behind the chapel doors and his face was lit with happiness as he saw the girls come out into the night with their basket hats and warm shawls wrapped round their shoulders. They breathed little puffs of mist as they talked to each other and he waited, reluctant to approach them. Perhaps he ought to go home after all, he was not going to find anyone among this lot.

But then one girl came out alone, standing still in the light from the doorway, her hair gleaming as it peeped out from under the brim of her hat. She hugged her shawl closer and Gerwin could see the small but womanly shape of her and his breathing became uneven. Why was she standing there alone looking up and down in the darkness? Was she waiting for someone?

The lights went out behind her one by one and still she stood there. Gerwin's heart dipped in pity; she was being rejected just as he was, but he would not let her be sad, he would take her to his home and look after her. He would watch for a moment longer, until the old lady and gentleman who were calling their good nights had gone from sight, then he would go to her and take her home.

Rhian was angry, but she concealed her feelings as she said her good nights to the Reverend Parker and his wife.

'Yes, lovely meeting, thank you. Of course I'll come again, it was very uplifting.' She watched them walk away and for a moment envied them. Mrs Parker was clinging to her husband's arm and he was leaning forward, giving her his full attention as though every word she spoke was a pearl of wisdom.

Rhian glanced up the lane. Where was Heath? He had promised to come and meet her after practice. He was being so offhand with her that it was driving her to distraction. He knew how she felt about him; was it her fault that she believed a girl should remain chaste until after the wedding ceremony. A trick to trap a man, that was the way Heath looked upon her scruples. She could hear the derisory tone in his voice even now.

'Girls do what they like with men nowadays,' he had said just before she left the house earlier. 'No need to wait for the wedding bells. Try it out, see if you like it first, for it's no good changing your mind afterwards.' He had laughed at her shocked expression, not knowing that she was picturing him in Carrie's arms.

'Never mind, you've got a lot of growing up to do yet, *cariad*.' But she was grown up, Rhian thought indignantly. She was a working girl earning her own living, paying Auntie for her keep. That she had been unable to work these last weeks because of her burned arm was not her fault. In any case, the laundry needed rebuilding and there was talk that it might never be opened again.

Rhian stirred restlessly, feeling the cold of the stone step bite in through the soles of her boots. Perhaps she should wait no longer but make her own way back home. She pouted, for she had looked forward to talking alone with Heath away from her aunt, who seemed to listen to everything she said.

She shivered and drew the shawl more tightly around her shoulders, deciding she would give Heath a few more minutes – perhaps he had been delayed. And maybe he wasn't coming at all, said a voice inside her. Anger was replaced by despair then and Rhian began to walk away from the silent empty chapel which stood over her like some great dark monster.

She thought she heard footsteps, slow and measured, following her along the lane towards the road, told herself sternly that she was being silly and allowing her imagination to get the better of her. Yet the footsteps continued like the dull thud of a heartbeat behind her.

Rhian quickened her pace, but as she looked over her shoulder she saw a large shape loom up behind her. She would have screamed, but a hand was across her mouth and dark eyes were staring into hers. The man held her against his body, talking to her and soothing her as though she was a spirited filly.

'There now, be quiet like and I'll take care of you. No need to be afeared of me, I shan't do you any harm. Just come home with me where we can talk.'

Rhian tried to protest but she was being dragged bodily along the dark lane. And although she attempted to resist, her struggles were useless.

'You're scared,' he said, almost in wonder. 'Your heart is beating like a little trapped bird.' His hand was on her breast and Rhian shrank inside herself.

'Don't be worried, I'm only taking you home. I've got a pocket full of money and I'll see you are all right. Gerwin Price is my name, perhaps you'll tell me yours when we get more friendly.'

Rhian felt blind panic race through her. She knew of Gerwin Price, he was the reason for her brother being behind prison walls. God, she couldn't tell him her name or he would kill her for sure. He believed that Billy was responsible for the death of his father.

She kicked out and then caught at the branch of a tree with her hands. Gerwin dragged at her impatiently and her arms were almost pulled from their sockets. She cried out against the palm that covered her lips with bruising strength but nothing, it seemed, would deter the man from his intention of taking her to his home.

She felt her strength ebb away. Her feet were dragging along the ground now, she was trembling with fear. Was there no one to see her and help her escape from the clutches of this madman? A faint moon crept from between the clouds, the streets were silent for Gerwin had taken the small byroads out of town.

As the twinkling, friendly lights from the houses faded away, Rhian's last hopes of escape died. Now she was being lifted bodily over a small wall, they were crossing a field and still the hand was clasped to her mouth until she thought she would never draw breath again.

A small cottage suddenly loomed up before them and he kicked open the door. Then she was inside and the foetid smell almost made her gag. He pushed her into a chair and lit an oil lamp and then he was holding it above his head, smiling down at her like some demon out of hell.

'Why have you brought me here?' Rhian asked, her teeth chattering with fear. He smiled and placed the lamp between them and Rhian saw that the table was filthy, the grooves between the planking filled with grease.

He ignored her question. 'You're a good girl, come from the chapel, haven't you?'

Rhian nodded. 'Yes, but I don't know who you are, so what do you want with me?' She must be calm, she told herself, talk to him nicely, not anger him and then perhaps he would not harm her. So suddenly that she screamed in fear, he snatched at her hand and examined it under the light.

'You haven't got a husband, see, there's no wedding ring on your finger. How would you like to stay with me?'

Rhian strove to control herself. 'I am promised to someone, though, and I must keep my word – you surely know that?'

'Look girlie, I may be drunk,' he said roughly, 'but I'm not soft in the head, mind. If you haven't got a ring, then you have never had a man between your legs, now is that true?'

Rhian began to cry, she could not help herself. Tears loomed up into her eyes and ran down her cheeks. Gerwin muttered an oath and went to the cupboard, taking out a bottle of gin and swallowing deeply. After a moment, he returned to her.

'Look, why don't you make us something to eat and tidy up a bit about the house,' he suggested, his voice slurred. 'I know the place don't seem much now, but women have got the knack of making it all look right.' He leaned over, his voice rising. 'And stop blubbering, I can't stand a woman who blubbers.'

Rhian got to her feet quickly and rolled up her sleeves. 'If you want me to do cleaning, you'd better build up that fire,' she said quickly. 'I can't do without hot water, can I?'

As she hoped, he needed to go outside for firewood. Rhian was halfway across the room when Gerwin returned almost immediately with an armful of logs. She hung her shawl on the peg behind the door, pretending that was all she intended to do. He looked her over approvingly as she stood rigidly waiting for him to tend the fire.

'You're a pretty girl, what's your name?' he asked and she spoke quickly, afraid of offending him.

'Rhian,' she said and then could have bitten out her tongue for telling him the truth.

'That's nice,' he said, nodding his head, 'it will do very well.' He smiled. 'How would you like to be Mrs Rhian Price, doesn't that sound good?'

'Give me that water quickly,' she said, trying to speak calmly, 'otherwise I'm never going to get the place cleaned up.' She pointed to the bottle of gin. 'Have a drop more why don't you? I'm sure you must be very cold waiting out there in the night air for me, the drink will warm you up a bit.' Perhaps he would drink himself senseless, she thought desperately and then he might fall asleep. In the meantime, she would keep herself busy and clean up the awful mess, though her stomach was turned by the stale smell in the room.

She scrubbed the table until her fingers were raw, but at last the wood showed from beneath the grease fresh and white in the lamplight. It took her longer to clean the floor and by the time she had finished her knees were sore and her back ached intolerably. Yet as she stood and surveyed the change her efforts had made in the small kitchen, she felt a strange pride. The fire glowed cheerfully in the grate and the kettle was singing on the hob. Gerwin must have sensed her feeling, for he smiled suddenly.

'You see, it will be a nice house when you have finished. Come and sit by here and I'll give you a cup of tea. I don't want you to work too hard or you'll think I'm a bully.'

Rhian needed to rest, she had never worked so hard in her life. Yet she approached the table carefully as though moving close to a wild beast and jumped violently when his hand reached out to cover hers.

'I'd treat you fine, like, if you'd stay with me,' he said. 'You wouldn't want for nothing.' She repressed a shudder, avoiding his eyes which were glazed with drink.

'I'm sure you'd make a very good husband.' She spoke carefully, as though rehearsing the lines. 'Any woman would be lucky to have you.' His grip tightened on hers. 'Do you mean that, Rhian?' he asked earnestly and swallowing hard, she nodded.

'Yes, but may I go home now? Auntie will be worried about me.'

He looked at her carefully and after what seemed an eternity he nodded. 'Yes, I'spects you should go home. I'll fetch your shawl.'

He picked up her Bible and flipped it open, frowning as he tried to make out the name inscribed on the cover. Rhian stood stock-still, fear crawling over her like icy fingers.

'Rhian Gray,' he said at last, then his head jerked up. 'Gray, you are kin to that Billy Gray, the one who killed my father!' He gripped her arm and shook her roughly. 'Don't deny it, I can see it in your face. I knowed I seen you somewhere before.'

Rhian had never been more frightened in her life, she thought she would fall into a faint for her head was swimming and the room spun around her. Gerwin lifted his hand and she felt a stinging blow catch her temple; lights spun inside her head, exploding like shooting sparks from the copper works and then she was on the floor, grasping at the table leg and trying to steady herself.

He was crouching over her, his eyes blazing, a muscle in his face twitching. Rhian tried to crawl away from him, but he leaned on her arms, pinning her to the cold stone which was still damp from her scrubbing.

Rhian shook her head, her body cold as though she was dying piece by piece. She knew what he intended to do and her mind rebelled. Her head fell back and her eyes rolled; she tried to scream but he placed one hand over her mouth, tearing at her clothing with the other.

It was a nightmare without end and Rhian was past tears or hope. She lay still while he debased her and even the pain could not rouse her to action. At last he crawled away from her grunting like an animal. Without a backward glance, he stumbled to the stairway and she heard him curse as he tripped over the step.

It was only the fear of his return, trickling slowly into her mind, that forced her into movement. She managed to rise to her knees and straighten her torn clothing, her movements jerky like a puppet with someone pulling the strings. Wrapping her shawl closely over her bruised breasts, she cautiously opened the door.

The cold of the night air hit her like a burst of icy water and then she was hurrying away from the cottage, stumbling over the fields, the silent moon above her giving her light. She did not cry for her world had come to an end – she would never be a whole person again, so what use were tears? She kept close to the wall, like a cat slinking unseen around corners. She could face no one, could never speak of what had happened to her this night. The only way she could bear to live was to try and put it all out of her mind. But she knew that in the deep of night she would lie sleepless in her bed, reliving the nightmare that had come true.

The house was silent as Rhian let herself in by the back door. Cautiously she lit a lamp and carefully and systematically, removed her clothing, wrapping the bloodstained garments into a bundle. Then she began to wash, the cold water stinging her torn flesh. The morning light was creeping in through the window by the time she felt able to go to her bed and search for the sleep that would not come.

Chapter Twenty-Five

A light powdering of snow covered the branches of the holly trees, lighting up the gardens like a scene from a Christmas card. Delmai stood looking around her as she entered the hall of Dean Sutton's house, her hands tingling with cold even though she wore good leather gloves. She rubbed her fingers together and Bertha looked at her sympathetically.

'Come in and sit by the fire in the drawing room, Mrs Richardson,' the maid said kindly. 'I'm sure Mr Sutton will not be long.'

'Thank you, Bertha,' Delmai said quickly. 'I've come to commiserate with Dean over the loss of his dear father.'

Bertha's eyes were sad and there were touches of grey in her hair. 'Aye, it's a sad time for the master, what with him losing his dear wife not so long back and now this…'

Delmai reached out a hand and touched the maid's arm comfortingly. 'I know it must be hard for you too,' she said softly.

As she sat near the fire she heard the sounds of the doorbell chiming in the hallway. She bit her lip; it seemed that Dean had other visitors and she had wished to speak to him alone.

'Delmai, how wonderful you look! I'm sure you have shed pounds, my dear, and all the better for it.' Marian Thomas came towards her, hands outstretched, an expression of curiosity in the narrowing of her catlike eyes. It was clear she was wondering just what Delmai was doing in the house of a man so recently a widower, and she a woman who had left her husband.

'I'm feeling fine, Marian,' Delmai forced a smile, 'and you?' Marian settled herself in an armchair near the roaring fire and peeled off her gloves. 'As ever,' she replied airily. 'But tell me, how are you finding life down in Canal Street? Wasn't that explosion in the laundry a dreadful affair – poor Dean, he's suffered quite enough in the past few months, hasn't he?'

Delmai nodded, 'Yes, he has.' She felt ashamed that she had come as much to ask Dean's help as to offer him sympathy, yet she thought he could do a great deal in the fight to free Billy Gray from prison. She reasoned that Dean, who had once been Billy's employer, would have nothing but good to say of him and apart from that, he had some pull with the dignitaries of Sweyn's Eye. It had seemed a good idea, but now she wasn't so sure. In any case, how could she possibly broach the subject with Marian Thomas sitting there waiting to drink in every word she spoke?

'Two funerals in as many months,' Marian was saying. 'What a dreadful blow for Dean to lose his dear father so quickly after poor Bea's dramatic death.' Delmai inclined her head, not disposed to answer. She was busy with her thoughts, wondering how she might corner Dean and tell him about her idea of offering a petition to the governor with a view to reassessing Billy's case. Her hopes of talking privately to him were completely dashed when he entered the room with Dr Thomas, who was talking in his usual ponderous way, putting his pipe in his mouth at every other word and sucking on it as though it clarified his thoughts.

'Delmai, I'm delighted to see you!' Dean came forward and took her hands and then turned to include Marian in his greeting. 'I'm sure honoured to have two beautiful ladies in my drawing room.'

Marian immediately engaged Dean in conversation and Dr Thomas sat beside Delmai, his kindly eyes resting on her.

'And how are you, my dear?' he asked in genuine concern. Delmai had the uncomfortable feeling that he understood a great deal more about her separation from her husband than he let on.

'I'm well enough,' she replied and feeling that she had been a little abrupt, she forced a smile. 'Canal Street suits me, though I was very perturbed by the explosion in the laundry.' She lowered her voice and the doctor nodded his head.

'Bad business, that. It wouldn't have happened if Mali had still owned the place. Scrupulous she was, and she had Mary Jenkins as overseer – a fine woman who knew her job down to the last degree. A pity old Mr Sutton saw fit to replace her.'

Delmai's eyes slid away at the mention of Mali Richardson. She was a remarkable woman and she had married the better of the two Richardson brothers, but Delmai could not help feeling that she was an upstart, a woman climbing above her station.

Yet she envied her too, the realisation was like the moon suddenly appearing from beneath the clouds. What would she give, Delmai thought, to move out of her own class and marry Billy Gray? The idea was preposterous, and yet she could imagine herself being happy with the gentle man who had managed to awaken her feelings and without hardly even touching her.

'You're far away, Delmai, a penny for them!' Dean was smiling down at her and Delmai glanced up at him quickly.

'I was just thinking it's about time I went home,' she said as she glanced out of the window. 'If it snows any more, I shall have all my work cut out to get down the hill.'

As she had hoped, Dean saw her to the door. She paused in the hallway and took a deep breath.

'You know how grieved I am about your father,' she said softly, 'that goes without saying. But apart from that, there's a favour I'd like to ask you.' She spoke as lightly as she could. 'I think Billy Gray deserves to have his case reviewed, I'm convinced he's innocent and I believe you are too.'

Dean had a thoughtful look on his face which Delmai did not quite understand. 'He's such a fine man,' she went on desperately, 'and from the talks I've had with him at the prison, I'm convinced that he did not steal anything and wasn't even at your brother's premises. It was an accident of circumstances, that's all.'

Dean was staring down at the young earnest face before him without really thinking of the words she was saying. The idea of allowing Billy Gray out of prison was a tempting one if it only served to spite Brandon. He burned with frustration and anger when he thought of his brother taking all that should have been his, for in Grenville Sutton's will he had left everything to Brandon. He would not stand for such treatment, though, and had already put the matter in the hands of his lawyer. Dean meant to contest the will and Brandon would find he had a fight on his hands.

Apart from that, there were still times in the sleepless hours of the night when he ached for Mary Jenkins. At such times he felt he could cheerfully kill if only he could possess her. What a fool he had been to let her go when he'd had her under his roof and could have rid himself of the fever of wanting her, except that his pride had been hurt.

But here was a way of spiking his brother's guns, he thought with satisfaction. If Gray was let loose, God knows what he would do when he found that his lady-love had played him false. It was adding insult to injury that the man responsible for putting him behind bars was now bedding his woman.

Dean smiled down at Delmai and rested a hand on her shoulder. 'Honey, I think you're right,' he said softly. 'I shall do all in my power to help you free Billy and I'm only surprised I didn't think of it myself.'

As Delmai walked down the hill through the lightly falling snow, her mouth was curving into a smile and her heart was light. She would go home and have a drink of port to celebrate, for now – with Dean Sutton on her side – she knew it was only a matter of time before Billy was freed.

Next time she visited him, she would have some real news for him and she could imagine even now the way his eyes would warm and his face come alive. Her heart ached and her arms longed to hold him. Then doubts rushed in – when he was free, would Billy be out of her grasp? If he returned to work for Dean Sutton, she would scarcely ever see him. How could she suddenly begin to visit *Ty Mawr* when she had not done so before?

However, there was a solution. She could offer Billy a job herself; she could buy a carriage and he could be her groom instead of Dean Sutton's. No one would take it amiss; she was a prison visitor, a do-gooder in many people's eyes and all she could be accused of was taking her position too seriously.

As for Mary Jenkins, she would pose no threat. Delmai was sure that she had turned Billy away from any thoughts of taking up his romance where it had left off. Mary was not the one for Billy, she was ambitious and proud and Billy needed love and gentleness.

As she passed the laundry gates, Delmai shuddered at the desolation of the ruined building. No steam rose from the rooftops and no smell of dirty laundry being boiled. Large boulders lay strewn across the yard and one of the trees had been torn from its roots to lie like a gaunt skeleton in the gloom.

Hurrying into the warmth and comfort of her house, Delmai did not know that she had given Dean Sutton ammunition in his fight against his brother. Had she been aware of the fact, however, it was doubtful whether it would have deterred her from taking the only course of action that was possible.

–

Brandon sat in his office with a sheaf of papers in his hands. He was frowning as he thought of the funeral, cold and stark, and of the cemetery that faced into the teeth of the winds coming in from the sea. He could still scarcely believe that his father was dead, and though in his heart he knew it was not Dean's fault, he could not help but feel bitterness against his brother. There had been an angry scene at the reading of the will and Brandon had felt an urge to punch his brother's face in fury until the pain that burned within him was extinguished.

Mark stepped into the office and Brandon looked up quickly.

'This is going to be better than the first handbook,' he said with forced cheerfulness. 'All that remains is for us to make sure it gets printed this time.'

Mark nodded. 'Aye, I'll keep my eyes skinned; there'll be no more fires, I'll make damn sure of that.'

Brandon ran his fingers through his hair so that it stood up thick and crisp, curling across his brow. 'I'm going to get off home now,' he said. 'You keep watch tonight and don't come in tomorrow. I'll see to everything at the works.'

He stepped out briskly across the fields, his hands thrust into his pockets for warmth. He should be feeling on top of the world, he told himself, since he was beginning to make headway at the steelworks, the profits though small were coming in regularly and now the handbook was almost completed. So why was there this niggling sense of discontent running through his veins?

He needed a woman, he told himself, someone warm and passionate and yet who would not attempt to bind him with promises. Mary Jenkins sprang to mind at once and he smiled to himself, for she was more likely to send him away with a flea in his ear than take him to her bed.

And yet the idea, once rooted in his mind, would not be shaken free. He thought of the cottage Mark had found for Mary; he had said it was situated in the valley between the Town Hill and the Kilvey Deep. Without conscious effort, Brandon found himself heading in the direction of the valley and cursed himself for a fool. Mary would hardly be in residence yet, last time he had spoken to her she had not even known about the place.

It was strange really how thoughts of Mary had haunted him. He had known many women, taken them into his arms, given of his passion until he was spent, yet never had he found a woman remaining in his thoughts so long after he had possessed her. Mary was passionate and yet she offered him more than mere sensuality – she offered him herself and he had taken of her freely. So different from the other Mary that there could be no comparison, he realised suddenly.

Mary Jenkins was a remarkable woman, with a good business head and a quick mind. She had courage too and beauty, but even though she was all these things, Brandon knew there was another side to her. She had run to his brother with information – it *must* have been her, there could be no one else. Perhaps she had given Dean the benefit of her beauty at the same time. The thought stuck in his throat and threatened to choke him and Brandon once more cursed himself for a fool. His footsteps slowed and he almost turned back in his tracks, yet something within him urged him to go on.

The cottage stood alone; it was unmistakeable, picturesque yet sturdy. The roof was covered in snow, the trees around lifting white fingers to the dark sky. The windows were ablaze with light and Brandon knew with a sudden lightening of his spirits that she was within.

He paused, wondering if she had company. She would hardly be there alone, not a woman like Mary. Perhaps even now she was lying naked in some other man's arms, and why shouldn't she have lovers? The very thought set his teeth on edge.

He walked around to the back of the small house and noticed the trail of smoke rising from the chimneys. The curtains were open and he saw Mary's figure through the glass as she bent over the table. His mouth tightened; the settings were for two people.

Impatiently he turned and strode away. There was a mist before his eyes and anger surged through him even as he called himself a fool. Well, he should learn a lesson and leave Mary Jenkins strictly alone. They had no place in each other's lives and the sooner he fixed that thought into his head the better. And yet as he strode through the darkening night, there was a strange feeling eating at the corners of his mind which not even to himself would he admit to be jealousy.

–

Inside the cottage it was cosy and warm and Mary looked up as Mali appeared in her kitchen doorway. 'I'm getting a bit lonely in there,' she said, but her smile belied her words. Mali was large with child, her eyes were shadowed with fatigue, yet there was a happiness about her that was plain to read in the contented curve of her mouth.

'Sit down by there,' Mary said quickly. 'I was going to call you as soon as the meal was ready.'

Mali settled herself into a chair and leaned back sighing gently. 'It's a nice house, Mary, it has a lovely feel about it as though the people who lived here were happy.'

Mary smiled, absent-mindedly moving the cutlery. 'Yes, I feel that too,' she said. 'I'm so grateful to Mark for finding the cottage for me. I think I was beginning to wear out my welcome at the Murphys'. It's nice to have my own possessions around me again too.'

Mary knew Mali's eyes were resting upon her and she continued to busy herself with the cutlery, but Mali would not be deterred.

'And what about you, Mary?' The question was light, softly spoken and Mary sank into her chair, staring at her hands.

'Me, I'm a business woman, you should know that – I always have been.' She shrugged. 'With Billy likely to remain in prison for the rest of his days, there's nothing else for me to look forward to except making as good a life for myself as I can.' She met Mali's eyes. 'At any rate I can make sure I don't end up in the poverty I was born to,' she smiled. 'Which brings me to rather an important matter. I was going to wait until after we'd eaten, but I might just as well give you this now.' She rose and from the cupboard took a tin box, smiling in delight. 'I've got your money, Mali! I said it would only be a loan, didn't I?'

'Oh, Mary! Sterling and I meant it as a gift, a thank you for running the laundry so well. I don't want it back.'

'But you must take it,' Mary said earnestly. 'I wouldn't feel right if you didn't.'

'Well, we'll see,' Mali said. 'Now put the box away and let's eat, I'm starving.'

The meal was simple but Mary saw with satisfaction how much her friend enjoyed it.

'This *cawl* is delicious,' Mali said, breaking a piece of bread and with a mischievous smile dipping it into the soup that was thick with meat and vegetables. 'Good thing Sterling isn't here, he'd give me a good ticking-off for eating like a hoyden!'

Mary glanced at the clock ticking on the wall. 'What time is he coming to fetch you? Not too early, I hope?'

Mali grimaced. 'Well, he won't be too late. He's determined to look after me as though I am a china doll to be wrapped in cotton wool.'

Mary smiled. 'I can see that you're still as much in love with your husband as you ever were. You don't know how lucky you are, Mali Llewelyn.'

'Mali Richardson, if you please, I'm a respectably married woman.' When Mali laughed, her whole face lit up and Mary didn't wonder that Sterling took such good care of her. She was small and dainty – the direct opposite to herself, Mary thought ruefully.

'Are you hoping for a girl this time?' Mary took the soup bowls away and placed slices of lamb on a plate, garnishing the meat with tiny baked potatoes still in their jackets.

'I'll be like an overfed monster by the time I've finished,' Mali protested, 'and yes, I would like a daughter. But for now I'll settle for some of those lovely Welsh cakes.'

'Eat up!' Mary said. 'There's two of you to feed, mind.' She smiled at Mali but there was an ache in her throat. She envied her friend the happiness that radiated from her. Mali had changed, become more confident, her manner polished and her head held proudly. She was a woman loved and it showed.

'Why are you staring at me? Have I grown two heads or something?' Mali laughed softly, brushing back a wisp of dark hair that had escaped from the confining pins.

Mary smiled. 'No, not grown two heads at all. I was just thinking that marriage and motherhood suit you down to the ground.'

Mali leaned forward earnestly, her elbows on the table. 'And making a career for yourself suits you too. I've never seen you looking so beautiful.' She paused. 'It's almost as though you've been sleeping and have woken up – there's a light about you somehow that wasn't there before.' She shrugged. 'I expect I'm talking a lot of nonsense. Let's have some Welsh cakes now, shall we?'

Mary moved about the room, bending over the fire to make a pot of tea, glad of an excuse for the sudden heat in her cheeks. Mali was too perceptive, she saw change but did not know the reason for it although Mary did. Ever since she had met Brandon she was a different person; it was as Mali had said, as if she had come out of a long sleep.

By the time Sterling called to take Mali home, she was flushed with laughter. She took her husband's arm and looked up into his face and the joy in her eyes was painful for Mary to see. She felt like an outsider, staring in at a fairy-tale world in which she could have no part.

'What do you think, Sterling?' Mali leaned against her husband's shoulder. 'Mary wants to give us the money back, tell her she must keep it!'

Sterling rubbed his hand through the thick golden hair and smiled at Mary. He was so handsome, it was no wonder Mali was head over heels in love with him, Mary thought.

'You must invest it, Mary,' Sterling said reasonably. 'Plough it back into the business and if you feel you owe us anything then, give us a percentage of the profit.'

Mary stared at him doubtfully. 'But I'm in a position to repay you right now,' she said. 'I was grateful for the loan, but I can't presume to keep it.'

Sterling touched her arm. 'This is business, Mary. I can see you are going to be a big success and I want a part in it. That's not charity, that's sound sense.'

'All right,' Mary said at last, 'consider yourselves shareholders as from now. I'll see a solicitor about it as soon as possible and keep it all above board.'

Mali leaned forward and kissed Mary's cheek. 'As if you would ever think of cheating us, don't be silly!'

Sterling opened the door and a flurry of snowy air blew into the house. 'Mary's right,' he said. 'Always be businesslike, that's the way.'

Mary watched the hansom cab drive away into the darkness and then returned to sit before the fire, staring at the flames, her hopes high as she planned what to do with the money she had saved so religiously. There were all sorts of possibilities open to her now that it was still hers to use.

She locked up the house conscientiously, throwing the bolts across and then drawing the curtains over the windows. She had been nervous of being spied upon ever since Gerwin Price had walked so easily into the kitchen of the house in Canal Street.

She washed the dishes and put them neatly away, then settled to some mending. She grimaced as she restitched a hem in one of her petticoats; far better if she had given the garment to Muriel to sew on the machine.

Her hands fell idle in her lap but her thoughts were racing, making the blood pound in her head. What if she were to buy a store, open up her very own shop? She could sell everything from underwear to fruit and vegetables in the same building and she would have no difficulty in finding people to work for her.

The money Mali had insisted on investing would more than cover a down payment. But then property on the scale that she envisaged buying would cost far more than she could afford. A smile suddenly curved Mary's mouth as she put aside her sewing. 'That's a very good idea,' she said out loud, 'and it would just serve the Cooperative Movement right!'

Chapter Twenty-Six

It was Christmas and Sweyn's Eye was covered by a benign layer of white that hid the ugliness of the town, beautifying even the scattering of buildings that sprawled along the banks of the river Swan.

Rhian dressed for the outdoors. Her fingers obeyed her, lacing up her boots and fastening buttons, but it was as though they had a life of their own and were not a part of her.

'Come on, *merchi.*' Heath stood in the doorway, coat collar turned up, a white silk scarf tucked in at the throat. His cap was pulled down at a jaunty angle over his brow so that Rhian could not see his eyes, but she heard the concern in his voice. He came closer to her and took her hand and when she stared down at her fingers lying within his it was as though she was not part of the scene but an onlooker, standing outside herself. She felt nothing, not even the warmth of his hand curling in hers.

'Auntie Agnes is as excited as a child to be going to Mary's for dinner.' Heath's voice was falsely hearty; he was trying to understand, to be patient, but he did not know of the horrors that haunted her imagination.

'All right.' She spoke slowly like someone waking from sleep. 'I'm ready.'

Heath put his hands on her shoulders and she looked away from him, wincing slightly. He spoke softly as though to a frightened dumb creature. 'Can't you talk to me, Rhian? What's been wrong with you these past weeks, what's happened?' He tipped up her face to look into her eyes and Rhian sighed heavily.

'The hansom cab is waiting,' she said and her voice was light, without substance.

'It can wait!' Heath said angrily. He drew her close to him and rested his chin upon her head. 'Why won't you tell me what's wrong? You're so thin and pale lately, I just don't know what to make of you.'

Rhian moved restlessly. 'We must go, Auntie will be wondering where we are.'

Heath shook his head, admitting defeat. 'If you won't speak to me then I can't make you, but I'm going to see Dr Thomas about you. There's something wrong and I mean to find out what it is.'

A small flicker of animation touched Rhian's features. 'Mind your own business, Heath,' she said. 'I don't want any interference in my life, don't you understand?'

Heath led the way out into the cold air without another word and Rhian looked around her at the white-covered trees, branches pointing starkly towards an overcast sky that promised more snow. The world was frozen just as she was inside, as she had been ever since... Her thoughts veered away from a subject too painful to even approach and she sank into the seat beside her aunt, the cold leather striking chill to her bones.

'Goodness, I feel like a child at a Sunday school outing,' Agnes said cheerfully. 'Wasn't it kind of Mary to ask us over to her new house? I'm just dying to see it.' Rhian felt the cab jerk into motion and she stared out of the window pretending an interest in the countryside as an excuse for not answering her aunt's question. She was aware of Heath sitting opposite her, a confusion of brightly coloured parcels in his arms. He frowned and Rhian glanced away from him quickly, reading the reproof in his expression.

Mary's house stood under the folding hills surrounded by ghostly trees, looking like a Christmas card. Rhian dimly heard Auntie Agnes croon with delight as Heath helped her through the laborious task of descending from the cab. Mary was at the door smiling with pleasure and Rhian noticed without real interest that she looked beautiful. She was dressed in a gown of rich ruby-red velvet with white lace ruffles at the collar, and her hair was upswept into glossy waves. She looked like a queen, Rhian thought, lovely and untouchable.

She shivered even as she moved into the warmth of the house behind her aunt, who was laughing uproariously at something Heath had said. Rhian stood still, looking around her at the glistening holly leaves rich with berries and the bright fire that roared in the open grate, but she still felt cold.

'Rhian, is your arm quite better now?' Mary was taking her shawl from her shoulders but Rhian held tightly to the heavy flannel, knowing that without it she would feel exposed. Mary looked puzzled. 'What's wrong Rhian? You look so pale and thin, not sick are you, *cariad*?'

Heath took his sister's arm and led her away. 'Put the kettle on, there's a good girl, let's all have some hot toddies, shall we?' Rhian watched with jaundiced eyes as Heath bent to talk to his sister. He was confiding in her, telling her about Rhian's strange behaviour, she knew it as surely as if she could hear the words. Mary glanced over at her and then looked quickly away, nodding her agreement to something Heath was saying. Rhian sat stiffly on a chair and stared into the flames of the fire, wishing she had pleaded a headache and stayed at home. But then Heath or Aunt Agnes would have insisted on sending for the doctor, she thought wearily. Why couldn't folk just leave her alone?

Rhian endured the parcel opening and the huge dinner of roast chicken and stuffing without too much difficulty, but when Aunt Agnes went to the piano and began playing carols, she felt she could not bear to be shut in the room a moment longer. She rose to her feet and moved to the door, unaware that Mary was watching her carefully.

'Off to look at the garden, are you, Rhian?' Mary said gently. 'Be careful out there, it's slippery, mind.'

Rhian nodded and let herself outside, breathing softly, her heart feeling as though it was going to stop altogether. She looked around at the bushes and trees that remained still and silent as though frozen for ever, and wondered would they bloom in spring as they did every year or had the earth simply died?

Then she left the garden and moved towards the pond in the shelter of the trees, staring at its glassy surface as though it offered her comfort. It would be so easy to slip beneath the ice, to feel the rest of her freeze by inches as her mind and spirit had already done. She moved towards the edge of the pond and her fingers rootled in the stiff grass to find a stone. She beat at the ice until it cracked and then she pulled away slices of it, making a hole big enough for a person to slip through. Rhian stood looking at the green water for a long time, unaware that her hands were as cold as the ice they had been breaking.

'Rhian!' Mary's voice broke into her thoughts. 'What on earth are you doing out here, you'll catch your death of cold.'

Mary took her arm and led her away from the edge of the pond, staring down into her face in concern. 'Won't you tell me what's wrong, *merchi*?' she pleaded softly. 'Something terrible has happened to you, I just know it has. Is it anything to do with Heath?'

Rhian shook her head dumbly. Her lips were pressed close together, and she could not even think of the horrors that had befallen her, let alone speak of them to Mary.

'Come on inside then and have a warm drink. Look, your poor fingers are blue with the cold, silly girl!' Mary's arm around her shoulder propelled Rhian back towards the house where the sound of voices rose and fell to the tinkling accompaniment of the piano.

Rhian sat in the corner and wrapped her arms around her body, wanting only to return to her own room where she could lie in bed and stare at the green-painted wall. She resented the prodding and prying of other people who only wanted her to relive the nightmare she would sooner forget.

Visitors came and went. Rhian stared without interest at Sterling Richardson, who had married a copperman's daughter.

'It's a girl, Mary!' he said excitedly. 'We've got a daughter.'

Why were some women's lives blessed and others like herself – cursed, Rhian wondered.

When Mary asked Aunt Agnes if she would like to stay for mince pies and a drink of porter, Rhian would have cried had she been capable of tears. She sank further back into her chair, refusing the wine and tried to shut herself off from the festivities around her. She had no reason to rejoice for she was an outcast, not worthy to associate with decent company. How they would all recoil from her in horror if they knew what had happened. Even Mary with her kind eyes and strong mouth would shake her head and somehow blame her. She was a bad girl, little better than a floosie.

'Come on, have some porter.' Mary held out a glass and reluctantly Rhian took it, sipping it obediently though she did not even like the taste.

She was relieved when at last Auntie Agnes, yawning widely, declared it was time she was going home to bed.

'That's all right, Auntie,' Heath said, smiling. 'I told the cab to call for us at about eight o'clock and it's nearly that now.'

'It's been a lovely Christmas party,' Agnes said cheerfully. 'There's good it is to see a girl like you getting on so well. Not thinking of marriage yet, are you?' She raised her eyebrows archly, but Mary simply laughed.

Aunt Agnes kissed Mary's cheek. 'Goodbye then, and a Happy New Year to you, my dear.'

Rhian was the first to settle into the cold seat of the cab. When she looked at the lantern swinging outside the window, the lights seemed to dim and shimmer before her eyes. She felt ill and weak and she wished Mary had not come along just as she had been about to find solace in the cold waters.

She was hardly aware of the drive home; her aunt was snoring gently at her side and Heath seemed to have given up the struggle to make conversation.

The silence of the familiar house was a welcome balm and Rhian hurried upstairs to her room without a word. She felt a small pang of guilt as she heard Heath help her aunt up the stairs, but she quickly silenced it as she began to undress. It was an ordeal to draw off her petticoats and she held her breath until her nightgown was safely over her head. The cold crisp cotton felt scratchy to her skin as she did up the buttons to the neck. She brushed out her hair, careless of the pins that still gripped some of the curls, and then crept into bed and lay staring at the shadows on the wall, trying to clear her mind of everything and to coax the elusive sleep that always evaded her.

Suddenly she became aware that her door was slowly opening and sat up, her heart thumping as she clutched the blankets to her thin body. A tall figure was framed in the doorway; he seemed strange and menacing and Rhian felt her blood turn to ice. It was Gerwin Price, she thought in panic, he had somehow invaded the privacy of the house just as he had invaded her body. She opened her mouth to scream and then, in the light from the lamp, she saw that it was Heath standing looking down at her, his hand held out to her as though to comfort her.

'Rhian, why are you so frightened? Let me help you,' he said softly. As he sat on the edge of the bed the springs creaked and Rhian moved back from him, her eyes wide.

'Don't touch me, please don't touch me, Heath,' she said tonelessly. His hand dropped on to the patchwork, his shoulders seemed to sag. She could almost feel sorry for him, which was ironic when only a few short weeks ago she had longed for him to ask her to be his wife.

'Is it anything I've done?' Heath persisted. 'Have I hurt you without knowing it? Come on, *cariad*, you can tell me.'

She shook her head dumbly. How could she tell him what vile things had been done to her, he with his fine clean masculine frame and his honest eyes. He would feel the need for revenge and then perhaps he would be hurt too. No, this weight on her mind that was bearing her down could not be shared, least of all with Heath Jenkins.

'Rhian, you're fading away before my eyes,' Heath tried once more. 'I know there is something worrying you, now be a good girl and tell me. I won't be shocked whatever it is, mind.'

The silence lengthened and he sighed. 'Is it my fault? I know you were angry seeing me with Carrie, but perhaps I can try to explain that to you.'

Rhian shook her head slowly. 'Will you just leave me to go to sleep, Heath?' she asked pitifully and on an impulse, he took her in his arms, cradling her close. She was rigid, her hands pushing at his chest, her back arched away from him as if his very touch repulsed her. Heath rose from the bed defeated and moved towards the door, pausing with his fingers on the handle. 'Well, if ever you want to talk, then come to me, do you understand? I'll never be too busy to listen to you.'

When he had gone, Rhian lay down and faced the wall and wished that she could find the relief of tears, but her eyes were dry and they burned in her head like coals in a fire. She was damned to hell on earth, she thought desperately and there could be no escape except in death.

Chapter Twenty-Seven

The dawning of the new year brought torrential rain, washing the streets clear of snow and casting a gloom over Sweyn's Eye. It was no longer picturesque, a Christmas card world of silent whiteness; it was a place where the streets were grey and windswept and the folks remained indoors, the smoke from many chimneys evidence of the fires roaring in the hearth. But Mary was abroad regardless of the inclement weather. She had a goal in mind and nothing, not even the teeming rain, was going to deter her.

She looked at many buildings, some on the outskirts of the town, one or two hugging the dockside, but at last her search was rewarded and she found just the premises she required. As she walked through the cold empty rooms, she furnished them in her imagination, placing curtains at the windows and carpets on the floor. There would be chairs, elegant and upright enough for the customer not to be too comfortable. And occasional tables, discreetly placed so that there would be need only for the minimum of traditional counters. It would be almost like a large comfortable home, Mary thought in satisfaction.

The price of the building made her gasp, but she had enough to make a down payment and that was all that was required for now.

She took out a list of names from her bag and stared at it with a smile curving her lips. Each one of the people on it belonged to the Cooperative Movement and heading the list was Mrs Asquith. But first, Mary intended to see her lawyer.

Gregory Irons was not a man Mary would care to have as a friend, but he was sharp and efficient and he could make sure that the property became hers without delay, which was all that she required of him.

His office was well carpeted and a cheerful fire roared in the grate. 'I shall refrain from asking why you need such a large building, Miss Jenkins,' he said smoothly, smiling at her from over the polished surface of his desk. 'But I will need a certain amount of cash as a down payment, I'm sure you understand.'

Mary nodded. 'I shall pay a substantial deposit, the rest of the money to be handed over on completion of the sale.'

Gregory Irons looked at the money Mary had taken from her bag, transferring the notes smoothly to a drawer in his desk. He wrote out a receipt with a flourish of his pen and handed it to Mary.

'I should have the matter concluded quite soon,' he said. 'There appear to be no other offers for the building, so far.'

Mary forced a smile. 'There will be no other offers, will there, Mr Irons? I'm sure we understand each other.'

He rose. 'I think we understand each other perfectly, Miss Jenkins.'

Mary took a cab to Singleton Street, as it was still raining and she did not wish to be at a disadvantage when she saw Mrs Asquith. Her visit was not a welcome one and Mary was forced to sit in the chilly hallway on a hard-backed chair, waiting until the lady of the house saw fit to put in an appearance. But she would be patient and bide her time and force herself to remember that Mrs Asquith would be invaluable to her.

She was thoroughly chilled by the time she was called to the drawing room. A huge fire roared in the hearth and the lady of the house looked up from her writing desk, her face a mask of coldness.

'I can't think why you wish to see me, Miss Jenkins,' Mrs Asquith said impatiently. 'But I should be obliged if you would state your business as briefly as possible.'

Mary smiled charmingly. 'I have a proposition to put to you,' she said. 'I have acquired a building on a prime site and I'm giving you first refusal of renting part of my premises from me.'

Mrs Asquith looked at her in surprise as Mary continued to speak. 'Only a select few will have the privilege of occupying a spot in the new emporium, Mr Phillpot for example.' Mary did not stop to explain that she had not approached Alfred Phillpot, nor was she likely to do so.

Mrs Asquith put her hand to the long jade necklace that hung over her ample bosom. 'Well, in that case, let's sit down and talk this over like businesswomen, my dear.'

Mary took a seat near the warmth of the fire and stared into the flames smiling in satisfaction. The first part of her plan had been the hardest and it seemed that now she was well on her way to achieving her goal.

For Mary the next few days proved to be busy ones. One by one she visited the people on her list and soon the outer portions of the large building were taken by prospective tenants, all of whom had eagerly agreed to pay a large lump sum on signing the agreements drawn up by Gregory Irons. The only person unaware of what was happening under his very nose was Alfred Phillpot, and it amused Mary to imagine his reaction when he found out that he was left out on a limb.

Gregory Irons was all smiles when Mary paid him yet another visit, and he took the money she handed to him with a satisfied smile.

'I have to admire your nerve, Miss Jenkins,' he said dryly. 'You buy an enormous building and by renting out parts of it have other people footing the bill.'

Mary returned his smile. 'Yes, they are all satisfied customers, but this way I keep the upper hand.' She rose from her chair. 'Thank you for your efforts on my behalf, Mr Irons. I'm sure we shall be able to do business again in the not-too-distant future.'

As Mary left the chambers, she failed to see Dean Sutton step out of his motor car. He watched as Mary walked down the street, her head held high in her usual proud manner and even now, he ached for her. In the lawyer's office he took a seat and asked the question that was uppermost in his mind. 'What was Mary Jenkins doing here?'

Gregory Irons looked at him in surprise. 'You know my clients' affairs are confidential,' he said, a little affronted by the American's brashness.

'Balderdash! I pay you to watch everything that goes on in this town. Now come on, what did she want?'

Gregory Irons leaned back in his chair, pressing the tips of his fingers together. 'As a matter of fact, the young lady has just concluded a very good deal.' He could not help but smile. 'She bought a huge building with only a few hundred pounds to put down on it, then she went round renting out parts of the building until the entire thing was paid for. She's a very clever lady, that one, even though she is from the lower orders.'

Dean leaned forward in his chair. 'I want to know every move that woman makes, do you understand?' His eyes were hard and angry and Gregory Irons longed to tell him to go to hell, but good sense prevailed: Dean Sutton was a very generous man.

'I shall do that, Mr Sutton,' he said smoothly. 'Now, what else can I do for you?'

'It's about Billy Gray,' Dean said more calmly. 'I think it's time his case was reopened.'

–

Mary strode along Wind Street and stopped outside Sutton's Drapers shop. The bell pinged on the door as she pushed it open and Mrs Greenaway shuffled in from the back room.

'Why, Miss Jenkins, it's you. Not looking for your old job back, are you?'

Mary shook her head, smiling. 'No, I'm not after work, I'm offering it. Where are the girls?'

Mrs Greenaway rubbed her hands on her apron and leaned towards the open door that led into the kitchen.

'Nerys, Joanie, there's someone here to see you!'

Mary sat on the upright chair and leaned on the counter smiling as the two girls entered the shop, knowing that in Nerys and Joanie she had two ready-trained drapery assistants. 'How would you like to earn more wages?' she said softly.

After only a week, the part of the building that Mary intended to use as her own store had begun to take shape. She employed men to paint the woodwork and on the lure of a bonus they worked like beavers.

Muriel had spent hours sewing curtains and covers, above which chandeliers hung from the ceiling like fairy lights. The floors were carpeted with jute, which had the virtue of being both strong and cheap. It was hard work, but Mary was exhilarated by it and she gained an added satisfaction in seeing the other parts of the building receiving similar treatment from her tenants.

She had taken care that not one site was let to any shopkeeper who would be in direct competition with herself. There were greengrocers and butchers, milliners and shoemakers, everything a customer could wish for all in the same building.

At the beginning of the third week, Mary had a visit from Alfred Phillpot. The little man was virtually bristling, his cheeks red and angry and his mouth twitching.

'Could you spare me a little of your time, Miss Jenkins?' he asked abruptly and smiling sweetly she led him into the newly decorated office with its imposing leather-topped desk and polished swivel chairs. She faced him across the room and could see that he was lost for words.

'I think it's time that the Cooperative Movement stopped fighting me, don't you, Mr Phillpot?' she said quietly. Both of them were aware that it was not the Cooperative Movement but Alfred Phillpot himself who had been the cause of all the trouble. He moved to a chair and, unasked, sat down heavily. She placed her hands on the desk and leaned over towards him and he seemed to shrink visibly.

'I have one site left,' Mary said gently. 'Would you like it, Mr Phillpot? The rent is very reasonable, mind.' He gulped hard and Mary saw with amusement the struggle he was having not to damn her to hell.

At last he managed to speak. 'May I have time to think it over, Miss Jenkins?' He ran his finger round his collar as though it had suddenly grown too tight for him. Mary smiled.

'Of course, but don't take too long, there is a waiting list the length of my arm for prospective tenants.' She stood up straight. 'Don't you think that "Mary Jenkins Buildings" is a good name for the place?' She glanced at the man from the corner of her eye and he seemed about to have apoplexy. When he rose to his feet and took a thick wallet out of his pocket, Mary knew she had won.

-

The beginning of the new year seemed a time of confrontation for Mary, for shortly after she had talked with Alfred Phillpot, Dean Sutton came to see her. She heard the engine of his motor car as it chugged up the hill and had time to take off her apron and fold it away before opening the door.

'What are you doing here?' She held her head high, for she owed this man nothing. Dean removed his hat and stepped forward and Mary had no choice but to allow him inside the cottage.

'You sure do take the biscuit for brass neck, honey.' His voice was heavy with sarcasm. 'You steal my employees from under my very nose and then ask me what I'm doing here as if I was some shoeshine boy.'

During the next few days, she was too busy working at the store and preparing for the opening to think much about Dean's visit. She had a difficult task convincing Katie that she would make an excellent second in command, but at last she succeeded. It seemed that everything was going well and then a note was delivered to her by hand, unsigned, telling her curtly that Billy Gray had been released from prison.

Mary's thoughts were in chaos so that she could not concentrate on the arranging of models or the displays of flowers in Grecian urns.

'I'm going home, Nerys,' she said. 'You'll be taking orders from Katie in my absence, remember.'

Katie followed her into the office. 'Come on out with it, something's bothering you as sure as God made little green shamrocks.'

Mary handed her the letter and looked at her levelly. 'I should be filled with happiness and joy, but I no longer feel close to Billy and I don't think I've ever been in love with him.'

Katie shrugged. 'People change, and don't I know more about that than most folks? Go home now, I'll take care of everything, don't you worry.'

Mary drew her thick woollen coat around her shoulders and pinned a velvet, wide-brimmed hat to her glossy hair. 'I must go and see Billy, I'll have to speak to him some time and it might as well be now as later.'

'He'll be at his auntie's house for sure,' Katie smiled. 'He'll be after seeing his sister and asking her about you.'

Mary hurried down the carpeted stairs and out into the street, knowing in her heart that she was afraid to look Billy in the face. She knew now what it was like really to love a man. All the same, face Billy she would. She must do everything in her power to help him, but there could be nothing more than friendship between them, ever.

Heath opened the door to her, looming above her tall and handsome, his eyes so like her own staring down at her.

'You've heard that Billy's home,' he said. 'Come on in, he's sitting talking to Auntie Agnes drinking tea, a stunned look on his face as though none of this is really happening.'

Heath rested his hand on Mary's arm. 'I'm not prying and you can tell me to mind my own business if you like, but go easy on him – he's had a rough time by the look of it.'

An awkward silence fell as Mary entered the parlour. Billy slowly put down his cup and rose to his feet, his eyes unreadable.

'Billy!' she spoke his name warmly. 'It's so good to see you home again.' She put her hands on his thin shoulders and kissed his cheek and the harshness of tears blurred her eyes. She loved Billy, but in the same way as she loved Heath.

'Isn't it wonderful to see our boy freed from that awful place?' Agnes smiled up from the comfort of her chair. 'Put the kettle on again, Rhian and make Mary some tea. We've all got such a lot to talk about.'

Mary slipped her arm through Billy's and felt that he was withdrawing from her. 'How did it all happen?' she asked quickly and he looked away from her.

'It was all Delmai's doing. Mrs Richardson got up a petition, believed in my innocence and Mr Dean got his lawyers to work on the case – found new evidence, they said.' He shrugged. 'So now I've a free pardon.' His voice was strange as though he was embarrassed, and there was something in his manner that Mary couldn't understand.

'Well, you know how pleased I am to see you again,' she said softly.

Rhian carried the tray into the room and set it down on the table. Mary glanced at her; she was still very pale and there was no light in the blue eyes.

'Aren't you pleased to see Billy home again?' Mary said, wondering if Rhian was feeling neglected. The girl nodded without speaking and sat in the corner, her hands twisted together in her lap.

'I hear you've gone up in the world,' Billy said. 'Quite posh you are now.'

'Well, I've gone into business if that's what you mean, I'm not sure about being posh though.' She forced herself to smile. 'Anyway, let's talk about you.'

Billy shook his head. 'Nothing to say.' There was an awkward silence and Mary looked down at her hands. She could scarcely talk about the issues uppermost in her mind, not with all the family sitting round.

'How about a job in my shop?' she said quietly. 'I'm sure you could be a great help to me.' His eyes stared at her, troubled, and

Mary changed the subject quickly. 'Let's have that tea, shall we? I'm parched.'

Later, Billy walked with Mary to the tram terminus. His overcoat collar was high around his neck, his cap pulled down over his forehead. It was almost as though he thought of himself as a fugitive hiding from the world and Mary's heart went out to him.

'Mrs Richardson has offered me a job,' Billy said slowly. 'Wants me to be her groom, but I don't think I'd want to be working for her. It would put me on the wrong foot somehow, as though I was getting charity and I don't want that from her.'

She was relieved when the tram came into sight. 'See you soon, Billy, and then we can talk some more.' She sank into her seat gratefully; it had been difficult being with Billy and not blurting out her true feelings. But how could she tell him she no longer felt the same about him. It would be like kicking a man when he was down? Yet she longed to be honest with him and indeed for Billy to be honest with her too, for it was clear that he had changed towards her.

As she crossed the dank fields and saw her cottage come into sight, she felt warmed. The small building nestling in the valley was her home now and no one could ever evict her. The thought took her back to Delmai Richardson; it was strange, Mary thought, that a woman like that was prepared to take such an interest in Billy. Mary felt guilt weigh upon her like a burden for she herself had done very little on that score; a few abortive attempts to visit him in jail and a letter or two was not much to give a man to whom she had promised herself.

Once indoors, Mary lit all the lamps and drew the curtains against the darkness of the night. The rooms looked warm and cosy despite the fact that the fire was not lit. She looked up at the clock – there was not much point in lighting it now, it was far too late. She would go to bed and curl up in the blankets.

But when she was in bed, she found she could not sleep but lay awake for hours watching the pattern of the moonlight dancing on the walls. She itched to speak honestly to Billy and she would be tormented until she had told him that she could never be his wife.

Mary rose in the morning feeling heavy-eyed and almost decided not to go in to the store at all. But there was so much still to be done. Stock to check and prices to be arranged, as well as the more mundane tasks like the placing of the chairs and tables.

She intended the opening day to be something of a spectacular occasion. She would invite the mayor to cut the ribbon across the doorway and then in the evening there would be a champagne party. After all, she was starting a new age of shopkeeping; it was surely something of a rarity to have so many shops under one roof.

Mary dressed quickly. She no longer wore flannel skirts, but good serge suits. As she pinned on her hat she stared at her reflection in the mirror, and recognised that she was a different woman from the one who had stood outside the prison gates so many months ago. She was a woman now in every sense of the word, and she knew just where she was heading. What is more, she would allow no one to get in her way.

She left the house and made her way along the lanes, avoiding the sodden fields. The sky was still overcast but the rain had at last ceased and there was the promise of a pale watery sun breaking through the clouds.

When Mary arrived at the store, she was met by an embarrassed-looking Nerys.

'There's a man in your office, says he knows you. I don't like the look of him though.'

Mary, staring through the open door, recognised Billy and her heart sank.

'It's all right Nerys, I'll deal with it,' she said crisply.

'Morning, Billy, it looks as though it might turn out to be a very nice day.' She sat at her desk, her hand trembling as she picked up her pen. 'I've just had a marvellous idea, why don't you take the van out into the valleys for me? I don't want to let my customers down, but I'll have very little time for travelling from now on.'

'You know I'll do anything you want, Mary.' Billy didn't smile; he stared at her, his eyes dark and Mary bit her lip, trying not to lose her patience with his hangdog attitude. It was a result of being at the mercy of a man like Griffiths, she told herself, but the knowledge did not help much.

'If you find Katie, she'll see that you're all right,' Mary said, staring down at the books on her desk as though they were the most important thing in her life. When the door closed, she sighed and leaned back in her chair, rubbing her eyes wearily. 'Oh, Brandon, if only you were here to help me,' she murmured. Proud Mary, he had called her, and yet she would lose her pride if only she thought he would come at her bidding. She removed her hat and coat and returned to her desk; there was work to do and no good could come of sitting dreaming.

The day dragged on and it was almost dark by the time Mary decided she should go home. She was the last one left in the building and as she switched off the lights one by one the fittings loomed like ghosts around her. She sighed; there was so much to do, so many complications in her life, and without a love to share it all what was the point, she asked herself?

It was cold out in the street with the lamplight shimmering on the rim of ice in the gutters. Mary stood looking up at the emporium, trying to be enthusiastic about what the townspeople were describing as Mary Jenkins' great achievement.

'Proud of yourself, I dare say?' The voice was low and vibrant and Mary would have recognised it anywhere.

'Brandon?' she said as the tall figure loomed over her. He smiled down, but the light from the lamp shining in his eyes made them appear hard and cold. 'So this is the wonderful new store I've heard so much about,' he said softly.

'I wouldn't have expected you to be interested.' Mary tried to speak normally, drawing her gloves on to trembling fingers. He put his finger beneath her chin and forced her to meet his gaze.

'I want you, Mary.' He was very close to her and she longed to cling to him. She had believed she would lower her pride, but now that the moment had come she felt only anger.

'*Want*, that's all you know, isn't it?' Her voice was low and fierce. 'Can't you think of emotions, ever?'

She began to walk swiftly away from the store and he fell into step easily beside her. 'Do you want me to lie to you, Mary?' he asked with wry humour.

She glanced at him with eyes full of tears. 'Just leave me alone, will you?'

But Brandon went with her across the fields, along the lanes and right to her door.

Inside the cottage, Mary took off her coat, acutely aware of Brandon standing watching her. She went to him and put her arms around his neck, feeling the crispness of his hair against her fingers.

'Lie to me, Brandon,' she said softly, 'and tell me that you love me.'

Chapter Twenty-Eight

Brandon was not in a good mood. He strode around the works finding fault, growling at the men in a way that was entirely uncharacteristic of him. The heat in the mill brought sweat glistening on his forearms and beading his face, but he ignored the discomfort, waiting impatiently for Heath Jenkins to swing a sheet of steel back over the top of the mill to the rollerman.

'Billy Gray is out of prison?' he said shortly. 'Is it true that he's been employed by Mary?'

Heath looked at him levelly. 'I don't know why you're snorting like a wounded bull, Mr Sutton, but aye, it's true.'

Brandon examined the pile of steel plates that still held a residue of heat. At last he looked up again and saw that Heath was watching him; the boy was far too shrewd, his raised eyebrows asking a question that he was too polite to put into words.

Brandon left the mill and strode across the sodden earth towards the steelworks where the blast furnaces rose like iron-clad monsters into the heavens. Trade had worsened; some of the steel workers from other companies were on strike and the situation was causing a great deal of suffering in the town.

The General Labourers' Union would not give up the struggle for a pay rise and Brandon knew that soon he would have to declare himself. He was in full agreement with the men, knowing that they suffered far more than the owners, but the Employers Association to which he belonged was arguing for a close-down of foundries, thus forcing the men to capitulate.

And yet it was not the troubles of the steel industry that were uppermost in Brandon's mind at this moment. He was remembering the way Mary had come to him, so softly so sweetly that he had almost believed she loved him. He was a fool, he told himself. Mary was simply having a last fling before settling down to respectability with her lover Billy Gray.

In the office, Mark was poring over the sales sheets. He glanced up as Brandon entered, shaking his head ruefully.

'Sales are down, sir,' he said slowly. 'Things are not looking good.'

Brandon rolled down his shirt sleeves and sat at his desk running his fingers through his hair wearily. He had been up most of the night trying to urge Evo into moving more swiftly with the handbook – he could almost believe that the old man was dragging his heels deliberately. Now he nodded at Mark and pointed to the pot bubbling on the stove.

'Get us both some hot strong coffee, Mark. I don't think this is going to be one of our better days.'

Mark grinned and pushed back his chair, moving over to the stove with quick lithe movements. He was a lucky man; his life was comparatively uncomplicated, Brandon thought with a trace of envy.

'How is that beautiful girl of yours?' He leaned back in his chair, pushing the seat on to the two back legs and swinging to and fro, his feet on the desk.

'As lovely as ever,' Mark replied. 'Working for Mary Jenkins, she is now, seems very happy too.'

Mark moved towards the desk with two cups of coffee black and steaming. 'That store is really something, you should see the way Mary has had it all done out; she'll have a little gold mine there, if you ask me.'

Brandon wasn't asking, but in spite of himself he was interested. 'Go on,' he said, picking up his cup. 'Tell me all about it.'

'Well, apart from the main part of the building where Mary will be selling clothing, there are the other sections rented by shopkeepers dealing with different commodities. It's an arcade of shops really and not only will Mary make a profit from her own sales but she will have rent from the other traders too. She can't fail.'

'Good!' Brandon said absent-mindedly wondering at the glow of pride which warmed him as he listened to Mark talking.

And yet he wondered bitterly how it was that Billy Gray had been so suddenly pardoned, surely the man was guilty as sin. He pushed the thought aside; it really was no business of his.

He looked over at Mark. 'I'm thinking of leaving the Employers Association,' he said bluntly. 'I know it will cause a stir in the town and no doubt I'll be ostracised, but I can't go along with what they are trying to do to the men.'

Mark looked up slowly. 'Think carefully before you make up your mind to anything, sir,' he said soberly. 'You've made yourself pretty unpopular already with your plans for the handbook. If you leave the Association, you'll really be out on a limb.'

Brandon rose and moved to the window, staring out at the large expanse of works spread along the river bank. It was his and he would run it how he saw fit and not in the way the Association demanded.

'The bastards want to cut the wages even further,' he said stonily. 'Not content with denying uniformity of pay, they plan to take up to thirty-one per cent off the wages. I can't go along with that, it's putting the trade back twenty years.'

'I know how you feel, but you can't fight the Association single-handed,' Mark said positively. 'Pull in your horns a bit just for now, cut down on costs yourself and perhaps we'll be able to weather the crisis.'

Brandon shook his head. 'The men have already taken a voluntary cut in wages, I won't ask them to take any less.' If only Dean had not contested their father's will, he thought in frustration, there would be no need for penny-pinching.

'We must get the handbook out, Mark,' he said firmly. 'It will change everything. Other employers would be bound to take notice of it, for all the unions would be holding it like a knife to the throat of the bosses.'

'And where will you be sir, down a pit without a light!' Mark shook his head. 'Perhaps you should be discreet for a month or two until trade figures improve.'

'The demand for steel is there all right,' Brandon said. 'It's just the unrest between boss and worker that's causing the trouble. As for us, our prices are still comparatively high, while other companies can undercut us because of the stranglehold they have on the workers.'

There was a knock on the office door and Mark rose to his feet. After a moment's hushed conversation, he admitted Ianto. The man held his cap between his fingers, twisting it nervously; he could hardly look Brandon in the face as he spoke.

'I'm quitting, boss,' he said quickly. 'Got to say the truth, been offered more money and I need it, see.'

Brandon leaned forward, elbows on the desk. 'Well, that's all right, Ianto. You have to go where the pay is good, I'll not deny that. Tell me, who will your new employer be?'

Ianto looked puzzled. 'I thought you'd know about it, boss. Mr Dean Sutton, your brother, put the work my way. The Duffryn foundry is taking on a few men. I think you'll be losing more workers soon, but the scum haven't got the guts to come and tell you face to face like I have.'

Brandon shook his head. 'Well, good luck to you, Ianto! Far be it from me to prevent you from leaving and thanks for talking straight.'

When lanto had left, Brandon thumped his fist on the desk in frustrated anger. 'The poor fools!' he said angrily. 'They don't realise they're simply being pawns in a tactical manoeuvre. My brother has only a few shares in the Duffryn, he doesn't care if it stands or falls and once he sees me ruined, the workers will be out on their ears so fast they won't know what's happened.'

Mark nodded. 'Aye, you're right, sir but if you try to tell them that the poor sods won't listen – just think you're trying to queer the pitch, that's all.'

Brandon drew on his coat and moved to the door. 'I'm going out to get some fresh air.'

A cold wind was blowing in from the sea as Brandon made his way to the dockside. It was here, staring at the sails billowing in the breeze and the old craft rising and falling on the waves, that he usually managed to put things in perspective. He walked along the water's edge reading absent-mindedly the names painted on the sides of the vessels at anchor. The *Sea Urchin* nestled alongside *The Spanish Main* and *Silver Maiden* bobbed cheek by jowl with a small craft imposingly called *Midnight Cloud*. If he had a ship of his own, he mused, he would undoubtedly call her *Proud Mary*. The thought jolted him to a halt.

He paused for a moment, unaware of the figure he cut as he stood outlined against the grey sky and pewter sea. He was thinking far too much about Mary Jenkins, he warned himself; she was beginning to get beneath his skin.

He should be searching for a well-bred young lady, one who could sit at home and care for his children and run his household – not wasting time thinking of a woman who could match him wit for wit in business acumen.

He moved along the quay towards the pier, feeling the softness of the wind ruffle his hair. It was good to get outside the works sometimes, to put all his problems behind him and just relax. Then he looked up and his footsteps faltered to a stop.

'Mary!' he said and she stood before him, more beautiful than in his imaginings, her skin warmed into rosiness by the sting of the wind, her eyes bright like jewels in her high-boned face. 'What are you doing here?' he asked and it was almost an accusation.

Mary looked at him defensively. 'This is a place I always come to when I'm troubled, don't you remember, Brandon?' She spoke softly and he stared at her for a long moment before walking away from her.

'Brandon.' Her voice halted him and he turned slowly, almost reluctantly. He didn't move, simply stared at her coldly. 'I heard you have taken Billy Gray to work for you.'

Mary hung her head. 'I can't just abandon him, he's had a bad time in prison. Try to believe me that he's innocent, even the courts say so now. And surely you can understand what it means to owe someone a debt.'

After a moment, Brandon nodded. 'You may be right,' he said more gently.

Mary moved restlessly, her fingers making pleats in her serge skirt. 'Billy is so vulnerable that I don't think he could take a rebuff. I feel I owe him a helping hand at least. He thinks I have grown far away from him because I now own a large store.' She sighed. 'I have a good business at my fingertips it's true, but not without a struggle, mind.

'Many problems I've had. The Cooperative have worked against me, trying to close me down, but by using my wits I've made a success of my life.'

Looking into her eager upturned face, Brandon felt a mixture of emotions that he could not explain. He moved away from Mary, her nearness was clouding his thinking.

'I don't know why you're telling me all this and I'm sure you'll do what you think best regarding Billy Gray.' He was aware that his tone was curt but he wanted Mary to have no false illusions.

To his surprise she came behind him and put her arms around his waist, resting her head against the broadness of his back.

'Brandon, don't you understand, even now? I love you. You are the only man I have ever allowed to get close to me, in any way.' She felt soft and warm against him and on an impulse he turned and took her in his arms, holding her close, smoothing her hair, kissing her forehead, her eyes, her lips, but after a moment he drew away.

'Go home, Mary,' he said, moving away from her. He thrust his fingers through his hair and turned to look out to the flat expanse of the sea, the waves tipped with white foam.

He was aware of her departure, though he did not turn to look at her. He strode along the beach in the opposite direction, knowing he was a fool to allow her near him. A woman could not change her wanton nature any more than he could make gold out of tinplate.

'Forget her!' he said angrily and as he reached the road he turned back towards the steelworks, his thoughts crystallised, his mind made up. He would leave the Employers Association, he would send in his resignation at once and be damned to them. His life was his own and he would run his works any way he chose, whatever the opposition.

–

The moon was a bright orb hanging over Kilvey Hill as Mary stared through her window. The kitchen behind her was lit only by the glow of the fire, and though the cottage was cosy and warm, Mary had never felt so alone in all her life. She could not rid her mind of the meeting that afternoon with Brandon, when it had seemed for a brief moment that she had evoked some sort of response in him. Not his usual quick passion, but a warmth and a caring that had touched her heart. But then he had sent her away and she knew that it had been only an illusion.

She sighed deeply and rose from her chair to move restlessly around the room. The piano lid stood open, the ivory keys gleaming like the teeth of some monster in the shaft of moonlight from the window.

She was possessed by a great restlessness, anticipating the impending opening of the Mary Jenkins Arcade and yet somehow, even that seemed an empty victory.

There was no love in her life, there never had been not since childhood. But she was being self-pitying she thought in dismay. Of course she was loved, she had her brother Heath and some very good friends. She should be ashamed of herself for falling into such a slough of despond.

She took her coat from the cupboard and shrugged into it, doing up the buttons tightly against the cold wind. She would walk down to the town, go to the store. Perhaps now was as good a time as any to talk to Billy.

Mary had installed him in the small flat in the attic of the emporium, grateful that he would be on hand to keep an eye on things during the night time. Not that she really expected any trouble, since the people who had once been against her now had a vested interest in the success of the venture, but it never did any harm to be careful.

She had not forgotten the break-in at Brandon's office or the fire that had gutted the press. Everyone had enemies. She thought of Gerwin Price and shivered.

The breeze blew the scent of the sea towards her as Mary walked along the silent lanes towards the lights of the town. Sweyn's Eye was a place with many faces. There was the heavy concentration of works along the river bank, the docks with the thrusting steamships and billowing sails, the countryside within walking distance and lastly the town itself – contained, compact, the streets winding, the buildings tall and dominating. She could not envisage living anywhere else in the world, yet on the heels of that thought was the knowledge that she would follow Brandon to the ends of the earth if he only asked her.

When she reached the streets, she saw how the lamplights washed down over the cobbled roadways. The sound of singing came from the public houses, lights spilling from windows scattered like bright shiny beads from a broken necklace.

The main road was lined with the more imposing structures of the town and Mary paused before the Arcade, her heart lifting with pride. This was her own achievement, won by the toil of her hands and the sweat of her brow.

She let herself into the building and along the broad passageway to where the door of her own store lay like a beacon before her. She stood in the silence breathing in the scents of new linen bales and freshly polished furniture, knowing with satisfaction that it was all hers.

The stairway at the back of the store was narrow and winding and Mary made her way upwards with care in the dimness of the moonlight. On the top landing she paused for breath and sounds she could not immediately identify drifted towards her. Frowning, she moved closer to the door of Billy's flat and turned the key in the lock.

'Billy, it's Mary, are you there?' she called. The gaslights were aglow in the living room and glinting on the table was a bottle and two empty wine glasses. A low laugh came from the bedroom and Mary knew suddenly that she was intruding on Billy's privacy.

She moved back so quickly that she collided with the table and a glass shattered on the floor. There was a moment's silence and then the door to the bedroom opened. Billy was standing staring at her, his mouth open in surprise. His hair was ruffled and the buttons of his trousers were undone.

'I see that you have company, Billy.' Mary strove to keep the sarcasm from her voice but failed dismally. To think she had been afraid to tell Billy that it was over between them and yet the moment her back was turned he was entertaining a woman!

She moved forward, suddenly angry. 'You have a nerve, to bring someone here onto my premises, Billy Gray,' she said sharply. 'Let's see which one of my female staff you've managed to coax into staying the night with you.'

Billy held up his hand but Mary pushed him aside impatiently. Then she stood in the doorway, dumb with surprise, for never in her wildest dreams had she expected to find Mrs Delmai Richardson naked in Billy's bed.

'I see you have expensive tastes, Billy,' Mary said quietly. 'What you do is no longer any of my business nor my responsibility, mind,' she said slowly.

Delmai Richardson slipped under the sheets and drew on a gown.

'Billy will be all right with me, don't you worry,' she said, staring up at Mary defiantly. 'Don't you realise that we love each other? Billy has never loved you, it was simply a childhood infatuation. I'm sure you must recognise that yourself by now.'

Mary sat down suddenly in a chair, her anger gone. How could she blame Billy for doing the same thing as she had done herself? She had been unfaithful to him long ago. Delmai misinterpreted her silence.

'I suppose now you mean to expose us to society,' she said breathlessly. 'Wife of one of the Richardson brothers in bed with a convict?' She caught Billy's arm and hugged it to her. 'You can say what you like about us, it doesn't matter any more; the only reason we kept quiet was out of respect for your feelings.'

Mary sighed and rose to her feet. 'I shan't say anything, don't worry,' she said flatly. At the door she turned and looked at Billy. 'I came here to tell you it was all over between us, anyway.' She heard Delmai sniff derisively but she had no heart to quarrel.

As she hurried down into the street Mary paused for breath, staring up at the clouds sliding over the moon. So it was finished – anything that had remained between herself and Billy was gone for ever. She could not help but feel saddened for they had been together since childhood and she had been so sure of his love. How could she trust any man when even Billy could change his affections?

She walked home at a steady pace, trying to calm her mood. Nothing must interfere with the opening of the store tomorrow, certainly not her own mixed emotions.

Mary sat at her fireside drinking hot milk and staring into the dying embers of the fire and suddenly she was crying, something she could not remember doing since she was a child. The tears fell bitter and hot onto her hands, for it seemed that she was a woman destined to live her life alone. She did not love Billy, yet his betrayal hurt her deeply and Brandon, the only man she could ever love, might as well be a million miles away for all that he cared about her.

After a time, she dried her tears and knelt down to rake the ashes from the fire. She must go to bed, she told herself, try to sleep, for in the morning, she must be fresh and rested for the greatest triumph of her life. But then why was it that she lay curled in her bed, alone and unhappy, feeling as if she had gained the world and lost her soul?

Chapter Twenty-Nine

Snow came again to Sweyn's Eye, a softly folding quilt that lay upon the streets, disguising rooftops, laying a sliver of ice across canal and river. January was not to be banished without leaving cold winter fingers over the town.

Rhian sat near the fire, a thick shawl around her thin shoulders, her hands chilled even though she rubbed them together for warmth. Carrie came into the room struggling with a full scuttle and knelt before the ornate hearth, placing coals upon the flames as though they were precious gems. She frowned as she turned to look at Rhian and sank back onto her heels.

'What's wrong with you these days, *merchi*?' she asked gently. 'You look so lost and sad.'

Rhian shook her head. 'There's nothing wrong with me, Carrie. Don't worry your head about me, I'm not worth it.'

Carrie's eyes were shrewd. 'There is something eating at you and haven't I known it these past few weeks! Changed you have, girl, not so damned selfish to tell you the truth. Time was when you wouldn't lift a plate and carry it over to the sink. Good help you are to me now, Rhian. Come on, Carrie will understand. Is it something to do with Heath and me?'

Rhian met Carrie's eyes and then looked away quickly, remembering her naked in Heath's arms. She shook her head. 'No, it's nothing to do with Heath or with you.' And yet it was in a way, she thought bitterly.

There had been a long train of nightmare experiences, beginning when Aunt Agnes had fallen sick and culminating in the night of Gerwin Price's attack. She moved quickly as though to dispel the dreadful thoughts that festered away inside her. So long as she did not allow herself to remember, she could survive.

'There's such misery in your eyes, *merchi*,' Carrie went on. 'I've seen nothing like it except in the expression of a beaten dog. Let me help you, I can see you're hurting inside.'

'There's nothing anyone can do,' Rhian said quickly. 'I'm going to my room. I'm feeling so tired, I'm sleeping on my nose.'

It was cold in the bedroom but fully clothed, Rhian climbed beneath the quilt and huddled there, knees drawn up to her stomach. She had been in bed only a few minutes when she heard footsteps mounting the stairs and recognised them as belonging to Heath.

'Are you sleeping, Rhian?' He knocked on the door, calling to her softly, but she remained silent, hoping he would go away. Her heart sank when she heard the rattle of the doorknob and she sighed heavily, turning on her back and blinking as the light from the lamp Heath was carrying spilled on to her face.

'We've got to talk.' Heath sounded strong and positive. He sat on the edge of the bed and Rhian resisted the impulse to move away from him.

'You're as jumpy as a kitten,' he said gently, 'and what's more, you're wasting away to nothing. There's something wrong. I must know about it and find out I will, even if I have to shake it out of you.'

He put his arms around her and in spite of her resistance drew her close. 'Come on now, there's a good girl, tell me what's wrong.'

She struggled against him but he held her fast. When he bent his head to kiss her cheek, she leaned against him as though too dispirited to fight any more.

'It's something I can't talk about,' she said woodenly. Heath held her at arm's length and stared at her, his eyes narrowing.

'Has someone been pestering you, some man?' He looked into her eyes and Rhian wanted to spill out to him all the horrible sordid memories that still festered inside her. He saw the weakening of her face and pressed the point.

'Look, Rhian my lovely, if anything has happened to you, don't I above all people have the right to know?'

She recognised the truth of his words that he was the nearest one to her. There was no one else in whom to confide and who knows, perhaps she would feel better if she spoke of the horrors that lived inside her skull.

Rhian began to talk in a low monotone, saying the things she had never believed would be spoken out loud. She spared Heath nothing of the sordid events of the night when Gerwin Price had taken her, used her and defiled her. She was so ashamed that when she at last stopped speaking she would not look up.

The silence lengthened and she wondered if Heath would leave her now in disgust, never to speak to her again. After what seemed an eternity he took her in his arms, holding her close and stroking her hair.

'You must not feel that any of it was your fault,' he said, though his voice was husky as if he was about to cry. '*You have done nothing wrong*, do you understand me?'

He smoothed her hair gently. 'I love you, Rhian. I think this is the first time I've told you so, but you mean more to me than anyone in the world.' He tipped up her chin so that he could look into her eyes. 'None of us is perfect, Rhian *cariad*. I've had so many women I've lost count, but when I'm your husband I'll be yours alone and we shall start a new life afresh together, do you know what I mean?'

Rhian nodded. 'I know only too well, Heath. You will try to forget that another man has entered the secret places of my body, has violated all that I thought I would have to offer my husband. How can I marry anyone, now?'

Heath became tense. 'You must tell me the name of the monster who did this to you, Rhian. I will wipe him from the face of the earth and then you will be at peace, you'll see.'

Rhian was suddenly frightened that Heath meant to kill in retribution for what had happened to her. She turned her face towards the wall and sighed heavily.

'It was dark, Heath, I couldn't see anything, only feel, just *feel* that's all.'

'Rhian, why are you protecting this bastard? Tell me his name, how can I rest until I've punished the man?'

'Vengeance is mine, sayeth the lord,' Rhian said tiredly. 'That's what the good book tells us, Heath and you can't do anything, so please forget about it or I shall be sorry I told you.'

He moved away from the bed and stood in the doorway, breathing heavily. 'I'll give you a few days to think things over, Rhian. Perhaps when you are not so upset you'll remember something that will lead me to the maniac who harmed you. I'll not let it rest though, never let it rest, so put your mind to that, girl.'

He went out and closed the door with a bang and Rhian covered her face with her hands as the memories evoked by the telling came flooding back into her mind.

-

With the onset of February the last of the snows vanished. Women queued at the soup kitchens of Sweyn's Eye while their menfolk stood on corners, shamed expressions on tired faces, jaunty white scarves hanging over threadbare topcoats, for the strikes were spreading. There were no wages for the men who thwarted their bosses and the living was hard in the small cottages and smoke-grimed terraces of the town.

Mary delayed the opening of her emporium and put her van to good use. Alone, she toured the outer limits of Sweyn's Eye with food and clothing and anxious faces stared up at her, thin and gaunt with fear. Mary dutifully wrote her accounts in a large book, knowing in her heart that none of the debts was ever likely to be repaid.

And yet her admiration for the people of the district grew as gifts were pressed upon her by proud villagers. She found she might be given anything from the most beautiful and intricate carvings to sacks of peat for the fire – anything at all, in fact, that would serve as a means of barter for much-needed food and clothing.

When Mary was asked to open a soup kitchen in Sweyn's Eye, she called on Mali for help and together they provided the necessities that were to feed the poor.

'It breaks my heart to see poverty in the streets of Sweyn's Eye,' Mali said as she was retying an apron around her slender waist. 'Now that I've children of my own, I can imagine what it must be to see them going hungry.'

Mary refrained from saying that she had known a much worse poverty, a grinding down of soul and spirit that came with an utter lack of caring. When they were children, she and Heath often did not have essentials such as bread to put in their hungry mouths. As for shoes, they were something others wore and until Mary was a young woman she had walked barefoot without thinking twice about it.

It was through Mali that Mary learned about Brandon's rebellion against the Employers Association. They had met as usual at the soup kitchen in the Strand and Mali put down her ladle and gestured for Mary to follow her into the back room.

'I must have a cup of tea, share one with me? I know you've been out in that old van of yours and you must need a rest too.'

Mary rubbed at her ankles ruefully. 'I do, my feet are so cold I swear I've got frostbite in every toe.'

Mali held out a cup of tea towards her. 'Drink this, it's strong as sin but hot and sweet, it will do you good.' The two women sat for a moment in silence, each busy with their own thoughts.

'I wonder how long these strikes are going to last,' Mary said. 'It seems wrong to open my store with all this poverty hiding in the backstreets of Sweyn's Eye.'

'Nonsense!' Mali said stoutly. 'You have to make a living. No good to man or beast if you become as poor as a church mouse yourself.' She stared at Mary over the brim of her cup. 'I'm sorry for Brandon Sutton though. Seems he's left the Employers Association, caused quite a stir among all the other bosses. He's keeping his works open while everyone else, even Sterling, has closed down.'

Mary felt a glow of pride at the stand Brandon was taking. She did not look up but stirred her tea vigorously, willing Mali to go on speaking about him. She had not seen him for days, not even caught a glimpse of him in the street and she ached for him. It was so painful that at nights she tossed and turned, trying to think of a way of going to him and begging him if need be to love her. But in the light of day such notions would vanish as quickly as they had come.

'He's losing orders,' Mali continued, 'and Sterling tells me that the other bosses are squeezing him out. Brandon needs funds and needs them badly, even to the extent that he's offering shares in the Beaufort Steel and Tinplate Company on the open market.'

Mary digested this in silence but inside she glowed with excitement. She could help Brandon, indirectly. She would go to Gregory Irons and instruct him to buy some shares for her without revealing her name. If she mortgaged the Mary Jenkins Arcade, she could raise a considerable sum of money.

'Still, I've enough to think of with the children,' Mali continued, 'without bothering my head about the works and such. Mary, you're not listening to a word I'm saying,' Mali laughed. 'You know you haven't seen my baby daughter yet. I want you to promise you'll come to see her before she gets too grown-up.'

'Yes, I will,' Mary replied absently. She was aching to be away; she wanted to make arrangements with the lawyer at once, but she knew she would have to act in secret because Brandon was far too proud to accept help from any woman, especially Mary Jenkins.

She looked at Mali's rosy face with a trace of envy. 'You're so lucky, Mali,' she said softly. 'You have the man you love and two fine children. I'm as jealous as a cat, you know that, don't you?'

Mali smiled affectionately. 'But in the nicest sort of way,' she said. 'Don't worry, Mary, you'll be getting married soon; you must be feeling on top of the world yourself now that Billy's out of prison.'

Mary shook her head. 'Billy and I have come to a mutual decision,' she said carefully. 'We both realise now that there was nothing but affection between us, like that of brother and sister instead of lovers. So we shan't be getting married and it looks as if your friend Mary is fast becoming a vinegary old maid.'

'I knew there was something wrong,' Mali said gently. 'You haven't been yourself for some time now, Mary, in spite of your fantastic business success. I'm so sorry.'

'No need to be.' Mary rose and put down her cup. 'This way, no one gets hurt. Come on, let's go and serve some more soup, there's an errand I must run before I get off home.'

If Gregory Irons was surprised at Mary's request to buy shares in the Beaufort Works, he did not show it. His eyes, sharp and unfathomable, watched her every action and took in every word – almost as though he was learning it off by heart, Mary thought in surprise.

'Why are you so interested?' She caught him off guard with her abrupt question and a slight colour rose into the lawyer's pale cheeks.

'I was just wondering if I should buy a few shares myself. You did such a wonderful deal buying your premises that I have the greatest respect for your business acumen.'

Mary wasn't too sure that he was speaking the truth, though his reply was plausible enough. Perhaps it was too glib, she thought uneasily. But then she dismissed her doubts for after all, what could the lawyer make out of the deal except to buy a few shares himself? She was becoming over-sensitive. She rose, picked up her bag and gloves and made for the door.

'I'd like you to keep this information to yourself,' she said firmly. 'I don't want anyone, not even Brandon Sutton, to know who is buying the shares.' As she hurried down the stairs and out into the street, Mary was still uneasy. She would have been more so if she could have seen Gregory Irons give his clerk a message, asking Mr Dean Sutton to come to his office at once.

Before returning home, Mary decided to call in at the Arcade to see that all the preparations were complete, for she had decided to go ahead and open the store. She was being harassed by her tenants who were worried about the loss of revenue and in all honesty she could not blame them.

She made a great clattering as she climbed the back stairs, for she had no wish to find Billy in the arms of Delmai Richardson again. But there were no lights in the building and the rooms up on the top floor were in darkness.

Puzzled, Mary tried the door and it swung open at a touch. It was eerie walking across the silent, shadowy room and she breathed a sigh of relief as the gaslight dispelled all but the deepest shadows. There were unwashed cups on the table and a half-empty toast rack, but there was no sign of life anywhere.

Then her eye was caught by a white envelope resting against the clock. She picked it up, opened it and stared unbelievingly at the words written in a hasty scrawl. After a moment, she crumpled the sheet of paper into a ball and threw in onto the floor. 'Silly fool!' she said, her voice sounding loud and strange in the emptiness of the room. She sat down heavily in a chair and stared around her, trying to examine her feelings.

Billy Gray and Delmai Richardson had run away together, it was unthinkable. By morning, the news would be all over town, for someone would have seen them leave either on an omnibus or at the station. She rose to her feet quickly; she must tell Rhian and Aunt Agnes, it was better they learned the truth from her.

She carefully locked the premises and hurried along the street. The air was chill, the darkness coming on early because of the overcast skies. Her mind was racing with questions: did Delmai Richardson love Billy, really love him, or was he simply a moment's excitement? She could never return to Sweyn's Eye – not now, not ever. For a married woman to run away with any man would have been a scandal, but with a man like Billy Gray who had been imprisoned for manslaughter it was unthinkable.

Auntie Agnes was drooping in her chair when Carrie showed Mary into the parlour. Rhian was nowhere to be seen and Mary looked questioningly at Heath.

'She's upstairs, she's always alone in her room these days. Mary, I must talk to you about Rhian, it's important.'

'All right, Heath, but not now,' Mary said quickly. 'Please go and fetch her, she has to hear this.'

Rhian came with obvious reluctance and stood in the doorway with an almost fey expression in her eyes. Mary stared at her anxiously.

'Come on, out with it,' Aunt Agnes said testily. 'There's a funny one you are, Mary Jenkins, coming round here in a great haste and then standing there gawping at our Rhian. Get on with it, girl.'

Mary dragged her gaze away from Rhian's pale face. 'It's nothing to worry about,' she said carefully, 'but I've got to tell you that Billy's gone away.'

Rhian did not speak and her aunt stared at her impatiently. 'Did you know that your brother was going away? No one tells me anything, think I'm senile they do, but I've got eyes and ears and I know what goes on in this town, don't you worry.'

She looked at Mary. 'Gone off with that lah-de-dah lady, I'll be bound – that Mrs Richardson and her a married woman, should be ashamed the pair of them.'

Heath frowned. 'What's she talking about, Mary? What has Billy got to do with Mrs Richardson?'

Mary shook her head. 'It's true, he's run off with her and tomorrow the whole town will be buzzing with gossip about it. How did you find out, Aunt Agnes?'

'Carrie goes to the shops for me, listens to people talking, maidservants and the like. Know all about their betters they do, and not afraid to spread the muck either.'

Carrie looked apologetic. 'Pumps me, she does, every time I go to the butcher's or the baker's, asks me to repeat every word I've heard and takes it all as gospel truth.'

Mary sighed. 'Well, no matter now, soon everyone in town will know. It's not the sort of thing that can be kept a secret.' She was about to rise to her feet when Rhian spoke in a low voice.

'Can't trust anyone, not even our Billy. Men are all the same, evil.' She looked at Heath. 'You're no different, though you'd like us all to think you are.'

She turned to face Carrie. 'So you tell Auntie everything, do you? Have you told her about you and Heath going to bed together?'

A silence fell upon the occupants of the room and Mary stared round from face to face in bewilderment. Was this what had been worrying Rhian for the last few weeks?

Carrie broke the spell by moving quickly to the door. She picked up her shawl and without a word hurried out of the house.

'Why don't you go after her, Heath?' Rhian said bitterly. 'Go and give her your false promises of love, for I don't want to hear them, do you understand?'

'Rhian...' Heath made a move towards her but she turned and fled up the stairs and he dropped his hands to his sides in despair.

'She doesn't realise how it is, Mary,' he said defensively. 'A man needs a woman, it's only natural if one is willing that you take what is offered.'

Mary stared at her brother, seeing not his young face but the strong chin and jaw and the turquoise eyes of Brandon Sutton. Was this how he saw her, as merely a woman to fill his needs for the moment? With an effort she brought her attention back to the present.

'Look, Heath, it might be just as well if you stay the night in the rooms above the Arcade. You can mind the place for me and give Rhian a chance to get over all this; it must have been a shock to her, you know.'

'I know more than you think, Mary,' he said bitterly.

She felt suddenly weary. 'I'm going home, I'm tired, we'll talk some more tomorrow. Good night, Auntie, and don't worry too much, I'm sure Billy will be all right.'

The old woman nodded. 'Aye, he'll go to hell his own way and whatever I say or do won't make a pennyworth of difference.'

'Let me walk you home, Mary,' Heath said, but she shook her head and kissed her brother's cheek. 'No, stay here, boyo, look after Rhian and Auntie Agnes. It seems you'll be the only man of the family from now on.'

Heath grimaced. 'Not if Rhian remains so set against me. I love her, Mary, I really do in spite of everything.'

'Well, that's big of you,' Mary replied tartly. 'Considering you were found out, I don't blame Rhian for not going into your arms like a falling flower.'

She gave Heath no chance to speak again, but hurried away along the dark street, wanting nothing more than to climb into her bed and sleep the clock around. She would forget everything for tonight, there was nothing more she could do. The story of Delmai Richardson and Billy Gray would ring through Sweyn's Eye for a few weeks, but then it would die away and be forgotten. And she would still be alone, Mary thought with a touch of bitterness.

She let herself into her cottage and closed the door, throwing the bolt home and sighing with relief. It had been a strange strife-torn day and Mary felt weary and low in spirits, yet surfacing from the gloom of her thoughts was the satisfaction that she had done something practical to help Brandon. With that knowledge hugged to herself, she slipped between the sheets and fell into a deep sleep.

Chapter Thirty

The rain fell softly on Sweyn's Eye, colouring the streets pearly grey, turning the waters of canal and river to pewter. The sea laved the shore with gentle attack, shifting shingle in ceaseless movement. Mary was dressed and ready to leave for the store, intent on checking the arrangements for the party that was to be held prior to the opening. She was dressed in a suit of deep plum with a hat to match, and even to herself she admitted that she was looking her best.

A loud knocking made her pause in the act of drawing on her gloves and she picked up her soft leather bag and opened the door, expecting to see the hansom cab she had ordered. However, a thin young man stared down at her, his smile self-effacing. It took Mary only a few minutes to recognise him as clerk to Gregory Irons.

'Please will you come to the office at once.' He stuttered slightly as though nervous and beneath his hat his hair hung damply on his forehead.

'Come inside,' Mary said. 'I'm expecting a cab to arrive at any moment, we might as well travel in comfort. Now, what's all this about?'

Tanner shook his head apologetically. 'I really don't know, Miss Jenkins, Mr Irons doesn't confide in me.' He did not meet her eyes and Mary began to feel uneasy. The young man knew more than he was telling her, but it was obvious he was not going to give anything away.

When the cab arrived she hurried out of the cottage, bending her face away from the rain as she climbed into the cold leather seat. The clerk sat gingerly beside her as though she might turn and bite him at any moment, Mary thought impatiently.

The streets were coming alive with traffic and Mary watched the milkman chivvy his horse as the animal ambled along the cobbled roadway, stopping outside the houses of the regular customers. As the cab paused to allow a tram to go by, Mary watched the dairyman measure the milk and tip it foaming into a jug. Then the cab was moving away, towards the main street where the offices of Gregory Irons were situated.

The lawyer was seated behind his desk, but he rose to greet Mary with a smile that she felt was intended to show sympathy.

'What's wrong, Mr Irons?' she asked quickly. 'I would prefer it if you would come straight to the point.' He returned to his seat and with a wave of his hand indicated that Mary sit opposite him.

'I'm sorry, Miss Jenkins. Bad news, I'm afraid. The banks have refused to allow a mortgage on the Arcade.'

'But I don't understand,' Mary said, frowning. 'Why should they refuse, when the property is worth far more than the mortgage I required?'

The lawyer put his fingertips together and examined them as though they were of great interest.

'I cannot comment on that, and I do assure you that I have done my best for you.' He looked up at her. 'Unfortunately, this means that you will have to forego the shares in the Beaufort Works, but I'm sure that is no great hardship – it was only an extra means of income, was it not, and you are still financially sound.' He looked down at a paper before him. 'You could buy a small amount of shares with the cash coming in from your tenants – not the volume you wished for, but as a small speculation it would certainly be viable.'

Mary shook her head, trying to understand the solicitor's words. 'If I am sound, as you put it, why won't the banks advance me the money?'

The lawyer shuffled the papers on his desk for a moment before answering. 'All the principal members of the town have your best interests at heart, Miss Jenkins, and the consensus of opinion is that you would be jeopardising your business by taking this step.'

'Surely that's my prerogative?' Mary asked at once and Gregory Irons smiled.

'Not if the bankers of Sweyn's Eye have any say in the matter. But let me put your mind at rest. There are other people, eminent people in the town who are only too willing to buy shares in the steelworks. One of them is a close, very close friend of yours and I shall not divulge any more information on that subject. But I want you to know that if your aim was to offer a helping hand to an ailing firm, then it will be done for you.'

Mary rose to her feet. She was still very angry, but mollified by the knowledge that Brandon would be out of trouble.

'Is the prospective shareholder Sterling Richardson, by any chance?' she asked and Gregory Irons inclined his head as though in acknowledgement though he didn't speak.

'Then I'll bid you good morning,' Mary said more cheerfully. 'Thank you, Mr Irons.' She let herself into the outer office where the clerk was bent industriously over his books. He glanced up as she passed and gave her a shy smile, leaping to his feet to hold open the door for her.

Mary found herself back in the busy street, her feelings mixed. What Gregory Irons had told her seemed a bit strange, but she acknowledged that she was a newcomer in the business world of Sweyn's Eye and thus ignorant of a great many matters. But Brandon would be all right now even without her help, and she gave a sigh of relief as she hurried along the pavement towards the Arcade.

As she stepped through the glass doors into her own store, she stared around her with a sense of pride. Everything was poised as though waiting for the great day when the sales floors would be a hive of activity.

Nerys and Joanie were at work on the drapery counter and as Mary approached, both girls smiled at her in delight.

'How are you settling into your new lodgings?' Mary asked, peeling off her gloves. It had been a good idea to ask Carrie to give the girls a room in her house because she was sure to keep a check on them. Joanie giggled nervously and it was left to Nerys as always to answer.

'It's lovely, Carrie gives us much more freedom than old Mrs Greenaway ever did, but good girls we are, mind.'

'I should hope so.' Mary smiled and waved her hand around her. 'And what do you think of my store – isn't it magnificent?' She felt buoyant, really alive as she anticipated the party that night to precede the opening the next day.

'It's a beautiful shop, Miss Jenkins, and I'm that thrilled to be in charge of my very own counter.'

'Who are the new assistants, miss, and when will they be arriving?' Joanie ventured to ask and Mary stared at her thoughtfully.

'Well, Katie will be my second in command, as you know, and Muriel is coming to work here as soon as she can give in her notice at *Ty Mawr*. I'm hoping to persuade Rhian Gray to take a position in the shop too. It would save me finding lodgings for my staff if I can employ local people.'

Joanie giggled nervously and Mary looked at her sharply. 'Have I said anything funny?' The girl covered her mouth with her hand and with a sigh Nerys pushed her aside.

'It's all the gossip, miss. It's running riot through all the servants' quarters in all the big houses.'

'What is?' Mary asked, but she could hazard a guess at what the girls were talking about.

'Billy Gray, miss. I know he was your friend once, but gossip says he's gone off with Mrs Delmai Richardson from one of them big houses up on the hill. You must have seen her, miss, sad face on her that would turn the milk sour.'

'It's all right, Nerys.' Mary felt her elation ebb away. 'I'm quite aware of the facts.' Her tone forbade any more discussion and as she walked away, she saw Nerys begin to write prices for the bales of cloth on the shelves behind her.

In the lounging area of the shop, where customers could take tea at their leisure, the small tables were set with pristine damask cloths. Shining glasses stood ready for the evening's festivities, which Mary expected most of the business people in town to attend. She knew that Mali and Sterling would be sure to come, and most certainly Mrs Asquith and the other tenants of the Arcade who would make the most of the occasion to advertise their own wares. Mary half-smiled as she thought of Alfred Phillpot; he had accepted her invitation, but she knew he would never forgive her for outsmarting him.

She moved into the office and stood looking around her, wondering with a sudden surge of fear if she would be able to cope with a big business. This was no van selling a few dozen shawls or a pair of boots here and there. The store would have a huge turnover in goods, and her customers would range from the poorest members of the town to the toffs from up on the hill.

Mary moved to the window and stared down at the streets, her hands gripped fiercely at her sides. She would make it work, she was determined on it. Some of the tension left her. Tonight was still a long way off and between now and then she had a great deal to do. She had promised to help at the soup kitchens again and the thought was enough to subdue her feeling of excitement.

For the trade situation was worsening, the strike had taken hold and the workers had become if anything more determined to fight the reduction in wages that was the aim of the bosses. Only Brandon Sutton among all the steel and tinplate owners seemed on the side of the men, and because of this he was gradually being frozen out, ostracised by the society of Sweyn's Eye who thought it strange that a man would allow some of his profit to go to his workers.

Mary looked around at the opulence surrounding her and felt a great burden of guilt. What right had she to all this when out there in the streets of the town her own people were starving?

'Don't be a fool!' she told herself out loud. Now she was in a position to help the folk who were living in poverty just as she had once been herself. She could afford to give the poorer of her customers the goods they needed on 'tick', the understanding being that they would pay when times improved.

She left the office and walked back down the broad elegant stairway towards the door, her head held high, and no one watching her would have known the mixture of emotions whirling within her.

Later, as Mary dressed carefully for the opening of the store, she found that her hands were trembling as she fastened the hooks on the back of her high-necked gown with difficulty and smoothed down her skirts, looking at herself in the long mirror of the wardrobe. She had fined down of late, she noticed; her waist was neat, her hips gently swelling. A mature woman she was now, and should have been long since married. She would be a success for she was bent on it, but she would have no one with whom to share her triumphs. Now was not the time for introspection or self-pity, she told herself; she should be at the Arcade before anyone else so that she could make any last minute alterations she might find necessary.

Her brother called to collect her and stood in the doorway smiling. 'Are you ready, Mary?' he asked.

She put her hands on his shoulders, drawing him inside.

'You look so handsome in your best Sunday suit, boyo, I wouldn't know it was my brother.' She kissed his cheek and Heath smiled down at her, his eyes warm.

'You look lovely yourself, Mary Jenkins,' he said playfully and then he sobered. 'I'm proud of you, mind. I know I don't say a great deal about it, but there's a fire in my heart that's just blazing with pride because my sister has made herself rich and famous.'

'Hardly that,' Mary laughed, 'and there's sentimental we're getting – anyone would think we'd been at the gin bottle.' She fell silent for a moment and both knew they were remembering their early days when the gin bottle had ruled their lives.

Mary slipped her hand through Heath's arm. 'Let's be off, we're standing here wallowing like a pair of hogs in mud!'

The Arcade was ablaze with lights, the windows gleamed, the doorways stood open and already the hubbub of noise reached out like fingers into the night.

'I'm late,' Mary said anxiously and Heath caught her hand.

'So you should be, the star always arrives last.' He looked down at her. 'Chin up, Mary, you're a businesswoman now, better than half these toffs gathered here and don't you forget it.'

As she moved into the lounge, she was accosted on all sides by eager faces; mouths opened and closed, offering her congratulations and as she reached the centre of the room, Nerys stepped forward with a huge bouquet of flowers.

Mary felt overwhelmed. She buried her face in the blooms and attempted to gather her thoughts enough to raise her voice and thank everyone for attending the opening night of the Mary Jenkins Arcade.

'Well done!' Mali was at her side, her eyes shining with happiness. 'I always knew you would make a success of your life, Mary. You had a star above you, somehow, I knew it all that time ago when I first came to the laundry.'

Mary handed the flowers to Joanie. 'Put them in water, there's a good girl,' she said and then turned and took Mali's arm and led her away to one of the corner tables.

'You haven't done such a bad job on your own life,' she said, smiling. Mali pushed back a stray wisp of dark hair, her eyes alight with happiness as they rested on her husband who was standing talking to Gregory Irons a short distance away.

'I'm content,' she said softly. Then she gazed at Mary once more. 'But I married into wealth, you have become a rich woman in your own right and I'm proud of you. You really are a remarkable woman, Mary, and you deserve all the luck in the world.'

Mary giggled suddenly and put a hand in front of her face. 'Don't look now, but there's Alfred Phillpot coming over to swallow his pride and say something fitting. He looks so pained you'd think his trousers were too tight for him.'

'Miss Jenkins, felicitations! Everything here looks beautiful, you are to be congratulated.'

'Thank you.' Mary inclined her head and watched as the man backed away with undue haste.

'I bet that dented his pride,' Mali said in amusement.

They saw the man scurry away with a pained look on his thin face. 'Dented more than his pride, dented his pocket too if you ask me,' Mary said, smiling.

'Wicked, that's what you are, Mary.' Mali hid her smiles behind her hand. 'But he deserves to have to eat humble pie; pulled a few dirty tricks on you, didn't he?'

'He's not important.' Mary was watching Gregory Irons talking earnestly to Sterling and Mali followed her gaze.

'I wonder what my husband finds to talk about to Mr Irons,' she said lightly. 'The lawyer is not one of Sterling's favourite people.'

'I think I know,' Mary said, smiling. 'Sterling is buying some shares in Brandon Sutton's steel company. Giving him a helping hand, he is really.'

Mali looked puzzled. 'No, you're mistaken, Mary. I happen to know that Sterling has no intention of buying any more shares just now. He has sunk a great deal of capital in a new copper company further along the river.' She shuddered delicately. 'He was saying that if war came, God forbid, there would be a renewed need for copper.'

Mary stared at her in bewilderment. 'But Mr Irons definitely said...' Her voice trailed away as she recalled he had said nothing specific when she had asked if the new shareholder was Sterling Richardson; he had merely inclined his head, allowing her to believe what she wished. An uneasy feeling gripped her – the man was up to something, but what? Why should he care one way or another who bought Brandon's shares?

'My dear Mali and Miss Jenkins, how wonderful to see you both together like this, two successful – er – ladies.' Marian Thomas was overdressed in a plush velvet of sherbet pink. Her hair was drifting free from its pins and she was slightly the worse for drink.

'And what's this I hear about your sweetheart, Miss Jenkins? Caused a stir by running off with poor Rickie's wife, I understand!' She shook her head. 'No telling what the lower orders will get up to next.'

Mary rose to her feet and stood before the doctor's wife, imposing in her anger.

'I have always wanted to tell you this,' she said quietly. 'You are a bitch! And at this precise moment, you are a drunken bitch.'

'Well! I've never heard the like of it in all my born days. I'll cross you off my visiting list, Mary Jenkins and as for you, Mali Richardson, you never were on it.'

Before Mary could think of a reply, Mali was speaking for her. 'Then you are doing both Miss Jenkins and myself a favour,' she spoke decisively and Marian Thomas backed away, her face red.

'I'm sorry for the doctor,' Mali said ruefully. 'He's such a kind man but that wife of his – she's lucky not to be burned as a witch.'

Mary smiled, her eyes twinkling. 'That reminded me of the Mali I used to know, flooring that Sally Benson outside the laundry and you such a tiny thing!'

Mali returned to her seat and sighed softly. 'Aye, it seems a lifetime ago and a great deal has changed since then. Who would have thought that we'd be sitting here in your fine big store, drinking your health in champagne?' Mali raised her glass. 'I wish you all the happiness in the world, but you know that, don't you?'

As Mary tipped up her glass, she saw a broad figure shouldering his way through the crowd towards her and she stiffened.

'Good evening, honey.' Dean Sutton leaned over her hand, speaking smoothly. 'I know you didn't send me an invitation to your little shindig here, but I guess that was an oversight on your part, little lady.'

Mary was vaguely conscious of Mali making her excuses and vanishing into the crowd. 'I think you've got a nerve coming here tonight,' she said in a low voice, but Dean sat down in the seat Mali had just vacated and continued to smile at her.

'I hear you've been trying to buy shares in my brother's business.' He twisted the glass between thick fingers as Mary, suddenly tense, gave him her full attention.

'I don't know how you've found that out, but in any case it's none of your business.' Her voice was low and in spite of her efforts it trembled. Dean's smile widened.

'Well, I made it my business. I went and bought those little old shares for myself. Got my brother hog-tied now, you must see that.'

Mary watched him carefully, her mouth dry. 'What do you want me to say?' She forced herself to speak calmly, but Dean was not fooled for an instant.

'In love with my little brother, aren't you?' he said conversationally. 'Must be, if you're prepared to put your new business premises in hock in order to help him out.'

Mary felt he was playing with her and anger began to grow, bringing rich colour to her cheeks. Her impulse was to order Dean out of the building but she hesitated, for she might as well know the worst.

'Is that all you've come here to say?' she asked, striving to speak calmly. He ignored her question.

'Ah, here is my brother now, talk of the devil!'

Her heart began to beat swiftly as she saw Brandon cross the room towards her, his face hard and his eyes like chips of ice as they took in the sight of Mary and Dean apparently having a cosy chat at the same table.

He stood before her, his face set and angry. 'I'm just about ruined because of you!' He spoke harshly, looking directly at Mary, and she put a hand to her throat in an effort to still the pulse that was rapidly beating there.

'Brandon, you don't understand…' she began, but he silenced her with a sweep of his hand. 'I understand that I've been double-crossed,' he said loudly. People were turning to look at them and Mary moved towards him, her hand held out pleadingly.

'Come to my office, we can talk more privately there,' she said urgently, but he did not move.

'Why did you do it, Mary?' he said. 'You knew I would never let the shares go to Dean and so you put in a bid for them on his behalf and like a lamb to the slaughter, I let them go.'

'I did intend to buy the shares for myself,' Mary protested. 'But the banks wouldn't allow me the money. I thought...'

Brandon shook his head. 'There's no point in lying to me, you were a front for my brother and I won't forgive you for that.'

Dean rose to his feet and put an arm on Mary's shoulder. 'You know how close we are,' he said triumphantly. 'Why shouldn't Mary help me?' He held on tightly to her, but she managed to pull away from his grasp.

He smiled down at her almost pityingly. 'You can't have both of us, honey, so you might as well settle for me.' He turned his attention to his brother once more, while Mary watched in dumb horror.

'And listen to this, boy, you'd better forget that handbook you intended bringing out if you want your business to survive.'

Brandon's eyes flashed and his chin jutted forward. 'Are you daring to threaten me?' he asked quietly. Dean shook his head.

'Not at all, brother, I'm simply talking for your own good. I'm a chief shareholder in your business now you put your signature to the documents and it's all legal and binding.'

Brandon moved closer to his brother. 'You know damn well I'd never have signed if I had thought for one minute you were the buyer.'

'Please, Brandon don't quarrel, not here in public.' Mary forced her way between the two men and Brandon shrugged and moved back a pace.

'I won't spoil your little party, Mary.' His eyes looked into hers with such depths of bitterness that she wanted to fling herself into his arms and beg him to believe her, but she heard a giggle behind her and turned to see Marian Thomas enjoying her discomfort to the full.

'Oh, get out of here, both of you!' Mary turned and walked towards her office, her head high but her throat aching with unshed tears. If Brandon had so little faith in her, then it was better that they never saw each other again.

As she sat at her desk, the sounds of voices rose and fell. There was the chink of glasses and the noise of laughter and it seemed that the party was in full swing again. Mary put her head down on the desk and closed her eyes. This should have been her night of triumph and yet she had never felt more miserable in all her life.

Chapter Thirty-One

February was whimpering its way to an end with no relief from the rain that beat an incessant tattoo on the dull pavements. The small shops in the *Stryd Fawr* no longer hung boots from a string outside the coffin-shaped doors or displayed scrubbing brushes and zinc baths where people could stop and look at them. And the rain was only an additional obstacle for the small traders of the town, for there were twin enemies which carried more force than the weather.

The strike was reaching unprecedented proportions, the men organising a mass meeting at the recreation ground with the result that the womenfolk kept away from the small shops, for money was scarce.

The emporium opened by Mary Jenkins was offering unheard-of bargains to the wives of striking men: cut-price garments, food at practically giveaway prices and, worst of all, no rush to make payment. Small shopkeepers grumbled among themselves, putting together a petition to stop her, but Mary Jenkins had the audacity to say that the poor had been exploited for long enough.

Even the story of Rickie Richardson's frantic efforts to find his wife took up only a small column in the local papers, for no one knew or cared where she had gone.

Brandon's thoughts were with Mary, he could not help but admire her. Devious she might be, but she took care of her own and he could only respect her for that. And yet he could not explain even to himself the depths of anger and even surprise he had felt when he had found how she had tricked him into selling the shares to his brother.

It was a chance meeting with the lawyer's clerk that had alerted him. Tanner was a thin pimply youth who had a fancy for hot toddies and when sufficiently full of them, every man was his friend. He spoke of Mary and of Dean both discussing shares in the Beaufort Steel and Tinplate Company with Gregory Irons.

And Brandon cursed himself for a fool for the happiness he had felt when he'd taken the lawyer's word that Mary was investing money in his firm.

What made a woman pliant and responsive in a man's arms one moment, only to turn to rend him like a she-wolf the next, he wondered. But he had told himself long ago not to try to understand a woman; he had learned that lesson young.

As Brandon made his way down the main street, he saw the long queue of women waiting with a variety of bowls and dishes in their hands for the soup kitchen to open. Even as he was about to pass, the doors were flung wide and he stood still, a mixture of emotions raging through him.

Mary was standing behind a long table, a thick apron wrapped around her waist. The colour rose in her cheeks as she saw him and for a long moment they stood like pieces of petrified wood, looking into each other's eyes. It was Brandon who moved away, thrusting his hands into his pockets and edging past the press of anxious women heading for the long table.

He strode on towards the press, where Evo was still working on the handbook. The man had become increasingly reluctant to continue with the project and it was only the inducement of more money that spurred him on. When Brandon had announced his intention of leaving the Employers Association Evo's face had been long with worry.

'There'll be trouble over this.' He had spoken in low mournful tones as though there had been a death in the family. 'Those toffs don't let no one get away with being different, you'll see.'

Brandon hadn't even bothered to answer the man. The intention to print the book had brought him to the brink of ruin, but the obstacles put in his way only made him more determined to succeed.

When Brandon arrived at the press, he knew with a sinking of his heart that something else had gone wrong. Mark and Heath Jenkins were there already, standing outside in the rain with faces puzzled and gloomy. Evo was almost wringing his hands in despair and as Brandon drew nearer, he caught his breath in anger. He looked at Mark and the manager shook his head.

'Someone's done a great job here, boss,' Mark said fiercely, his eyes filled with anger.

Brandon moved nearer, seeing the sea of papers littering the floor and the machinery smashed beyond repair. Evo was swaying to and fro on his heels like a mother nursing a child. 'Don't ask me to get mixed up with the likes of this again, Mr Sutton, for I shan't.'

'Not a hope of salvaging anything from this mess,' Mark said through his teeth. 'Whoever it was did a good job.'

'Caught sight of the devil who did it,' Evo said glumly, 'I'm sure it was Gerwin Price – I'd know that haystack hair anywhere.'

'I'd like to strangle the bastard!' Heath's big hands were clenched together.

'Price may have been the instrument, but whose hand wielded the weapon?' Brandon said heavily. He stared at the wreckage before him in despair. Months of work had been ruined in one night and it seemed he would never get the handbook published. He was beginning to wonder if there was any point in continuing to try.

'Will you give up now, Mr Sutton?' Evo asked anxiously and a quick rage ran like a fever through Brandon's veins.

'I'll be damned if I will!' he said harshly. 'I'll start again as soon as possible. I still have my own original copy of the handbook and get it printed I will if it kills me. Mark, you can take it with you – go as far afield as you like, but get it published!'

Mark nodded. 'I'll do that, sir,' he said, his eyes alight. 'We won't be beaten, boss. We'll show them all, you'll see.'

'That's all very well, but what about my press? Who's going to pay for all this mess?' Evo said mournfully.

Brandon smiled grimly. 'Don't worry, Evo, you'll be paid. Mark, Heath – come along with me. We'll get the manuscript and then you can get on your way as quickly as possible, Mark.'

Later, as the three men sat in the offices of the Beaufort Steel and Tinplate Company, Mark stared at Brandon with his eyes full of sympathy.

'I'll see that the book is printed, boss, don't worry about that, but what are you going to do about the works? Can you keep going?'

Brandon sat on the edge of the desk swinging his leg, a frown crossing his brow.

'I can't sell, that's for sure, not without my brother's agreement. He will probably try to force the men out on strike to keep in line with all the other works, and in that way ensure his money is no damn use to me.'

Heath rose to his feet. 'Well, I'll go and see Gerwin Price. I may get something useful out of him.'

Brandon shook his head. 'I doubt it. He's an animal, not a brain in his head. He destroys for the sheer pleasure of it, so don't bank on getting anything there.'

He reached into his desk and threw a blackened ornament towards Heath. 'Take this, you may at least be able to tie Price in with the fire. I found it in the mess we cleared up afterwards. And thanks, both of you!' He sat down in his chair and drew out a ledger, staring down at the figures before him and Mark and Heath glanced at each other, knowing that they were dismissed.

As Heath made his way out of the gates, he stared at the tall stacks of the blast furnace, seeing the smoke rising to mingle with the clouds. Deep within him he felt that the fight Brandon Sutton was facing to get the book published was bigger than he had imagined. Heath had liked the boss from the first, but now his respect for him made him eager to help in any way he could.

He looked down at his working clothes, for he had been about to start a heat when Mark had asked him to accompany him to the press. Perhaps he ought to get off home and change and then go and search for Price, see what he could get out of him.

The metal eagle in his pocket seemed to burn a hole as he fingered the rough edges and thought of how he would like to rearrange Gerwin Price's face. Unthinking animal he might be, but the sod knew the difference between right and wrong.

So immersed in his thoughts was he that he almost collided with Mary as she left the soup kitchen.

'Steady on, you lout!' she said, laughing and Heath held her in his arms for a moment, love for his sister warm and serene within him.

'Far away you were then, boyo. What's wrong? Lost a fortune and found a penny, have you?'

He drew her hand through his arm. 'Not exactly,' he replied, 'but you're right about one thing. I'm madder than a bull in a field of cows.'

'Come on, tell Mary all about it.' She squeezed his arm and Heath stared down at her, frowning.

'I don't know what happened between you and Mr Sutton,' he began, 'I saw that you were quarrelling with him on the night of the party, but he's being wronged and I'm not going to stand still and do nothing.' He saw the light vanish from Mary's eyes.

'Has he been blaming me for the business of the shares again? I swear I didn't know anything about Dean Sutton buying them – that rat of a lawyer led me to believe that it was Sterling Richardson.'

Heath shook his head. 'No, not blaming you, Mary, something else has happened to put the business of the shares out of Brandon Sutton's mind for the moment.'

'What's gone wrong now?' Mary asked and though she spoke calmly enough, Heath could see that she was breathing rapidly. She cared about Mr Sutton, it was as plain as the nose on his face.

'The press has been destroyed, the books torn and thrown all about the place. Such a mess you've never seen in your life!'

'*Duw*, there's a fighter he is and he'll win in the end or I'm not Mary Jenkins.'

Heath noticed absently how Mary fell back into the Welsh idiom when she was disturbed. He put his hand in his pocket and encountered the metal eagle.

'You haven't by any chance seen this before, have you, love?' He held it on the palm of his hand and felt Mary stiffen at his side.

'Yes, I've seen it before, on the coat of that waster Gerwin Price.'

Heath saw that Mary was trembling and he drew her into the shelter of a shop doorway and stared down at her, his arms on her shoulders.

'Come on, Mary, I know you when you're upset. You'd better tell me all about it. When did you come to see this button?'

Mary took a deep breath. 'It was when we were living in Canal Street,' she said. 'You must have been working I suppose but at any rate I was in the house on my own.' She paused as if the memory still had the power to shake her.

Heath put a finger under her chin and looked down into her eyes. 'Go on Mary, I'm your brother – you can tell me.'

Mary shook her head, placing a hand on his cheek. 'I'm half afraid to say for fear of what you'll do.'

Heath shook her gently. 'Tell me what happened, Mary, I mean to know.'

'All right.' She leaned against him as if suddenly wanting to talk. 'He saw me in the bath. Peering through the window he was, came in and attacked me. Didn't get nowhere with me, though, don't you worry, boyo. Interrupted he was when Brandon Sutton came just in time to throw the monster out.'

The breath hissed through Heath's gritted teeth as Mary's story suddenly made everything crystal clear to him. He saw again Rhian's pale face and defeated eyes as she told him about the man who had violated her – now Heath knew who that man must be.

'I'll kill the bastard!' he said under his breath. 'He doesn't deserve to live.' He looked down at Mary. 'Get on home with you, out of this rain, I'll be seeing you later.'

Mary caught his arm, a look of fear on her face. 'Please Heath, don't do anything silly, now. You're just a boy and I don't trust that Gerwin Price any further than I can see him.'

Heath smiled grimly. 'Not a boy any longer, a man I am now, Mary, or haven't you noticed?'

As he moved down the street, he did not glance back. He had a job to do and nothing would deter him, not even his sister's pleading looks. Gerwin Price must take his medicine and Heath was just the one to administer it.

–

Rhian was seated in her customary position near the fire, for the cold seemed to have entered her very bones. She glanced up without warmth as Mary entered the parlour and looked away again quickly. There was something in Mary's bright intelligent eyes and animated features that was almost painful for Rhian to look upon.

She shuddered. Would she never feel clean and wholesome again? Mary Jenkins seemed everything that was wholesome and clean and in that instant Rhian almost hated her.

Mary made small talk with Auntie Agnes and Rhian was satisfied to be silent, lost in her own thoughts. She watched as Carrie brought in the coal and pushed the kettle onto the fire and was startled when Carrie spoke to her.

'Do you want a nice cup of tea, then?' she coaxed. It seemed she was always trying to be kind and though Rhian had forgiven her for stealing Heath away, they never spoke of it. Rhian was aware of Carrie's feelings of guilt and felt sorry for her, but she carried her own burden of guilt that was far greater than anyone could ever know.

'There are some Welsh cakes in the tin,' Auntie Agnes was saying and Carrie fetched plates and bustled around with the tea tray. Everything seemed so sane and normal on the surface, but Rhian felt she was an outsider looking in.

Carrie went away to wash the dishes and Auntie began to doze, her head on her chest. Rhian did not want to look at Mary, but she was forced to do so for Mary brought her chair closer and Rhian could smell the fresh scent of her.

'I know you're upset about Heath and Carrie,' Mary began, 'but please try to understand that he didn't mean to hurt you. Since he was little more than a boy he's gone out tomcatting and I always told him he'd get into trouble one day because of it.'

Rhian shook her head. 'It's all right, Mary, don't trouble yourself with me. I'm not worrying about Heath or anything else for that matter.' She saw the look of doubt on Mary's face but turned away and stared into the flames, pleading silently to be left alone. But Mary continued speaking.

'Well, I'm worried about him.' She spoke now as though not aware of Rhian's presence, more as if she was thinking out loud. 'Gone looking for Gerwin Price, he has.'

Rhian's heart jerked painfully and she swallowed hard on the bile that rose to her throat. She saw again the cruel eyes and tufted hair and felt hands holding her, hurting her.

Mary's voice broke harshly into her thoughts. 'It seems that Gerwin started the fire at the press some time ago, something of his was found in the wreckage. Now the press has been smashed and the papers torn to pieces and Heath is going to see what Gerwin has to say about it all.' Mary paused and Rhian felt as though she had fallen into the coldness of the ocean and was being sucked down by the waves.

'I had to tell Heath that I had seen that eagle button before. It was the night Gerwin attacked me. Would have done me harm, too, except that someone came to the house just in time.'

Rhian stared at Mary. 'Gerwin Price attacked you too!' Her voice seemed strange even to herself and she wasn't surprised at the way Mary was suddenly staring at her.

'What do you mean, "too"?' Mary asked slowly 'Rhian, is this what's been the matter with you all this time? Did Gerwin Price…?' Her voice trailed away as Rhian hung her head, the colour ebbing from her face.

Tears came then and Rhian felt her body shudder with the force of her sobs. Mary's arms were around her, holding her and after a moment, Rhian relaxed, feeling that she was not alone in her misery after all. Mary had been the target for Gerwin's cruelty too, so Rhian could not be entirely to blame for what had happened to herself. Then Mary was suddenly holding her at arm's length. '*Duw!* Did Heath know about this?' Her tone was urgent, breaking through Rhian's confused thoughts. After a moment, Rhian nodded. 'Yes, he did, I told him… but not the name of the man.'

Mary breathed in deeply. 'I think he must have put two and two together, Rhian, for he was muttering something about killing Gerwin. I thought it was in the heat of the moment, but now I see that Heath meant every word.'

The two women sat clasping each other in silence and it was Mary who moved first.

'You sit by here, *merchi*. I'll go and see if I can find out where Heath is gone.'

As the door closed behind Mary, Rhian rose to her feet and stood trembling for a long moment, staring around her. The clock ticked loudly, the coals shifted in the grate and in her chair, Aunt Agnes still snored gently. Rhian seemed suddenly to breathe again, her senses came tingling back and for the first time in weeks she was afraid for someone other than herself. If Heath caught up with Gerwin, there was no knowing what would happen.

She moved upstairs to fetch a shawl and saw that the light was on in Heath's room. As she stood in the lamplight staring around her, she saw a poster lying across the bed. She leaned closer to read the words and saw that a mass meeting had been arranged for the following day at the recreation ground. Perhaps Heath had gone there, just to check that everything was all right. At least it seemed like a promising place to begin.

To think about leaving the house was one thing, but as Rhian wrapped her shawl around her shoulders and opened the door to the night, she shuddered. She had not been in the darkness once since the attack. She took a deep breath and moved down the street, thankful for the pools of light shed by the gas lamps. She stared up at the shooting sparks from the works and a strange desperation seized her. She could never be happy now, not while she lived in Sweyn's Eye. Whatever happened tonight, as soon as was possible she would get right away. In time, her broken spirit might heal and she could look herself in the face again.

Her footsteps sounded loud in the quiet street and Rhian walked more quickly, thankful to hear the sound of singing from the public bar of the Cape Horner. It was not far now but the streets, although broader, were even more silent.

The recreation field lay long and dark in the shadow of the trees and Rhian shivered but forced herself to go on. A dais had been set up at one end of the ground and it jutted out deep and black, the fluttering of flags the only thing that moved. Rhian wondered if she had guessed wrongly, perhaps no one had come this way at all tonight and she might just as well turn to go home again.

Yet some perverse instinct forced her on. She skirted the dais carefully, drawing closer, like a huntsman nearing its prey. Then she heard sounds, low animal grunts and the hair rose on the back of her neck. She put her fingers to her throat feeling she could not breathe. Once more she was being crushed beneath the weight of the man who was tearing and rending at her. Then the darkness receded and she was still standing at the edge of the dais, listening to what she now recognised was the sound of men locked in combat.

She fell on to her stomach, ignoring the dampness of the grass. Carefully she lifted the canvas that hung from the dais down to the ground and the bright light of a lantern dazzled her eyes for a moment. Her vision cleared and she saw with horror that Heath was lashing out at the red and bleeding face of Gerwin Price.

Heath glanced towards her. 'Get out of here!' he shouted. 'The fool is messing about with explosives!'

Gerwin took advantage of Heath's moment of distraction to strike and the two men fell onto the ground, Heath's flaying arm knocking the lantern from its hook. Gerwin Price grunted like an animal, going for Heath's throat, his eyes widening in terror as he caught sight of the burning end of a fuse moving insidiously towards the charge.

'Let me out of here!' he screamed. 'It's not my fault, Dean Sutton paid me to set the charge to go off tomorrow. He's the one to blame, not me!'

He raised a fist, intending to smash it down into Heath's face and Rhian was hardly aware that she had picked up a stone until she heard it strike with a dull thud.

Gerwin turned with a look of surprise and Rhian held her breath, rooted to the spot with fear. He pitched onto his face and with a sob Rhian grasped Heath's arm.

'Get up, Heath!' she begged. 'We must get away from here before the whole lot goes up!' She slapped Heath's face and though he still appeared dazed, he managed to crawl from under the platform. Rhian pushed him onward, stumbling awkwardly over the uneven ground.

'Come on,' she said breathlessly. 'Hurry, for God's sake!'

Heath pitched forward and Rhian threw herself over him. There was a sound like the crack of thunder as though the heavens were split asunder, and as she looked back fearfully over her shoulder Rhian saw the entire platform lift in the air as though held by a giant hand. Then a splintering of wood fell like a shower back to earth.

She sat for a long time, cradling Heath in her arms, crying into his shoulder. There were streams of people running like ants across the ground, asking questions and getting no response. But at last Heath sat up, shaking his head as though to clear it.

'Thank God,' Rhian whispered softly. He rose to his feet and put his arm over her shoulder, ignoring the crowds that thronged around them.

'So this is all Dean Sutton's doing, is it?' he said raggedly. 'He paid Gerwin Price to murder Brandon and God knows how many innocent people.'

He sighed heavily. 'I think, somehow, that Mr Dean Sutton is going to sign the shares in the Beaufort Works back over to his brother.' He smiled in the darkness and then seemed to become aware of Rhian at his side.

'Come on,' he said gently, 'I'm taking you home.'

Rhian clung to him and suddenly she began to cry in great gulping sobs and it was like the melting of the winter snows.

Chapter Thirty-Two

The day was bright and sunny, a gift of spring bestowed on winter, when even the air was as sweet as wine and the chill breeze carried with it the scent of salt and sea.

Sweyn's Eye was awake early as men arrived from hill croft and valley pit, converging on the town from every direction.

Folks came in carts or charabancs, on horse or on foot. Comedy bands dominated the streets, the men ghostly with painted clown faces and slashed red mouths. Blaring discordant notes issued from brass trumpets, arousing laughter from the onlookers lining the streets. And it seemed that no one gave a thought to the explosion at the recreation ground or to the fact that a man was dead.

Mary for her part felt only relief that Heath was safe. He sported a black eye and a swollen jaw and she realised that without Rhian's intervention matters might have taken a very different turn.

Rhian was a changed woman; she seemed alive now and in command of herself once more. She was determined to leave Sweyn's Eye and begin afresh in a place where she was not known. And in her heart Mary could not blame her, in spite of the hurt her decision caused Heath.

Through the window of the store, Mary heard the marching of the massed bands. She leaned on the sill and pressed her face to the cold glass, her breath misting it like white crystals of snow.

After the bands came the men on strike, carrying brightly painted banners calling for equality for all. Mary had seen such marches before and knew that the crowds would make frequent stops at the public bars on the way, growing more angry and less sober as the day wore on.

The store was an empty shell, since no one cared to shop on a day like this. Mary had given her staff the day off, realising that all of them would want to watch the parade. As she stared down into the busy street, she wondered what the outcome of the rally would be. Brandon meant to address the crowds – a strange thing, she thought, when a boss was on the side of the workers. And yet she was achingly proud of him.

Mary glanced at the ornate clock on the wall, but it was still early, the meeting would not start before noon. The morning was a time for laughter and frivolity and only later would the business of the day begin in earnest.

She felt very alone as she moved around the store. Rich materials hung on display frames and the shelves were stocked to capacity. In spite of the strikes, Mary could consider herself a rich woman. Yet happiness was another matter entirely and the nearest she had come to it was when Brandon held her in his arms. But love was for the favoured few, not for the likes of Mary Jenkins.

She moved abruptly to pick up her coat, thinking that she might just as well lock up and go home for there was little point in remaining in an empty store.

She moved down the wide staircase, feeling the coarseness of the jute beneath her feet, telling herself that soon she would have splendid rich carpeting. Yet there was no excitement in the prospect. What was success if there was no one with whom to share it?

She was at the door when a figure huddled into a shawl came towards her. 'Bertha, what on earth are you doing here and covered up like that, is something wrong?'

'Yes, there is and Mr Dean would kill me if he knew I was here clecking to you.' She glanced over her shoulder as though afraid she had been followed.

'I heard Mr Dean talking. He's got a bunch of men together, mercenaries he calls them, going to disrupt the meeting. He and

Mr Rickie Richardson were discussing it. I know your brother works for Brandon Sutton and I was afeared that something would happen to him, he being all you got in the world.'

'You did right to come to me.' Mary tried to be calm, though her heart was thumping so loudly she could scarcely think. 'You must do one more thing for me – call round the houses of the men who work for Brandon. Women like the wife of Joe Phillips, they'll stand by me, I'll be bound.'

'But you can't interfere in what's going on at the recreation ground,' Bertha said in horror. 'I wanted you to stop your Heath going, not to join in the fight yourself.'

'Just do as I say, Bertha,' Mary said firmly. 'Trust me, I know what I'm doing.'

She watched Bertha leave and then hurried along the main street which was silent and empty now, littered with papers and discarded bottles. As she turned the corner past the Cape Horner, she heard the sound of drumbeats and they seemed to echo in her head, part of her own pulse. She moved as quickly as she could, hampered by her high heels and narrow skirt. There was no point in going for the tram, for the traffic would be stopped in honour of the parade.

The canal was golden with green fronds of fern drifting on the surface, and to her right stood the laundry – desolate and ruined, a mere shell. It was difficult now to imagine the old days when she had worked with Mali and when Mr Waddington was the kindly owner who encouraged his girls to better things.

The Sutton family had catapulted into Mary's life bringing with them destruction and hate, yet from the ashes Mary had risen to become a rich woman in her own right. She brushed her thoughts aside, her breathing uneven as she neared the docks where the steamships rolled at anchor and where one lone sailing vessel stood proud and tall in the sunshine.

Here it was she had met and talked with Brandon at the spot on the quay where they both sought solace for troubled minds. They had so much in common, Mary thought, and yet they were divided by a gulf of mistrust and doubt and by the heritage of wealth.

Soon Mary was in the broad tree-lined avenue that led towards the recreation ground. She heard the voice of the crowds like a roaring of beasts and the beat of many drums competed with the rolling of the waves.

The meeting had not yet begun and she sighed with relief. There was still time to warn Brandon about his brother's plan to send in mercenaries to disrupt the proceedings. She looked frantically around her, trying to spot a familiar face, someone who would know where Brandon was.

A man leaned over her, his face painted ghastly white, his eyes rolling in his head and his breath smelling of ale. He was like some monster dragged up from a nightmare and Mary pushed him aside angrily.

A makeshift platform had been erected on the grass not far from where the old one had stood. Mary shuddered, seeing splinters of wood still littering the ground and realising that Dean had meant the charge to go off when Brandon was speaking.

'Cain and Abel,' she muttered under her breath.

There was a drum roll and a cheer went up from the crowd as Mary saw Brandon climb onto the platform, his hands held out for silence. He looked tall and handsome and Mary loved him so much that she could hardly bear it.

She was pushed roughly aside then and glancing up she saw a stranger, his eyes hard, his lips a thin mean line. He was carrying a thick stick and Mary knew with a sinking heart that he was one of the mercenaries Bertha had spoken of. She looked round carefully, spotting other strange faces among those of the townspeople.

As soon as Brandon began to speak, he was heckled by the man grasping a stick. 'This is a boss speaking to us, he's no right to be here. Bosses are liars, we all know that!' There was a murmur from the crowds as the man continued to speak.

'This Sutton fellow can't even run his own business – got to close down any day now, you ask him. And this handbook of his, where is it? We're all tired of waiting and of promises that are never kept.'

Brandon was unruffled. 'If that man who is so brave in the crowd would like to come and face me, then we can talk.' His voice was clear and strong, obviously making a good impression on his listeners.

Suddenly, Dean Sutton was leaping up onto the platform and the brothers stared at each other in silence for a moment before Dean began to speak.

'I know my brother for a failure and a fool,' he shouted. 'He's sold you men out, letting me buy shares in his works knowing I'm a supporter of the Employers Association.'

There was a buzz of excited voices and Dean held up his hand. 'You know where you are with a proper boss. Come over to the Association's way of thinking, fit in as you've always done and there will be no more disputes. Seek fair wages the right way, by negotiation with your bosses. Get rid of men like Brandon Sutton, he's a traitor to his own class and he'll be a traitor to you.'

The man at Mary's side waved his stick aloft. 'Let's teach this Brandon Sutton a lesson he'll never forget.'

Mary looked round frantically. There was no sign of Joe Phillips's wife or of the other women, but something had to be done and soon. On an impulse she pushed her way through the crowd and stepped up onto the platform.

'I'm Mary Jenkins, but then you all know me,' she said loudly. 'I'm one of you, born and bred in the slums of Sweyn's Eye and always one to speak plain, mind.'

Mary felt Brandon grip her arm. 'Get down from here, you don't realise how dangerous this situation could become.'

She gave him a quick look. 'You are the man I love and I'll not leave you alone in trouble,' she said.

A voice called to her from among the people. 'Might have been one of us once, Mary Jenkins, but rich you are now.'

She faced the crowd, her head high. 'Aye, rich I am and haven't I shared what I have with you all? Ask any housewife in Sweyn's

Eye and you'll get the same answer – Mary will wait for any money that's owed!'

Her words were greeted by silence and, encouraged, Mary continued. 'This man Brandon Sutton is honest, trying to help you, but you poor fools can't see it. Had trouble printing his book, press burned down, machines destroyed – and why? To keep you workers getting what's owing you. Open your eyes, which of these two men up here would you rather trust?'

For a moment, it seemed as though Mary had won and then one of the mercenaries was moving forward. 'Are you a lot of petticoats to be swayed by a woman? Fight for your rights the way the men of the valleys have always needed to fight.'

As the mass of people pushed forward like a restless sea, Brandon thrust Mary from the platform.

'Get out of here as quickly as you can honey,' he said loudly. 'It looks as if I'm going to have my hands full.'

It was as though all hell was let loose, women were screaming and fists flying. Mary looked back and was horrified to see the platform swamped by mercenaries.

'Brandon!' She cried his name, but her voice was lost in the animal noises of the crowd. She was frightened, her head spinning as she tried to push aside the people who were crowding her. She cried out as a flying arm caught her a blow on the side of her face and she hit out blindly.

Separated from Brandon by a crush of fighting men, Mary saw Joe Phillips throw a great fist in the face of a mercenary. The man fell like a log, blood pouring from mouth and nose and she felt a savage satisfaction in knowing that Brandon's men were still on his side.

She found herself on the edge of the skirmish, her hair hanging loose down her back, her good serge jacket torn from her shoulders. A whirl of flying fists and lashing boots knocked her sideways and she fell on to the hard ground gasping for breath.

A tall figure stood over her and Mary looked up fearfully into Dean Sutton's face. His eyes glittered with anger as he reached out and caught her arm, jerking her roughly to her feet.

'Can't mind your own business, can you?' He ground the words from between clenched teeth. 'Well, you've chosen the brother who is nothing but a failure, do you understand? Brandon is through, finished and you two deserve each other.'

Panting, Mary tried to pull away from him. '*Duw*, I'm glad I never let scum like you put a finger on me!' She stared at him scornfully. 'You tricked me over those shares of Brandon's, didn't you? Somehow you must have bribed Gregory Irons to let you have them instead of me, after I'd signed papers and all.' She paused for breath. 'What sort of a man would bring mercenaries to fight his brother? A coward you are, Dean Sutton, a coward!'

His hand lashed out catching her a blow that sent her reeling against the rough bark of a tree. Dazed, she looked up in time to see Brandon launch himself on his brother and bear him to the ground.

Brandon's fist smashed home once, twice and then a third time. Dean tried to get to his feet, but Brandon was like one possessed.

Gasping for breath, Mary rose to her feet, catching Brandon around his waist and shouting at him to stop, trying to penetrate the mists of rage that clouded the turquoise eyes.

'Please, you'll kill him and he's not worth it.'

Brandon moved away from his brother and stood looking down at him in disgust. 'So you tricked Mary over the shares, did you? And as for all this,' his hand swung out, encompassing the crowds of fighting men, 'I might have known you were behind it.'

He paused for a moment as though to control the anger that was plain to see in the set of his mouth. 'About those shares, I think you are going to have to sign them back to me, unless you want your exploits to be exposed to the whole of Sweyn's Eye.'

Dean stared up at him truculently. 'I don't know what you're talking about; accusations are one thing, proof another.'

'I have witnesses,' Brandon said calmly. 'Two respectable people who heard Gerwin Price blame you for the charge that was placed under the platform.' Brandon stared at his brother and shook his head. 'Oh, I might not make it hold up in a court of law, but remember this, Dean, mud sticks and even the most shady inhabitants of Sweyn's Eye would draw the line at murder. And one more thing, Father's will. I don't think you'll be contesting it after all.'

Dean stared at his brother with the eyes of a man who knows he has been beaten. Brandon took a step towards him. 'If you come near me or Mary again, I'll kill you.' His voice was flat, unemotional and the more frightening for the lack of anger in it. 'Now get out of my sight before I start on you again.'

Dean lurched to his feet, rubbing his hand across his mouth and without a word, turned and lurched away into the crowd. Mary was about to speak when her attention was caught by a loud cheer and she looked along the length of the recreation ground and saw Rhian at the head of a band of women. They all wielded weapons: broom handles, rolling pins, even stone water bottles.

Joe Phillips's wife stood on a box and shouted at the top of her voice. 'We fight for Brandon Sutton and we fight our own menfolk if need be.'

The women banded together and Mrs Phillips lashed out at the nearest man with her broom. He yelped like a dog and ran into the crowd and a wash of laughter swept through the onlookers. In no time at all, the mercenaries seemed to vanish and men were picking themselves up from the ground, shaking their heads and holding hands over blackened eyes. Mary took a deep shuddering breath; it seemed the fighting was over.

'Mr Sutton!' A voice called loudly with a note of excitement that attracted everyone's attention. Mark pushed his way through the crowd with Katie close behind him. He was holding aloft a book, the pages shivering and moving in the breeze as though with a life of their own.

'Here it is, men!' Mark said jubilantly. 'The handbook we've all been waiting for! There's no going back now, thousands of these have been printed and the bosses will have to take notice of our claims.'

Brandon was surrounded by a press of cheering men, then lifted high on the shoulders of his workers and carried triumphantly through the grounds.

Alone, Mary moved towards the beach and walked along the golden sand, uncaring of her dishevelled appearance. Her feet sank into the golden sand and the wash of the waves was an accompaniment to the tears falling down her cheeks.

At the quayside, she sat on the wall and stared out at the ships riding high in the harbour. The sky was overcast and the threat of rain was in the air. Mary felt as though she was suddenly the only person left on earth. The silence was deep and heavy, without even the hoot of a tug boat to send the gulls crying into the air.

She heard distant footsteps and glanced up quickly, her eyes narrowing so that she could see better into the distance. There was no mistaking the tall straight figure coming towards her and Mary got to her feet and stood trembling, her hands clenched at her sides.

'Brandon!' She sighed his name, love washing over her. And then, unbelievably, he was holding out his arms to her. She paused, her heart fluttering like a caged bird, then she began to run, her hair streaming in the breeze. The distance between them seemed great, but Mary knew with a deep conviction that she would reach him in spite of the difference in their worlds. She flung herself against him and Brandon cradled her close, his lips on her hair.

A ray of sunlight pierced the clouds, bathing them both in a golden pool. 'My proud Mary, I won't let you run away from me again, not now or ever,' he said softly.

She put up her hands and cupped his face, her eyes shining. He kissed away a tear as it coursed down her cheek.

'You know I can't promise you an easy life, don't you?' he whispered, his lips still against her cheek. 'I may have nothing to offer but constant battling against the Association.'

He paused and looked into her eyes. 'Well, Mary, will you have me?' he said at last.

She was trembling so much that she could hardly speak. 'My love,' she whispered. 'Don't you know you are all I have ever wanted in this world?' She drew his mouth down to cover hers and it was as though the earth had begun to sing.